RETRIBUTION

BOOK THREE IN THE DOMINION SERIES

S. E. LUND

ACADIAN PUBLISHING LIMITED

FOREWORD

Though the mills of God grind slowly, yet they grind exceeding small;
    Though with patience He stands waiting, with exactness grinds
He all.

Friedrich von Logau—*Retribution.*

To be left alone
And face to face with my own crime, had been
Just retribution.

Longfellow

CHAPTER 1

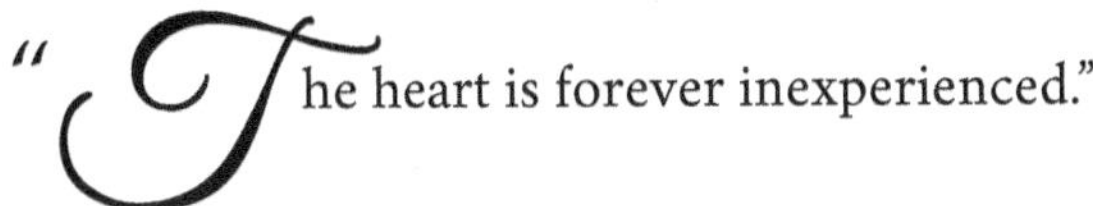

"The heart is forever inexperienced."

Thoreau

MICHEL CLOSES his eyes for a moment, inhaling as if he's trying to gain control over himself. When he speaks, I can barely hear his voice.

"How much have you read?"

"Hardly any," I lie. I didn't even know I'd written down my experiences in an online password protected blog. It reads like a dark fantasy romance – not like a real journal. Ancient French manuscripts. Vampires. Fallen Angels. Murders. Monsters planning for Dominion. It's all there – a record of my thoughts since I found the manuscript after the university released my mother's research files back in May.

I squeeze my nails into my palms. I don't know much about my past with him, but I read far enough to know that pain blocks his touch telepathy and prevents him from reading my mind.

"Don't block me, Eve," he says and takes my hand, lifting me up so that I stand before him. "Not now. Not after everything."

He looks down at my palms, which have been injured from my nails. Blood seeps out of two wounds on one palm and from a single wound on the other. He shakes his head, and sighs heavily. Then he tilts my head up and strokes my cheek, and he must release some kind of calming endorphin because my sadness evaporates, my shock at learning the truth about myself receding into nothingness. All I see are his black-lashed blue eyes, which are huge now, the pupils dilating, the whites bloodshot as he transforms into a hunter, an ascended vampire – or whatever it is that he has become. I don't really understand what I wrote in my journal. All I know is that huge black and steel-grey wings unfold behind him, and for a moment, awe overwhelms whatever he's done to calm me.

Then he lifts my palm to his mouth, his lips open against my skin, his tongue touching the wounds, tasting my blood. We connect in that strange way I experienced on the beach and when we made love earlier. I relive a memory he has of doing the exact same thing. He did it on that first night we met at the Linguistics Building and I realize that for him, everything that happened with me from then on was a foregone conclusion once he tasted my blood.

It seems like so long ago, but it's really only a few months and to him, it's like we just met for his memory isn't like a human's – fragmented, abstract. It's whole, physical, emotional, as if he's reliving the moment as it happened.

MAY 17TH. Not even four months ago. There's a knock at the door to the office he hastily commandeered in the Linguistics Department at Boston University where I'm a student. He compelled the real owner, Professor Steve Cormier, to stay away for the evening so he could use the office to meet me, review the manuscript, see if it was the one he'd been searching for.

To see if I was the one he was hoping not to find...

I look so much like her – Danielle. His first and only love. The years have not dulled the pain he feels at her loss and he relives her death again in the few seconds that he stands at the door and stares at me, a vampire's memory far too vivid and far too long for it to have faded even these eight centuries later. Time stands still for him when he relives the memory. It is that vividness that keeps the memory and his love for her alive.

He remembers emerging from Soren's compulsion, finding Danielle dead in his arms. He remembers Soren throwing her lifeless body over the wall onto the city's garbage heap. He remembers digging her grave outside the walls of Carcassonne, his vision clouded by tears, his fingernails ripped off as he claws at the hard dirt with his bare hands.

His physical pain doesn't matter. His wounds will heal, just as his immortal body heals of every insult – but his immortal heart? It never heals, the wounds still fresh like they were made just yesterday. He remembers covering her lifeless body with the hard clumps of earth, cursing the day he was so weak that he returned to her when he knew he shouldn't. Knowing even then that it would likely mean her death but lying to himself so he could have her.

I am the perfect tool Soren could use to entrap him and make him comply. Anger at his own weakness fills him briefly, so bright and sharp that he can't breathe for a moment. Hatred for Soren tears at his heart.

He tried so hard not to look for me. He tried so hard not to find me. He succeeded for ten long years, dampening down his curiosity so he wouldn't seek me out, check up on how I'm doing to see what kind of woman I've become. Just another decade of loneliness, self-denial, and abstention from his more human needs. He's used to it by now, but his baser desires still dog him despite the constant prayer and the aesthetic lifestyle he's adopted. The rigorous physical demands he puts on himself are intended to drive out all lust and desire. To deny them.

A century of denial.

And then, there I am at his door, so young and fresh, my skin so creamy white like my northern Irish ancestors, the hazel eyes with flecks of every color fringed by thick lashes from my French side, a slight blush to my cheeks from the unnaturally cool weather the region's experiencing. A spray of freckles over the bridge of my nose making me look younger than I am – just twenty-one.

A flash of fear crosses my face and he knows immediately that I suspect what he is and my expression makes him hate himself even more, if that's even possible. He's tried so hard not to be that monster, denying his most basic nature. With the rare exception, he's fed primarily off donated blood since transfusions were discovered earlier in the 20th Century after the Spanish Civil War, from glass bottles and then plastic bags, but it never fully satisfies, for vampires crave that connection to humans that a feed from their bodies allows. He's rowed competitively, he's fenced for sport, he's run endless miles, he's pumped iron, he's swam hundreds of thousands of laps, all of it to quash the lust that he can't deny through force of will alone.

He's too weak.

He's barely touched a human in the past one hundred years except to compel them. He hasn't even been with another vampire sexually or to share blood in an effort to completely eradicate any lingering physical desire. He's tried to live as the priest he always intended to be, but it's still there, simmering just under the surface.

And then, there I am at his door.

He holds a mug of coffee in his hands to warm them so I won't flinch when we shake hands, because he has to read me, see what I know, how much I suspect.

"Are you Professor Cormier?" I say, my voice shaky.

He doesn't want to lie and so he evades the question.

"Eve?" he says, extending his hand so that I have to take it or look rude. He doesn't let go, and in the brief moment he enters my mind, he sees that I know all about vampires, and that I suspect he's one but my desire to get the manuscript translated makes me hesitate and not follow my first instinct to flee.

I smile back and hold up the envelope. When he sees my dimples, desire fills him, for my dimples are like a gift – like brief flashes of sunshine through the clouds on an otherwise-dismal day. He opens the door and waves into the interior, forcing me to turn sideways to avoid touching him. As I walk by so close, he catches my scent. It intoxicates him, the combination of my human scent, my female scent, my blood, my perfume – gardenia, citrus – and something else he can't place. He imagines how soft my naked skin would feel against his fingers and mouth. He tries to keep those thoughts out of his mind.

He can tell I'm forcing another big smile, trying to look like I'm not afraid, but he knows all I really want is to run away. My need to know what the manuscript says despite my fear of him and what he might be keeps me there, and part of him wishes I was more afraid and would run right now. He could catch me, but if he had to restrain me, he's afraid where such rough physical contact would lead.

Already, he admires me. He thinks I'm brave. He thinks I'm strong, despite everything that's happened to me.

Above all, he wants me.

He's sure I'm her – the girl he tried to forget but never could entirely, my fate a mystery, one he hoped would remain that way for my own sake. But in his eight-century long existence, stranger things have happened. He has to be certain.

He asks me questions and then he's certain it's me for he remembers a conversation he had with my mother when I was just a child performing at a recital in London.

My mother wanted to call me Lilith but my father said no.

When he sees the manuscript, he can't believe he's finally found it. The pages are old but well-preserved, the ink still dark, the colors barely faded. He touches the vellum and it's smooth under his fingertips.

He asks me how I came into possession of it, but he already knows. He's just testing me to see how I respond and he sees that I can't lie. He can read the lie in my face and in my body language, in the tone of my voice. This makes him both pleased and sad, for he sees that I'm lying to him, but he also knows that he can tell when I lie just by my face and body.

Then, as much as he wants to just accept this turn of events, take me into his life, hide me away in his estate and have me as his pet, his blood slave, and eventually turn me so I'll be his eternal companion, he knows he shouldn't. If he does, my life will be at risk. Unless he turns me, I'll most likely die in the line of duty as has every other Adept who has worked for the SCU. My mother tried so hard to keep me out of this life, wanting me to be a dancer or musician so badly, and he feels an obligation to see her wishes come true in some kind of repayment for her own sacrifice.

He knows what he must do – he must compel me to forget the manuscript, forget about vampires, forget about him. He must wipe my memory of his face and of this meeting. Send me on an entirely different path – one in which my gift for music, rather than my gift for seeing death and violence, will be nurtured and preserved.

When he refuses to translate the manuscript, using the excuse that he has to verify it wasn't stolen, he enjoys my resistance and wishes so much that he could have me as his and his alone, for it's been so long since he had someone and he would so love to train me as his Adept. It would be such sweet reparation for all his long years of sacrifice.

When I go to the door to leave, my emotions at the surface, tears of frustration in my eyes, he's so tempted to kiss me just once and show me what I'll be missing even as he plans to wipe the memory from my conscious mind. Surely one kiss wouldn't harm anything. Hasn't he suffered enough loneliness all these years?

He forces me against the wall, enjoying how his blood responds to my nearness, his heart rate increasing to match mine, his arm on the wall beside my head. He senses my attraction to him and it momentarily unsettles him for he was sure I'd find him horrific because he's a vampire. When my body responds to his nearness, his responds with lust, and he wants so much to have me, to just break all his own rules for me.

God must understand...

My tears move him, not because he wants to see my pain but because I feel so much emotion and it reawakens his own, reminding him that he can feel. That to feel is human and he wants to be human again – the way he was before he was damned, innocent of the bloodshed and death that surrounded him in the secret world he now inhabits.

He runs his finger through my tears and they taste like me, the way my body would taste if he were to lick me. I taste salty, with just a hint of my genetic inheritance. He's already sensed it in the scent of my blood on my breath, which he can't ignore despite his strength of will.

He demonstrates his power to affect my body, touching my cheek, causing my brain to release pleasure endorphins so intense that it makes me weak-kneed and forces me to close my eyes. He loves how I look when I'm in the grip of that much pleasure and he knows that's how I'd look when I'm in the throes of passion. He wants so much to watch, so he can feel it with me for there's nothing that breaks down walls between a man and a woman more than shared pleasure.

He smells my hair, enjoying the fresh scent of shampoo on it, how my perfume clings to it and mixes with the oils in my skin to deepen the scents. He looks into my eyes, noting the flecks of violet – just like Danielle. His gaze moves to my freckles – just a spray across my nose, giving me a youthful look, a bit mischievous. He imagines I'd be a handful to try to control. If I were his, he'd keep me on a long leash just so he could enjoy reining me in when I rebelled too much. He'd want me to rebel. He wouldn't want me to be completely compelled into obedience.

He'd want me to choose him freely.

That thought almost makes him lose control and throw away all his plans to let me go, wipe my memory and send me back into obscurity. My dimples save me. They remind him that I'm just a girl, barely out of my teens, innocent despite the pain I've experienced in life. I deserve a life.

I don't deserve a monster.

He doesn't want to forget my dimples. He wants to make me smile once more before he sends me away so he can see them again. He can't help but imagine waking me in the morning, me all warm and still sleepy, kissing my neck and seeing my dimples when I smile, my eyes still closed. He imagines kissing each cheek, dipping his tongue into each dimple to make me think of him dipping his tongue somewhere else.

He could overwhelm my resistance with pleasure but then, he knows he'd never be able to stop himself from claiming me as his own.

But he can't resist at least one kiss. God knows he's denied himself so much this past century, he deserves just one ...

He takes my face in his hands and presses his mouth against mine and it intoxicates him, the warmth of my body against his, the softness of my lips against his cold ones. The press of my breasts against his chest. Despite everything, I want him. Despite him being a vampire, pale and undead, a threat, I want him.

He can't help himself. He opens the door between us to show me what could be if only he could have me, to claim me. How good it would be to know how he feels, how his body responds to me, how his blood responds to mine.

When my legs weaken from the intensity of his senses and emotions, he is so tempted to pick me up and carry me to the couch and take me, but he fights it with every ounce of will that remains.

Seeing my response, feeling it, isn't much consolation, but it's all he has and it gives him pleasure to know that if I were his, I would be so responsive to him. When I finally gave in, I would be his willingly, despite how my mind rebels against the thought.

Then he tries to make me forget, regretting every word, his heart sinking more and more as he commands me to forget him, his face, the meeting, the manuscript. When I don't respond the way I should, he's unnerved. He tries once more, gripping my face more firmly, but he can't tell if it's taken. Perhaps it will take effect once I'm out of the building but a fear is growing in his mind... My mother was immune to being compelled. He never thought I would be as well for it's such a rare freak of genetics, it rarely occurs in successive generations.

He takes me down the stairs, trying not to look at my face for he fears his resolve will crumble if he does. By then, his emotions are so high that when he pushes me down the steps to the sidewalk, he uses too much force and he sees me fall to my knees on the hard cement. He curses himself for losing control – he who prides himself on self-restraint and continence.

He watches through the window as I drag myself to my feet, cradling my hands because of the pain. He thinks that he's seriously screwed. If the compulsion doesn't take effect, he'll be forced to deal with me. He'll be unable to resist me – he knows how close he is to the edge.

One misstep and he'll fall.

When he sees my scraped palms, hears me call him a bastard, he knows his compulsion has failed and what he must do. I must become his Adept. He can't control me using compulsion. There's only one way to control me. Love. Even now, he knows he will love me. He's not sure yet, but he hopes that I could love him. He'll have to build trust between us, so that I'll be his willingly. He'll use the lust we both feel for each other to cement the bond.

He's existed now for eight long centuries. He knows how this works.

He returns to the office and quickly retrieves his coat and the manuscript, tucking it into his messenger bag. He tries to damp down the elation he feels at this turn of events even as he tries to pretend he doesn't feel elated.

Then he follows me to the bus stop.

"Sorry to have to tell you this," I say to him, tears of pain in my eyes. "But your little trick with the Vulcan mind meld didn't work. I remember everything."

He gets the reference to Star Trek and enjoys it. Even now, faced with a monster who could kill me in a moment, I'm a brat. I'm defiant. I am a hunter.

"No, it's me who's sorry." He takes my hands and examines them, clucking his tongue in disapproval. He looks into my eyes. "What kind of prick would do this to you?"

He throws that back at me, letting me know he can read my mind. Then, because he can't deny it any longer, he bends his head to my palm and tongues my cuts. My blood brings out the vampire in him, his bloodlust raging, his vision focusing in on me, his sense of hearing focusing on my heart pounding in my chest. His teeth elongate, and an ache builds in his body. A delicious ache, but so intense it feels more like addiction than just pleasure at the taste.

An addiction that, once activated, can never be slaked or overcome.

"Oh, Eve, now look what you've made me do..."

CHAPTER 2

"*M*emory is the diary we all carry about with us."

Oscar Wilde

Michel releases me, our shared memory dissipating, and I blink rapidly as I struggle to recover from its effect.

I know now with certainty that he didn't want this existence for me but due to some quirk of my genetics, my inheritance from my mother, I'm resistant to compulsion and he failed to make me forget. I turn away from his overly-emotional expression. I know he's waiting to see my response, to know if this shared memory can overcome my anger and shock at what I've read.

I don't know if it can.

I sit on the couch for a moment, trying to catch my breath. Trying to sort through the conflicting emotions that fill me.

He sits beside me and takes my hand but I pull it away. "Enough, Michel. I need some distance."

"Distance is the last thing you need now, Eve. Let me show you more. Don't go by the things you wrote in your journal. People change. Feelings change. You loved me when we parted and that's all that matters. If you give yourself a chance, you'll rediscover that love."

"I don't remember any of it. It's a story about some woman I don't even know."

"Did my memory feel like a story?"

I shake my head. It felt real. Almost as if I remember it as well. My body remembers it but my mind doesn't.

"Then let me show you one more memory," he says, his voice pleading.

"Which memory?"

"Whatever one you want."

I think for a moment back to what I read. There are so many I'm curious about. The first time we had sex, but that's too dangerous. When he took me to his mansion and played Chopin for me. When he returned from Pittsburgh. When he came to me on the beach in Ipswich.

"The bombing," I say and I know immediately that's the memory I want to see. It's one I never wrote down in my journal of course. I lost my memories because of it. All I have is an entry the morning of the bombing, expressing my excitement and fear about going to meet with members of the Council of Clairveaux to discuss their plan to kill Soren. That's the very last entry. Two months ago to the day.

He sighs and says nothing for a moment and I know he's not happy that I picked that memory of them all.

"*Eve...*"

I turn to him and take his hand. "You said any memory. I want your memory from that day. From the time we went to meet the Council. I know from reading news reports that we were in the car traveling along the waterfront when the bomb exploded. Show me your memories of what happened."

"No," he says and shakes his head. "No, because then you'll know things you shouldn't – things that would still put you at risk. Eve, I've done *so much*, I've given up so much to protect you. I can't have you at risk ever again."

"Michel," I say and touch his cheek, cup it with my hand. "*Please.* Show me what you think I can see safely. I need to know…"

He closes his eyes and leans into my hand for a moment.

"Kiss me first," he says.

"Why?" I say, frowning.

"Because I'm afraid you'll never kiss me again."

"You're scaring me, Michel."

He just shakes his head. Then I close my eyes, leaning my face up for him to kiss me.

"No," he says, "You kiss *me*." He pulls me onto his lap so that I'm sitting with my legs on either side of his hips. He places my arms around his neck. "Like this."

I lean down and press my mouth against his, and when I do, he opens himself to me once more, our minds connecting as our lips part. I'm lost in the kiss, lost in his arms and in his memory.

He GLANCES *around my tiny apartment, seeing it again with a mixture of melancholy and pleasure. He'll have to close it up after, pack up my things, such as they are, and put them in storage. I won't need my apartment or my things any more. He'll sort through some possessions that might be meaningful to me and set them aside. They can go with me to my new life.*

He has so many pleasant memories of my apartment. That first day when he saw how Spartan my life was – how different from his life of opulence. How fearless I was to stand up to him, despite knowing what he was, Samurai sword in hand. How unwilling I was to let him in that first night. How, despite my fear, I put up a brave front. The first time we had sex – it's memorable because of the intensity and his surprise that it happened at all.

He sees my old piano and is determined to buy me a nice baby grand for the cottage where I'll live up north in Ipswich with my foster parents. The cottage they already have is tiny and there's not enough room for one so he'll have to find a bigger place for us to live. I must have a piano worthy of my talent.

He goes to my vanity while I'm busy feeding the cats and picks up the bottle of my perfume from France, determined to keep it for himself. He knows it will be torture to have my scent surrounding him, but it's the one thing of mine he'll allow himself to keep. He'll spray his sheets with it and lie naked in bed, thinking of me safe, out of the world of vampire hunters, studying music instead of science. I'll probably meet some young musician and fall in love, marry, have children of my own, teach at a university. It's too late for me to become what I should have been – a concert pianist – but I can still have a life filled with music.

The thought of losing me chokes him momentarily but he's determined to see this through. He's been too selfish for too long. He refuses to let another woman he loves die because of him.

The time comes to leave my apartment, to get in the car and take me to meet my new destiny. A sense of numbness fills him as we drive along the waterfront, as if he's shutting off his emotions in preparation for what is to happen next. If all goes as planned, I'll drink the drug to make me forget, the blast from the bomb will provide a diversion, and an already dead but soon to be burned and maimed body will be buried in my place, complete with long fair hair like mine. The coroner has already been compelled to identify it as mine.

My death will throw everyone off my trail for good. Soren. Blackstone. Julien.

He squashes down the guilt that wells up inside him at betraying his brother, but he knows that Julien will never leave me alone – not now that Julien and I have been together.

Aside from Michel, only my foster parents will know who I really am. They've been given new identities and compelled not to divulge my existence to anyone. If all goes according to plan, in a week, I'll be safely tucked away in Ipswich and Michel will never see me again.

He's made a vow to God to give me up. He'll provide me with a steady supply of his blood to keep me healthy, but in all other respects, I'll be allowed to live a normal life – without him in it.

I sit beside him on the seat, and when he takes my hand, he can sense that

I'm nervous and a bit excited at the prospect of meeting the Council and finally getting my revenge against Soren. He thinks I am so brave and so damn stubborn. If only I'd been compellable, none of this would be necessary, but my will is just too strong.

This is the only way he can think of to save my life, to prevent me from suffering in a future he can barely stand to imagine taking place. A future with me as Soren's weapon, making him the biggest monster to ever walk the face of the Earth, with Michel at his side but unable to help me, forced to watch me fall into perdition. A future with me being worse than dead, a soulless blood slave to Soren and his pantheon of hybrid vampire-Ancient-gods.

Michel would rather suffer my loss than to see that future and he intends to prevent it. Losing me, faking my death, will give him time to do just that.

The road ahead is blocked by a fire truck that has responded to a car fire.

"Looks like a fire of some sort," I say, unaware of the danger I'm about to face.

That's Michel's cue. He turns to me and takes my face in his hands, grief and tenderness for me making his throat choke.

"Eve, I love you." He kisses me, his emotions washing over me, bringing tears to my eyes. "Don't forget that." He reaches into a pocket and takes out a tiny glass ampoule and breaks the tip off it. Inside is a drug to erase all of a certain type of memory made in the past decade. He must erase them – my memories of names, faces, and events back to my mother's death. "Drink this."

He knows I can't be compelled to forget but forgetting is the only way I'll give up my vendetta, the only way I won't fall into Soren's trap. He must use this drug, despite the damage it will cause to me.

I take it from him and examine it. "What is it?"

"It's to protect you." He pulls me closer, close to tears, his resolve to carry through with this plan waning just a bit as he thinks of the price I'll pay.

I drink it down, trusting him totally, and he wishes – he just wishes I felt that trust long before this day. Instead of having to send me into oblivion, away from him forever, he and I would be living somewhere along the Welsh coast that I love so much.

But that will never be.

"You're so brave." He buries his face in my hair, his mouth on my neck.

*"Whatever happens," he says, his lips at my ear. "Remember that I love you."
He pulls his small crucifix over his head. "This is for you," he says and slips it
over my head. I examine the crucifix.*

"It's beautiful." I look up at him. "It's Marguerite's."

*He nods. "It's very old." He holds my face in his hands. "Eve, when you
look at the cross, you'll remember that the vampire who gave it to you loved
you."*

*"I'll remember," I say. I smile at him and he makes a sound deep in his
throat and kisses my cheeks, his tongue touching each dimple, one after the
other.*

*Then an explosion rocks the car and he knows this is the moment that I
leave him forever and he can't bear it. He can't bear to have it happen
without me saying the words once more.*

"Tell me you love me."

I smile. "Of course I do."

"Say it."

I kiss him. "I love you, Michel."

He kisses me back, deeply. Then he brushes my hair off my cheek.

"That should make you feel a bit dizzy."

As if on cue, I grab hold of the seat.

"I'm so sorry..." he says, "...but I can't let you go to him."

*He thinks of the plan he's made for me. I'll be whisked away to a safe
house with a physician to examine me and a nurse to tend me until I wake
up from the effects of the drug. Then, I'll begin a new life.*

*But fate intervenes. Another explosion right next to us rocks the car again
with its shockwave, this time more intense. Michel wraps his arms around
me, covering me with his body. A huge black cloud of smoke and fire envelops
the car.*

And then, darkness.

*Even Michel is taken by surprise. He tries to shield me from the blast
wave but the concussion is so intense. Michel recovers enough to drag me out
of the broken windshield. A medic is already at our vehicle, and checks me
over as I lie unconscious on the pavement. He pushes a distraught Michel out
of the way, tending to me, checking my pupil response, my breathing, my
pulse.*

"Head injury. Her pupils are unequal. We have to get her to a hospital."

"No," Michel says and leans over me, touching me to see where I've been injured, using his powers to heal what he can but I'll need his blood. "Take her to my estate as planned."

While they load me into the ambulance, Michel checks on Vasily, who's been seriously injured, his face covered in blood, his legs mangled. He runs his hands over the damaged arteries, sealing them off to prevent blood loss. He can't do anything immediately about the broken bones, but will provide some blood to help him heal.

"Take him to the closest trauma center."

They comply, one ambulance whisking Vasily off, the other driving me to a house of Michel's outside of Boston. I'm intubated because my oxygen is too low. Michel asks the medic for a syringe and withdraws a vial of blood from his arm.

"Give her this," he says, handing them the syringe. "It will stop any further damage from taking place."

"Will it heal her?" the medic asks, examining the tiny vial.

He shakes his head. "Too late for that. It will only stop it from progressing. Give it to her now."

They inject Michel's blood into me and that stops further damage, but the injuries I've received will require extensive physical therapy. But my life has been saved from the future he fears. The future he can't bear to see come to pass, but which dogs his dreams, turning them into nightmares.

I'm taken into his safe house where a team of doctors and nurses wait on me, checking me over. Once Michel is certain I won't die, and that the damage done to me has stabilized, he leaves and goes to the hospital to see Vasily. He's been in surgery for a broken hip and fractured leg, and despite Michel's attempt to heal him, he has lost a lot of blood. Michel provides a second vial of blood, which will help him heal, but even so, Vasily will never be the same. Michel isn't as powerful as Soren. He can't fully heal a human who's received so much extensive physical damage. All his blood and touch can do is prevent the damage done from getting worse.

None of this was supposed to happen.

Someone discovered Michel's plans and tried to turn it to their advantage, planting a bomb that was meant to kill me. It can only be Blackstone. They want to prevent me from being used by Soren. My death would prevent him from taking power until he can create another.

Michel sits at Vasily's bedside and tries to think through who betrayed him. He looks back in time at everyone he's come into contact with but he can't think straight with both of us, Vasily and me, having been so near to death.

Someone betrayed him.

I'M INTUBATED *for a brief period until my brain swelling goes down and my breathing stabilizes. Michel sits by my side, holding my hand the entire time. Once I can breathe on my own, they put me in a medically-induced coma. When I've recovered enough, he'll leave me for good. But for now, he sits at my side and cares for me as much as he can, stroking my cheek, holding my hand, kissing my forehead, giving me his blood.*

Then the day comes for them to take me out of the coma and he must say his final goodbye and part of him is starting to crumble, his resolve weakening. But he sees that this is the only way for me to be spared from the future he dreads.

He leans down and lifts me into his arms, kissing my mouth, my cheeks, my forehead, my neck where he bit me, tears blurring his vision. He hugs me tightly, wanting to prolong this as long as possible, hating this fate, but finally, he lets me go, laying me back down on the hospital bed.

He nods to the doctor, who infuses my I.V. with a drug to slowly wake me and Michel backs out of the room, standing in the shadows to make sure I do awaken. When the doctor nods to him, Michel knows it's time. Everything is in place to move me from the safe house once I'm stable. I'll go to the cottage in Ipswich where my foster parents wait for my return.

He leaves the room, the house, the neighborhood. Driving away, his intention to never see me again is firm even as his heart breaks. He thinks briefly of killing himself as a way to ensure he never comes back but now, in his transcended state, nothing but Soren's own hand can kill him.

He thinks of a way to achieve just that end. He must find a way to destroy both Soren and himself so that neither can threaten me. Planning this is the one thing that will keep Michel away from me, and will keep him from just immersing himself into one of the stasis tanks at the SCU for the next century, until he knows for certain I'm dead and gone.

❧

WE PART MINDS and my face is resting in the crook of Michel's neck, my tears on his skin. I touch the ornate gold crucifix on a chain around my neck.

Michel gave this to me...

I sit up and look in his eyes, shaking my head, unable to speak. He tried so hard to avoid this. I can't blame him. I can't hate him, despite all the lies and omissions since we met. They were all motivated by a desire to be good, to be strong, to do the right thing. I'll stay with him, despite what I've read and his role in everything. All the lies – what do they mean when compared to his love?

Finally, I kiss him again because I know he's waiting to see my response, and when I do, relief floods through him and he chokes up for a moment, pulling away from our kiss.

"I'm so sorry about everything," he says, his voice breaking. "I'll make it up to you. We'll stay here, away from that life. You'll study music. We'll move away, go to Wales if you want."

"No. I can't leave. We're going to find a way to stop Soren."

"No, *no*," he says. "Not after this."

"Yes," I say. "It's our duty. You know that. We can't run away."

He shakes his head. When he starts to speak again, I silence him with another kiss, not letting him try to talk me out of it. Now that I know the whole story, how can I be selfish and ignore my responsibility? I don't let him pull away from me when he tries, and instead, I grind myself against him, my hands pulling him closer.

"I need you *now*," I say, kissing him, and I can feel his immediate response to the sound of need in my voice.

He can't resist me. I'm counting on it.

"Oh, God, *Eve*..."

I know he didn't believe this would end the way it has and hope fills him.

"Feed from me," he says, and I stare at the blood. I read about doing this in the journal, but since we've been together, I have only consumed blood from the vial he provided me. I hesitate, but then I cover the wound with my mouth and suck and his body shudders from the pleasure. When the blood hits my brain, I'm in another place with him, and that place is pure pleasure that seems to go on and on...

I know he'll fight my desire to kill Soren, but I won't give in until he complies.

That, or I'll leave him and I doubt he'll let me leave him ever again.

CHAPTER 3

"You ou shall know the truth and the truth shall drive you mad."

Aldous Huxley

THE NEXT FEW days pass much as they have since the bombing. Michel and I walk the beach together, stopping to remember when we met – again – and the few days we're back together are so happy and filled with pleasure, I shut off my mind for once, just letting things happen. He shows me memory after memory so that I start to feel our shared past rather than just know about it from reading my journal.

He can't deny me this time. When we've had our fill of each other, he'll let me back in to the life he tried so hard to keep me from so we can kill Soren. He's not said it in so many words but I've felt his resignation about it. He knows that unless he wants to go through the whole *drug me to make me forget* exercise again, I won't give up until we face what lies ahead. Until we find a way to destroy Soren and prevent Dominion. He's tried to keep me from being involved and it nearly cost me my life. Now, he *must* understand that I can't let it go.

It's my calling – to do what my mother failed to do. Help in the fight to 'cure' vampirism and prevent new vampires from being made.

To help prevent Dominion.

THAT NIGHT, we wear sweaters as we walk along the shore because the nights are now cool, the air crisp with a hint of Autumn. After our walk, we lie on a blanket on the beach and watch the stars, our hands clasped.

I want him to show me his memory of my mother's death. I haven't asked him yet, and have been blocking him from my mind so he won't know. But all day, I've been thinking of it – wanting to know how he felt and what he was doing when it happened. They knew each other and he was her liaison to the Council. As we're lying on the beach, I decide to ask.

"Take me back to the day my mother died. When you learned about it."

He says nothing for a moment. "Why?"

"I want to know what you know, how you felt."

He sighs. "That is not a memory you should have, Eve. It's not a good memory nor is it safe for you to know. It will put you at risk."

"How? I just want to know how you felt about it. What you know."

"I can tell you that Soren was responsible. He wanted your mother to turn over research to him, research she was doing for the Council to find a silver bullet to kill us all. He tried to compel her but she was immune, just like you. That's where you got it. When she wouldn't comply, she died."

"Wouldn't killing her mean he'd never get her research?"

"No," he says. "There were others working with her. He wanted her on his side. He wanted to develop his own silver bullet – not one that would kill us all, but kill selectively so he could use it against those who resisted him. She was key, but her colleagues would be just as useful."

"I want your memory," I say, my voice firm. "You used your memories to convince me to stay with you. It's not fair that you get to use them for your own goals but not for mine. *Show* me."

He turns on his side and reaches out to stroke my cheek. "Please Eve. I'm asking you not to demand this. Ask me for some other memory – *any* other memory. This is somewhere you don't want to go."

"Or somewhere *you* don't want me to go," I say, and pull my hand out of his. "What is it about her death that you don't want me to know? "

He doesn't say anything for a moment, his expression haunted, his eyes huge.

"I was there."

"What?" A shock rushes through me. "You were *there*? When he killed my mother?"

He sighs heavily.

"You have to understand, Eve, that I was susceptible to his compulsion. I had no ability to stop what happened. I didn't *know* what was going to happen and even if I did, he controlled me."

I reach out to touch him, to try to connect with him to see into his memories, but he blocks me, pulling away.

"Eve, *no*," he says, frowning.

"Michel," I say and tuck his hair behind his ear. I move closer and kiss him. "Tell me the truth. Do you think I won't stay with you if I know the truth? Isn't telling the truth better than lying to me?"

"I'm not lying. I was there. I couldn't stop it from happening." He shakes his head. "You won't understand."

"Try me," I say and kiss him again.

Then he kisses me back forcefully, almost angrily, his arms wrapping around me, his mouth opening, his tongue touching mine. I feel his emotions when we connect and he tries to drown out my questions with pleasure, squelching my ability to push because I'm almost blinded by it. He rolls me over and lies on top of me, his wings unfurling, spreading out above us. He kisses me, my face, my neck, the curve of my breast as he unbuttons my sweater.

"I want you right now, here on the beach," he says, his voice breathy. His need ignites my own and I don't resist.

"You won't get out of this so easily," I say, smiling in spite of myself.

We'll see about that," he says, pulling my jeans off, the cool air making me shiver. He practically rips my panties off and then kneels between my thighs, pressing them apart, kissing all around my hips and thighs before claiming me, his mouth covering me, his tongue finding my clit.

I gasp from the pure pleasure of it, my fingers tangling in his long hair.

Overhead the stars are unmoved by the show of passion taking place beneath them, between some kind of strange and powerful vampire-angel hybrid and a small human female. I'm barely able to focus as Michel's tongue swirls around my clit, while he sucks it, making me shudder with pleasure. He slips fingers inside of me, stroking me.

"You're so nice and wet, Eve.

"It's all your fault," I say, smiling.

"I'm going to love fucking you."

I close my eyes and inhale when he begins to suck and stroke at the same time. It doesn't take long and soon, I know I'm close.

Then he removes his fingers and rises up, freeing his erection from his jeans, and he slides into me with a tortured grunt, his wings half folded. I wrap my legs around his waist and pull him against me with each of his thrusts and I'm so worked up, so swollen and ready that, soon, my eyes roll back in my head from the pleasure.

I hear him gasp as he starts to climax, my orgasm bringing on his, and the combined sensation is almost enough to make me pass out from pleasure.

WE LAY TOGETHER for a few moments, recovering.

"If you think I won't ask again just because you're so good at this, think again." I swallow, my heart rate slowly decreasing.

He sniffs my skin, kisses his bite mark and I know he'd love to bite me and drink my blood right now, but he wants to wait until it's time for my feed.

He'll have to let me in, let me experience his memory of my mother's death, or I'll leave, and he knows that. I relent and won't push right now. This is too good. I want this moment to last for a while. But I won't let it rest for long.

I have a plan…

THE NEXT NIGHT, after a long day of walking the beach and then sitting in the silence of the house reading, we stand side by side at the island in the kitchen in his cottage and prepare fresh spring rolls for dinner.

While I slice the vegetables and stir fry the thin strips of marinated tofu, he prepares the wrappers, soaking them in hot water and then blotting the excess moisture with a paper towel. In the background, Debussy is playing on the sound system – *Reverie*. One of my favorite pieces.

We don't speak, just move around each other while we work, both of us listening to the music, enjoying the comfortable silence. He moves behind me to get a new roll of paper towels, and touches me as he passes, his hands resting for a moment on my hips. He kisses my neck briefly from behind. I smile, and keep chopping the carrots, slicing them into thin strips. I pop the end of a carrot into my mouth and chew while he hums along with the music.

This is so nice.

I glance over at him and he's smiling to himself while he works. Then I go behind him to get the cilantro from the fridge and touch him as I pass, my hand sliding down his back to his butt, which I give a soft squeeze.

This goes on for a while longer, both of us making every excuse to touch each other. Still, there's no discussion, for even at a distance, I can feel him through our shared connection as his blood slave. He's content. He's happy. He knows we're going to have sex before we eat. All the touches are just foreplay. He's trying to decide whether I should feed before dinner or after. If I wait to feed, it means we'll have sex twice this evening and that just feels right.

Michel *wants* me. He wants to be *mine*. Michel wants all of me and to be everything to me. That's pretty powerful. He wants to fulfill my every need – except for my need to kill Soren.

From what I read in my journal, Julien said he could never give me what I needed. That I had to just take what he could give, which was pretty much just good sex. A good fuck now and then. But Julien was totally committed to fighting Dominion and letting me play my part. As his partner. His equal.

Sadness fills me for some reason, despite all the good feelings between Michel and me. Michel senses my shift in emotion. He puts down his rice wrapper, takes the knife out of my hands and turns me toward him, wrapping his arms around me. He releases some kind of endorphin in my brain that drains the sadness out of me, replacing it with a deep sense of warmth from him, of love.

"He's moved on, Eve," he says softly, his lips against my neck below my ear where he bit me that first time.

I nod, certain from the entries in my journal that I meant little to Julien, or at least, he's occupied with whatever woman he's with at the time. Another vampire, probably. Some call girl that he had to have sex with as part of his cover infiltrating Blackstone like he did when I was with him. I'm glad he's moved on. I don't need that kind of disruption in my life. I *love* being with Michel. He feels so strong and so certain, like a powerful force that will protect me. That will completely possess me. From my journal, I know that Julien always just upset me, frustrated me, and made me feel unsteady, like I could lose my grip and fall.

Michel takes my hand and pulls me away from the island. "Come," he says and I know he wants us to have sex now, so I'll forget this little mental reverie about Julien.

"But the tofu…"

Michel stops and turns the stove off and then takes my hand, pulling me into the bedroom. I let him of course, smiling once more at the thought of the pleasure I know I'll feel.

Once we get to the bed, he sits on it and pulls me between his thighs and starts to unbutton my blouse.

"You think you can make everything better with an orgasm," I say, grinning at him. He responds immediately with his own smile.

"Everything is better with an orgasm, Eve."

And he's right.

I'M FAMISHED by the time we've finished preparing our meal of fresh rolls and Vietnamese beer. We sit at the table by the window and before we start, Michel makes the sign of the cross, his head bowed for a moment. I frown – he's still so religious. He's unable to completely escape the Church – escape being a priest – despite all these centuries.

I eat my meal with relish, dipping my fresh roll in the peanut sauce Michel made. We're sitting at the small table by the sliding glass doors that look out over the ocean. The doors are open, admitting the sound of the ocean in the distance and the scent of fresh salt air. On the sound system, a selection of Gregorian Chants provides a somber but beautiful ambience. It reminds me of what Michel is at heart – a priest. A man of God. How sad for him that Marguerite took that away from him. Despite how hard he tries to live a chaste and priestly life, he fails. He kills in the service of the Council, he has sex with me, and he plots and plans, lies and cheats.

His life is as far from the priesthood as it could be.

I reach out and take his hand, overcome with love and sympathy for him. He looks up from his glass of beer and smiles.

"I'm happy, Eve. Here with you, like this."

"Would you have preferred to remain mortal, taken your place as Bishop of Carcassonne? Lived and died in the Church?"

He puts his glass down and wipes his mouth on a napkin. Then he looks up at me, his expression thoughtful, a distant look in his eyes.

"I've lost my immortal soul," he says. "To a priest, that is the worst fate possible."

I frown. "I don't believe in souls, immortal or otherwise."

He smiles softly and returns to his meal.

"So you're just giving up on fighting Dominion? You and I will just live out my life apart from the battle and let whatever happens happen?"

"Yes," he says. "That is my desire. If we become involved in the fight, you or I – or both of us, will die. I couldn't stand for you to die because of this insanity."

"My mother died because of it. I need Soren to get retribution, Michel. You have to know I won't rest until he does get it."

He turns to me, his expression just a bit frustrated. "After all this effort to get you back, do you really think I'll just let you put your life at risk?"

"Yes," I say. "You and I – we can't have a normal life. Not while vampires are planning to take over. Not while Soren is free."

His blue eyes are huge. "I don't want to lose you. I don't want you to sacrifice yourself."

"You really think you can sit by and ignore the war you've told me about?"

He takes my hand once more. "I'll do my best. No one knows you're alive except Vasily and your parents. Whatever happens, you and I will remain apart from it. I've lived too long and sacrificed too much. I'm not giving up anything else. There are others who can fight this war. I'm out."

He turns back to his last fresh roll and eats it without looking at me as if that's his final answer. I sit and stew for a moment, knowing that I can't accept that. I can't stand by while Soren and his servants prepare to take power.

I say nothing in reply, sticking to my plan. I don't want this sour feeling between us. I want to enjoy Michel while I can. Just the two of us alone.

It will be time to leave this little haven he's created soon enough.

WE GO for our nightly walk on the beach, Michel's arm around my shoulders. While the days are still warm, they're getting shorter and it's already dark when we walk along the shore. There's a half-moon and its light glows on the surf. The sky is clear and the Milky Way is a long dusty arc in the sky above us. The exercise will invigorate me, make my mind clear for a while before my feed.

Now is when I most want to talk to Michel about Dominion, press him for more details, but I bite my tongue and wait. When we get back to the cottage, my stomach is already full of butterflies, thinking of our feed and what I want to happen. I've been planning this for a few days, giving Michel some time to calm down about me wanting to relive his memory of my mother's death. Tonight, I want him to drink my blood as I drink his. It will maximize our connection, and when he's under the influence of my blood, I'll see if I can find his memory of my mother's death.

That's my plan. I think I've been successful in keeping it from him, for if he knows, he doesn't show it.

We both know what happens next when we arrive back at the cottage. I go to the bathroom and start the water for a nice warm bath. I pour in some of the bath salts Michel had prepared that contain my perfume. There are no words between us as we undress and step into the tub. Michel sits across from me, his pale skin so beautiful in the soft overhead light. Michel takes one of my feet and washes it with some soap.

It tickles me a bit and I can't help but giggle.

"Oh, your feet are ticklish, are they?' he says, a devilish grin on his face. "Now I know a surefire way to make you smile and show me your dimples."

I try to pull my foot away, because I can barely stand him touching the sensitive bottom. "Don't, Michel!" I laugh when he refuses and continues to wash it. Then, when it's rinsed of soap, he starts to suck my toes.

I hold my breath because I'm torn between the eroticism of it and how his touch still tickles. I don't know whether to groan or giggle.

"You have such nice toes, Eve," he says, and tongues my baby toe, sucking it briefly before slipping his tongue between it and its neighbor. He kisses the bottom of my foot and then my ankle and calf. I know where this is leading.

"Oh, God," I say, and close my eyes. "I'm ready right now."

"I know you are," he says. "You've always been so responsive. Have I said that I love that about you? Despite everything that happened to you, you haven't shut off."

I open my eyes and look at him. Despite everything that's happened to me. Of course, he means Thompson. He means my mother's death. He means everything that's happened since we met.

He pulls me over to him so that I lie on top of him in the bath, my arms around his neck and I can't help remembering a journal entry where I was in a tub in Julien's warehouse, lying just like this.

"I wish it had been you who killed Thompson," I say and tuck his hair behind his ear.

"I had so many plans to be your first in everything, to be your champion, and yet I find my brother replaced me in them all."

"You gave me to him like some spoil of war," I say, unable to keep a tiny bit of hurt from my voice despite the fact that I have no memory of it, just the words written in the pages of my journal.

"I had no other choice. It was Julien or Soren."

"Julien could never replace you," I say. "He admitted it to me. All I'd ever be to him is a good fuck."

"He did care for you," Michel says, frowning. "In his way."

"Then, was he at least upset to think I was dead?"

"He was," he says, glancing away from my face. "Upset. Yes. But you've read your journal. He's glib. He thinks life is a big game. A joke."

"I think he was upset because he thought I was supposed to be his Adept, not yours."

Michel shrugs. "Let's not talk about him. He's moved on and so must we. Now," he says and moves my hair from my neck.

I smile at him, a thrill going through my body when he kisses my neck. He makes that throat sound and pulls me close, kissing my cheeks, one after the other.

"Temptress," he says and helps me up.

Then he pulls me to the bed and we roll together in the bedsheets, losing ourselves in each other's touch.

When he finally bites my neck and drinks my blood, the pain is sharp and bright as his teeth break my skin. It makes my back arch, pressing my body against his, but it also clears my mind.

In that moment, when he's drinking my blood and his blood is in me, we connect so deeply, our minds and bodies almost fusing as one. I search his mind when he's in so deeply, he's lost all control. I find the memory, and in this moment of time standing still, I relive it.

He can't stop me.

~

"YOU'RE GOING to keep your mouth shut, Michel. I don't care what you think. If she doesn't comply, she dies."

Soren holds Michel's chin in his hand, using his powers to force Michel's compliance. Michel's helpless to resist.

They enter my mother's laboratory. It's a Tuesday evening just before Christmas. She's working late on a report and has me with her, because my father is practicing with the Boston Chamber Orchestra. Soren goes right into my mother's lab. Michel peeks in the office and sees me sitting there on the floor by her desk, old issues of National Geographic spread out beside me. Soren has no idea I'm here, so intent on getting to my mother that he fails to notice my scent but Michel can't miss it.

"Hello, Eve," he whispers. "You stay here. Your mother has some business to attend to. I'll be back in a minute. Do you understand?"

I nod, and barely acknowledge him, more interested in what I'm reading than my mother's visitors. He follows Soren into the laboratory where my mother sits at a desk, going over a report, checking results.

Soren already has my mother by the throat, and it's clear when Michel enters, that she's refusing him. Soren leans closer to my mother, his face next to hers, and she looks determined, as if nothing could make her comply.

He raises his hand and slaps her across the face. The blow makes her head jerk back, knocking her face to the side. Blood dribbles out of the corner of her mouth.

"Stop!" Michel says, lunging at Soren, but the larger man merely grabs Michel by the head and compels him once more.

"You're going to stand there and say nothing. Do you understand?"

Michel is helpless to refuse him. "I'm going to stand here and say nothing."

"Good."

Soren goes over to my mother and strokes her cheek. "Poor Natalia," he says. "Mean old monster going to hurt you because you won't comply. How much pain do you think you can take? Shall I use a closed fist this time?"

"You'll do what you want," my mother says. "Don't hurt Eve."

"She's mine now. You made your choice."

Soren turns to Michel. "Kill her," he says. "Drink her blood. Then find the whelp and send her to one of our families."

Michel steps back, shaking his head.

"No," he says, his voice breaking. "Don't make me do this. She's my friend."

Soren takes Michel's face in his hand. "Drink her blood until she's dead like a good servant."

Michel is helpless to refuse him once again, his mind blank. He goes to my mother and takes her in his arms. He's doing things without knowing what he's doing and can't stop. Soren's compulsion is too powerful.

"Protect her," my mother whispers in his ear. "Give her a new life. Don't let her be like me."

"I can hear you," Soren says, his voice impatient. "That's enough good-byes, you two. Do it, Michel. I'll be waiting in the car."

Soren leaves the room.

～

*W*HEN *M*ICHEL'S FINISHED, *when my mother's heart stops, he comes out of the trance-like state he's been in. Grief overwhelms him – how many humans has he killed for Soren over the centuries?*

Too many to count.

He lays her down on the floor, hatred for Soren growing to such a great degree, he feels as if he'll explode. Then he sees me standing in the doorway, my face white. He wipes his chin and his hand comes back stained red, my mother's blood is covering it.

My eyes are huge. "What did you do to my mother?"

He stands helpless, wiping his face while I run to her, my hands on the wound on her neck as I try in vain to stop the bleeding but it's too late. I turn to him, my eyes wet. "You killed her!"

He pulls me off my mother's lifeless body and makes a split-second deci-sion. He removes a small ampoule from his pocket. Inside is a new drug that destroys all memories for names and faces and events for the past day. It was meant for my mother if she agreed to comply with Soren and turn over her research, so she wouldn't remember in case the Council decided to evaluate her. Instead, he uses it on me so I won't remember seeing my mother's dead body, or remember seeing him with blood on his mouth. He could try to compel me, but Soren could always make him reverse the effect, and Michel doesn't ever want me to remember this moment.

I won't remember seeing him or Soren in the office. I won't even remember waking up that morning, excited because Christmas is only a few days away. He breaks the tip off the ampoule and forces it between my lips. I grimace at the taste, try to spit it out, struggling in his arms, but he holds his hand over my mouth.

I can't help but swallow.

"There, there, Eve," he says, his voice soft. "It will all be over soon. You'll forget everything and start a new life."

After a moment, I stop struggling as the drug takes effect – the drug that will wipe my memory of the events of the past twenty-four hours.

Michel leaves me by my mother's dead body, unwilling to let Soren know I was here, calling the SCU's EMS team as he leaves the building so I'll be found soon. He wants to ensure I get medical treatment because the drug is so new. It's only after he escapes Soren's watchful eye hours later that Michel learns the drug was too powerful for a child of my size. It eats away at my longer-term memory. It almost kills me, causing my brain to swell, affecting my breathing so that I'm intubated.

He visits me in the hospital and makes a vow then and there that he'll hide me from Soren and this life as my mother begged. He'll do whatever he can to prevent me from being brought into this world of vampire hunters and Adepts. He owes it to my mother, whose trust he couldn't help but betray.

He vows that he'll kill Soren one day if it's the only thing he does before he dies.

CHAPTER 4

"*A* kiss makes the heart young again and wipes out the years."

Rupert Brooke

"Eve, *no*..."

Michel pulls out of the stupor he was in from my blood, but it's too late. In that strange suspension of time I experience, I'm able to relive the entire memory, even though in reality only a few seconds pass. I see enough to know that *he* killed my mother. That it was *him* who made me forget, not my own weak mind.

"*You* killed her." I struggle beneath him, but he holds me firm. I stop fighting him and stare up at him, my vision blurry. "*You* killed my mother. But how..." I search his face. "I read you in the SCU that time I was tested. I saw your last kill..."

"I'm so *sorry*," he says, panic in his voice.

"But my journal says I read you, when you drank my blood that first time, and I almost died. I thought *Soren* killed my mother."

He shakes his head.

"Tell me!"

Finally, he closes his eyes and exhales heavily. "I'm eight hundred years old. I know how to block someone. Control what they see."

Numbness fills me, my body tingling as if I'm going to faint. "Have you ever *once* told me the truth?"

Again, I struggle beneath him, my horror growing with each minute.

"Eve," Michel says. "It wasn't me. It was Soren's compulsion. I would *never* kill your mother. You must see that from the memory!"

I can't even look at him, turning my head away, my emotions starting to choke me. He tries desperately to turn my face back, but I keep my eyes closed. Even his attempt to release some kind of calming hormone fails to comfort me.

"Let me *go*."

"No," he says, "not until you understand."

"How can I *ever* understand?"

He finally rolls off me and I crawl away from him. I run to the bathroom and kneel down to vomit in the toilet. He follows me and stands over me, holding my hair as I retch.

When I'm finished, I turn around and push him away. "Leave me alone!"

"No," he says and lifts me up, using his superior power to restrain me. His expression is almost desperate but also angry. He presses me against the wall, taking my face in his hands and I'm powerless to stop him.

"*I* didn't kill her, " he says. "Soren did. I was just his weapon."

"Don't," I say. "How can I be with you knowing this?"

"Eve, don't do this," he says and turns my face back. "You're not thinking straight. You must understand I was compelled to do it."

"You were *with* him."

"I was trying to find a way to *stop* him."

"I'm leaving."

"I won't let you," he says. "I've paid such a high price for you. For all of this." He waves his hand to the cottage, pointing outside to the ocean. "I can't have you misunderstand. I can't have you hate me." He presses his body against mine and his voice is almost a whisper. "I can't bear it."

A rush of something like Nirvana floods through me and it's so intense, I can't keep my eyes open. All my anger and sadness dissipate and I feel nothing. When I open my eyes again, I'm staring into his blue ones, and his eyes are wet.

"Eve, I *love* you. I think I've loved you since I saw you perform on stage in London. I know that sounds wrong, but you can't know what it's like to watch mortals being born, growing up, growing old and dying. For eight centuries I've watched while the mortals I've known have died. I've tried to give you up, but I can't." He sighs and leans his arm on the wall, pressing his forehead to mine. "I just *can't*. I gave up everything to save you. Don't misunderstand what happened."

He takes in a ragged breath and runs his finger along my bottom lip, his mind searching mine for any shred of understanding.

"You also gave me that drug to make me forget but it made me forget too much," I say, "and I almost died."

He closes his eyes. "I was trying to prevent you from being traumatized by what happened."

"You mean remembering that it was you who killed her," I say.

"*Eve*," he says, frustration in his voice. "Let me explain…"

"Stop," I say and hold up my hand. "I've heard enough. I don't want to hear any more. I can barely stand to look at you."

I cover my eyes, trying to regain control over my emotions, for whatever he's done to me is wearing off.

"I'm going back to my parents' cottage and try to figure all of this out. When you're ready to tell me only the truth, *all* of it, you can come to me."

"I'm *telling* you the truth."

"I need to be away from you so I can think for myself."

He shakes his head. "You're not leaving me."

"I *am*. The only reason I didn't leave you when I first learned that you lied to me was because you had me so wrapped around your little finger."

"You want the truth?" he says and I can hear in his voice just how close he is to losing control. "I *never* had you wrapped around my little finger. If I had, none of this would have happened. If anything, it was the other way around. I could never refuse *you*. *You* wanted *me*, Eve, and I gave in to you despite my better judgment. *That's* the truth."

"You gave in to *me?*" I'm unable to comprehend what he means. "Are you saying you didn't want me?"

"No," he says and I can hear frustration in his voice. "No. I wanted you. *God*, I wanted you. But I didn't want you to be in this world of ours. If you had to be, I wanted to give you the choice. I wanted you to be free to choose. You did. You chose *me*."

"That's the biggest lie of all. All you ever talked about was me obeying you. Giving in to you and your need for control."

"It's the truth. You just don't understand. You've always had the power, Eve."

I shake my head and turn away. "It's the other way around. You're the powerful vampire angel. I'm just a mortal."

He shakes his head. "Eve, I *want* you. To have you, I'll do whatever you want. I'll give you whatever you need. *Whatever* you need. But what you think you need and what you really need are two different things." He takes my hand and something sweet rushes through me. "It's always been that way with you." He moves even closer, his fingers brushing against my cheek. He looks in my eyes. "You don't know what you want because you're fighting for your life, every moment of your life. You're so afraid to stop fighting and listen to your heart."

I shake my head, for it doesn't make sense.

"I really want to be equal."

"You really want *me*," he says, his voice soft. "I know it." He wraps his arm around my shoulders and presses his forehead against mine. "You want to sit on my lap with my arms around you. You want me to protect you. You want to be safe, completely safe for once. You want to be absolved of guilt for what Thompson did to you." He closes his eyes. "I can make you feel safe. I can make you feel alive. That's what all this is about. That's why I've done everything that I have – so you can finally be safe. All you have to do is just let me take care of your every need. Your every desire."

"Surrender to you."

He opens his eyes. "Surrender to *yourself*, Eve."

I'm so confused by his words, my mind shuts down.

"You'll have to force me to stay."

He frowns. "I will."

"I'll hate you for it."

"You *must* be safe," he says, his jaw clenched. "I've given up every-thing for you. I can't have you taken from me. I almost lost you," he says and covers his eyes.

"Then protect me," I say, unable to look at him. "But I'm going back to my parents. I won't stay here. I'll contact you if and when I want to see you."

I go to the bedroom, dressing quickly. He follows me and stands in the doorway watching me. He's devastated but so am I. Even though we just had sex, I feel *nothing* but numb. He's beautiful, but he's ulti-mately a stranger who I don't remember. Worse, he's the vampire who killed my mother. The one who left me alone with her bloody body on the floor in her lab.

I push past him, grab my overnight bag and march to the door.

"It's the middle of the night," he says, holding the door closed with his hand. "You're not going anywhere now."

"You can drive me back," I say, not looking at him. "I have a key and the cottage has an alarm system. I'll be safe."

"You'll never be safe unless you're with me."

"Obviously, I wasn't safe with you. What if Soren compels you to kill *me* now?"

He shakes his head.

"Eve, I *love* you. You love me."

I shut his words out of my brain because while they're pretty, they mean nothing to me. They're just words.

"If you're worried about me, send your security team back to guard the cottage."

"They're not available tonight."

I throw my hands up in exasperation. "Then stay outside in your car. I'm not doing this," I say and point to the cottage. "I'm not going to be a fuck toy for my mother's killer. I'm not going to be your little Adept. Your little blood slave."

I reach for the doorknob and open the door, but he refuses to let me leave and grabs my arm, squeezing hard.

I glare at him. "Are you *actually* going to stop me from leaving?"

"I've never been able to stop you from doing anything." He slams the door shut, his brow furrowed, his lips thin. He closes his eyes for a moment as if trying to control his anger and then he shakes his head.

"Eve. This can't be happening." He presses his body against me, his hands cupping my face. "I *love you*. How many times do I have to say it?" He presses his lips against my mouth and it's only because he's affected my brain that I don't push him away and he knows it. After a moment, when he feels no response from me, when my body is silent, unaffected by his kiss, he pulls back, his eyes searching my face. Then his arms drop and he glances away, giving in.

He goes to the bedroom and quickly dresses then returns to me, opening the door. I go outside to the driveway where his car sits. We drive the short distance to my parent's cottage and he joins me as I open the front door.

"Eve," he says, before I can close the door. "You're not even going to say goodnight?"

I look at his face. He's so beautiful standing there, his hair a mess, hanging in his blue eyes, his face filled with pain, but I feel nothing for him. Nothing but anger. No, actually I *enjoy* seeing his pain.

Nothing more.

I close and lock the door, then set the alarm. I stand in the darkness of the foyer feeling like I can't catch my breath and watch as he stands there for a moment with his head down. Finally, he returns to his car and just sits there, pulling his collar up, his arms folded across his chest.

He's actually going to sit there the rest of the night?

I turn and my father's standing in the hallway in his pajamas and housecoat. He rubs his forehead, brushing his grey-brown hair out of his eyes.

"What's the matter? Why are you back? I thought you'd gone to be with Michel…"

"I know everything," I say, going to him and hugging him, the tears starting. "He killed my mother. I'm not staying with him."

He takes in a big breath and hugs me back.

"I'm sorry. We had no idea. We agreed to his demands so we could have you back with us. After the bombing, when we almost lost you, we would have done anything to get you back."

"I know. I don't blame you."

"If you need to talk…"

I shake my head.

"This is something I have to figure out myself."

I go to my bedroom and crawl under my covers, tossing and turning for hours, unable to sleep.

CHAPTER 5

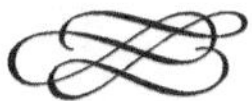

"*A* very small degree of hope is sufficient to cause the birth of love."

Stendhal

THE NEXT TWO weeks pass pretty much as they had before Michel returned to my life. I get up and have breakfast with my parents, walk the beach, and sit on the patio to eat my lunch while watching the ocean. Michel doesn't intrude. He gives me the space I asked for.

Security has returned and so I have the time to think about my life and what I want now that I know the truth. I go over the journal again and again. It's clear that I loved Michel. It's clear that he loved me but how can I be with the vampire who killed my mother? I realize he was compelled to do it, but he was *with* Soren. He's complicit in what happened. And then there's Julien – could I love him? I can't believe I had sex with both of them. My journal says I thought Michel was gone for good and that I eventually turned to Julien out of loneliness and despair.

I don't know what I want anymore. I know nothing about who I am inside. Despite knowing I wrote the journal, it feels like it belongs to someone else. I lost the person I'm reading about in the pages of my journal.

I need to find her again, or create a new person.

I read the newspapers, read the coverage of the bombing now with different eyes. Michel never intended to take me to meet with the Council to talk about killing Soren. He doesn't really intend to let me take up that cause again, and is just humoring me, hoping I'll give it up eventually. But I won't give up the cause and now that I've recovered, that means the mission can still go ahead, if I can meet with the Council. I may have to do it on my own. I think about Terri and wonder if she'd help me...

I try to track down where my possessions went after the bombing but it's impossible. Michel took everything and now, unless I go back to him, I can't even read my mother's research to try to figure out what she knew. I have only my journal notes to go on and most of the time, they were more focused on my feelings than on specific details.

At night I sit and watch the stars, a profound loneliness filling me. I know I can have Michel if I want him but knowing that he killed my mother saddens me for how can I want the man who destroyed my life?

I don't know if I want him on his terms. As much as my journal claims I was falling in love with Michel, I'm just so angry and shocked to learn the truth about him that I don't know how I feel about him now. All I have is this story about a woman who wanted revenge and a vampire-killing vampire she thought she loved and who she thought would help her get revenge. Another vampire she thought she could love who got between them. She had sex with them both.

Other than Michel's memories that he shared with me, I remember *none* of it. It's a story. It's fiction. I feel so detached.

Now, when I walk the beach, I notice the man trailing me about five hundred feet behind. I notice the car parked on the shaded street across from the cottage. I notice the security cameras set up around our property, which I never thought to ask about before.

I'm a prisoner of this life, I'm *his* prisoner, with no real memory of who I am.

~

IT'S on Saturday as I'm on the beach for my morning walk when I see a figure approaching me in the distance. He's barefoot, his jeans rolled up as he walks in the surf. I wonder if my security team will go to him or stop me from getting too close to him but they don't.

He's not looking at me, but stopping to pick up stones, throwing them out on the water. He bends down to pick up shells, using driftwood to move some kelp. He kneels and examines the shells, holding them up one by one in the sunlight.

Finally he rises and starts walking towards me again, not looking at me, just walking with his head down as if his mind is busy. He looks like Michel – except he has shorter hair and quite the growth of whiskers. He's wearing a pair of faded jeans and a white t-shirt, a wooden cross on a black leather rope around his neck. Sunglasses hide his eyes, but his face is the same as Michel's. I stop in the sand, waiting.

He glances up and when he sees me, he falters, his mouth opening.

It's Julien – it *has* to be. He looks identical to Michel but has a long scar on his cheek. According to my journal, I had sex with him after an intense and unconventional courtship, vampire style.

He stumbles, and falls to his knees, removing his sunglasses as if he doesn't believe it.

"Dieu..."

He sits back on his heels, his head bowed, his hands on his knees as if he's unable to remain upright. Huge dark wings unfurl behind him. He shakes his head, his lips moving and I can barely hear what he's saying. He's speaking in French – cursing in French. Curse after curse.

"Sacristy..." he says. *"Crisse. Batard...."*

He rises and staggers towards me. I step back, afraid of him, those wings making him look like some wild fallen angel. I'm shocked at the intensity of his emotional response. He grabs me, crushing me against his body, squeezing hard, harder, breathing fast.

"Oh, God, *oh, God...*" he whispers, taking my face in his hands, his blue eyes on mine and his eyes are brimming.

Then, he kisses me, one long intense kiss and when a connection forms between us, his emotions explode into me, leaving me breathless. He ends the kiss, his forehead against mine.

"I thought you were *dead*," he says, his voice breaking. "I saw your body. I saw your *hair...*" He runs his fingers through it then over my throat where Michel bit me. He looks down at the gold crucifix around my neck and touches it, shaking his head.

"I thought..." he says, touching the crucifix around his own neck that looks identical to the one I'm wearing. "That *bastard...*"

He struggles to speak for a moment and when he does, he's so emotional, he can only whisper. "They identified you through DNA because your body was so badly disfigured..."

"That wasn't me," I say, trying to pull back but he won't let me, his arms going around me, his face in my neck, his tears wet on my cheek.

"Oh, *God*," he says, squeezing me so tightly I can barely breathe. "Oh, God you're *alive...*"

Then, he must finally realize I don't remember him and he pulls back. He grimaces as if in pain, brushing the hair from my face.

"You don't *remember* me?"

I shake my head. "I know you must be Julien," I say quietly. "I can tell because of your scar. I read about you in the journal I kept before the bomb."

He shakes his head as if he can't comprehend what I'm saying.

"But we were *lovers...*"

"We had sex, *twice*," I say, emotion filling me, making my throat choke. "We *weren't* lovers."

"*I* loved you. You said," he says, his voice breaking. "You said you could love me."

"It doesn't matter." I try to step away. "I don't remember anything because of the head injury." I turn away because the pain on his face is just too blatant and brings tears to my eyes.

"What?"

"Retrograde amnesia and some agnosia caused by a Council drug your brother gave me. The damage was to my frontal lobe. I lost everything so far back, I can barely remember my mother's face. No recent faces. No events since I was ten, according to my neurologist. Just body memories, sounds, smells, but I have no idea how I got them."

He's breathing fast. Faster.

"That *bastard...*" he says, his voice barely audible. "I'll kill him. I'll fucking *kill* him," he says, and his fists are clenched, his lips pressed thin.

My emotions rise. He's just so upset, this beautiful stranger who I don't remember but who acts as if I'm his, and I don't know how to take it.

"He didn't want me to try to kill Soren," I say, unsure why I'm defending Michel.

"No," he says. "He just wanted you all to himself." Then he glances past my shoulder and I hear someone coming up behind me. I turn as a man dressed in a black suit and white shirt, sunglasses, a wireless headset in his ear, comes along the beach towards us, struggling to run in the sand. He goes to Julien and tries to shove him away.

"Julien, leave now," the guard says, his chest out, but Julien just takes the much larger man by the throat and lifts him up, squeezing. He's a fearsome sight, his face a mask of rage, the vampire coming out, his eyes red, his fangs extended, his wings spread out wide. The guard chokes, his limbs flailing, his face becoming purple.

"Stop!" I cry out to Julien, but it's as if he doesn't hear me. "Don't, Julien please! He's only doing his job."

He turns to me, his face changing, eyes returning to normal as if I've called him back from some very dark place. He drops the guard, who falls onto the sand, choking, his hands at his throat as if he can't breathe.

"You've hurt him," I say, kneeling down to the man, who still can't breathe. I glance up at Julien. "Help him!"

Julien shakes his head. "I'm not a medic, Eve. I'm a vampire. I kill. I don't heal."

"But you *can*," I say, tears in my eyes. "Do something…"

Finally, Julien's wings fold up until they disappear and he kneels beside me, taking the guard's head in his hands. He runs his fingers over the man's throat as if he's molding the man's windpipe, and after a moment, the guard starts to breathe again, inhaling loudly then coughing. Julien takes the man's face in his hands once he's breathing more normally.

"You're going back to wherever you came from and you're going to forget you saw me here. As far as you know, Eve's fine. She's safe. There's nothing to worry about. Do you understand?"

The guard blinks. "She's safe. There's nothing to worry about."

"Now go. Tell any other guards that Eve's safe. Tell them she went with Michel and she'll be gone for a while."

The guard struggles but manages to stand, straightening his jacket and adjusting the headset. He turns around and goes back in the other direction towards my parent's cottage.

"Thank you," I say to Julien when he turns back to me.

He just stares at me, his gaze moving over my face.

"What am I going to do with you now?" he says quietly. "I'm not letting you out of my sight ever again."

I shake my head.

"No," I say, moving away from him. "Don't you be like Michel. I don't need two of you trying to treat me like I'm some kind of possession."

"You *are*," he says, his voice choked. "You were *meant* for me. I claimed you first."

I frown and turn away, remembering another entry from my journal that it was Julien who bit me first.

"Do you have *any* idea how ridiculous that sounds? You sound like a spoiled child."

"I *was* spoiled. I had you and then Michel took you away from me. Then, he led me to believe you were *dead*," and even now, his voice breaks. "Eve, I didn't know if I could go on when I thought you were dead..."

"But you did go on."

"No I didn't," he says and his voice is almost a whisper. "I went back to the monastery. I quit fighting. I couldn't imagine what I'd be fighting for anymore."

"Stop it," I say. "That's ridiculous. You're a knight. You're a soldier. You told me it's what you do, fight. Kill enemies. Besides, we were barely even together."

He's silent for a moment.

"You don't believe in love at first sight?"

Yes, I *do*. Or at least I thought I did. But my love at first sight wasn't for Julien. It was for Michel. That much I do know from my journal.

"You had a strange way of showing it."

"I didn't *want* to love you," he says. "I couldn't help it."

I dig my nails into my palms and don't respond.

"Eve, I thought my enemies won," he says. "And I stopped caring anymore. But now..." We just stand there in an awkward silence. Finally, he speaks and his voice is barely above a whisper. "Are you," he says. "Are you with him again?"

"Not anymore," I say. "I found my journal and read everything. Until then, I had no memories of anything after my mother died. I didn't even know vampires existed. Michel and I met again. Then I learned the truth – that it was Michel who killed my mother. I left him."

"You *left* him? He *let* you go?" He shakes his head, disbelief on his face. "Soren compelled him to kill your mother, Eve," he says. "He wouldn't have done it himself."

"It doesn't matter. He killed my mother, Julien! He *lied* to me," I say, tears in my eyes. "All this time. He lied to me all along and so did you. You never told me the truth either."

"What good would it do to tell you?" he says, an edge in his voice. "You'd only obsess about it, plan some way to get revenge, and get yourself killed in the process. That's exactly what you did, once you found out that Soren was responsible," he says and waves to the beach, "All this is because of your vendetta against him. We were both right not to tell you the truth."

"The truth is always preferable to lies."

"You think so?" he says, his voice suddenly hard. "You've barely been alive. You know nothing about existence. Believe me, sometimes a lie makes existence bearable. Like I lied to myself about you. That if we'd met first, you would have loved me instead of Michel. Believe me, that lie kept me alive during very dark times."

I deliberately shut those words out of my mind.

"I've lived too many lies, Julien," I say, glancing away from his too-blue eyes. "I only want the truth from now on. All of it. Only the truth."

He just stands there, staring at me.

"OK, I'll tell you the truth," he says, his voice hard. "It's either me or Michel for you. There's no one else you can be with, so *choose*. If you choose neither of us, by default, you choose Soren. He'll deploy you like a weapon with no regard for you as a human. He'll pass you around his lieutenants like a cheap bottle of wine."

My body tenses at that.

"He won't love you like I do," he says finally, his voice soft. "Or Michel."

"You and Michel keep saying you love me, but it means nothing to me. *Nothing*." I turn away, hating that I have no memories of my life.

"You wanted the truth, Eve. No more lies." He takes my arm and releases a calming endorphin that saps my ability to resist him physically. He turns me back around and holds my shoulders, bending down so his face is just inches from mine.

"I *love* you. I wish I didn't. I *hate* loving you. I thought I'd given up on love centuries ago, but it's so hard to live forever without it. I can't do it anymore."

Then he pulls me along the beach, going back in the direction he came from.

"What are you doing?"

He doesn't answer, just keeps walking, my hand in his, our fingers threaded together.

"I followed Michel here on a whim one weekend," he says, laughing ruefully. "Just to see where he was going and I find he's bought this cottage on the ocean. What's he doing here, I wondered. I staked it out. Didn't see anything but him and Vasily staying here, so I thought maybe he bought it for Vasily because he was hurt in the bombing. I come out here today to check on things because I was starting to *miss* Michel and who the *fuck* do I find but you, wandering the beach, security detail trailing you like the fucking queen. Jesus *Christ.*"

We climb up the dunes to the road and his car, which is parked down a tree-lined side road. He opens the door for me and I climb in, my mind resisting but my body betraying me, as usual. He fastens my seatbelt like the chivalrous knight he once was, except of course, that he's taking me against my will.

I can't even speak. I just sit there as he gets in the driver's seat and takes out his cell. He speaks into it briefly, relaying two words.

"I'm coming."

"My parents…" I say.

"I'll call them later."

We drive off and I watch out the car window as the landscape passes us by on the road back to Boston.

WE DRIVE to a suburb and to a stately mansion in a grove of trees. The house is old, with huge windows looking out over a large green space of manicured lawns and shrubs, a fountain in the center. There's heavy security and a guard at a gate admits us, nodding as Julien rolls down his window. We round the circular driveway to the huge double doors where another guard stands.

"I thought you lived at the monastery."

"I have several properties."

The guard opens my door and Julien comes around and takes my hand. I can't resist him, because the endorphins he's released in me are still too strong. We enter the house, and I stand in the huge foyer with a cathedral ceiling and a large winding staircase up to a second floor. The floors are marble, as are the walls, and the furnishings ornate and antique. It looks like it's been transported from some grand home in eighteenth-century Florence or Paris.

"This doesn't seem at all like you," I say. "Not from what I read in my journal."

"You don't know me," he says, his brow furrowed.

He speaks with someone who looks like a servant or butler and then he comes to me, taking my hand. He pulls me up the staircase to the second floor and into a huge reception room, past an ornate grand piano and several instruments – a cello, violin, and bass. We walk through the reception room, through a hallway and then into a bedroom with a magnificent bed all draped in sheer white curtains. He closes the door and his wings unfurl as he leans against it, his arms slipping around my waist, pulling me against his body.

"Don't," I say in protest but my heart is racing just from his touch and his intensity.

He shakes his head.

"I'm not arguing with you anymore," he says and his voice is breathless. "I'm listening to your body from now on, not your words or your mind. You want only the truth? I'll tell you the whole truth. All of it. But I want only the truth from you, Eve. You lie all the time, to yourself, to me. Your body doesn't lie. It's the only truth that matters now."

He kisses me, his mouth soft on my lips, holding them there as he threads his fingers in my hair.

"Please," I say again when he pulls back. I'm barely able to speak. "Don't." But my body has already warmed from his touch.

"Shh," he says, pressing a finger against my lips. "No more lies between us, Eve."

He kisses me again, this time his kiss is more intense. Despite my mind telling me this shouldn't happen, my body responds to him when his tongue touches mine. He makes a sound deep in his throat.

My heart responds to the blatant desire in his face, to the need in his eyes, a thrill of lust shocking through my body. As we kiss, he opens himself to me and I experience everything from our shared past through him, how he first saw me when I was a child in the darkened hallway in our house, how he felt that night at the diner when we first met, how he followed me to the crime scene, to everything afterwards when he and I were together in Boston, then the moment he saw me on the beach, the image of me standing there making him fall to his knees, overcome, covering his eyes. His memories and his emotions speak more loudly than any words ever could and in that moment, I know he *loved* me – he *loves* me.

He pulls me against him tightly and there's nothing I can do to resist him. So I don't.

I don't even try.

When he feels me give in, he pulls back from the kiss and exhales heavily, his forehead against mine. He drops his arms and stands there not touching me, just looking in my eyes.

Then, he offers his hand to me and I look at it and I know what he's doing. He's giving me a chance to choose. I hesitate. There's no doubt that I'm aroused by his touch. I know he loves me from our shared memories. He needs me in an almost desperate way.

I take his hand.

He exhales heavily and for a moment just squeezes my hand in his. He pulls me over to the bed, sitting on it, his wings folding up. He guides me between his thighs and embraces me, his arms around me, his lips pressing against my neck.

We remain like this for long moments. His tongue is wet against my throat where Michel bit me – where *he* bit me so long ago – and it sends another shock of desire through me so that I can't help but gasp.

He lies back, pulling me on top of him so that I'm resting on my elbows, my face above his. He brushes my hair back, tucking it behind my ear and I stare into his eyes. He's so beautiful, I can barely stand it.

Then I lean down and kiss him, his mouth opening against mine, his arms squeezing me more tightly, his emotions surging through me as we connect again, and whatever my mind thinks about what I'm doing, my body doesn't care any longer. *I* don't care any longer. I only know that this feels as if it could finally fill the void in my body, in my heart, that's been there for the past two months since I woke up.

Perhaps my entire life.

Then he bites my neck, the pain is brief and bright, and I come again, all my senses overwhelmed and it's just too much to bear.

CHAPTER 6

"To fear love is to fear life, and those who fear life are already three parts dead."

Bertrand Russell

I WAKE IN THE NIGHT, my body starting to feel the effects of my blood addiction. Julien isn't with me and I get up and tiptoe to the bathroom, where I find a large towel, using it to cover my nakedness.

I go out into the main reception room and he's standing at the window, naked, talking into his cell. He hears me, of course, and turns, the phone at his ear. He waves to me and I join him. He pulls me against his body with one hand and continues to speak softly into the phone for a few moments.

"Tell him those are my terms. If he doesn't accept, I'm gone for good and so is she."

I frown. What plans is he making for me?

"I won't hear any counter offer. That's final." He ends the call, tapping the screen and turns to me. "Why are you awake? You should be sleeping."

"Who were you talking to," I say, unable to read him.

He puts the phone down on the windowsill and brushes the hair off my cheek.

"Vasquez. I told him you were coming back to work for the SCU and I was going to be your partner."

"You did?" I say, surprised that he's going to let me work again. "How can that be? You were implicated in the River Man killings."

"Since O'Neil's death, there's been a shake-up in the SCU. Files were lost. My case in particular. You and I will work together. This is what we were meant to do, you and I." He bends down and kisses me briefly. "I know you won't rest until you follow your mother's path. Michel won't give you what you want, Eve, but I will. I'll give you everything you want. *Everything.*"

"That's what he said as well," I say. "I don't know what I want anymore."

He smiles briefly. "Yes you do. You just don't want to admit it. Listen to your body and your heart. Don't listen to that moralizing superego that haunts you, telling you that you must atone for wrongs you never did. For bad things for which you had no responsibility."

I try to ignore his words because that sounds too much like what Michel said.

"I need your blood," I say plainly, rubbing my hands over his bare chest.

"How do you want me?" he says and I can hear the instant transformation in his voice at the very thought of it. I search him out with my mind and he's immediately choking with lust at the prospect of me drinking his blood, being on a blood high.

I close my eyes and lean against him.

"Where do you want me to feed?" I say, barely able to speak, I'm so overwhelmed with desire.

"No, this is all about you," he says, pulling the towel off me, his hands stroking down my back as he pulls me against him.

But I catch a hint of what he wants – a brief vision as he's imagined it and he wants me drinking from his neck and that image is now what I want as well.

I sit on his lap, my hands on his shoulders, and stroke his face.

"Now," he says, and uses the corner of his fingernail to open a thin seam on his neck below his ear, just beside the Lorraine Cross tattoo that looks more like a brand than ink. I kiss it first, wondering what it means, and then press my mouth over the wound, sucking at it, nursing, the blood trickling into my mouth, the effect immediate.

My body trembles with pleasure as the endorphins hit my brain and I can't imagine a more intense experience than this, our minds connecting, the effect of his blood magnifying everything ten-fold.

It's almost too much to bear.

Almost.

But I can bear it because it's washing away the pain and grief over learning that Michel killed my mother. I will bear it because this is what I need to forget him. I shut off my mind and let my body lead me where it wants me to go – where my heart wants to be.

Then Julien bites me, the pain sharp and short and we wallow in pleasure too intense to describe.

THE NEXT MORNING, I wake and he's naked on his stomach beside me, a pillow over his head. I'm surprised to see him there and that he wants to sleep with me. He always left before.

"What's going on in that too-busy mind of yours, Eve?" he says, his voice muffled under the pillow. "You think too much."

I smile. "How can I not think with you lying there like that?"

He pulls the pillow off his head and rolls onto his side, reaching to run his fingers over my cheek, aiming for my dimple.

"I was thinking that you never slept with me before and wondering why you are now."

"I've changed," he says softly. "Before I thought you'd died, I thought I had time to position myself so I could win you back from

Michel. I can't wait anymore. I have to take what I want or Michel and Soren will."

I don't know what I think of this possessiveness of his, other than it thrills me a bit and scares me at the same time. He's so powerful now as a vampire since he and Michel took the waters of life, but it's just the force of his personality that's also so powerful.

"I don't like it when you talk that way. I'm not a possession."

"I should never have let Michel take you back when he returned from Pittsburgh, but I didn't want Soren to take you. I *love* you, Eve," he says softly. "Whatever you want. Anything you want. *Anything*." He sits on the bench and turns my face to him. "I'm yours, in case you didn't realize it. I'll do anything you want. Just say the word."

I look at him for a moment, at the blue eyes, the dark brows. The thin silvery scar on his cheek.

"I read in my journal that you said you couldn't give me what I want. What made you change your mind?"

"Time," he says and shakes his head, brushing the backs of his fingers along my chin. "Time changes us all."

CHAPTER 7

"March on and fear not the thorns, or the sharp stones on life's path."

Khalil Gibran

"The first thing you have to do is get trained," Julien says as we sit at a small table in the reception room and a servant brings a tray of food for our breakfast. I select some scrambled eggs and toast, with a cup of coffee and orange juice. I'm starving, having barely eaten since Julien found me on the beach.

"What will that involve?"

He scrapes eggs and bacon onto his plate and digs in, as if he's ravenous.

"You need to learn how to use your powers," he says between bites, eyeing me. "You beat Michel in the dojo but that was just one on one. If you have several opponents and some of them are also Adepts with fight sight, you'll need to know how to beat them. You're going to a special training facility in France."

"France?"

He nods, takes a sip of coffee. "They specialize in Nitō Ichi fighting. You need to know how to fight with two weapons – a stake and a sword. Or a gun and a stake. The trainers there are the very best. You'll be there for two weeks to get the basics and then you and I will practice for a while. You'll be tested when I think you're ready. If you pass, no one will be able to beat you without a very tough fight."

"I can't beat either you or Michel any more, can I?"

He shakes his head, takes a long drink of orange juice, looking at me intently over the rim of his glass.

"No. Not since we both transformed."

"Since you both can now manipulate our minds, make us think you have wings or can disappear."

"Oh, ye of little faith," He says and shakes his head, grinning. "You are *so* stubborn."

He turns back to his food but now, he's a bit less focused, like he wants to say something but thinks better of it.

"What?" I say, knowing he wants to speak up but he doesn't.

He shakes his head. Puts his fork down and pushes back from the table.

"Nothing," he says. He regards me from under those dark brows. "It'll be a tough two weeks, Eve. You'd better eat up. You'll be worked like you've never been worked before. The mental and physical discipline will change you."

"How?"

"You'll become tougher. Wiser."

"Wiser?"

"It's not just a physical discipline. It's mental. It forces you to focus on what matters. It centers you spiritually."

A thrill goes through me at the thought of training and becoming stronger. I took some Kendo as a teen, using wooden katana. I knew that Nitō Ichi was double sword fighting.

"What about Michel?" I say, wondering how he'll respond to the fact that Julien has me and is planning on training me.

"What about him?" he says, and I can still hear a thin note of anger in his voice. "You're mine. I made that clear to Vasquez. Michel's out of this as far as I'm concerned. Things are the way they were supposed to be so forget him and his grand plan of manipulation."

"What plan?"

He just waves his hand in dismissal. "He thinks he can control everything. He's self-deceived."

I try to push Michel out of my mind, but I know he'll be upset that I'm with Julien. Right now, I'm still too shocked by his revelation to know how I feel. I sigh and drink down the rest of my coffee.

"What about your blood when I'm at the facility?"

"I'll make sure you have a supply to keep you healthy. Mine has the strength of ten vampires so it will help you heal from any wounds or bruises you get from training."

"When do I go?"

"Tomorrow. We fly tonight."

"You think I'm ready?"

"If you aren't, you'll get ready really quick."

"Will I see you at all?"

He shakes his head. "Not until your training is over. I'll see you the last day when you're tested."

A sense of apprehension fills me. Going to France, staying at a training facility for two weeks away from everything I know.

It will be a real test.

THAT NIGHT when it's time for my blood feed, I'm in no mood for sex and Julien retreats when he feels me so apprehensive, his lust doing nothing to arouse me.

"I'm sorry," I say when he pulls back so I no longer feel his desire. "I'm nervous."

"It's OK. You'll feel better soon."

I feed on his neck as he likes me to, and when I have enough, I just lie in his arms, the endorphins from his blood relieving my anxiety. He lays me back on the couch and rolls on top of me, his face in the crook of my neck, breathing in my perfume. Soon, I start to respond again to the feel of his body on mine, of his lips pressed against my neck. He doesn't want to feed on me tonight. He wants me to be as strong as possible for my training.

But he thinks one last fuck won't hurt me and I see his mind and how he wants me. He wants to fuck me missionary style, my legs wrapped around his waist, him resting on his elbows, his face over mine so we can watch each other's pleasure.

So we do.

~

JULIEN SPENT the night preparing his blood for my stay in France – fourteen small vials of his blood so I won't go through withdrawal and we can still connect.

We fly on his private jet. The flight is long and my nerves are on edge as the plane taxis down the runway of the private airport where he keeps his plane. He takes my hand and relieves some of the anxiety I feel and we sit like that for a long time, side by side, hands joined across the narrow aisle between the seats.

After a night of flying, we land in France and drive the rest of the way to Carcassonne. Being there brings a sadness to Julien that I can sense even at a distance. So many memories he has about this city and his transformation. So many battles fought in the surrounding areas during the crusades.

"It makes you sad to be here," I say as we walk arm in arm along the cobblestone streets of the old walled city before the drive to the Abbey where I'll train. "I don't remember reading the manuscript but I know you and Michel lived here when you were children and then later… after…"

He threads his fingers through mine. "It's been so long since I've been here. It's a bit hard, the memories."

We stop in front of a stone dwelling, with new windows and white plaster on the outside.

"This is where she lived," he says, his voice soft.

"Who?"

"Danielle. The one you resemble."

I remember what I read in my journal. Soren compelled Michel to kill Danielle. Just like he compelled him to kill my mother. I didn't judge Michel so harshly when I read that journal entry. Part of me knows that Michel wasn't responsible, but my feelings are still so raw.

"You loved her?"

"In my way. The way a seventeen-year old boy-man loves. With total abandon, but incredibly shallowly."

"How is love different now?"

"It's deep," he says and squeezes my hand. "But the abandon isn't there any longer. That's a thing of youth and innocence. It comes from the belief that love never ends. Now, I think there's always a bit held back. For protection."

"That's sad."

He smiles briefly but even now, there's a touch of pain in his eyes.

"Scar tissue is a great motivator."

Poor Julien – to think I was dead all that time... My throat constricts and I squeeze his hand more tightly.

WE DRIVE through the countryside towards the Pyrénées Mountains and anticipation builds inside of me as we near the Abbey. It's nestled in a high mountain valley, surrounded by forests, the old stone building with a walled enclosure and a huge garden inside.

The guard at the gate takes Julien's and my passports and reads them over then motions Julien through. We arrive at the massive front doors of the Abbey de St. Michel, and I get out and stand in awe at the ancient building.

I sign papers and Julien meets with the trainers while I receive my gear and have my blood taken by a medic with a tray. Then it's time for Julien to leave and I tear up, suddenly afraid and surprised that I already miss him.

"Shh," he says and wraps his arms around me, his chin resting on the top of my head. "You'll be fine. You're very gifted. Just try to focus on the training, do everything to the best of your ability, and think of me at night when you're lying in bed. I'll feel you thinking of me. They say you shouldn't masturbate during training so your energy won't be wasted and so I won't either. But I will think of you and we can connect for a while." He bends down and looks in my eyes. "But if either of our minds go there, I'll shut you out, so be warned. I want you to pass with flying colors, Eve. No hanky-panky."

"Hanky-panky..." I say and blink away tears.

Then the moment comes to part and I stand there, wiping my cheeks. He walks down the hall and away from me for two weeks.

I follow one of the trainers to my little cell of a room with a narrow single bed and dresser, a desk with a light and a crucifix on the wall over the head of the bed. These rooms, she tells me, were once meant for monks who lived in total silence. All residents are expected to maintain a vow of silence while at the Abbey except during training and to talk with officials and trainers. No talk with other students is permitted. Lights out at 9:00 p.m.

She leaves me and I sit on the bed as darkness encroaches on the Abbey. It's now 8:30 and I have half an hour to get settled, so I unpack the few possessions I am allowed to use – pen and paper, my clothes, toothbrush, bar soap, shampoo and conditioner, brush, comb and medications if needed. Everything else is provided by the Program.

Finally, I drink down the vial of Julien's blood and lie down on the hard little bed and close my eyes, the endorphin rush overwhelming me. Sleep is a long time in coming. When my mind searches out Julien, he's still on the road back to Carcassonne, and I feel a brief rush of love from him and then he shuts me out.

TRAINING IS INTENSE.

If I thought I was worked hard as a child at my father's knee, it was nothing compared to training at the Abbey. We work all day, starting at dawn, doing work to improve all aspects of our physical health, from balance to strength to reflexes. We learn about weapons, about fighting tactics. We learn about making weapons from everyday materials in case we're ambushed.

Each night I go to bed aching from the day's exertions, drinking down the small vial of Julien's blood. Then I lie in a kind of stupor as it heals me of my pain and fatigue. It's then I want to connect with Julien, but he denies me for fear we'll both succumb to our lust. Instead, we connect right before I drink it when I'm still exhausted and aching from the most recent bouts.

I lose fat while I'm there, and gain muscle. I can start to see definition in my muscles that I never had before and when I look in the mirror, I'm different. My face changes – my chin is sharper, my cheekbones more defined.

Julien was right. This is changing me. I am stronger. I feel more confident.

FINALLY, we each get our own sparring partner, who we'll work with for the last three days of training. Mine wears a traditional Japanese costume, a Ninja-like outfit, except for the ornate scowling mask covering his entire face. He stands stiff while I enter the dojo during our first session and bows to me when I take my weapons and stand before him.

I bow back, and then my coach signals that we can start fighting and I lunge at him. He's fast, so I gather that he's another Adept who has already gone through training. I've improved tremendously during the past ten days, but he's still better than me, always seeming one step ahead of me when we fall into fight trance.

Still, either I'm really good or he just keeps a bit ahead of me, letting me show my ability without shutting me down, but we seem to be almost equals. The fight goes on and on, much longer than normal and by the time our weapons are locked together, sweat is dripping off my face and my cheeks are hot, my breath ragged.

"You're good," he says, his voice muffled from behind the mask. "One of the best."

He pushes me, managing to get his foot behind me, and I trip and fall back and he's on top of me, his swords crossed and it's a good thing they're wooden or I'd be dead.

Then he pulls his mask off and it's Michel...

CHAPTER 8

"*Love is a better teacher than duty.*"

Albert Einstein

"Julien really thinks he can protect you. That you can protect yourself," he says, and his voice is hard, his blue eyes hooded, his hair falling in his eyes. "He can't even protect you from me." Michel is barely out of breath while I'm gasping. He's lying on top of me, his body heavy on mine. "If I could find you, how much easier would it be for Soren?"

I blink the sweat out of my eyes.

"If Soren wants me, he'll take me. I'm resigned to that. He obviously doesn't want me or he'd have taken me by now."

"Or maybe he just wants to torture me a little longer by letting you stay with Julien before he does decide to take you from both of us."

I try to wriggle out from underneath him, but he's too strong and keeps me pinned beneath him.

"Are you going to let me up?"

"Have pity on me, Eve," he says, his gaze moving over my face. "Considering I had you back with me for so short a time before losing you again, you might just stay like this for a moment," he says. "Indulge me. It reminds me of another time we fought and the positions were reversed. Do you remember?"

"You know I don't," I say. "I've read a passage about it in my journal, but that's it."

Then, he joins his mind with mine, showing me the fight through his eyes.

Michel stands at the ready, waiting for me to enter the Dojo. I walk in, my cheeks bright pink from the chill air, the umbrella in my hand, my Boston U backpack over one shoulder, my hair a bit mussed from the wind.

I feel a surge of desire from him as he sees my face. His lust is mixed with a deep fondness for me that surprises me. Then I watch through his eyes as I run for the wooden practice swords and fight him, easily beating him, and I appear to him like a blur. Finally, he sees me as I lie on top of him and he's thinking that I'm amazing. I'm magnificent. I'm far too beautiful.

He wants me. He's already falling in love with me and can't resist me. Most of all, he wants me to kiss him as I lie on top of him.

He wants me to choose him.

Then he releases me from the shared memory and I'm back in the dojo in France, with his body still heavy on top of me.

He's here to take me back.

"Don't think you can just take me and I'll go along with you. I'll fight you every step of the way."

He smiles, his smile lopsided, his blue eyes dark. "I once told you I love brats, Eve. I do. Don't think that would dissuade me."

"Does Julien know you're here? If he doesn't, he will soon enough. He'll come to rescue me."

"Forget about Julien for just a moment. You need to listen to me, Eve. I've stood on the sidelines just to see what his game was, and I've seen it now. I'm here to ask that you come back to me."

"You're *asking* or telling?"

He closes his eyes for a moment and exhales, his usually soft lips a tight line.

"Asking."

I consider for a moment. He's actually *asking* me? Part of me doesn't believe it.

"Why would I come back to you, knowing what I know?"

"You know I didn't do it under my own will."

"Tell me everything or you might as well leave now."

He sighs. "Julien wants to use you as an ordinary Adept, finding rogues and prosecuting them like you're a pair of police detectives. He has no ambition except to keep you by his side. That's a waste of your gifts, Eve. I need to use you as you were intended to be used – to fight Soren. We're going to join his coven and discover just what his plans are. You'll be my pet."

"Julien wants me as his partner. As equals. Why isn't that good enough for you?"

"I've already explained this. I have to trust you completely. You have to trust me completely. Soren has to believe you are under my control."

"You aren't in danger anymore. You don't need my protection. Besides, I thought you wanted to keep me out of this life."

He says nothing for a moment. "You want back in, and I know now I can't stop you. I tried and failed. I want you. I need you to stop Soren."

I can't believe he's actually here, thinking he can just take me back, especially after what happened between us. I decide to hear him out.

"And if I say yes?"

As I say the words, I swear I can see hope in his face, his eyes almost pleading.

"If you say yes, we're going to do this right. The way I planned on doing it from the start."

"What does *that* mean?" But I know what he means. For me to be his obedient pet, the way vampires and humans are together. With me as his little blood slave. His Adept, sitting on his lap, my arm around his shoulder, feeding on him, killing for him, protecting him.

There is a part of me that responds to that despite my need for equality.

He must feel it for he leans his forehead against mine for a moment as his breathing quickens. We remain like that for a moment and I push the thought out of the way, hating my weakness. My heart screams that he killed my mother… My mind counters that he was compelled to kill her just like he was compelled when he killed Danielle. Not of his own choice.

It was Soren. My hatred for Soren almost makes me change my mind.

He exhales heavily, making that sound in the back of his throat. Then, he pulls back, his face serious once more.

"You'd need to obey me without hesitation. If I tell you to do something, you must do it. I have to know with complete certainty you won't question me."

"I don't really think I want this," I say, but I know it's a lie. There's this part of me that wants to go fight Soren. If Julien really only wants me to be an ordinary Adept, and not fight against Soren, I'm not sure it's enough.

"Eve," he says, his voice soft. "This isn't about what you want or what I want anymore. If it was, you and I would be living in Wales on the Pembrokeshire coast. From there, we could watch the stars at night and walk the beaches. Listen to the birds nesting in the cliffs on Skomer Island. Make love to the sound of the surf."

I stare at him for a moment. Despite everything, it still touches my heart that he wants us to be together somewhere far away, but I must fight Soren. Maybe I'm starting to accept that Michel isn't truly guilty, that Soren was the one truly responsible for my mother's death.

But still… I'm with Julien now. I love *Julien* and it's only in that moment that I realize I *do* love him.

"If you want me to come with you, you have to tell me everything. Tell me how you knew my mother."

He sighs. "I met your mother before she joined the Council as a researcher. Then she married your father and she wanted a child so much but she was infertile, her tubes blocked and scarred by an infection she got when she was on the streets. I told her about a Council program which would provide her with IVF if she agreed to carry at least one child to term for our use."

"So you blackmailed her."

He exhales. "We gave her what she wanted most in life. A child. You think what she wanted most was to kill all vampires, but you're wrong. She wanted you."

"You preyed on her desire for a child to get your prized Adept with fight skills."

"Eve, do you have any idea how important you are?"

"No," I say, anger filling me once more, despite his powers. "You've never really explained."

"At first, your kind – the new group of enhanced Adepts – were intended to protect vampires like Julien, who'd be fighting those out for Dominion. To protect them as well as work cases."

I nod. "My mother could fight. How was that possible?"

"She was one of the very few natural anomalies found due to genetic screening. They were fast, but they didn't have fight sight. That was just your group. Eve, your DNA was enhanced using Ancient DNA, and from them, DNA from the Grigori."

"Grigori," I say, scoffing. "I don't believe in any Fall."

He sighs. "Regardless, when the Grigori fell, they infused their DNA into that of humans and it's been passed on for thousands of years, mostly silent. When it is expressed, it causes more problems than it solves. Your mother's abilities caused her so many problems until she understood they were gifts."

I frown, not knowing what that meant. "What problems?"

"Like you, she had touch telepathy and saw violence in the objects she touched. But unlike you, she grew up in a very violent home and so she was almost driven mad by it. She ran away, lived on the streets, was a prostitute and drug addict in Brooklyn. Like Kate. That's how she became infertile."

"Kate was an Adept?"

"Yes," he says, shaking his head. "She was a natural anomaly like your mother. But she wasn't discovered until it was too late for her.

She couldn't be saved. All I could do was care for her until she died. I couldn't cure her, even after I transformed."

I exhale, wanting to keep pushing him to get more answers.

"You met my mother because of your work."

He nods. "I was in New York for a while doing outreach for the Council. We looked specifically for runaways and street youth. Because of their gifts, natural Adepts most often had problems in school and with their families. I found your mother and realized she was an Adept. I brought her to our rehab facility. She blossomed. Went to school, got her degrees, met your father…"

"Julien said I was meant for him. My mother wanted me to be his Adept, if I chose to join the Council when I reached eighteen."

Michel looks away and I follow his gaze out the window at the mountains surrounding the Abbey.

"*Technically*, you were intended for one of us. Your mother wanted it to be Julien because she trusted him. I wasn't an operative at that time, but Julien was, so you would never have been mine."

"An operative?"

"Undercover," he says. "Working to infiltrate Blackstone. I was at the SCU."

"Why are Adepts like me so important?"

Finally we sit up and he takes my hand, leading me to chairs along the wall. I sit and he stands in front of me. I look at my coach and he's standing with his head down. Michel must have compelled him to comply, no questions. Michel sits beside me on a chair, one arm on the back behind me. I move away from him.

"We discovered that those of you created under the new program have this unique ability. When you drink our blood, you can connect telepathically to us and we can connect to you. If you drank the blood of ten vampires, you can connect us all. Genes we didn't understand from the Grigori were transferred, giving you this ability. You're a conduit."

I move farther away, for when he's so close, I can't help but feel something from him.

"Why is that important?"

"It would link all of us together so we'd know exactly what each one was doing and thinking. Like a collective. Like the Grigori before they fell. It would be amazing for warriors. Or strategists. Or angels who just want back a bit of the heaven they lost when they fell. That's why Soren wants you."

"This is insane," I say and turn my face away. "The Grigori. Fallen angels. I don't believe it. They're just mutated humans. They have some ability to project into our brains and make us think we're experiencing things. Like you making me see wings, manipulating my dreams or my mind. That's it."

He sighs. "You just won't believe, will you? No matter what."

"I'm a skeptic," I say and look at him. "I need proof. Evidence."

"Haven't I given that to you? What more do I have to do?"

I shake my head.

"How can you prove it isn't a mental projection? You can't. I know some neuroscience. Real experience or stimulating a memory – there is no ultimate difference to the brain or the person experiencing it. Until you can prove it, projection is the simplest explanation. I tend to accept those over the more complicated ones that rely on some improvable deity."

I'm so confused and squeeze my fingers into my palms to clear my mind.

"Regardless of what you believe, believe this. I didn't want this for you. I wanted you to study music like your parents did. But what I want isn't the point. This is about fighting Dominion," he says, "and both you and I have a responsibility to join the fight. *This* is what your mother would have wanted for you, had she known how close we are to it. Julien's so infatuated with you, he won't let you be used the way you should be, but Eve, as much as I love you, I know I have to put my personal desires aside and use you the way you were meant to be used."

"As a weapon?"

He nods, closing his eyes. "*Yes.*"

"I hate the thought of leaving Julien."

"You'll hate yourself even more one day if you don't come with me."

"Why can't you and Julien just cooperate and fight against Dominion together?"

He shakes his head. "Because we both love you and want you for our own. Neither of us wants to yield to the other."

"Why can't I choose between you?"

"You *can*. I just wanted to give you time. I wanted to see how Julien would use you and now I have." He shakes his head. "In the end, he's too selfish. He wants a happy little life with you as his partner, fighting crime like you're some ordinary Adept. You're *not* ordinary and you were meant for this war."

He shakes his head for a moment as if fighting his emotions.

"I can't lie, Eve. I was just as foolish and selfish. I thought I could make a new life for you and escape this future but I was wrong. I understand now that I must follow this path, however much I wish to avoid it. As much as I love you – as much as I want you, I need you with me to win this war even more."

"So I can choose?"

"Yes, but please," he says and takes my shoulders in his hands, staring in my eyes. "Consider what I've said seriously. I'm giving you this choice. By rights, I could just take you, the way Julien has. He *didn't* give you a choice, did he? He took you and you were far too overwhelmed by him and by everything that's happened to you to refuse. I *will* give you the choice. I've *always* given you the choice. But let me warn you again – things have gone farther than I thought they would. Time is not on our side, Eve."

"Tell me so I understand."

"I would but I don't want to frighten you." He shakes his head. "I don't want to break your heart."

"It's that bad?"

He nods, and brushes a strand of hair off my face. "If it wasn't, I'd let you stay with him without making this offer. I won't lie to you. He can make you happy. I know that."

"So if I say I'm staying with Julien, you'll just up and leave right now?"

"I let you stay this long. I didn't try to take you back. I wanted to see what he'd do and how you'd respond. I've made my offer. You have until the end of the course to decide. At the end of your test, Julien will be here and he'll take you with him. Or I'll take you with me. It's your choice. You'll have to live with the consequences."

I don't know what to do or say, so I just sit there, staring at his beautiful face, so filled with concern.

"I want you to be happy, Eve," he says and leans in, kissing me softly. "I'll do everything I can to make you as happy as possible if you agree to help me. But I can't promise you happiness. You may chafe at what you must do, what you must be when we're on stage and you're seen as my pet. As my blood slave. It will be dangerous. You may even die."

"If I decide to stay with Julien?"

"I'll leave and I won't come back unless you ask me to. Even if you do decide to stay with him, at any time, you need only contact me and I'll come for you. It will break my heart if you choose him, but I want you to be free to choose. To be happy."

Something's building inside of me. Emotions are filling me up, making me close to tears. I bite my cheek for a moment.

"What about your happiness?"

He shakes his head. "I'll be happy once we stop Dominion. Not until."

I close my eyes and take in a deep breath. "I'll decide when the time comes," I say.

He nods and releases my shoulders. "Have you fed yet today?"

I shake my head. "I usually do before they shut out the lights. The blood heals me of any wounds I receive during training. Then Julien and I connect."

He nods. "I want you to have my blood tonight. If Julien knows I've made this offer, there's no telling what he might do."

"He'll be worried if I don't connect with him."

"Your trainer will call him and tell him that they had to feed you ordinary vampire blood because the facility experienced a power outage and the blood went bad. He won't be happy, but he'll wait. I know he's busy in Boston. He's planning on flying to France tomorrow night so he'll be here for your final test."

"That's devious."

He cracks a grin. "I'm eight hundred years old, Eve. I've had lots of practice."

I can't help but smile back at his playful tone and that lopsided grin. Then his grin disappears and he pulls me into his arms, his lips finding my cheek, his tongue touching my skin. I feel such a wave of love and desire from him that it almost makes me pass out, but I push him away.

"Michel," I say, trying to escape his arms. "I can't..."

He sighs, his hands cupping my face. "I'm sorry. You must understand how I feel..."

I do understand. I feel it when he touches me. He loves me. He wants me. His heart is breaking at the thought that I love Julien.

Despite everything, this feels so right – being with Michel. This could happen so easily between us...

I pull back and there are tears in his eyes. The expression on his face is haunting in its sadness, as if he already knows that I'll choose Julien.

But even I don't know what I'll choose. Who I'll choose.

CHAPTER 9

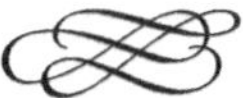

" There is no I or you, so intimate that
your hand upon my chest is my hand, so intimate that
when I fall asleep your eyes close."

Pablo Neruda

I SPEND the rest of the afternoon and evening in class, studying for our final written test. The instructor goes over the different fighting techniques, weapons, tactics, and other information we've received over the course of the past week and a half. All the while I can't stop thinking about Michel and what he's offered. He's actually giving me the choice to go with him or to stay with Julien. Some part of me can't really believe it – will he renege on his offer and take me if I decide to stay with Julien?

Will I stay with Julien? I think back to our time together, as brief as it has been, and my heart swells with emotion for him. He's so beautiful and so attentive and so erotic... The thought of us working together as partners makes me happy.

But Michel... He's so serious. His words are so somber and scare me. Dominion – it's just a concept to me – the rule of Ancients and vampires over mortals. I remember reading in my journal what Julien said to me at the hotel in Norfolk – how the Ancients were planning to strike against technology. Millions – perhaps billions – would die in the coming war.

I'm so torn.

~

LATER, after I shower and dress in my pajama top and bottoms, I'm finally alone in my tiny bedroom, sitting on my bed waiting for my nightly dose of blood. The door opens and it's Michel. I realize he must have compelled everyone in the building if he can just come and go at will. He closes the door and sits beside me on the bed.

"You need to feed," he says, his voice low, husky.

"You have a vial of blood for me?" I say, but I know he wouldn't bring a vial. I know that like Julien, this appeals to him so much – my need for his blood. My feeding off his body.

"No vials of blood between us, Eve," he says and pulls me into his arms. I stiff arm him and don't let him embrace me.

"No," I say. "I can't just do this so easily. I'm used to Julien..."

He exhales heavily.

"Do you really want my blood in a vial?"

I hesitate. I can't deny that the idea of sitting on his lap as I have with Julien, drinking his blood from his neck appeals to me, but I suddenly feel all shy with him. He's so much like Julien, except the longer hair and clean shaven face, but the eyes and thick black lashes, the square jaw and soft mouth are the same.

"It would give me some distance. This is all so," I say and struggle for words. "So overwhelming. I just can't go between you two like this. You can't expect me to."

"I know," he says and strokes my cheek, releasing an endorphin in my brain that makes me relax. Before I know it, he's pulling me onto his lap, into his arms. I can do nothing, my body so relaxed I'm practically like a rag doll. He positions my arms around his shoulders and tilts his head to the side, dragging his nail down the skin on his neck below his ear. A thin line of dark blood forms and begins to drip down his neck.

I don't hesitate, pressing my mouth against it, sucking.

He sighs, his arms tightening around me. The taste is so sweet and intoxicating, different from the tiny vial of Julien's blood I've been drinking while at the abbey because it's fresh and not adulterated with preservatives and anti-clotting medications. I don't need much to feel satisfied – just a mouthful or two – and as I fall away from his neck, he lays me down on the bed and lies on top of me.

I spread my thighs without thought and he lies between them. He moves and presses against me, and although my body is ready, my mind still fights.

"Please," I manage to say, turning my face when he leans down to kiss me.

Finally, he sighs and rolls off me.

"I'm sorry," he says.

"You have to understand. I've just been with Julien. I can't just fuck you. It's the blood."

"It's OK," he says and exhales. "I understand. I can wait. When you've existed for eight hundred years, you learn patience. When this happens between us, I want you to be absolutely certain. I want you absolutely present with me, willing, ready." He kisses me and strokes my cheek. "I'm a very patient man, Eve. I can wait for you."

It's then my thoughts turn to my future and a cold sensation takes hold of me. I still don't know what my decision will be.

Beside me, Michel exhales heavily and pulls me tightly against him.

WE SLEEP on the tiny cot, nestled against each other, him spooned against my back. I'm surprised he stays, but he must have every guard and trainer under his power. Of course, when I wake with his body beside me, I want him but I dig my nails into my palms.

"It's OK, Eve," he whispers. "I won't push, but you'd better leave, quickly, or I might not be able to control myself." He kisses my neck and his lust momentarily makes me dizzy, my eyes closing. I see into his mind and detect his plan to masturbate in the shower when everyone's in class and he'll be alone, with thoughts of my naked body in his mind's eye.

I roll over and I'm unable to keep the smile off my face when I see his wide grin.

"I'd better leave. I'm not even allowed to masturbate while I'm in training."

"It's a male plumbing thing," he says. "I have no choice in the matter. It's part of the lifestyle."

I recognize the Seinfeld reference and smile against the pillow.

This is too good. This feels too perfect. *I could be happy with this —* the way it is right now between us. So light, so happy, so filled with lust and love. If it could be like this always... But the things he said yesterday suggest it will be otherwise and that worries me. I never was an actor. I could never hide my true feelings even if I lied to myself about feeling them. I don't know if I can do what it is he says I'll have to do to be with him.

I push the thoughts out of my mind and get up, leaving him alone in the bed. Before I go, I take one last long glance at his half-naked body sprawled on the bed, his skin so perfect and pale against the dark wool blanket, his muscles well-developed, the dark thatch of hair running down from his navel beneath his boxer briefs. Just seeing him lying there almost naked sends another jolt of desire through me and part of me wants to just go to him. But I don't. I can't be that woman — the one who cheats on her lover. I can't be Marguerite who moved between the two brothers, having both at the same time.

Instead, I head to the showers and the cafeteria to start my day.

~

I'M busy in class all day, reviewing before the big written test but thoughts of Michel masturbating in the shower as the water runs over his naked body distract me from my work, a pleasant ache in my groin.

Late in the afternoon, Michel watches me while I spar with two fellow students, practicing with a set of short swords, one wooden, one metal. He's dressed in a black Japanese-style uniform, soft trousers and tunic, his feet bare. He circles us, his arms crossed, stepping in to give us direction. He seems to have taken over Julien's role. Julien was the Knight, the soldier, the warrior. I wonder why he isn't here instead of Michel. Why didn't he decide to take part in my training the way Michel has?

Regardless, Michel is focused, watching me, judging me, stopping the fight at various points to make a comment about technique, adjusting my stance and even his touch arouses me. He rolls his eyes at me once when he stands in for my opponent, adjusting my body so I'm in a better position and I feel a stab of desire at his touch.

"Eve," he whispers in my ear as he leans in briefly, squeezing my shoulder. "Concentrate."

It's so hard for me to concentrate when I know what he's done earlier.

He grins and pushes me away. All the while, his eyes are on me and I feel self-conscious. Despite his brief indulgent smile, his face is dark as I fight, his eyes intense. I'm a bit hesitant for fear I don't perform up to his standards.

LATER, we eat together in the cafeteria after the other students have finished, and he tells me about my performance against multiple opponents. I have slightly better fight sight than the students I fought against today, and it gives me an advantage.

"Physically, you're now strong enough to fight, but you still must develop judgment. That will only come with time. You and I will need to practice frequently, to ensure you have faced every possibility and found a way to survive, succeed."

I don't say anything. He's planning as if I *will* go with him but as much as I desire him, I haven't decided. While I sat in class earlier, instead of listening to the instructor review a section on weapons, I thought about my choice. I can't deny my attraction to Michel – he's so calm and strong and makes me feel safe and loved. His willingness to let me choose makes my emotions surge. But he killed my mother, and there's a part of me that can never forgive him.

Then I think of Julien…

Julien's so *passionate*. When I'm with Julien, I feel as if we're just completely absorbed in each other. He loves me. He *needs* me in a way Michel doesn't seem to. Michel will let me go, but I know Julien wouldn't.

I feel as if Julien and I are equals. I know we aren't – he's eight-hundred years old. He's a vampire – more than just a vampire now that he's transformed. But when we're together, I feel as if he treats me like an equal – as two humans instead of a vampire and human, the way Michel does. I'm Julien's partner as well as his lover. He wants us to be a team to police the treaty and stop Blackstone. His humanity seems closer to the surface. Despite our intimacy, Michel still seems otherworldly to me and there's this distance I feel from him, like a separation that can never be breached, no matter how much mutual lust I feel from him.

Now, as I sit across from Michel while we eat our meal, my gut wrenches about the decision I must make tomorrow. No matter what I decide, someone will be hurt. Michel said it would break his heart, but it must not break it that much if he's willing to let me go. I know Julien wouldn't let me go without a fight.

That must mean something…

I choke up at the thought of this choice and for a moment, I put my fork down and try to calm myself, taking in deep breaths, biting my cheek to gain control. Tears bite at the corners of my eyes. Across from me, Michel looks up and frowns, wiping his mouth on a napkin and pushing his plate away. He reaches across the table and takes my hand and if he's reading me, if he knows my thoughts, he doesn't say. He doesn't protest. I don't feel him in my mind and I wonder if I've blocked him or if he's just that much more powerful now that he can enter my mind without my knowing it. I have been drinking his blood.

He squeezes my hand, his face so earnest, his eyes haunted. He stands and comes around beside me, pulling me against his chest, stroking my hair as I struggle to regain my composure.

Still, he says nothing. Just holds me tightly.

He *knows*...

Then he lifts my chin with a finger, wiping my tears away with his other hand.

"You are so beautiful in every way."

He leans down and kisses me, his kiss chaste. When he does, I wish I'd never met Julien. But I have and now I can't get Julien out of my mind. Part of me wants neither of them, but as Julien said, if I don't choose one, by default I choose Soren, for he's the most powerful of the Ancients – or whatever he is. I still haven't figured that out yet.

Michel sits back down and we continue to eat in silence. My mind is unable to leave Soren behind and I decide to push Michel for information. He can't protest – he wants me to make this huge decision and I need to know more before I can.

"What *is* Soren?" I say. "He's not just an Ancient."

Michel sits back, frowning. He doesn't say anything for a few moments as if debating with himself on whether to tell me.

"What do you think he is? You met him."

"That's not fair," I say. "You *know* what he is. Why won't you just tell me? He told me that I was wrong about what he is. That must mean he's not an Ancient. Is he Grigori?"

Michel pushes food around on his plate without looking at me. Finally, he speaks and his voice is almost a whisper.

"He is less than Grigori. More than an Ancient. When he fed the first time, it wasn't on a human. It was on his maker – his father. He killed his father, a Nephilim. That made him more powerful."

"What *is* his plan? He doesn't want to lead Blackstone. What does he want?"

"Eve," he says and shakes his head. "I can't tell you. How many times do I have to repeat that?"

"Why? You want me to just trust you, come with you, to be your little blood slave, and help you stop him, but you won't tell me." And then I pull out my trump card. "Julien would."

He doesn't respond so if my barb hit its target, I can't tell.

"Julien doesn't see what I see."

"What do you mean? See what?"

He shakes his head quickly, and I can see the internal struggle written on his face, his jaw tensing, his brow furrowed. Finally, he glances up at me, his eyes pained.

"Even telling you this much changes everything and I have to try to see my way through all over again. I wish I could tell you, Eve. You don't know how much. I just *can't*."

"Why? What do you mean, see your way through all over again?"

He bites his bottom lip as if to stop himself from speaking. He's completely unnerved by this conversation. What is he hiding? Why does he feel so afraid to tell me the truth?

He leans forward, his eyes downcast, and whispers as if he's afraid to say the words out loud.

"Every word, every act, every decision," he says, his voice shaking, "changes *everything*. I can see all ends and I'm trying so hard to find the one that protects you but even just saying that much changes it all once more. Soren and I – we're playing a game of chess, both of us assessing each other's moves. We can both see every possible outcome, every possible future." He says nothing for a moment as if overcome, struggling with his emotions, then he looks at me, his gaze moving over my face. "I wish you could just obey me, Eve. Just *obey*. It would be so much easier."

"I can't until you tell me why I have to."

He closes his eyes, raising his hands as if in surrender. "That is my dilemma. I must not tell you, I must not force you because if I do, it will lead to the end I fear the most. I must keep you in the dark and let you choose."

"You're not making any sense."

He shrugs, his eyes dreamy as if he's seeing something in the distance or in his mind's eye.

"It all keeps changing, shifting, the ground moving under my feet with each word and each action. I try to do the right thing, keep on the right course, but I am unable to control everything. I fail to control you." Then he glances back at my face. "I have to be so careful..."

"You sound insane." He does. What he's saying makes no sense. "Tell me, Michel! Tell me what's going on."

He shakes his head as if helpless.

I put my napkin over my plate and stand. If he's going to keep up this mystery man act, I can't go with him. Julien promised to tell me the truth, always. Why can't Michel?

"I'm going to my class. I guess I'll see you later at the final bout."

He nods without looking at me as if he's already off somewhere else, trying to see his way through it – whatever *it* is.

AFTER ANOTHER HOUR IN CLASS, we go to our sparring practice and Michel is there, waiting for me, short Wakizashi swords in hand. This time when we fight, he keeps just ahead of me, pushing me, challenging me, forcing me to always be on the defensive. And then he hurts me, by accident I'm certain, but he hurts me all the same. He slices my arm and the blood pours out of the deep cut, so much so that it scares me.

I crumple to the ground and try to stem the flow of blood. He grabs my arm and applies pressure to the wound, his brow furrowed.

"I'm so sorry," he says, holding the edges of the wound together with his fingers. Slowly, the edges knit together and the flow changes from a gush to a tiny ooze but I've already lost a lot of blood.

He carries me to my bedroom for I'm weak from blood loss.

"Don't let me die," I say, as darkness closes in on me.

"You won't," he says, biting his own wrist, holding it up to my mouth. "Drink."

I do, for I know it will heal me, replenish the blood I've lost. Soon, I feel strength return to my body and my vision, which had dimmed, clears so I see his beautiful face poised over mine, his eyes dark.

Soon, I'm able to sit up and I examine the thin line where the wound used to be.

"Soren healed me completely without making me drink his blood."

"He's more powerful than I am."

"What *is* he?" I say, touching his arm. "What does he want?"

"He wants to be a god," he says, and then helps me up. "A god of war reborn. He wants to claim the Roman Church for his own. Use it to rule over all."

"And you? What will you be to him? He wants you with him."

He nods. "He wants me as his High Priest. His Pope."

He raises his eyes to meet mine as if he's embarrassed to admit this to me. Finally! Michel tells me something I didn't already know.

"And are you?" I say, heat rising in my face at his admission. "Are you his High Priest? Will you be his pope?"

He exhales. "I will. He wants Julien as his warlord."

A chill goes through me, my body numb. "And me? What am I supposed to be?"

His jaw tenses for a moment as if he's grinding his teeth.

"His Medium."

I frown. A Medium? "Do you mean like a psychic Medium? Is this what you meant by me being a conduit?"

He nods. "You'd channel – focus the powers of those you join with, giving Soren more powers. Powers he could tap and use to do miracles. Feats of wonder to ensnare unwitting believers. But he's not a god. He's an abomination. He's a monster. What did Yeats write?" He pauses for a moment, as if remembering and then he recites the poem, his voice grave.

"Things fall apart; the center cannot hold;

Mere anarchy is loosed upon the world,
The blood-dimmed tide is loosed, and everywhere
The ceremony of innocence is drowned;
The best lack all conviction, while the worst
Are full of passionate intensity."

"I know that poem," I say, remembering it from high school English. "How does it end? Something about a monster being born."

"What rough beast," he says, his voice a whisper, "its hour come round at last, slouches towards Bethlehem to be born?"

"It was about the post-war years in Europe," I say in protest. "After the First World War."

"It's an allegory, using Biblical imagery. But what I'm talking about is Biblical, Eve."

"You mean like the Anti-Christ? You're saying Soren is the Antichrist? And you support this?"

"Not the Anti-Christ, no. But a monster none-the-less." He frowns at me, his blue eyes dark. "I don't support him. He's an abomination to me. I'll fight him. I have to find the right way to do so."

"By looking like you support him. But Michel, he's compelled you. How do you know he doesn't already know your plans to fight him?"

He shakes his head and turns his face away from me. Then he sighs heavily. He pulls me closer, his arms going around me. He leans in, his lips next to my ear.

"All I know is that he's trying to make sure I have no other choice but to comply with his wishes to save your life." He squeezes his arms around me so tightly that I can barely breathe. "Oh, God, Eve," he says. "I'm so tired of this. Trying not to say the wrong thing. Saying enough to convince you but not kill you. So tired..."

I pull away and he releases me, and there are tears in his blue eyes. "Tell me!"

He cups my cheek, and strokes it with his thumb.

"I see it all," he says. "Every different future. Each decision, each word makes one future more likely to come true, and others less likely. Eve, if you could only just obey fully, I could save you but you have to fight me every second of the day..."

"Save my life? You mean I'll die if I don't obey you?"

He says nothing, just brushes a strand of hair from my cheek.

"There are things worse than death."

"Quit being so cryptic!" I hit him, pound his chest for I'm angry and scared. He sounds demented. "Tell me or leave."

"Don't you *understand?*" he says and grabs my shoulders, shaking me, his face filled with grief. "I sentence you to death by telling you. I *can't* tell you. I've already told you too much. If I do tell you, you *will* die. This is my test – the test of what future I will allow to come and what price I'll pay..."

I push him away and stand up. "You're deluded."

I back away from him, but he won't leave me alone. He rises from the bed and follows me until he has me cornered. He presses against me so that I'm trapped, one of his arms on the wall beside my head.

"If I tell you, you'll die. Even telling you this makes it more likely and I'll have to scramble to adjust, recalculate, re-plot my course, alter my plan. Eve, I have to watch every act, every word," he says and shakes his head. "Every breath."

"You can't tell the future!"

He shakes his head sadly. "I can. With each word," he says and strokes my cheek. "We change it. Every time we speak, every time we make a decision, the future is altered. Don't you see? There are so few good futures for us, Eve. So many bad ones. I see them all, I see them change each time I talk of this with you. Please, just stop asking me. Just obey me and let me save your life. I can't stand a universe without you beside me."

His expression of need for me touches my heart but I shake my head, unable to accept his words. He thinks he can see the future? It's impossible. It hasn't happened yet. He can't see it.

He *can't.*

He's deluded. This is what Julien was speaking about – Michel's obsession with controlling everything so he can affect the future.

"If you can see the future," I say, frowning, "then you knew you were going to cut my arm. You let it happen."

He sighs. "I saw myself cut you. I saw you bleeding, Eve. I saw you survive. I saw how that act cascaded forward into the future, altering it ever so slightly in my favor so I *let* it happen," he says and presses his finger against my lips. "Now please, go to sleep."

He leads me back to the bed and I lie down but sleep is long in coming, for I have his blood in me and his body is right there, pressed against mine.

I know he's aroused.

This could happen so easily. I can't let it.

I owe Julien that much.

CHAPTER 10

"My love is selfish. I cannot breathe without you."

John Keats, Letters to Fanny Brawne

I WAKE with a start out of a bad dream in which I fall with someone's sword in me, the blade piercing my heart, my hands around the sharp edges. I'm panting and Michel's staring at me when I open my eyes, his brow furrowed, his expression dark.

"I saw myself being killed," I say, barely able to speak.

"I know." He doesn't say anything more, but heaves a heavy sigh and cups my cheek. "You needn't worry. I won't let it happen."

"That wasn't a vision of the future." I sit up, my heart rate slowly returning to normal. "It was just a dream about my test today."

"Eve," he says, closing his eyes briefly. "You are so stubborn. You saw into my mind when you were waking."

I shake my head, refusing to believe something that's impossible. "I'm just anxious about the test."

"Don't worry," he says and strokes my cheek. "The tests will be a breeze for you. You have nothing to fear."

He pulls me into an embrace and I'm distracted from the dream of my death. I haven't decided yet. I won't be able to make my decision until I see Julien and talk to him.

The thought chokes me up and I hug Michel tightly, despite my vow not to encourage him. He knows what I'm thinking through our connection and pulls me even closer against him.

We just lie there for a moment, wallowing in the sensations of sadness and his attempt to calm me doesn't stop my fear about my decision.

I GET up and before I close the door to leave, I turn back and stare at him. He turns on his side to face me, and his face has this haunted look, his blue eyes huge. We say nothing. There's no need to speak.

Then, I go to the showers, a choke in my throat. When I'm done, he's gone. I go to the cafeteria before preparing for my tests.

The written tests are first thing this morning, and are short. Most of our testing will be through performance and fighting later this evening. We have several hours off in the afternoon to study for our fights and I wonder where Michel is. I return to my tiny room but he's not there. I sit and go through my notes on various stances and moves and do some practice in the dojo, but he never shows up.

I wonder if Julien is already here and what he'll do when he comes for me. My stomach is in knots just thinking of it.

I go back to the cafeteria and eat supper by myself, surrounded by almost two-dozen other students, all eating, deep in thought as we mentally prepare for our bouts tonight.

FINALLY, my trainer arrives and takes me out to the garden where floodlights have been set up and the other students are standing in five rows of four students. The sun has set and it's about nine o'clock at night. We start going through the routines, the instructor barking commands at the front of the field. With my two wooden Wakizashi swords in hand, I perform the moves, my braid tucked into my tunic and my feet bare in the cool grass.

Movement in my peripheral vision distracts me and I glance to the right of the field where three priests in black vestments escort three tall men onto the field from a doorway. Dressed all in black and carrying black-visored helmets, the tall men have Wakizashi swords – *real* ones, similar to the wooden ones we used for practice.

Adepts with fight sight – it must be.

They march to the rear of the field and each one stands inside one of three rings marked out in chalk lines on the grass.

I glance back to the doorway when we switch to a series of side thrusts, and watch as a dozen observers in street clothes enter the field, speaking with the priests, but I don't see either Michel or Julien. The new arrivals walk up and down the rows of students. Two stop beside me, watching me go through the routine.

"How do you think they'll do?" a woman says.

"It's sink or swim," a man says, his voice smooth and foreign, sounding British. I see him out of the corner of my eye when I perform a side lunge.

A priest.

"This is their final test. They have to beat an experienced Adept in battle. This will separate the wheat from the chaff."

As I go through the routine, I wonder if I'll be wheat or chaff. Julien promised to be here to watch and I glance around but don't see him. I don't see Michel either, but perhaps they don't want to distract me. I can only imagine what's passed between them if they've met up before the test.

The trainers start pulling students out of the formation, taking them back to the rings. I hear shouts, cries of pain, the collective 'oohs' and 'ahhs' from the observers, scattered applause, but I'm unable to turn around and watch. Finally, one of the trainers motions to me, taking his baton and placing it in front of me so that I have to stop.

"Your turn," he says and motions towards the back with his head. "Move it!"

I run to the rear of the field and what I see turns my blood to ice. The three Adepts fight students inside the circles, and as I wait, one pushes a girl out of the circle, wounding her with a slice to the arm. She's unable to beat the Adept or fight to a draw, which is required to pass. Medics tend several of my fellow students who failed the test, gashes on their limbs.

I step up, watching as the Adept takes his place in the center of the ring once more. He wears a visored helmet so I can't see his face. The guard shoves me from behind and I step into the circle, my heart racing and my wooden weapons at the ready. In a crouch position, I wait. The Adept bows to me but I don't bow back. We fight for the required three minutes and the official raises a flag, signaling an end to the match. I've fought to a draw.

I've passed.

Standing at the edge of the field I see Julien. He's dressed all in black with a long black leather trench and a blue scarf around his neck. Perhaps he didn't want to distract me, but regardless, I run to him, ignoring the calls of the guards behind me. He's smiling when I reach him, his arms open, his blue eyes wet. We kiss, the kiss deep and passionate and I feel a rush of love and some surprise from him, as if he didn't believe I'd choose him. He must know Michel's been here.

"I knew you'd pass," he says, his face in my neck. "They trained you well."

We kiss again and he pulls me against him so tightly, I think he'll break my back.

"Julien," I say and pull back. "Michel…"

"I know," he says and cups my cheek. "We've," he says and hesitates. "Spoken."

"Then you know I have to choose…"

He nods. "Of course you'll come with me. You *have* to." He takes my face in his hands, strokes my cheek with a thumb. "You don't want that life – the one Michel's promised you. A life with him as his blood slave fighting some ridiculous war for control of the world," he says, his voice angered. "You want to be with me as my partner. My *love*."

I step away, shaking my head.

"Michel said something very bad is coming. He said he needs me to fight Dominion."

Julien shakes his head. "There's more than one way to fight Dominion, Eve. You were meant to work as a Blood Witness. With me. It's what your mother wanted. This is what we were meant to do."

"Michel said—."

"I *know* what Michel said, Eve," he says and steps closer again. "He doesn't know everything. He thinks he can predict the future, control it. He's a bit insane, I think."

"We've been together, " I say, but quickly add. "We haven't had sex, but he fed me and we slept in the same bed."

He nods. "I'd kill him if I could bear it, cut off his head and burn his body, but I can't. He only did what I would have done if the roles had been reversed."

"You aren't mad at me?"

"How could I be?" he says and shakes his head, touching my face with the backs of his fingers. "What we're doing to you..." He sighs. "Now, go back to your room and pack up your bags. I'll send some guards with you. Michel's ... busy. He won't bother you. Then, come to me. You don't want to go with him, Eve. He's trying to defeat Soren all by himself, but he won't be able to without risking your life. I *won't* do that. I'll protect you. Don't let his talk of doom and gloom make you choose out of fear. I *love* you. I'll love you completely and totally. You are *everything* to me. I'll give you everything you want." He kisses me. "I'll make you happy. He won't."

He turns me around and points to the entrance to the dorm. "Now, go. I have to sign you out and then I'll be waiting by my rental car in the parking lot. Hurry. We don't have much time."

"What do you mean, much time?"

"Just go."

I leave the field, and two of the guards follow me into the dorm and stand outside the door to my tiny room. I pack up my things, my hands shaking, my heart pounding in my ears. I'm not really even thinking. I just pack, my mind blank.

Then I hear a scuffle outside my door.

I turn to face it and when the door opens, it's Michel. He closes the door behind him and adjusts his clothing, which are bloody and there's a hole in his shirt over his heart as if he's been staked.

He's just taken down both guards outside my door. Julien's guards.

When I see him, my heart jumps. "Michel," I say, my throat closing up. "What happened to you?"

"What do you think happened?" he says and touches the fabric. "Julien staked me."

"With a wooden stake?"

"Yes."

"He wouldn't."

"Oh, he would," he says, shaking his head. "He planned on keeping me in stasis for an indeterminate time back at the SCU. What he didn't know is that I'm immune to that now."

"You can't be killed with a stake?"

He shrugs his shoulders. "Hurts terribly and disables me, but is no more effective now than a metal weapon."

"Because of your ascension. But why doesn't Julien know?"

"He doesn't know everything, Eve. I can't even tell him or risk his life as well."

"Michel, you can't *do* this – you can't try to save the world all by yourself."

He steps closer to me. "I have no choice."

I feel incredible guilt that I was going to leave with Julien. "Michel, I'm going to--."

"I *know* what you were going to do," he says and takes my hand, immobilizing me with his powers, pulling me over to the bed. He sits down and then pulls me onto his lap so that I straddle his hips the way I did that day in his cottage.

"As usual, Julien sweeps in like some conquering warlord and overwhelms you with his words of love, his passionate nature. He's relying on his ability to overwhelm you, Eve, to convince you to go with him – just like he did that day on the beach."

"Maybe I *want* someone like him," I say and I can see those words, that thought, hurt him, watch the pain cross his face as if he's been struck. "And what about you?" I say, angered despite what he's done to me. "What are you relying on to convince me to go with you?"

"Only your sense of duty."

I shake my head. "Julien says you're deluded."

"He's hardly unbiased."

"What am I supposed to do, Michel?" I say, genuinely confused. "I love you both, each in your own way."

"I know," he says and brushes hair off my cheek. "But come with me, help me stop Soren. I *need* you."

I look at him, at his beautiful face, his eyes so blue, thick black lashes fringing them, his long hair a mess, tucked behind his ears. I stroke his face, his cheek, and he leans into my hand, his eyes closing. When he opens them again, his eyes are wet.

"Julien *wants* me."

"*I* want you, too. Every moment of every day, Eve. Don't think he loves you more than I do."

I don't know what to say. Julien loves me more intensely. I feel the difference when they touch me. When they connect to me. Michel's passion is steady and strong, but Julien… Julien's passion is almost desperate. Like he'd do anything for me. Michel will follow his course, no matter what I choose. The mission comes first, like he said.

Julien will give up the fight.

I don't know whether to believe this vision of a hellish future Michel talks about.

"I can't go with you if you lie to me. If you hide things from me. I have to have the truth. All of it."

He inhales deeply, his brow furrowed.

"What did Huxley write? *You shall know the truth and the truth shall drive you mad.*"

"Better a cruel truth than a comfortable delusion," I reply. "Edward Abbey."

He closes his eyes for a moment.

"I can't *tell* you the truth, don't you understand?" he says and pulls back, taking my face in his hands. "If I do, I kill you! How many times do I have to tell you this?"

"You're insane."

I try to push him away, try to extract myself from his arms but he won't let me go, and he's almost desperate, pulling me against him, using his greater power to lift me up and turn me over, pinning me beneath him on the bed, his hands holding mine above my head. Only a day ago that would have aroused me, but now it only feels like assault.

"Eve, I *love* you," he says and kisses me, forcing himself on me, his hand cupping my cheek.

Finally, when I don't give in, he stops and breaks the kiss, momentarily pressing his lips against my neck where he bit me. Then he rises up and lets go of me. He wipes his eyes and adjusts his coat. He walks stiffly to the door, leaving me on the bed, my heart pounding.

He stands in the entry for a moment as if he's trying to regain control over himself.

"When you realize the mistake you've made, send me a message if you can. Find a way. If I don't hear from you when it all falls apart, I'll come for you."

Then he leaves.

I sit on the bed and cry, weeping, because despite my anger at him for all the lies and deception, part of me knows he did it all out of loyalty to his mission. He thought he was doing the right thing. It wasn't because he wanted to win me. It was because he felt he needed to keep me from knowing his plans. But I can't be with a man who doesn't trust me enough to tell me the truth.

I go to Julien.

CHAPTER 11

"If I had a flower for each time I thought of you I could walk through my garden forever."

Alfred Lord Tennyson

We drive away from the abbey and when I glance back, Michel is standing at the courtyard gate, watching. I can't help it. Tears fill my eyes and I hate myself for hurting him. It *will* hurt him to see me go. It will break his heart – he said it would. But I can't go with him to this life he told me about based on nothing more than his visions of some dark future that hasn't happened.

More than that, I can't imagine saying no to Julien. He needs me more than Michel. Michel will go on with his grand plans to be the hero no matter what I say.

If I chose Michel, Julien would give up completely and join a monastery, go into cloister, until I'm dead. I've seen it in his mind. He can't face a future without me. Michel needs me for his plans. Julien needs me for his very existence.

How can I say no to that kind of love?

"You staked Michel," I say, my voice breaking.

"It was the only way to stop him. I see it failed." Julien takes my hand and squeezes when he sees the tears on my cheeks. "I'm sorry," he says, and he releases an endorphin in me to make me less sad. "I did it to protect you."

"Don't," I say and pull my hand away. "Let me feel my emotions." I just sit there as the French countryside flies by, barely noticing the beauty of the tall trees surrounding me, highlighted by the full moon. I blink away my tears and bite my cheek to keep my emotions from Michel, just in case he's reading me from a distance and knows I'm sad. I don't want him to take hope from it because if he knows how hard this is for me, he might take it as a sign to come after me. I need some time with Julien. Just Julien, so I can know how I feel.

"You should never have met us." Julien drives through the hills down the mountain towards Carcassonne. "You'd be in school now, studying cell biology and molecular genetics and would be a blissfully normal cat lady in waiting."

"Don't remind me," I say, and I don't even smile at his attempt at humor. I know that will hurt him but right now, I'm not feeling the bliss I thought this decision would give me. I only feel conflicted.

He says nothing in reply.

Then I feel bad for hurting him and take his hand once more. "I'm sorry. I just need some time to process all this."

"I know." He squeezes my hand, threading his fingers through mine. "We'll stay in Toulouse overnight and then fly back to Boston tomorrow morning. I'm afraid you won't have much downtime. Vasquez wants us working right away on the River Man case. There's been a new development and we've got a new murder to investigate upstate."

"Julien," I say as exasperation builds in me. "I already told you Soren is the killer. I felt it when I met him and he held my hand."

Julien smiles at me, staring at my mouth. "You are so *tempting*, Eve. But Soren's got an alibi for every murder. He's not the one."

I shake my head at him. Soren's compelled him to believe that. There is nothing I can say that will change his mind. I have to just ignore it, but if I'm right, and I know I am, the River Man case will continue on and on without any resolution.

WE ARRIVE in Toulouse much later and I'm so tired after all the stress and emotion that even after I drink Julien's blood, I'm in no mood for sex and he doesn't try to convince me. He doesn't even try to get me in the mood. He lets me sleep alone in the other double bed, giving me the distance I need without protest.

It feels so strange for him to be there on the other bed after we've been parted for two weeks. But I'm overwhelmed with sadness and confusion about this choice I've made. We lie there in the darkness, and his breathing is loud in the stillness of the hotel room.

"Do you hate me for being with him? Nothing happened," I add. "But he slept with me in the same bed, kissed me, fed me his blood..."

The sheets rustle on the other bed, and he sighs heavily.

"No, of course not," he says, but there's a hint of pain in his voice that he can't disguise "What we're doing to you – it's almost unforgivable. But you have to understand us, Eve. We love you. Neither of us is willing to give up. I'm surprised Michel has, but I suspect he's just lying in wait in the hope I'll fail to make you happy and then he'll step in, the hero. But I won't fail, Eve."

"He said you would make me happy. He also said the sky will fall and I'll go with him to help save the world."

"He's insane."

I lie in the darkness and wonder what Michel's doing. Where is he staying? Carcassonne? Is he in Toulouse as well? Does he know, even now, what's passing between Julien and me?

"Go to sleep, Eve. We have an early flight. If you need me to, I can put you to sleep."

I start to cry at that and in an instant he's there, lying beside me, cradling my head in his arms. He strokes my cheek and the last thing I feel before sleep overwhelms me are his lips pressed against my forehead.

~

I WAKE in the morning and don't feel much better. My sleep was interrupted during the night with dreams of vague danger that never seemed to take full shape. Julien's already up and has showered. He comes out of the bathroom with a thick white towel wrapped around his waist and he's so beautiful my heart squeezes at the sight of him. His hair is wet, his lashes clumped together. Beads of water form on his bare chest. He just stands at the window and looks out the window at the courtyard below our room, toweling his hair dry.

He's mine now. That thought gives me a little jolt of lust but it's still too soon for me to just be with him. I'm still guilty for what happened with his brother for although I didn't have sex with Michel, I wanted to. I kissed him. I slept in the same bed with him. I *wanted* him.

I think of Marguerite having them both, one after the other in front of each other and it makes me sick. I will *never* be her. I will choose *one* of them.

I can't believe I've just thought that I *will* choose one of them, as if I haven't just chosen.

What's *wrong* with me? Why is there still a question mark in my mind?

~

AFTER A QUICK BREAKFAST in a quaint café down the street from the hotel, we take a taxi to the airport and start our long journey back to Boston. Julien sits beside me and holds my hand and I'm only too happy that he releases some calming endorphin in my brain to take away my fear of flying. I doze through the long flight and through our connection to Boston, the time passing like I'm in a drug-induced dream.

He practically carries me into the warehouse and deposits me on the bed in his white bedroom, almost twenty-four hours after leaving France. When it's time for me to feed, he offers me his wrist instead of his neck as I normally would have chosen. The blood does nothing to arouse me. It merely takes away the ache in my body.

I fall sleep and when I awaken, it's night and I'm alone in the bed. I get up and have a much-needed shower. The door to the shower opens and Julien is standing there, naked.

"May I join you or is it too soon?"

I shake my head, my heart heavy, suddenly shy. "Too soon."

He nods and closes the door once more, leaving me alone with shampoo in my hair. I finish washing and get out of the shower, dry off, then wrap my bathrobe around me.

I go to where he stands by the window, looking out over the Boston cityscape. He's no longer naked, but is wearing only his boxer briefs.

"You must understand," I say and take his hand, squeezing it briefly. "I feel like such a…" I say, struggling for words. "Like a whore. A heartless bitch, going between you two like I have."

"Shh," he says and cups my cheek, his blue eyes so soft. "Hardly heartless. Quite the opposite. And not a whore – *never*. How could you even use such a word for yourself? It's us, Michel and me, who should feel bad, forcing ourselves on you. Never you."

He pulls me into his arms and I let him, not fighting his touch for I need it now. But even so, despite the closeness of his half-naked body and the delicious ache of need I feel in him when we connect, I resist him and he once more lets me, not pushing.

WE EAT A MEAL, and I feel Vasily's absence.

"Where's Vasily?" I say, glancing around.

"Still in Ipswich and back with Michel now. He's semi-retired, I guess. Still does some work for Michel, but it's mostly management rather than security." He takes a drink of coffee and grins. "Just you and me, babe. No servants yet. I haven't even looked. Been too busy trying to win back the love of my life."

I smile, my heart aching. I reach out and take his hand. "I don't need a servant. I just miss him."

He squeezes my hand back. "We'll get someone to come and clean the place, do the shopping and maybe some cooking. You're not a housekeeper, Eve. You're not a cook. I've been a bit distracted from that kind of thing. Drink up," he says and points to my coffee. "Vasquez is meeting us at the SCU. Guess he's putting on civvies and is taking over Ed's place, if you can believe it. They wanted me to run the joint, but I'm more of an operations kind of guy and hate administrative bullshit. Like to get my hands dirty."

As we drive to the SCU, Julien fills in the details of my last days there as a Blood Witness working for the Council. I was fired, according to my journal.

"Why did Vasquez fire me?"

"He threw you to the wolves because Soren didn't accept his bait. Vasquez wanted to bring Soren into his plot for Dominion."

"Vasquez is out for Dominion? Why is he working for the SCU?"

"We're letting him. There's an old saying that is very true, Eve. Keep your friends close, and your enemies closer."

"He sent me to Ramallah to tempt Soren into taking me as his Adept, right?"

Julien nods. "Soren doesn't want to head Blackstone. He has his eye on bigger fish."

"The Church."

"Yes," he says. "Vasquez wanted Soren at the head of Blackstone as a figurehead because of his power with the military. When Soren didn't bite, Vasquez decided on a different course."

"Why is he even working for the SCU then?"

"So the Council can keep an eye on him. See what his game is."

"I don't get it."

"The SCU is the front line against Dominion. Once we found out that Vasquez was for Dominion, we wanted him close so we could use him to get inside Blackstone. I've compelled him to comply. He thinks he's this big double agent, working for Blackstone and the Council. He thinks he's fooled us all. It's himself he's fooled. That's OK. He gives us an in to Blackstone. He'll lead us directly there. You watch."

"I thought you weren't interested in fighting Dominion," I say as we drive through the streets to the building near the waterfront.

"I said there are more ways than one to fight it. Blackstone thinks they'll subvert our defenses from within and strike at us that way. Michel's obsessed with Soren, but he's nothing. I'm after Blackstone." He glances at me. "I have my reasons..."

"They betrayed you." I remember reading journal entries about our trip to Virginia after Michel went to Pittsburgh.

"They turned me into a day-walking vampire super-warrior and then tried to kill me. Besides their role in bringing about Dominion, they're responsible for the deaths of my fellow operatives. It's time for payback."

I HAVE no memories of the SCU but it feels perfectly right to sit at my little desk by the window. I touch my things – the computer I must have used, the files, and pens in the drawer.

Vasquez is a tiny man with beady eyes and sparse graying hair on his head. He's dressed in civilian clothes – a suit and tie, suspenders and a photo ID around his neck. He looks like a real cop and not a bishop, but he has no idea he's been compelled. I watch Julien with him and Julien seems to enjoy treating Vasquez with extra deference. Nodding when Vasquez speaks, his face all serious. But Julien glances over to where I sit and has this look in his eyes that speaks to me of barely-suppressed mirth. Because I'm his blood slave, I can feel his mind at a distance when he lets me, and I know what he's thinking.

He loves this game.

"Come here, Eve," Vasquez says. "We've got a case to investigate."

I join him in Ed's old office and Julien and I sit side by side in old wooden chairs in front of the desk.

"A new River Man case." He hands Julien the file. Julien flips through the papers inside and I lean closer and look at them. Grisly crime scene photographs of a decapitated and drained body, the head in the shackled embrace just like all the others. What does that mean? What is Soren telling us?

It's then I realize that we aren't really investigating Blackstone if we pursue this case and these murders. We're really going after Soren.

"I've already said that it's Soren behind these murders," I say to them both, unable to keep frustration from my voice. "I touched him when we were alone and I held his hand on the plane. He's the murderer."

Julien reaches out and takes my hand, squeezing it and a current of lust from him goes right through me. He looks at me, and deliberately licks his bottom lip. *What?*

Vasquez looks at me as if I'm a child. "Eve," Vasquez says and I can hear impatience in his voice. "Soren's a bit player in this. He has his own agenda and it's not the main problem we face. We're after Blackstone. These are Blackstone killings of Adepts in their control. This is the third Adept to be killed in this community and we suspect there is a cell there, operating out of the town. We have to find the killer and he or she will lead us to Blackstone. I'm sending you and Julien to investigate. The fact that there's another murder in this small town suggests that whoever is killing Adepts lives there. In fact, our geographical profilers suggest that the killer may actually reside there but has been expanding his range to kill others where they live, returning to his home base."

I sigh, and give in. Neither Julien nor Vasquez are able to hear what I'm saying so I might as well shut up.

~

LATER THAT NIGHT, as Julien and I pack our bags for our trip tomorrow, I sit on the bed and try one more time to get through to him.

"Come here," I say and pat the bed beside me. He smiles and sits, his arm going around my shoulders. When he tries to kiss me, I put a hand up between our lips to stop him. "No," I say. "Not that. I want to talk to you."

"Oh, damn," he says and grins. "I was hoping you were finally overwhelmed with lust for me and couldn't wait until after your feed..."

"*Julien,*" I say, unable to keep a straight face because of his leering one. "I'm serious. We have to talk."

"OK," he says and plays with my hair, making a mock serious face. "What is it you want to talk about?"

"Soren has compelled you."

He keeps smiling, twisting a lock of my hair in his fingers, bringing it up to his nose to smell. He looks in my eyes, tilting his head to the side.

"You are *so* cute," he says and touches my nose. "Have I told you that I love your freckles?"

"Stop!" I say and push his hand away. "Julien, Soren has *compelled* you to think he's innocent."

It's like he can't hear anything I say about this. Instead, he leans in closer.

"Just a few of them over the bridge of your nose, like you've just been out in the sun. Makes me want to ravish you."

I take his hand and try again. "Julien, Soren has *compelled* you to think he's innocent."

He doesn't hear me or ignores me, smiling broadly. Then he nuzzles my neck, licking his bite mark. He tickles my waist and I can't help but giggle.

"Stop!" I try to push him away.

"Oh, that *smile...*" His voice is thick with lust and he pushes me down on the bed, his weight holding me down, my hands trapped in his over my head. "When I see you smile, I want to fuck you, Eve. *Hard.*"

"Julien! Soren's compelled you!" I say, almost shouting.

"God, Eve, you're driving me *crazy*..." He's breathing deeply as if my words arouse him. Then he kisses me passionately, his tongue insistent, and with his free hand, he starts to explore my body.

What – has Soren *compelled* him so that if I try to reveal what I know, he gets aroused and takes it as an invitation to have sex? The harder I try to convince him of Soren's guilt, the harder he tries?

What a *bastard*...

"Julien, Soren's compelled you to think he's innocent," I say once more to test my theory.

"God, Eve, what are you *doing* to me?" Julien says, the need in his voice almost anger. "Fuck," he says exhaling heavily. "I need you right *now*."

"Soren's *compelled* you," I say once more, swept up in his desire. Part of me almost laughs at how Julien is responding, but it's not funny. Each time I say it, he's more desperate.

"Julien, Soren's compelled you," I say again, barely able to speak from the overwhelming need I feel from him.

In response, he lies on top of me, breathing deeply, his lips pressed against his bite mark.

That *bastard*.

~

LATER, after we've had a shower, we sit in our towels by the window, me on his lap, his arms around me and I feed from his neck the way he likes.

"I don't know what got into you tonight," he says to me, kissing me, brushing hair off my cheek. "But it was good."

I shake my head and run my fingers over his mouth. "You got into me. Twice."

He grins that characteristic de Cernay grin and my heart does a little flip flop. When we lie down, he's asleep in moments and I lie awake, my mind unable to shut off from the effects of the blood.

I wonder what game Soren is playing with us. Whatever it is, I can't even talk to Julien about it without him getting all randy and shutting me up with his mouth. I realize that was Soren's intent. He's probably smirking to himself, knowing that I'll be unable to convince anyone of what I know to be the truth.

I sigh and snuggle into Julien's embrace, closing my eyes in the hope that sleep will finally claim me, wondering what this trip will bring.

CHAPTER 12

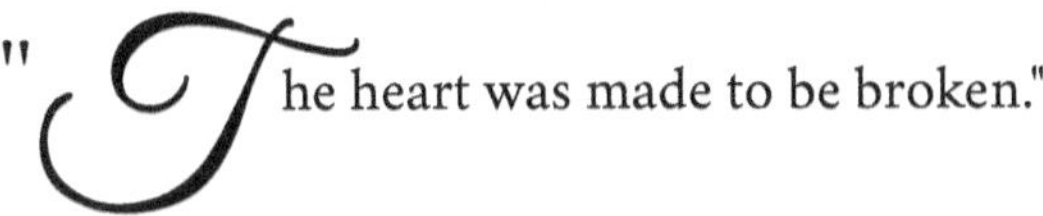

"The heart was made to be broken."

Oscar Wilde

WE TAKE the interstate up the east coast, on our way to a small town near Salem where the most recent murder took place.

While Julien drives, I'm in the back seat, reading files on the Blackstone Group that the SCU has amassed over the years. The file contains bits and pieces of intelligence they've been able to glean from captive Adepts and humans who worked for Blackstone and were either turned to our side or were killed.

Julien yells something from the front seat, but I can't hear because Joshua Bell is playing Vivaldi on my iPod, giving me shivers. I pull out my ear buds.

"What did you say?"

"We're almost there." He points to the GPS screen on the dash-board. "Just making sure you're ready. I have enemies everywhere and so we have to be on guard. I don't expect trouble but you never know."

I smile and hold up my stake and pistol loaded with silver bullets when I see his reflection in the rear view mirror, doing my best to channel Will Smith in Independence Day.

"Locked and loaded, and whatever it is you say when you use a stake."

"Sharp and pointed?" Julien says. When he sees my smile, he shakes his head, smiling back.

He's listening to jazz on satellite radio. "What is this?" I say, pointing to the radio on the dashboard.

"The Köln Concert by Keith Jarrett."

I'm not much of a jazz fan but I turn off my iPod. *This* I like.

I stuff a handful of bullets in my vest pocket. I never saw myself as a gun-toting vampire killer. I thought I'd be more like my mother – research scientist searching for a medical silver bullet, but this is fun.

While Julien sits with one arm out the open window, the wind blowing his dark hair around, I check my pistol. We're entering into some other vampire's territory and if confronted, will have to make a show of obeisance despite the fact that Julien is perhaps the second most powerful vampire out there next to Michel. Above him, there are only Ancients. I lean forward onto the seat and wonder how it will go when we meet our first vampire.

"Won't the local vampires know you from your car? It's not very forgettable."

"Any vampires in town will know who I am no matter what," he says. "What they won't know is where my loyalties lie. Always keep them guessing, I say." Then he frowns. "Put your seatbelt back on."

I knock him on the shoulder and sit back, strapping myself in.

We pull up to a motel on the edge of Davis Cove just after nine. Julien registers us, and hauls our suitcases and file boxes into the room. We get settled in, and then Julien takes off his boots and jacket before pulling out his laptop. I brush my teeth and get into my night-gown, the local paper in hand to read over the news coverage of the series of murders that the SCU is investigating. They're part of the same case as those in Boston. Soren's really shaking things up.

We'll visit the local Sheriff's office tomorrow and meet our

Council contact – the Sheriff himself – and look for potential cases. Tonight, Julien will check around in the bars and backstreets, looking for vampires who might be connected to the Blackstone Group and he'll meet up with his contacts. Then we'll decide what our next move is.

While Julien works on his laptop, downloading information so he can check out the most likely hangouts, I read the paper about the murders. There are several articles covering the coroner's report and on personal safety. If this latest death is a vampire kill, officials will claim it's due to the sick serial killer in Boston.

I read over the file Vasquez prepared. This case is different because the victims are all female, decapitated, drained and dumped on the beach. Soren is sending a message loud and clear. They were all young Adepts, same age as me, part of the new batch the Council created. He's picking them off because he knows we're meant to fight against Dominion.

Why hasn't he killed me? I can't talk to Julien about this unless I want to get him all excited. I have to figure this out myself.

"Anything in the paper?" Julien leans back in his chair and cranes his neck to see me on the bed, his blue eyes intent.

"Lame coverage of the serial case," I say and shake my head. "They're calling him Vlad."

Finally sleepy, I put the newspaper down, pull the covers up to my chin and turn my back to Julien, who's checking something out on the web. If I feed now, I won't be able to go to sleep for a while but I have an early morning. I wonder how long I can go without his blood. Maybe I'll wait for him to return from his stalking and feed then.

"You going to sleep for a while?" he says, glancing over at me.

I nod. "Wake me when you get back in."

I don't even hear him leave.

SOME HOURS LATER, it's still pitch-black out, but I hear him return and open my eyes. With my night vision, I watch him move around the room, taking off his jacket and scarf, his sweater, his shoes and socks. Then, I hear him washing his face and then brushing his teeth in the bathroom. He comes to the bed and stands beside me for a moment, as if listening for my breathing. Finally, he reaches down and pulls the covers up over my shoulder and goes to the bar fridge to get out a bottle of blood. He likes to drink before he feeds me so he doesn't feel as tempted.

The clock reads 4:30 a.m. The sun will rise in a couple of hours. It feels strange not to have him in bed beside me, but for some reason, he's staying up, talking softly on the phone to someone. His voice, deep and warm, fails to lull me back to sleep because of the ache that's building in me.

When he ends the call, tapping his cell's screen, I sit up.

"Julien, I need you."

He's there, beside me on the bed in a second. I rest my hand on his bare chest and can feel his heart start to beat faster under my touch at the thought of feeding me. This never fails to arouse him, this need I have for his blood. It makes him breathless and his excitement feeds my own.

"I wish you could bite me," he whispers in my ear when he pulls me against him. "Bite my neck."

"*Julien*," I say, surprised at this admission, a little titillated by his thoughts. "I'd have to be a vampire to do that."

"It's the most erotic thing of all, to feed another vampire. To feed each other."

"Why?"

"Mutual blood lust. Like sexual desire and addiction all mixed up into one. Joining with another vampire while you both feed…"

His lust fills me, his thoughts of other vampires he's had sex with before surfacing, his memories so real they make me almost pass out just from the sensations.

"Oh, God," I say and pull away from him, trying to block out his memories because they're too powerful. "I *never* want to be a vampire."

"I know," he says, and his voice sounds as if he's hurt. "It's horrible.

The bloodlust is rarely ever fully slaked. You don't want it. Being a blood slave is nothing compared to it."

"Don't ever let me become a vampire," I say, my voice breaking. "I'd rather die. Kill me first, Julien. I *mean* it."

He brushes my hair from my cheek.

"Okay."

But I see into his mind – a brief flash of resistance to that idea. He won't kill me if it happens. He'll let me become a vampire and then enjoy me the way he really desires. He doesn't want me to ever die.

I block him from my mind, shut him out.

"Julien," I say, angered. "*Never*. I'm mortal. I want to stay that way, even if it means I die."

He says nothing. Just pulls me into his lap and prepares to open a seam on his neck for me but I stop him, pulling his hand back, pushing away from him. I sit beside him on the bed.

"Your wrist."

"No," he says, his voice soft but insistent. "Don't do this. I love it when you feed from my neck."

"I don't *want* to be a vampire," I say, trying to sound as firm as I can. "You're going to have to promise me, truthfully, that you won't let it happen, or no more neck. Just wrist."

"*Eve*," he says, exasperation in his voice. "You're so cruel. I can't help how I feel."

"You can promise not to let me become a vampire, despite how you feel."

He doesn't say anything and I can feel his frustration. "You can't make me promise that, Eve. I *can't* promise. I'd do anything to save your life."

"There are things worse than death."

"You sound like Michel," he says. "Believe me, death is worse because it's eternal. Pain you can tolerate because it ends. Loneliness? It passes eventually. You can always start over every day. Being a vampire? It's bad. It's a curse but it's beautiful as well because you get to see so much, experience so much. But death? It's forever."

He takes my face in his hands and strokes my cheek with his thumb.

"You have to know that I'd turn you to save you. I wouldn't let you die. I *won't* let you die. Thing about vampires? We live forever, but those we love, we love forever. It's why Soren can't let go. He loved Marguerite. He'll never get over her death."

"I didn't think he could love anyone."

"You'd be wrong. He loved her. He loves Michel."

"Michel?"

"Oh, yes. Soren tried to hate him, but can't."

"I thought he hated Michel for killing Marguerite and staked you to torture him."

"No, the opposite. He staked me to get Michel on his side."

"Michel said Soren wanted him as his Pope." I glance at his face to see his response. "And you as his warlord."

Julien nods and brushes my hair away from my neck.

"He has plans. We'll use those plans to get to him one day. But now, we've got to keep after Blackstone. I have a feeling Vasquez has sent us here for a reason."

I watch his face for a while, entranced once more by his beauty, his large expressive blue eyes, his brows, the square jaw covered in a few days growth of beard. And the fact he has no idea he's been compelled.

"Julien, I don't want you to *ever* make me a vampire."

"Eve, I *love* you. Don't ask me to make that promise. I can't."

"Fine," I say and pull away from him. "Give me your wrist."

He does without hesitation, no more argument in him. He's already run a nail across his vein so that blood drips from the wound. I drink, a mouthful and then two. It's enough to satisfy me and I hand his wrist back and he licks the wound to heal it.

Then I lie down on the bed and pull the covers up, my back to him, the endorphins already making me feel warm. With his blood in my system, I can feel his sadness from a distance and it softens my heart towards him.

"It's really sweet of you to care enough to want to turn me, Julien,"

I say, "but it's the very last thing I'd want, considering what happened to my mother."

He says nothing, but I hear him finish undressing. He gets under the covers and lays without touching me. On my part, the blood is starting to work its magic and warmth spreads through my body and I need him. I can't deny it. I dig my nails into my palm in an attempt to block the desire from building, and to keep Julien from sensing it.

"I already know," he says and sighs. "Why are you so damn stubborn? Why don't you want me?"

"It's the blood, Julien." I breathe deeply to try to gain control over myself. "Nothing else. Besides it's really late. We have to work later. I need to sleep."

He turns over and it's only hours later that I do fall asleep.

WHEN I WAKE, he's asleep on the bed beside me. I should be with him, but it's still too soon. I need to find my way back to him.

While coffee perks on the small wet bar counter, I perform a series of yoga positions to limber up. Then, I go through my morning routine of Nitō Ichi martial arts moves – the moves we did to start our day at the abbey.

For that, I have my two short Wakizashi swords forged in Japan. One is a blade, one is a stake. I pull them from their cases and quickly clean them to keep them in good shape. I hold the blade up and run a cloth over the edge, remembering the night I passed the test. After I finish my routine, I shower while Julien sleeps, a pillow over his head.

After he's up and showers, we sit at the small table and plan our day.

"If there are any vampires here, they're in deep cover. I saw no one last night, on the street or in the bars. After we get a look at the body, we'll talk about our strategy. We may have to settle here if anything suspicious turns up in the police and coroner records. The term at the Catholic College started last week. If you need to, you can register and become a student. Fit in. All three victims attended there."

"Catholic college? I don't know if I want to do that. I'm not a practicing Catholic anymore or a good actor."

"Come on, Eve. You can do it if it means getting to know the victim's friends."

I nod. It will be a real challenge.

"We'll look for a cottage somewhere on the coast if we do stay," he says and that thought appeals to me. If so, I wonder what kind of place we'd find. I'd like a cottage overlooking the ocean – like Michel's back in Ipswich.

"I'll check out the town and see what I can turn up," I say. "I'll come and get you for lunch then we can go to the sheriff's office."

"I've got someone local to ghost you, make sure you're safe. If you get in trouble, look for a man with a red cap." He puts the pillow back over his head. "Make sure you have your gun permit with you."

I pat my pocket. It's there, right next to my Alcohol Tobacco and Firearms ID – the ATF being our current cover.

"Yes," I say. "Don't go all big brother on me."

"Just looking out for my secret weapon. Don't want them hauling you in for possession of a firearm without a permit. Red cap won't be able to help you if that happens."

I let the door slam behind me, smiling despite my best intentions.

CHAPTER 13

"*N*othing is meaningful except surrendering to love."

Rumi

I WALK DOWN the street to a large community information kiosk in the town's main square, looking for directions to the Catholic college. I notice a man following me a block behind, wearing a red cap. It makes me feel a little safer.

The map shows Bishop McDermott College is located a few blocks from the main street. I put on my best imitation Catholic college student's face and walk down the quiet streets to check out the red-brick building.

The campus is small, with a huge football stadium out back with stands. They take their college football seriously, despite being a small private school. Students mill about the grounds, entering the old building up a flight of stone steps. Some sit in groups under ancient trees.

About a century old, the building has ornate brickwork and quaint ivy-lined walls. I feel a bit of anxiety about attending here, but I remind myself that I'm a survivor first and foremost. I'll just have to swallow my unease at lying about who I am, try to fit in, but stay under the radar. Not that it will be easy for a new girl in town to slip under anyone's radar, but I'll try.

I walk to the Sheriff's office, which is located in one of the older buildings in the town square. Julien and I will come back later to speak with him. The SCU has already contacted him about us, telling him we're with the Council and that our cover is that we're ATF agents on a mission. He'll give us whatever resources we need.

Next, I make my way to the water because I have time to kill. I look behind me and about a half block away is red cap. He's carrying a newspaper and stops when I do, leaning against the wall of a building on the wharf. I've barely met anyone on the streets. It's off-season and the tourists have all gone back to their homes. Kids are all in public and high school.

I love the ocean, having lived near one for part of my childhood, when my father had a position with the local symphony orchestra in Cardiff and we spent time in Wales. Summers found us on the coast in a cottage overlooking the Celtic Sea. The scent of brine brings back so many memories of better times when I was just a girl learning piano, enjoying life with my family in our cottage on the coast. It also reminds me of my time with Michel, after we met again and he spent those strange days with me, walking the beach, looking at stars. I feel a surge of sadness but quash it. I'm not going to let guilt over Michel ruin my time with Julien.

I stand at the top of a hill overlooking the bay and breathe in the salty air. Vampires would like my memories. Due to my amnesia, my childhood is all I do remember. Sharing memories with humans is what vampires crave most besides blood. Even Julien wants our human experiences, to feel our emotions, using telepathic connections with us to keep his human side alive.

Now, some of them want to be our rulers. They want us, not as prey they have to hunt down and kill, or as suppliers of blood in vials, but as slaves and cows, as Julien said, providing them with blood. I'm not ready to let them take our world just because they're sick of hiding in plain sight.

Overhead, gulls wheel through the sky, gliding on the breeze and cry. I could live here for a while, if needed. Julien and I need time to get to know each other in more than just a carnal way. A month or two living here undercover would be like a vacation – or a honeymoon.

I find a quaint coffee shop on the picturesque wharf and get a pastry and cup of coffee. I find a table on the deck overlooking the water, open my iPad and read the morning headlines. Red cap gets a coffee and sits a few tables away from me.

If it wasn't for him, I'd feel almost normal.

TOWARDS NOON, I return to the motel and wake Julien up. He dresses quickly and we walk to the waterfront, hand in hand. We eat our lunch on a bench overlooking the bay with seagulls as our audience and I decide to have fresh shrimp, editing my vegetarianism so that it excludes only mammals and birds. Since I've been a blood slave, I feel a desire to eat flesh. It must be the blood but whatever it is, my compromise is that I'll eat crustaceans and smaller fish because, well, they seem to have less personality.

The local marina is filled with sailboats and yachts and there's a dock where fishing boats fuel up. An indoor farmer's market is located just a block from the water. I plan on going there for fresh fish, if we end up staying here for any length of time. I haven't had much chance to learn to cook, but if we stay here, I'll get a chance to play a normal twenty-one year-old woman and that appeals to me. Maybe, I'll even get to go to a bar with Julien and we can be a normal couple.

I feel as if I've missed so much since losing my memories and being a single-minded vampire-hunter in the making.

Next, we make our way to the Sheriff's office, located a couple of blocks from the water. Sheriff Steve Conyers is a man in his late forties and he looks like he belongs in the Marines instead of small town Massachusetts. His hair is salt-and-pepper which he wears in a brush cut and has dark eyes that seem to read you like a book. He shakes Julien's hand and then mine, eyeing me over.

"Isn't she a bit young for this kind of work?"

Julien laughs. "Special Cases Unit, special regs."

We sit in his office and Julien presents our papers. Sheriff Conyers checks them over and rubs his chin. He turns to his computer screen and logs in, then clicks through some screens for a moment before turning back.

"I got an email from Bishop Vasquez, telling me you'd be arriving yesterday and the whole story. I'll cooperate in any way I can."

Julien nods and changes positions in his chair. "We need to look at the case file if possible, so you'll have to tell your staff we're here undercover for the ATF. But if we decide to stay, we'll want to blend into the community as quickly as possible. Our cover with the civilians will be that we're here to escape the big city, and that Eve wants to attend college somewhere quiet. We'll try to infiltrate whatever group exists in town."

"No problem. I've got a copy of the forensic report right here. Dead girl's name was Christie Hamilton. Had the lead in the college musical. Just got the part and was all excited. The vampire who killed her and the other two should be staked and pissed on and I'm all for helping you do it." He hands Julien the file. "If you want, I'll just say that you were looking for advice on where to live in town. My sister is a real estate agent."

Julien examines the file, flipping pages. "Did you get the request for special blood and tissue tests?"

Conyers pulls out another file, handing it to Julien. Julien checks it over and then passes it to me. I read the results of the blood test – extremely high levels of oxytocin – far higher than normal and extremely low levels of dopamine. Both are signs that the victims were long-time blood slaves. I glance at Julien and he nods to me, understanding at a glance why I'm smiling.

Blood slave. Adept. We'll be staying. I'm almost happy.

Make that I *am* happy.

"What does that mean? Those tests?" Conyers asks, pointing to the sheet of paper I hold.

"It means that I'm going to college and we need a house to rent," I say and smile at Conyers. "What's a good neighborhood to live in?"

The Sheriff leans back in his chair and regards me for a moment. "You going to McDermott?"

"Hope so."

"Smaller than most colleges. Only two hundred students. Have a great football team, and their drama and music departments are first rate, from what I hear. They put on plays and concerts at the old theater downtown. Got a couple of new teachers from England in a few years back. Students rave about them. As to a house, my sister can hook you up with something. Lot of absentee landlords here who rent out houses on the coast to vacationers. It's off-season, so you might get a deal if you sign for three months."

I raise my eyebrows at that. Julien throws me a look. I might like to stay for three months.

"Semester started last week, so you're a bit late getting registered."

"Eve will have no problem getting in. Right now," Julien says, "I'd like to spend some time going over any other deaths you've had recently. Any the coroner ruled natural causes."

"Our coroner is pretty on top of things," he says.

"We might have to have more tests run on any that look promising, see if the deaths were connected. If so, we likely have a Blackstone cell located in town and will have to stay, gather evidence and then take it out once we're sure."

"You have my full cooperation," Conyers says. He stands. "I love Davis Cove. I'll do whatever it takes to protect our people."

SHERIFF CONYERS LEAVES us alone in a small office in the rear of the building. We spend an hour going over the most recent deaths for the town and there are a few that seem like they might need a second look.

"Look at this one," Julien says, handing me a file as we sit with the case files from the coroner spread out on the table. "A woman with cancer died in her sleep in the palliative care wing of the local long-term care facility where people who are dying are placed for the last days of their lives. The coroner's report failed to mention that she'd lost all her blood."

I take the file and read through it. She was in her sixties and had lived in town all her life. She'd have ample memories for a vampire to feed on and although she had cancer, her prognosis said she probably had weeks to live beyond what she did. Like Julien and Michel did eight hundred years ago, vampires sought out the dying in order to benefit from their blood, bringing them a peaceful death instead of one in pain, then compelling any family or officials to ignore the loss of blood as a cause of death. It was perhaps the only thing they did that had any value – giving the dying a peaceful death. I check the photograph, but there was no autopsy due to her prognosis.

About a half-hour in, I find another case that looks promising.

"Here's one," I say and flip a page in the file. "Older man. Lived alone and was in good health, other than being depressed because his wife had died earlier in the year and he missed her. Supposed suicide. Hung himself in his basement."

Julien glances up from a document he's reading. "Did they do an autopsy?"

"Nope, due to the noose and suicide note."

"Suicides are always suspect. Easy to compel folks because it's so horrific to deal with, people don't want to pursue it."

Finally, Julien finds a case that's a year old. "Here's a fourteen-year-old kid with terminal cancer who died in the hospital one night when the parents thought he'd be OK and left him alone, sleeping in their own bed for a change instead of on a mattress on the floor. When the nurse came in the next morning, the kid was dead. No sign of a struggle. Peaceful. Blood loss wasn't mentioned in the coroner's report but our tests will pick it up."

I finish my coffee. "How can they be sure these were due to blood loss? Won't the bodies be too decomposed?"

He put down a file and rubs his eyes. "There are tests to check for the normal and abnormal decomposition profiles. When you have a full volume of blood in you, the breakdown products are different than if you're drained. We'll have to check all their contacts as well."

It's unlikely that there'll be only one vampire here. Most likely several. Could be anyone, but most likely new residents. We'll get a list of all new residents in the town and start investigating each one.

I remember the Sheriff saying that the drama and music teachers moved to town from England a couple years earlier. One of the first things I'll do at school is sign up for the drama and music courses.

THAT AFTERNOON, we go to McDermott College to register. The registrar is only too happy to enroll me once Julien finishes speaking with her. She makes everything so easy from then on – the paperwork, picking up classes, even permission for me to go into the music class despite it being full, due to my background.

"Professor Rhys will be only too happy to have you in class," she says. "She studied at the Royal Northern College of Music in Manchester, England, and is very talented as a teacher."

I smile. She'd be the first person I'd check out, and I'll know immediately if she's a day-walking vampire or Adept. As one of the newest residents in town, and one of the dead girl's teachers, she'll be a prime suspect. I also manage to get into her husband's drama class. I'm a little more concerned about that. I'm such a poor actor, despite trying to act happy for years, act sane, act anything but who and what I am.

I need the practice at deception.

The rest of the classes don't really matter – even Catholic Ethics. I'm an atheist, but enjoy reading and learning about religion so I don't care what faith it is. I do like Catholic churches and music though, so Catholicism isn't so bad. It reminds me of my life before my mother's death, when I was a good little Catholic and believed in God.

"You start tomorrow," the registrar says as she hands me my timetable.

After I register, Julien and I meet with the Sheriff's sister about renting a house. We go to see three cottages on the coast that are available. We chose one high on a hill overlooking the ocean. It has three bedrooms, a fireplace and a great yard. Nestled in a grove of trees, it's a short walk to the hilltop and a narrow walkway down to the beach. I can't believe our luck and finding such a gem.

I *love* it.

I could be really happy here. It reminds me of our cottage in Wales. There's a sense of peace in the cottage, and in this small town that I haven't known for a very long time.

All it needs is a piano and perhaps, a violin. I'd love to play a duet with Julien one day.

"When can we move in?" I ask, as we stand outside overlooking the beach.

"You can have the keys once you put down a deposit and pay the rent."

I look at Julien, who's also smiling. He loves the ocean as much as me. I hug him. I'm actually *happy*.

Julien gives the real estate agent a check for three months rent and a damage deposit and we have the keys. The cottage is fully furnished with plush overstuffed furniture and we're able to move our paltry belongings in that night, checking out from the motel a day early. I'm glad to be out of there, and even more glad to have our own bedroom. The house is equipped with a security system, but even so, Julien has arranged to have a security detail on the cottage, just in case.

Our bedroom is at the front of the cottage, looking out over the ocean, sliding doors to a small stone patio and I'm ecstatic. The room is a bit prettified for me, all pink and white roses, with a four-poster bed and ornate dresser with a full mirror. A hand-made quilt covers the bed, and a hooked rug with a cabbage rose pattern lies on the floor.

It smells of fabric softener and looks peaceful. Julien takes a room beside it as an office, putting the bed away in the shed outside and moving the desk in from a foyer. Once the computers are up and running, it will be tech central during the mission. We have a special encrypted phone to use in case we need to contact the SCU on any matter and I'll see about buying some whiteboards so we can track evidence.

I'm just so excited to finally be in a real house. My first real home outside the apartment and my foster parent's cottage.

I go out to the hill overlooking a rugged beach down below and breathe in the briny air. One day, I want to live in a place like this. I look up into the growing darkness as the first stars peek out in the night sky. With the sound from the ocean and the silence of the coast, it's as close to heaven as I can imagine.

JULIEN GOES OUT AGAIN at night to put in a few applications for jobs so he can look as if he fits in. He doesn't need a job, of course, but this way he'll be able to meet the town regulars. He will also go out to check in case any vampires are out. He turns the security alarm on when he leaves and kisses me while I sit on our bed, reading on my iPad.

When he comes home much later that night, he wakes me when he moves around our room, undressing.

I sit up in the darkness. "Did you find anything?"

"No vampires," he says. "But I did get a job as a relief bartender at the Cove Bistro and Lounge. My first shift is Friday night. Luckily, their relief bartender left town and they had a vacancy."

"How does it feel to have a real job?"

He chuckles. "Bartending is a great job for meeting the regulars."

"Maybe I could get a job as a hostess or waitress there."

"I'll ask the owner when I go in on Friday. You could always be a busgirl."

I throw an extra pillow at him and he catches it, his reflexes faster than mine. I check the clock radio, which reads 2:30 a.m.

"I have my first day of college tomorrow. I'm really curious to meet the Professors Rhys."

"They're definitely high on the suspect list," Julien says from the bathroom doorway. "I don't need to warn you not to let anyone touch you."

"Then *don't*," I say, trying hard to keep frustration out of my voice. I have to tell myself that he's only being careful, warning me about the risks of going up against a vampire or another Adept with their touch telepathy.

He returns to bed and creeps in beside me, waiting to see if I'm open to him or not. I don't have to touch him to know he's already excited about my blood feed. I can feel his desire from a distance. I think that tonight, I'll let him feed me from his neck the way he likes.

I feel happy for the first time in a long time, here, with Julien. Doing what I was meant to do – police the Treaty.

I climb onto Julien and he gasps out loud when he realizes I finally want him. As I straddle his hips, he sighs.

"I could get used to this, Eve," he says before I silence him with my mouth.

CHAPTER 14

"The only abnormality is the incapacity to love."

Anaïs Nin

MY STOMACH IS all butterflies in the morning as I dress for my first day of college. I chose a navy blue long-sleeved t-shirt with a white camisole underneath and a pair of jeans. I usually wear Doc Marten's, but that might label me as a tough chick, so I put on a pair of black high tops instead. My hair is freshly washed and still damp. It's long enough that it will take at least an hour to dry, but I don't care. I put on only the most minimal amount of makeup – just a bit of lip gloss and a touch of mascara – don't want to look too made-up. It's a Catholic school, after all, but what do I know? Are there priests and nuns? I have no idea.

I don't have any real school supplies, so I take a notebook from one of the files and rip out the pages of notes. Along with some pens and pencils, that's it. I stuff them in my backpack, slip my cell into a pocket of my hoodie and put my ear buds in loosely.

I enter the bedroom and turn on the light. When I shake Julien's shoulder, he snorts awake.

"What's the matter? Are you OK?"

Julien sits up on the bed and watches me as I turn in a circle.

"Is this appropriate for a Catholic college?"

"You look demure." He rubs his eyes and then grins. "Little will they know that underneath the prim exterior is a vampire's lover and very brazen temptress."

"So I look like a normal college student?"

"Yes."

"Good," I say and take in a deep breath. "I'm more nervous about this than killing vampires."

"In my experience, Catholic college is hell but that was back in the day when the brothers patrolled the hallways with willow branches." He lays back and smiles at me, his hands behind his head on the pillow. "Killing vampires is easy in comparison."

"They have a cafeteria so I'll probably stay and eat there, check out the other students."

"Be careful. Don't take your gun or you'll set off the metal detectors, if there are any."

"Julien!" I say, frowning. "I'm not a total idiot."

I pull out my small wooden letter opener. It looks harmless, but I could kill a vampire with it if I have to.

He sighs heavily, sounding more like a frustrated parent than a partner and lover.

"You going to be OK? You feel nervous. I can help you with that..."

I grin. "I don't have time. Wish me luck?"

"You won't need it. Call me at lunch, let me know how things are going. Red cap will follow you there and back."

I nod and check my watch. I have enough time to stop by the coffee shop on the way to the college, get a coffee and grab a bagel. I'll eat on the way. I'm so nervous, I wonder if I'll even be able to swallow. I tell myself that this is nothing compared to what I do for a living, but it's small comfort.

~

THE HARDEST PART is walking up to the school through the throngs of students hanging around the front entrance and on the grassy field in front of the building. They stand in clusters, their chatter not making it past the music blasting on my cell.

Many of them turn when I walk up the path to the entrance. I'm probably one of the few new faces around. I keep my head forward and eyes on the path, pretending not to notice their eyes on me, but I feel them. When I walk up to the front doors, someone – a young man with blond hair – opens the door for me.

I smile at him and say a faint 'Thanks' and then go in to find my locker. I walk along the rows of lockers, looking for my number, and there it is. It's in the middle of a row, the only one that hasn't been claimed. I bought a lock from the registrar the previous day and so I open the locker and stare at the empty interior, uncertain what to do with it.

Classes don't start for ten minutes, and so I take out my lone notebook, a pen and pencil, and stuff my backpack into the locker. Then, I remember my letter opener – my weapon. But I could, if needed, kill or disable someone with my pencil, so I relax. I take out my class schedule with room numbers listed, and walk the halls, looking for my first class. It's on the third floor, so I walk up the stairs and search the hallway for room 312. Biology 325 – Marine Biology. The only biology class I could get into. Even Julien couldn't compel his way to get me into something more interesting – to me – and more relevant to my aspirations.

There are only a few students in the class – probably the other loners or brainiacs who want to get a great seat at the front. I take one in the middle of the far row beside the windows and sit down, staring out the window at the football field where some players are practicing.

So this is what school feels like... I have no memory of my years at Boston University.

Students filter in over the next few minutes, and finally, the teacher arrives. Professor Grant. In his forties, with black hair and black horn-rimmed glasses, a blue shirt and paisley tie and brown corduroy pants. He starts writing on the blackboard while students slip inside, taking their seats.

"You're in my seat."

I glance up, startled at the sound of a male voice beside me. A tall guy, dark hair and eyes, wearing a team jersey. Number twenty-three. Johnson.

"Oh. Sorry," I say and fumble with my things, glancing around, looking for another empty seat.

"You can have it," he says. "Just don't ever say I never gave you anything." He smiles an All-American smile. He's actually quite cute.

"Thanks," I say, sitting back down.

"You're obviously new. I'm Nathan Johnson, but my friends call me Nate."

"Thanks, Nate," I say and smile back. "Eve Hayden. My friends call me Eve." Out of habit, I extend my hand to shake and he chuckles and takes it, bringing it up to his lips in a mock kiss.

Stupid *me*. My first five minutes in class and I've already let someone touch me. Julien will be furious. Normally, Adepts wear gloves when they're operating to keep from touching other people skin on skin, which is the only time our telepathy works, but gloves would definitely be a tip off in college…

Nate winks at me and takes another seat in the row beside me, plopping his books on the desktop. I feel the eyes of every student turn to me. I remember what Julien said when we talked about me going to college. He said that the girls would consider me competition, while the guys would wonder what kind of woman I was and whether they'd have a chance with me.

I don't really know. I don't think I fit into any category. I'm just me. Eve Hayden, vampire killer.

Freak of nature.

~

FROM OUR RESEARCH, I know that the Professors Rhys have a daughter who is in her junior year and in several of my classes. So far, roll call hasn't revealed her presence. She's supposed to be in my biology class and my history class, but she isn't in either. I do get my first glimpse of one of the famed Rhys teachers in Drama.

Drama class is very dramatic. It's being held on the stage in the assembly hall. The curtains are drawn, creating a cozy little room, the sound muffled by the huge red-velvet drapes. On stage is a set with ornate couches and chairs. Almost two-dozen students sit or stand or lean against the furniture.

Professor Rhys is quite the character. He's in his late forties, with longish graying hair, a grayish moustache and droopy eyes that are extremely expressive and large. His accent is northern British and has a soft lilt that makes him seem all the more exotic. No strange paleness so he isn't a vampire. He parades across the stage as he talks to us about the play we're reading – something by Chekov – taking time to introduce me and forcing me to say a few words about myself.

"What do you want to know?" I say, uncertain what's expected.

"Tell us about your family, why you're here of all places," Professor Rhys says. "We consider ourselves a family here at Bishop McDermott, Eve. We like to know each student."

I take in a breath. "I live with my boyfriend, Julien. My mother died when I was eleven. My dad played with the Prague orchestra for a while but he's ill now and in an institution."

There's an awkward silence for a moment. I bet they weren't expecting to hear about my tragic life.

"Did you go to school in Prague?" a student asks.

"No, I was home-schooled. I studied piano and practiced all day."

The students ooh and ahh at that, looking at each other as if I'm something exotic.

"Why did you decide to move here, of all places?" Professor Rhys asks, examining me closely.

Julien and I have already thought up a good cover story. "My father spent some time here in the summer when he was a kid. I remembered him telling us about it and how if he moved back to America, he'd want to live here. He almost got a job in Boston and would have liked for us to move here, so this was the first place I thought of."

"Well, welcome to Davis Cove. We're glad to have you, Eve."

He seems really nice. He isn't a vampire – I can tell that right away. He might be an Adept, but there's no good way to tell that without touching him. There's still his wife to check out and of course, their daughter. From what the Sheriff said, they also have two sons, one who's studying at MIT and one at St. John's Seminary in Brighton. As new residents, each one is a possible suspect but I doubted either one is a vampire. More likely Adepts, if anything. Their kids are about my age. Maybe my crop of Adepts.

I MAKE it through the morning without major incident and when Julien calls, I'm sitting alone in the cafeteria in the corner of an empty table, eating my sandwich.

"How's things? Any football players hit on you yet?"

I laugh. "Well, one did kiss my hand this morning."

"*Eve...*" He doesn't laugh.

"It was my fault," I add quickly. "He gave me his seat and I introduced myself, and tried to shake his hand without thinking. He kissed my hand instead."

"No strange vibe?'

"Nope."

"What about the students and teachers? Anything there?"

I glance around the room at the collection of students, none of whom seemed interested in me.

"Not so far. Nothing. The one student I was looking for didn't show up in class today."

"Hmm," he says. "Sounds suspicious. Or a pure coincidence."

"I have music class this afternoon and history. We'll see how that goes. What are you doing?"

"Just ordering those test results. Should be here in a few days to a week, depending on how busy the lab is."

"Ok. I guess I'll see you after school."

I hang up and finish my sandwich, reading web news on my iPhone until my first afternoon class.

WHEN IT COMES time for music, I enter the classroom to find an older woman with grey bouffant hair at the front. She'd written her name on the board and it isn't Professor Rhys. It's a substitute teacher. I won't get to meet the elusive Professor Mrs. Rhys or her daughter today, but I suspect that there's nothing to be found in that family. Likely, they really are just new residents to America who found jobs at the school together due to a lucky coincidence of openings.

There are ten other new residents in the past few years we have to investigate, and so while they aren't a dead end for certain – I won't know until I've seen them all up close – I expect the Rhys family is just a family.

So my first full day at college isn't as bad as I feared. It's pretty tame. No one tried to strike up a friendship with me, and other than Nate kissing my hand, no one has even spoken to me.

I can do this.

"HOW'D IT GO TODAY?"

Julien stands beside me, chopping up some vegetables for a stir-fry.

I shrug. "Nothing spectacular happened, with the exception of Nate kissing my hand."

"Nate, hmm?" he says, frowning a bit. "Sounds awfully familiar, considering you just met."

"What?" I say and push his arm playfully. "You're not jealous are you?"

He pops a piece of broccoli into his mouth and chews, grinning sheepishly.

"Me? Jealous of some mere *human?* He's got nothing on me."

We sit down at the table and eat, Julien filling me in on what he's been up to while I was pretending to be a student.

"Our victim was friends with the Rhys girl," he says, raising his eyebrows.

That makes my skin crawl. I could see them both maybe being caught up in a vampire's circle, becoming blood slaves with him – and it was likely a 'him'. Few vampires chose Adepts of the same sex unless they're homosexual. The relationship is far too erotic. Most straights prefer the opposite sex.

"There's probably a vampire recruiting young female Adepts," Julien says. "You should get to know her and see if you can get into their little group – if there is one."

I push my food around on my plate at the thought. Of course, I suspect Soren's the one responsible for these killings, although there's a chance it's someone else.

"I think it's Soren who's responsible." I watch his response.

He leans over and takes my hand. "You are so *cute*." He kisses my knuckles as if to overwrite what Nate did earlier in the day. "Tell that Nate kid to keep his hands off you or your monstrously strong eight-hundred year old vampire boyfriend will come after him with everything I've got."

"Julien!" I say, laughing. I stab a piece of mushroom with my fork. "You have nothing to fear. No one," I say and lean forward, pushing my fork towards him, "could ever measure up to you. *No* one."

Through our connection, I get a momentary glimpse into his mind before he's able to shut me out.

Except Michel...

He looks away, not meeting my eyes, squeezing my hand.

I sigh.

"Whoever is responsible," I say, my voice a bit choked from his thoughts. "I look forward to finding the bastard and killing him – or them."

Julien shakes his head. "Eve, it's a job. It's an important job. You should do it because it's necessary – not because it gives you pleasure."

"You're one to talk."

He heaves a heavy sigh and leans back, releasing my hand. "You're too young to feel this way." He takes a sip of his beer and looks at me over the bottle. "You should be going on dates, deciding who you are as a person, falling in love."

"I *am* in love," I say. "I barely know who I am as a person but from my journal, I've known for years that I was going to be a vampire hunter. You have to remember what happened to me. I'll never be normal."

He won't meet my eyes. I don't know why he feels bad for me but how could he expect me to be 'normal' after all that's happened – whatever normal means.

It just isn't in the cards for me.

THE NEXT DAY, the Rhys girl finally shows up, and I know from the start that she isn't an Adept. She's wheelchair bound and on a respirator. She's in biology class, her chair a few rows over and at the front of the room.

Sarah Rhys, twenty years old and sweet with wavy red hair and glasses. So much for this family being part of any vampire coven – they're probably just what they seem – a family moved here from England for the chance at a new life in America, both parents teaching at the same college. Another candidate struck off our list.

After class, I make the exit first and then stand just outside the doorway, watching Sarah as she maneuvers her wheelchair out of the class, using a straw to control the motorized chair. Two of her friends flank her, and she smiles at me as she goes by. One of the girls with her knocks into me, and I manage to drop my book and pens. From roll call, I know she's Brenda Lane, a short blonde with clear blue eyes. She apologizes profusely for her clumsiness. We bend down together to pick up my things. When she hands me my pen, she touches my hand. She gasps briefly and looks at me, her mouth gaping. I freeze, staring at her, looking more closely.

"What's the matter?" I say.

"Oh, I," she says and stammers. "I got a shock or something."

I *didn't* get a shock, but I smile and try to brush it off. Is she's an Adept? If she *is*, she might know what I am. I have to cover quickly.

"Sorry. I'm Eve Hayden."

"I'm Brenda, and this is Sarah and Miriam."

I smile and nod to them all.

"I've heard of you," Sarah says, her voice with that characteristic soft Northern British lilt. "You're the new student. You're in my father's drama class and my mother's music class."

I nod and point down the hallway. "I have to go," I say, holding up my watch. "English."

She smiles and turns her chair to leave, her friends in tow. As I walk in the opposite direction down the hallway, I turn back and see her surrounded by her friends. Brenda glances back as well and our eyes meet. She's frowning.

Oh, oh...

I have a bad feeling about this.

Is Brenda an Adept? Is she involved in a vampire coven here in Davis Cove?

I CAN BARELY FOCUS during English class, and I sit and think about what happened and what I'll say to Julien. I fear Brenda has touch telepathy.

English drags on as does Christian Ethics, and finally, I'm released for lunch. Instead of the cafeteria, I go outside with my sandwich and apple so I can call Julien and relay my suspicions.

"You should really avoid touching people," he says, his voice sounding frustrated. "You *know* that."

"I know, I *know*," I say, knocking myself in the forehead with a fist. "She was the one who touched me this time. She deliberately took my fingers in her hand. Most people avoid touching a stranger so I didn't expect it."

I feel a bit nauseated at the thought she might be an Adept working for Blackstone.

"Sarah and Brenda are both in my history class this afternoon," I say. "And Sarah's mom teaches my music class. What should I do? Should I just leave now? Should we abort?"

"If she only touched you for a second, she wouldn't get very much. Maybe just a brief sense of your emotions. Maybe not enough to even know that you're a hunter and Adept. Do you remember what you were thinking when you touched her?"

"I was thinking she wasn't a suspect."

He exhales loudly. "Damn. That's not good. Let me call Vasquez and get back to you. We might have to call it off."

I turn my phone off and manage to chew down a few more bites of my sandwich, but I have this sick feeling in my gut that I've blown my very first undercover operation.

About fifteen minutes later, he calls back. I'm sitting under a tree in the shade, my sunglasses on, my Biology text open to the chapter we were reading, eating an apple.

"What's the plan?"

"Vasquez says to sit it out – go to class this afternoon, see if anyone makes a move towards you. I'll swing by and pick you up after school so you don't have to walk home alone. Don't agree to go anywhere with anyone – not during class, not after. Do you understand?"

"Yes," I say, swallowing, a lump in my throat. "I'm so *sorry*, Julien."

"It's OK," he says, his tone lightening a bit but I know it's just him trying to be gentle. "I'll see you at 3:00."

I'm not afraid. I'm disappointed. It's just that I really *like* it here. I really wanted to do this job, live here for three months with Julien and learn what it's like to be his, in such a nice place.

CHAPTER 15

George Chakiris

I FINISH my apple and make my way back inside the college to my locker, where I pick up my notebook for my classes in the afternoon. Nothing seems amiss in history. There are no strange glances from Sarah or Brenda nor does Mrs. Rhys look at me pointedly in music class. No one approaches me or appears to avoid me.

Just before the end of the day, as I go to my locker to pick up my backpack, Nate shows up at my side and leans against a locker.

"Hey, Eve."

"Hey," I say back. He's smiling that brilliant smile again. "The Junior Pub Crawl is on Friday night. A bunch of us are going as a group and you're welcome to come with us."

I'm so surprised that he's inviting me, I'm at a loss for words. My cheeks burn, but I smile and try to push my way through the awkwardness.

"Thanks. That's really nice of you." I close my locker and turn to face him. "I'm not sure I can come."

"Why not?" Nate said, frowning. "Your boyfriend? He can come, too."

"He's working."

"So he doesn't allow you to go out without him?" he says, smirking.

"No, I can go out!"

"Just kidding. If you can, it'd be fun. Everyone goes to this. It's tradition."

"I've never been to a pub crawl. If I can go, is there," I say and hesitate. "I mean, is there anything I should wear?"

"You've never been to a pub crawl? You're a junior. Where'd you go to university before?"

"Boston U. But I was a bit of a, I don't know – shy." I shake my head, embarrassed.

"I get it." He nods. "You're a genius, right? One of those brainy girls who's going to do a PhD or something?"

"Hardly!"

"Totally casual," he says. "I can pick you up at about ten."

"That's OK," I say quickly. "I'll get a ride."

"Great. Invite your boyfriend. He's welcome."

I smile and he smiles back, then he leaves me at the lockers. I stand for a moment, a little dazed. His joke about me being a brainy girl going to do a PhD makes me a bit nervous. Where did he get that? I walk to the front door. Julien will be waiting for me and I don't want him to worry.

He's leaning against his car at the end of the walkway, dressed in his usual uniform – white v-neck t-shirt, faded jeans, thick black belt, black leather jacket, dark sunglasses, several days worth of scruff on his face, his hands in his pockets. Gorgeous, in other words. I walk through the thinning crowds of students, and feel their eyes on me as I approach him. They've all seen the new girl in town. Now they'll get to see her boyfriend.

When I get to him, he takes my hand and pulls me into an embrace. Then he kisses me, his arms around me, pulling me against him. I try to pull away, but he holds me there, not letting go. Finally, he releases me.

"Julien" I say, my cheeks hot. "What are you doing?"

He grins. "Just showing all the little boys who you belong to."

He opens the passenger door for me and I get inside.

"I think they got the message loud and clear."

He hops in beside me and puts his arm over my seat and kisses me once more.

"I hope so." He guns the engine, the tires squealing as we drive off.

At least we leave in style.

"I'VE BEEN INVITED to the Junior Pub Crawl," I say as we sit at the kitchen island and eat our supper.

"No way," he says, shaking his head. "Too much drinking and touching, Eve."

"It's tradition," I say. "Besides, it will give me a chance to meet people. See what the Rhys girl's friends are up to."

"Booze and young college-aged guys mean attempts to pick you up," Julien says. "An excuse to get all snuggly with a girl so I'm voting no."

I bang my knife down on the counter, and then get hold of myself. "What if I don't drink?"

He rolls his eyes at that. "The whole purpose is to drink, *cheri*. I've been to a pub crawl or two hundred in my time."

"I'll just say no. I'll drink soda. Besides," I say, trying hard to rationalize, "maybe Brenda really did get a shock and I didn't notice. You can send Red Cap to shadow me."

Finally, he lets out a huge sigh of resignation.

"Forget Red Cap. I'm going with you."

I smile. I'm going to the pub crawl.

~

THE NEXT DAY, Sarah Rhys and her friends are absent from school, and the Professors Rhys as well. The funeral for Christie is this afternoon and a lot of students have taken the day off so they can attend. I want to go and check out who attended, but we'll have to rely on the Sheriff for that. I have no reason to go and so Julien asks the Sheriff to have someone tape the funeral unobtrusively just in case. It can't be overt – the coroner ruled the death an accidental overdose and so there'll be no police investigation.

At the end of the day, Nate is waiting at my locker, leaning against it, smiling.

"Hey, Eve."

"Hi, Nate," I say, a bit of warmth in my cheeks.

"We're going down to the beach for a swim. If you want, come and join us. I have my car."

I hesitate, fumbling with my books in my locker, stalling for time to think of an excuse. I want to go, see what these students are like, but I know Julien will say no to that as well. Who knows what kind of touching and feeling might happen at a beach...

"Isn't it a bit cool to swim? The season's over."

"Nah, it's still great. The sun's out today. The beach is sheltered. It'll be fun."

"I better not. I have a job interview at the Cove Bistro at five."

"Cool. You could always come along, go for a swim, and then take off when you have to."

I shrug. "I'll see."

"Gotta check with your boyfriend?" He chuckles. "I saw him yesterday. Nice wheels."

I smile. "He's proud of that car."

"He should be. He's also a bit overprotective."

I sling my backpack over my shoulder and start down the hall with him to the exit.

"*Definitely* overprotective," I say, smiling.

He holds the door open. "If you can join us, it'd be great."

I go to where Julien stands at the end of the sidewalk.

"Hey."

"Hello," I say. He pulls me into another embrace and kisses me pointedly.

When I pull away, I swallow hard, wondering how to word my request.

"Nate wants me to come for a swim down at the beach."

"Eve," he says, shaking his head. "Hasn't he got the message that you're taken? Besides, you don't go anywhere alone. Where you go, I go."

"Julien, I'm a hunter," I say. "I could kill these guys with a pencil in ten seconds if I wanted. I'm only in danger from another hunter or an ambush."

"Which he could be and which this could be," he says, his voice firm. He frowns down at me, his hands on my shoulders.

"Why don't you stalk me?" I say, unwilling to give in. "You know, use your skills in surveillance you bragged about when we were in Norfolk. I could go alone, have a swim, act like a normal college student my age, see what they're up to, and you could watch from a distance. If anything looked suspicious, you could swoop in and rescue me like the superhero you are."

He just looks at me from behind his sunglasses, his lips pressed thin, his jaw clenched.

"Jesus *Christ*." Finally, he exhales and glances away from me. "All right."

"This is what we're supposed to do – infiltrate."

"Yeah, but to me that means we infiltrate *together* so we can watch each other's backs."

"You mean so you can watch *my* back, don't you?" I say.

"Don't forget that you can still be beaten if you're ambushed."

I hold my hands up in surrender. "OK, I admit it, but you have to let me go on my own sometimes."

He nods but says nothing more, not looking at my face. "Tell your *friend* you'll meet him there. I'll take you home to get your swimsuit and I'll drop you off. Then I'll find a place to watch. Those are my terms. Take them or leave them."

"You can't tell me what to do."

He jerks his head back. "Yes, I can. *Don't* make me."

"Julien, I don't want to fight with you over this. You said partners. This is what partners do. Get each other's backs."

We stand for a moment without speaking.

"OK," he says, and brushes a strand of hair from my face. "I'm just worried about you. I know you think you're all tough now that you've graduated from fight training, but you're a long way from being able to defend yourself on your own."

"Thank you."

I turn back and walk up the path to where Nate stands.

"Your boyfriend giving you a hard time?"

I laugh. "Why would you think that?"

"He doesn't look happy."

I ignore his words. "I'll go home and get my bathing suit and meet you there."

Nate smiles. "Bring him along if you like."

"Can't. He's busy."

"Too bad. I'll see you at the beach."

I go to the car where Julien waits, already in the driver's seat. I get in and slam the door a bit too hard.

"Hey, welder's daughter. Don't slam the door."

We drive off.

I DON'T SAY anything on the way home. When we arrive, I go to the bedroom and change into my bikini and then go to the hall closet to get a beach towel.

Julien stands at the end of the hall, watching me. "You don't have something a little, I don't know, less like a bra and panties?"

"Julien, are you jealous?"

"Oh, *cheri*," he said and shakes his head. I can tell his emotions have gotten the better of him because when they do, he drops into his French accent. "How could I not be? You look like something from a Victoria's Secret catalogue."

"That's where I got it." I turn to him, and do a pirouette. "This is what normal girls my age wear when they go out and, you know," I say, struggling for words. "Do normal things with other college students, have fun, *socialize*. I read about it in a magazine. Saw it on a television show, so it must be true."

"You didn't socialize much at Boston U."

"Not that I remember," I say.

I pull a sundress over my head and slip on my sandals. Finally, I put on my sunglasses and grab my bag.

"Let's go," I say when he follows me. "I know, I know. No touching."

I FEEL a bit nervous walking down to the water after Julien drops me off – not because I'm worried I'll be ambushed by vampires out for my blood, or turncoat vampire hunters, but because all the eyes are on me, judging me. My stomach's all butterflies as I walk up to Nate, who leans against a picnic table, drinking a beer.

"Hey," he says, smiling. "I wasn't sure your boyfriend would let you come."

I laugh. I drop my bag and take off my sundress.

"You look nice," he said. "Come on. Let's go for a swim."

I follow him down to the water where several other people I recognize swim or stand in the water. A few are out in the waves with surfboards and wetsuits. I stand at the edge of the surf. It's bloody cold but Nate just runs in, splashing through the waves until he dives in head-first.

He turns around and swims back, then floats a few feet away from me as I edge into the water. I know he's going to splash me.

He does. "Come in – get it over with. Or I'll come and get you!"

I laugh, and evade him, swimming out a bit and tread water. He follows me and we just laugh and have fun, like I imagine normal people my age do. Normal people my age swim and go to pub crawls and have fun. They're not vampire hunters who see and feel violence in the world around them.

After swimming, we throw a Frisbee around while other students play beach volleyball.

Then, someone I haven't noticed until now, sitting in a recliner with a large brimmed hat and sunglasses, stands up and starts walking towards us. He's tall, maybe six foot four, very pale and well-muscled. He takes off his sunglasses and I gasp out loud.

Soren.

He smiles, his ice blue eyes gleaming.

"Hello, beautiful Eve."

~

I STAND and gape at him for a moment, speechless. Beside me, Nate's grinning. I see Julien racing down the street, then he swoops down the dune to the beach and is by my side so quickly he's almost a blur.

He stands in front of me, his arms behind him, holding me.

"Go, Eve," he says, his voice low and full of fear. "Get your things and leave."

"No, I don't think so, Julien," Soren says and steps forward and before Julien can respond, Soren has his hand on Julien's neck, squeezing, lifting Julien up off the ground as if he's nothing more than a feather.

"Don't, please," I say, stepping closer to Soren. "Don't hurt him."

Soren looks at me as he holds Julien up by the neck.

"So sweet that you care about him," Soren says. "I just love a good romance. And you two are just so sweet together! All that beautiful lust and love. I can't resist you two. But poor Michel, Eve!" He throws Julien fifteen feet through the air, where he falls among the rocks along the shore. The students ignore what's happening, and continue to play volleyball. I turn to run to him, but Soren stops me, one hand gripping my arm like steel.

"Poor Michel" he says, pulling me closer. "All alone after breaking his vows for you. How cruel are you to do that to him? Reignite his eroticism, then cast him away for his brother? I had *no* idea you were so heartless. I like it. I can use that heartless side of you."

"I'm not heartless!" I say, angry and fearful at the same time. "You're the heartless one, playing these two brothers against each other, compelling them so that they can't even hear the truth."

"Ahh, you discovered my little trick." He smiles a wicked smile. Then I feel his mind searching my memories. "You loved it, I see."

My cheeks burn that he can just see what's transpired between Julien and me.

"Don't worry," he says quickly. "Michel's got a replacement for you. I found someone for him to assuage his broken heart. Her name is Gabrielle. He doesn't love her but he surely is getting some much-needed solace from her."

At that, my heart squeezes. Michel is already with someone else?

"You'll like her, Eve. She's just about the opposite of you in every way. I figured he needed someone totally different to wash you out of his memories. Make new ones. Beautiful breasts, Eve. Perfect – large, firm, probably three times the size of yours. A man could drown in them. But there's one thing the same. I want to remind him of what he's missing. Long blonde hair, flaxen, like a river of silk." He laughs softly. "Every time he fucks her, he has no choice but to think of you. It's perfect."

"You're a monster. You're probably compelling him to be with her." He shakes his head.

"Not at all. He needs someone, Eve. He's been so lonely all these years. I care enough about him to help cure that loneliness. Poor Michel. She's obedient. You know how much Michel loves to control things. Sweet, soulful Michel, damned if he does, damned if he doesn't? How could you possibly turn him down?" Soren smiles. "My little Marguerite was like that as well, but a bit naïve about things, which led to her destruction."

"You abandoned her," I say, unable to keep my mouth shut. Julien has recovered and is by my side. "She abused Michel and Julien. She enslaved them."

Julien steps forward as if to stop me.

"Only fitting and just for my progeny." Soren pulls me closer and places his hand over my chest, above my heart. "Don't even think of trying anything, Julien. I'll have her heart in my hand in a second if you do."

"Please don't hurt her," Julien says and steps back. I can hear the submission in his voice.

"I don't *want* to hurt her, Julien, but I will if I have to. I'll just have to get my scientists to go back to the drawing board and make another one of her."

"What do you mean?" I say, weakness flooding through me. "Make another one of me?"

"Oh, that's right. No one's told you the truth, have they? Even Julien, who promised to tell you everything…"

"Tell me now."

"Oh, I don't think so. Let Julien tell you."

"What *do* you want from me?" I say, my hands fisting. "Other than to use me to torment Michel and Julien and get your sadistic pleasure."

"Oh, Eve, have I told you I love your saucy mouth?" Soren says and smirks. "Most normal humans with any sense would be down on their knees right now, terrified of me, but you? You never fail to stand up to me. I *like* that. You can't be intimidated. You will make a magnificent High Priestess."

"I'll never be your *anything*."

He steps closer and takes my chin in his hand. "You will be mine, Eve. Don't worry. I'm not interested in you sexually. But you will be my creature. You *are* my creature. I decide what happens to you. Now, I've had enough sun for one day. I'm hosting a dinner party at my home tonight. You and Julien will come. Dress in something risqué, Eve. I want Michel to see how happy you are with Julien. It will keep him all motivated. I want you to see him with his new blood slave. She actually wants him, Eve. It will be good for you to see them. It will keep *you* all motivated."

With that, he turns to Julien and cups his cheek, staring into his eyes.

"Bring Eve tonight. You are so looking forward to it. We're going to have fun." He releases Julien and faces me.

He turns away and Nate follows him, smiling back at me. "See you at school tomorrow, Eve."

Julien seems to be released from whatever power Soren had over him and comes to me, turning me around, checking me out, his gaze moving over my face and down my body.

"Are you OK?"

I nod but when he pulls me into his arms, his face in my neck, I can't help but tear up.

"He's a monster," I say, my voice breaking.

"I know."

"We won't go, will we?"

"Of course. We're going to have fun."

I look into his eyes. He has no idea he's been compelled.

I have a very, *very* bad feeling about this.

CHAPTER 16

"*If* an injury has been made to a man it should be so severe that his vengeance need not be feared."

Niccolo Machiavelli

WE DRIVE BACK to the cottage and my mind is numb from our encounter with Soren.

"We won't go, Julien. We *can't*. I can't stand him."

"We have to go," Julien says, glancing over at me as we drive along the road that borders the coast and leads to our cottage. "Soren invited us."

"I'm not going. I *won't* go. Michel will be there with some woman Soren's probably compelled to be his blood slave."

"We're going," he says and turns to me. "I *have* to take you. He expects us there."

"Do you do everything he says?"

"We'll have fun, Eve," he says and smiles as if this is just a nice party among friends.

I'm so frustrated that Julien doesn't realize he's been compelled. There is no way I can get through to him.

~

ONCE HOME, I shower and dress for my interview at the Cove. Julien drives me there and goes in to start his first shift as a bartender, working over the dinner hour with the usual guy to learn the ropes while I meet the manager for the interview. Mr. Taft is an older guy, looking close to retiring, a buttoned-down kind of person more suited to the boardroom than bar. He tells me he's an escaped Corporate America type who came here for small town life. He's nice and offers me a job working twice a week, Tuesdays and Friday during the dinner hour.

"What time do I finish on Friday?" I ask, hoping it won't prevent me from going to the pub crawl – if I survive tonight, that is.

"Five to ten's the usual Friday shift."

I cringe. "Can I start on Tuesday? I was planning on going to the pub crawl at the College..."

"I'm actually short-staffed, Eve. That's why I agreed to hire both Julien and you. The job's yours, but I need you on Friday to help out. Take it or leave it."

I take in a deep breath. "I'll take it. There'll be another pub crawl."

Mr. Taft extends his hand for a shake. I do as well, but I get no strange reaction when he shakes it. He's no Adept. I'm suspicious of everyone now.

"Wear black pants and a black long-sleeved t-shirt. We'll provide the apron. If you get here about fifteen minutes early, Carrie will do your orientation, show you the schedule and everything."

"Thanks," I say. "I appreciate the opportunity."

~

"YOU'LL BE happy to learn that I can't go to the pub crawl."

I stand at the kitchen island and watch as Julien hangs up his leather jacket. It's after seven and Julien is just home from his supper hour shift at the Cove.

"Why?"

"I have to work until ten. Besides, now that I know Nate is with Soren, I don't want anything to do with him."

He shrugs. "Go after. Make friends with the others. Maybe some of the Rhys girl's friends will be there."

I shake my head. "It's no use. I know that these murders were Soren's doing. There's no need to infiltrate. He's behind all this."

"Eve, Soren being here is just a coincidence," Julien says, shaking his head. He comes to me and takes my face in his hands and kisses me. The kiss is passionate. Every time I mention Soren's guilt, Julien gets all aroused. "Now, quit being so tempting and get ready."

He goes to the fridge and takes out a bottle of blood. "I'll be done at ten on Friday so I'll take you. I wouldn't mind checking out the locals."

I shrug. It's useless. He won't hear anything about Soren's guilt. He doesn't seem to care that Soren's here. He's blind to the danger.

"Whatever."

"Don't get all 'whatever' with me. Remember, we're here to hunt down Blackstone. I know you dislike Soren, with good reason, but he's a side issue."

That makes my pulse quicken and I have to bite back an angry retort. Surprisingly, tears bite at the corners of my eyes.

"I don't want to go tonight," I say, a choke in my throat. "I'd rather stay and look over my files. Whoever's doing the murders, we've got to find out who might be an Adept in town and who's got a thing for beautiful college girls."

"*Eve*," he says, tilting my chin up so I can't avoid his eyes. "Every man has a thing for beautiful college girls." He leans down and kisses me. "Look, I understand, I really do. You hate Soren. You have a vendetta against him." He sighs. "We can't be sidetracked by personal vendettas. We're on an operation to infiltrate Blackstone. This is work."

I nod, and he pulls me into his arms, his warmth enveloping me, and he calms me, my anxiety about tonight dissipating.

I *hate* that he can do that to me. While he can't compel my mind, he can affect my body and my ability to resist him. I bite my cheek. The pain helps block him.

"Eve, why must you always fight me?"

"I don't like it that you can just manipulate me, make me feel things or not feel them against my will."

"I'm a vampire, in case you forgot. You're lucky I can't compel you."

"If you could, what would you do?"

"I'd compel you to go get dressed in that pretty black velvet dress Luke gave you when he held you at his warehouse," he says, sighing when he feels me block him out. "But do what you want. I'm going tonight. I'll have a shower and then, if you want, you can come with me. If you're not with me, who knows what he might compel me to do. Or who to be with."

"Would he have to compel you?"

"Eve," he says, exhaling. He brushes hair off my cheek. "Of *course* he would but if he did, I wouldn't even know it. I don't want anyone but you."

"So you do realize he's been compelling you not to think he's the one responsible for the River Man killings, right?"

He smiles, his mouth quirking in that grin of his. "Eve, you are *sooo* cute..." He bends down and kisses me. "Now go get dressed before I ravish you right here on the floor."

Soren is *such* a bastard...

I PUT on Luke's dress and brush my hair, put on a bit of makeup. Julien dresses in something a bit more formal – a black suit with white shirt and black silk tie. He looks devastatingly handsome with his dark hair and blue eyes, a few days-worth of stubble on his jaw.

"You look good enough to eat," he says and pulls me against him.

"Don't worry about tonight, Eve. Just be with me. Ignore what goes on around you. You and me – we're together and that's what matters. Soren will try to shock you. He loves getting a reaction from people, testing their limits, seeing how far he can push them to go beyond their normal behavior." He runs his fingers through my hair and strokes my jaw with the backs of his fingers.

"Don't think you can outwit him. Don't look him in the eyes unless he tells you to. Don't talk back to him – at least not too much. Actually, I suspect he loves it when you resist and when you fight him, Eve. He needs you but he could decide to just kill you if you were too much trouble."

"What did he mean when he said he would just make another one of me?"

He exhales heavily and sits on the bed, pulling me between his thighs. He runs a hand from my cheek to his bite mark, which he touches softly, down my shoulder to my hand.

"He used DNA from the Grigori to create all the new Adepts in your group."

"He *created* us?" I say, shocked, adrenalin flooding through me.

"Not him personally, but his scientists."

"But I thought he was out for Dominion... I thought we were created to fight those out for Dominion."

"He wants his own version of Dominion. Instead of a military structure, he wants a religious one."

"The Church."

Julien nods. "He thinks he's one step ahead of Blackstone and will just swoop in and take over when they make their move, using your group of Adepts to do so. I don't know all the details, but he's maneuvering himself into place to take power when the opportunity arises."

"You think Blackstone's the real threat?"

"They most definitely are. They're the ones who will send things into a tailspin. Soren's hoping to take advantage, fill the power vacuum. In times of crisis, people turn to religion. They need to believe in something. He wants to be the one thing they can hold onto in times of chaos."

"Why haven't you told me this before?"

He shrugs. "Before the bomb, I figured there was only so much you needed to know. Things changed when I thought I'd lost you. When I thought you were dead."

"So you're less concerned about Soren than Blackstone."

He nods. "If we stop Blackstone, Soren's pretty much out of luck. He's hoping they'll succeed and then he can launch his strike and then take over. I have to prevent that."

He pulls me close and kisses me, then kisses his bite mark on my neck.

"Things will be uncomfortable for you tonight with Michel there. I can drug you so that you're not upset."

I take in a deep breath, and wonder what to expect. With Soren, I just don't know.

"Let me manage on my own. I have to get tough if I'm going to be of any use to you. Besides, I *chose* you."

"You did. I hope you don't regret it."

"Never."

I cup his face in my hands. He's so beautiful with those black-lashed blue eyes, that soft mouth. I lean down and kiss him.

"You smell so nice," I say as he pulls me into an embrace.

"Sandalwood."

I pull back. "You like it, too?"

"You like it," he says, a wistful smile on his face as he brushes hair off my cheek. "I want you to be happy."

"It doesn't bother you that it's Michel's scent?"

"You like it. That's good enough."

"I love you," I say and kiss him, running my fingers through his hair. I pull back and stare in his eyes. "I'm afraid of Soren."

"You don't show it," he says and smiles. "He really thinks that when he needs you, you'll just do what he says. He has no doubt. If he threatens you, it's just for show. I doubt he'd kill you no matter how much you resist him."

"Why is he so sure?"

Julien shrugs. "He'll just use his secret weapon."

"Which is?"

He strokes my hair. "He'll just threaten to kill us and you'll have to choose between our deaths and compliance."

I close my eyes. When I open them, his face is somber.

"It can never get to that point, Julien. *Never.*"

SOREN'S PLACE is just as ostentatious as I expect. I step over the threshold into one of the most beautiful homes I've ever been in. The opulence overwhelms me. White marble floors and walls, pink sandstone tiles on the floor, a huge crystal chandelier in the foyer. Art from every era hanging on the walls.

I stand in the entrance and my heart rate increases as I see all the vampires standing around in their finery, beautiful women draped over them. I'm afraid to look around too closely in case I see Michel. Beside me, Julien slips his arm around my waist and pulls me closer.

A servant comes to us and takes our coats, while another one escorts us into a large room with several seating areas set up where couples stand and sit, drinking champagne and eating canapés. They're all beautiful – vampires and their pets. About ten couples in total. I don't see Michel or Soren and I take in a deep breath and try to relax.

Julien squeezes my hand. He knows how I feel.

"If at any time you need help, just let me know."

I squeeze his hand back. "I have to be tough. I made my choice."

Julien leans down and kisses his bite mark on my neck. "I'll do everything I can so you don't regret it."

We go to a set of wingback chairs by a floor to ceiling arched window. I sit while Julien stands beside me, one hand on my shoulder. I take a big sip of champagne punch from a tall crystal glass a servant offers me. I need the courage.

"Watch how much you drink, Eve," Julien says. "Remember your lips become even more loose when you're tipsy."

"Don't remind me."

"Personally, I love it when you're a bit stoned or drunk," Julien says and squeezes my shoulder. "You're so funny. So honest. No lies."

"If I lie, it's because I have to in order to get through the day."

"I know."

It's then that Soren chooses to make an entrance and what an entrance he makes. He's wearing all black – a black silk suit with black shirt and tie. His hair is down and almost platinum in the light from the crystal chandeliers. His skin is so pale he looks Albino.

He's beautiful in a cold feral way. On his arm is a blonde beauty with fair skin and light blue eyes. She's wearing something that looks right out of Ancient Greece, with diaphanous material that reveals almost everything. She has an ample bosom, full and firm but supple. Even from where I sit, I can see her pubic area and she's waxed bare. Her eyes are downcast, her face demure despite the voluptuous curves and revealing fabric of what could be called her gown.

It's then I see Michel. He's walking behind them a few steps back. The sight of him makes my heart skip a beat, adrenaline coursing through me. He's so beautiful he takes my breath away.

His hair is long and a bit disheveled, tucked behind his ears, his face vampire-pale. He has on a white linen shirt, which is untucked and hangs over his dark pants. Overtop is a long black jacket to his knee, unbuttoned, with a tab collar and dozens of small covered buttons down his lapel. A large black cross is on a leather strap around his neck.

He looks almost priestly. A vampire priest – Soren's High Priest. His Pope. I suspect that's the effect he and Soren are going for.

Soren glances around the room and the other vampires all bow to him as if he's some great lord and their master. His eyes rest on us briefly, and beside me, Julien bows his head. I refuse and don't avert my eyes as Julien instructed. I hate Soren so much right now, I'm almost choking.

Then Soren turns to Michel and hands the woman to him. The two men exchange her like she's a possession and she goes to Michel, taking his hand. She's almost as tall as Michel is in her stiletto heels.

It's then I know she's this woman that Soren spoke of earlier. *Gabrielle*.

Michel pulls her against him briefly, his mouth bending to her neck, and then he turns his attention back to the room.

The woman – *Gabrielle* – stands beside him, his arm still around her tiny waist, her eyes on his face.

I drink down the rest of my champagne and reach for another one when the servant comes to me.

The party continues and remains uneventful for a while. Classical music plays in the background, and people chat with each other as Soren, Michel and the woman make their way around the room, greeting each guest.

I dread them coming to us. I wish Michel would just stay across the room and not come over. I'm relieved when he does exactly that, stopping at a couch by a window to our left. Gabrielle sits on the floor at his feet. He glances down at her and she tilts her head up and he cups her face with a hand. Then he bends down and kisses her, the kiss long and passionate.

My heart squeezes to see him with another woman, and her acting all submissive, but how can I be upset? Here I am with Julien beside me on the arm of the chair, hovering over me, one of his arms around my shoulder, his hand on my neck touching his bite mark.

I hate this.

I hate Soren for making us do this.

I hate him so much, I want to take a stake and drive it through his black heart. I don't know that I've ever felt so much hatred.

Julien exhales and squeezes my shoulder, releasing something in my brain to calm me. I sigh, the hatred seeping out of me. It's replaced by a warmth I've never felt before – a deep almost over-flowing sense of love and peace. And a touch of lust. Is it from Julien? I only know that once the hatred dissipated, this euphoric sense of warmth replaced it.

"What did you do?"

"I just calmed you. Reduced your anger."

"I feel so … strange."

Soren chooses that moment to make his way to us, and I fight hard to be angry with him, despite hating him only a moment ago.

"Well, hello beautiful Eve and Julien. The lovely couple."

"Soren," Julien says, his voice soft. Soren extends his hand and Julien takes and kisses the ring on his index finger. I can barely work up any hatred at what I see. Instead of making me angry, it amuses me. He's kissing Soren's ring?

Then I remember reading in my journal of the other vampires kissing Julien's and Michel's rings when they killed Luke and took over his territory.

Soren turns to me and smiles, extending his hand. I offer mine in return, surprised that I'm so willing to shake, and of course, he takes the opportunity to kiss my knuckles.

When he releases my hand, I lift my champagne glass to my lips but before I can drink it, he intervenes, pulling my hand away.

"Is that your second glass?" he says, smiling pleasantly while he takes the glass in his hand.

"Yes," I say, smiling back. "It's delicious."

"That's quite enough for you," he says. "This is a special blend. I don't want you too much under its spell or you'll go to sleep and that is *not* what I have in mind for this night."

"What *are* you planning?" I say, curious, upset that he's drugged the champagne but not so much that I feel like insulting him.

"A night of pleasure, dear sweet Eve. I want you warm but not too warm."

"You're a monster," I say, but smile in spite of myself. I try to hate him, but I'm filled with this sense of acceptance. "Did you drug everyone or just me?"

"Some of us don't need any help," he says. "We can't control your mind with our powers, Eve, but as Julien learned, we can affect it through drugs. I thought a little MDMA – *Ecstasy* – might soften your hard heart a bit."

"My heart isn't hard," I say.

"*Au contraire, mon petit.* It's far too hard. I aim to soften it a bit. What happened to you so long ago made you protect your heart. I intend to break that hard shell you have around it. Seeing Michel happy with Gabrielle will go a long way to that end."

Even hearing him say that makes my heart squeeze just a bit.

"You're wrong about me. I love Julien."

He tilts my chin up. "Your heart is hard, Eve. That's why you're able to break both of their hearts, one after the other. You broke Julien's heart when Michel returned from Pittsburgh, after you made him break his own rules about falling in love with humans. How you play these men against each other... Leading them both on. Even now, you lead poor Julien on, making him think, *hope*, that you've chosen him for good. But in his heart he knows that you'll pick Michel when it comes to it."

"I never led either on. You staked Julien so Michel would be forced to come to you to save him. Then, you stole Michel, leaving me with Julien. Forcing Michel to make a choice. He came back and I," I say and stumble.

"You went back to him after sleeping with Julien."

"I *loved* Michel. I thought I'd never see him again. I was..."

"You want them both – admit it. How could you not? This thing with Julien is just a temporary arrangement."

"I *picked* Julien."

"For now," Soren says. "But enough of this disagreement between us. It's so not what I had in mind tonight." He hands the champagne glass back to me. "Perhaps you should drink this after all."

"I won't. You're not going to manipulate me." I hand the glass to Julien.

"I already have." Soren turns to Julien and takes his chin in his hand. "Make your lover drink the rest." He turns back to the room. "Let the games begin!"

Julien hands the glass to me. "Drink up, Eve."

I take the glass and throw it on the ground.

"Eve," Julien says and takes my hand. "Just comply tonight. Now is not the time to fight."

All the good feelings from Soren's drugged champagne seem to dissipate. "You think I'm just going to join some orgy Soren's arranged?"

He squeezes my hand to calm me down once more. Then he makes me stand. He sits on the chair and pulls me down onto his lap, draping my arms around his neck.

"Now, kiss me, Eve."

I do, for the fight is out of me. Besides, he looks so beautiful sitting there, his eyes half closed, his mouth soft, waiting. I kiss him, his mouth so willing. Then I pull away and I lift my eyes, turning to the corner of the room where Michel sits with Gabrielle. She's on her knees beside him and he's stroking her head like she's a prized pet, her adoring eyes on his face while he speaks with Soren. He looks, if not happy, then completely relaxed.

She leans her head into his cupped hand and he bends down and kisses her, his kiss long and deep. The image of him kissing her is like a knife in my heart. I press my fingernails into my palms.

I shouldn't feel this way. I chose *Julien*. I *want* Julien...

Soren turns away from them, his hands clasped behind his back, walking to another couple already engaged in an embrace. Before he does, he glances my way and our eyes meet. For a moment, I feel as if he's in my mind, searching for my response to seeing Michel with Gabrielle.

He smiles and raises his eyebrows.

Bastard.

Julien pulls me against him. "*Eve...*"

I can't help it. Tears bite at the corners of my eyes.

"He's doing this to torment me," I say, staring in Julien's blue eyes. "Why?"

"Who can say why?" Julien says and there's a hint of frustration in his voice. "He loves to torment. He's the god of mind-fucks. It's best not to try to understand because then you're pulled down to his level." Julien brushes the tear from my cheek, and runs his fingers through my hair. "Just try not to think of everything that's going on around us, Eve, and kiss me." He pulls me closer. " I can't make you forget, but please let me try to make you happy," he says, his gaze moving over my face. "Your happiness is the only thing left in this life that matters to me."

He slips a hand behind my head and pulls me down to his mouth, kissing me. His kiss is like a salve on my wounded heart, a flood of love moving through me, momentarily taking away the pain. I could almost forget about Michel being with Gabrielle.

Almost.

Except that when I pull away, I see them again, and now she's kneeling between his knees, kissing him, her arms around his waist, his arms around her shoulders. Throughout the room, the other couples are likewise busy with each other, at various states of undress.

"Eve," Julien says, taking my chin in his hand, turning my face away. "Stop doing this to yourself. Michel's with her now. You're with me."

But Gabrielle is opening Michel's shirt, unbuttoning it, then kissing him, her mouth moving from his neck to his chest, then lower, her hands already on his belt buckle. I can't stand to watch, but can't tear my eyes away either. Is she really going to do that now, in front of everyone?

Of course she is. That's the whole point of all this. Soren's making me jealous.

Why? Does he want me with Michel?

Julien pulls me back to him and tries to kiss me again, but I don't respond to him, my mind fighting the endorphins he's trying to release in me to gain my compliance.

"Stop," I whisper. "Let me be what I am. Let me feel what I feel."

He frowns, exhaling heavily.

"You really prefer pain and heartbreak?"

I don't know what I prefer. "It's what I know."

"Eve, *stop*," Julien says, his voice harsh. "You're with me. Look at *me*."

It's just too much. I can't sit here and watch any longer.

I push away from Julien, turning to find Soren. He's standing off to the side of the huge room, leaning against a large marble fireplace mantle, watching his servants perform.

I stride over to him, my anger overcoming me.

He turns and sees me, then raises his eyebrows, standing straighter.

"Eve," he says, as if a bit surprised that I'm approaching him. "I can see Julien didn't make you drink the other glass of champagne. Pity."

"What is it you want from me?" I say, my voice breaking. "Did you want me to choose Michel? Is this what all this is about?"

I wave my arm around to the room where the other couples are in various states of undress and in different lewd poses and postures. I am barely able to hold back my tears of anger.

"This is about pleasure, Eve," Soren says. "Something you need far more of, apparently." He smirks. I see Julien approach and hold my hand up to stop him. He does, his face searching out Soren, who nods.

"I just thought it would be good for you to see that Michel has moved on. You made your choice. You should know the price. He needs someone now that you've woken his libido once more."

"I did no such thing. He did that all on his own."

"And what was he supposed to do once he found he couldn't compel you to forget everything as he initially planned? He had to claim you, or I would."

"Why haven't you claimed me if that was your goal?"

He smiles briefly. "You're far too much trouble for my tastes. In contrast, Michel always liked a challenge. I figured he'd control you for me. He might have been able to but I don't think Julien can. I don't think Julien *wants* to control you. He likes you like this, doesn't he? All wild and untamed..."

"I can hear you," Julien says.

"Of course you can, Julien. If I didn't want you to hear, I'd have sent you away."

Julien comes to my side and slips his arm around my waist, pulling me close to him.

Behind us, I hear a woman moaning and the three of us turn to watch as Gabrielle arches her back, her long blonde hair falling down her back as Michel kisses her neck.

"That Gabrielle is such a good little performer," Soren says, chuckling. "So responsive. Michel will be in seventh-heaven. I love how generous I am, Eve, to turn her over to him, considering he killed her what – almost eight-hundred years ago?"

I stand in shock, my mouth gaping. What does he mean?

"That's Marguerite?"

"No," Soren says. "Just her clone. I dug up her ashes and charred bones and found enough of a hip bone with preserved genetic material in it to make a copy. We always thought that burning would destroy a vampire permanently, but you mortals and your genetic technology, we're able to overcome that barrier to immortality. It's not her of course, and this one's a lot more shy and retiring. I trained her well, right from her first blood. She'll be some solace to Michel, considering he wanted you so badly."

I turn to Julien. "Did you know she was Marguerite?"

He frowns. "What are you talking about?"

I point to Gabrielle. "There. With Michel. It's Marguerite!"

Julien frowns. "It's not her. I don't know who she is."

I turn back to Soren. He only smiles.

"Compulsion is such a neat trick, Eve." He steps closer to me. "You read the manuscript. Can you imagine how wonderful it feels for Michel to have Marguerite at his command instead of commanding him? It totally blows his dirty little mind." He twists his hands together conspiratorially. "To have her so compliant, so malleable."

"You're a *monster*..." Tears cloud my vision. "You still haven't told me what you want from me," I say.

Soren regards me with an expression of triumph.

"I don't intend to. As I said before, when you figure out what I am and what *you* are, then you come to me. We'll talk. Now, if you're not going to take part in the festivities, please leave. Julien, take her home. She's destroying the pleasant buzz all this has given me."

Julien pulls me away, but before I leave, I catch one last sight of Michel and Gabrielle – *Marguerite*. Michel bends her over the chair, her gown pulled up around her waist. Then, he bites her shoulder as she arches her back in pleasure.

That would have been me, if I'd have chosen him and my body can't help but respond to the sight of them.

I turn and rush away, getting to the door where I turn around. Julien and Soren stand close to each other, and Soren takes Julien's face in his hand. He speaks to Julien, but I can't hear what he's saying.

Then Julien comes to me without a word, walking past me to the door. I follow him out of the huge room, away from the ornate tapestries and chandeliers sparking in the candlelight and out to the car.

We drive home in silence. I lean my forehead against the cold window and bite my cheek to gain control over my emotions. Julien says nothing, but I can hear his breathing and it's fast, as if he's fighting his emotions.

Soren created a clone of Marguerite? He trained the clone to be a proper little blood slave? He gave her to Michel?

I can't believe what a monster he is.

We arrive at our cottage, and I rush inside once Julien unlocks the door. I go to our bedroom and into the en suite bathroom to wash my face. I feel soiled, having been in Soren's presence and want nothing more than to get out of Luke's velvet dress and into my own clothes. I brush my teeth, staring at my bloodshot eyes, my nose still red from crying.

On top of it all – the anger at Soren, seeing Michel with Gabrielle -- *Marguerite*, the despair at Michel's apparent happiness with her, I feel the need building in me for vampire blood. I need to feel Julien's arms around me. I need to feel that sweet oblivion that his blood and body give me.

I leave the bathroom and he's not in our bedroom. He's not in the office, checking emails. He's in the kitchen standing at the island with a knife and a small crystal goblet. Blood drips from his wrist into the glass. When he sees me standing in the entry to the great room, he looks back down to the glass without a word.

"What are you *doing*?" I say in shock.

He doesn't reply. Instead, he licks the wound he's made. He picks up the glass and walks to me.

"Here's your blood," he says, his voice low. Then he goes to the closet and takes out an extra blanket and pillow. He throws them both on the couch and sits down, removing his shoes and socks. "I'm sleeping here."

"*Julien...*" I say, my voice breaking.

"Don't talk to me, Eve. Just go."

"Soren's done this to you," I say.

"No, *you* did this to me."

He can't understand. I drink down his blood quickly, then I go to him and kneel on the floor beside the couch where he lays, with his back to the room, the blanket over his shoulder. I pull the blanket away and run my hand down his arm. I take his hand in mine, threading my fingers through his. "Don't shut me out."

He pulls his hand away quickly and then turns over to face me, but his expression is hard.

"I thought you made a choice. It seems you still want Michel."

"I chose *you*," I say. "But you have to understand..."

"I *don't* understand, Eve. You say you love me, but why are you so jealous of Michel with Gabrielle?"

I shake my head, unable to explain.

"I loved him," I say weakly. "It's just too soon to see him with someone else. That's all, Julien."

"I can't be with you tonight, Eve. Don't touch me again. Just go to bed. We'll talk in the morning."

"No," I say, desperate now to have him forgive me. The blood has started to work on me, and I feel so warm and aroused, and he's so beautiful in his heart-broken way, his blue eyes huge. "Please..." I lean closer to him, wanting to kiss his mouth, but he turns his head away.

"Don't," he says and pushes me away forcefully so that I sit back on my heels and steady myself on the floor with my hands. "Not tonight, Eve. I need time." He turns over, his back to me and pulls the blanket back over his shoulder.

I struggle to get up and just stand by the couch for a while. Finally, I turn away and go to the bedroom. Perhaps in the night he'll come to me, forgive me. He has to understand. It's just too soon.

Soren's just such a bastard.

I lie in bed and squirm, for the blood is making me so aroused despite my sadness and regret. I toss and turn like this for an hour until finally, I get up to go to the bathroom to take a sleeping pill.

I should be with Julien right now, giving him the pleasure he needs, receiving the pleasure *I* need. Instead, he's turned me away. Has Soren compelled him to fight me?

I tiptoe back into the bedroom and lie in my bed, my face crushed into my pillow to silence my tears.

CHAPTER 17

" *L* ove and desire are the spirit's wings to great deeds."

Goethe

THE NEXT DAY DAWNS, and when I wake, I'm still alone in bed. Julien is still on the couch, the blanket twisted around him, the pillow over his head, his feet sticking out over the armrest. I go to his side and listen to his breathing, which is deep and slow. I wonder what Soren said to him last night – what new bit of compulsion he's inflicted on Julien to manipulate him and through him, me. I kneel beside the couch and rest my hand on Julien's arm, which hangs out from the blanket, his hand resting on the floor. I try to read him, but can't.

"Julien," I whisper. I run my hand down his arm to his hand and take it in mine. "Wake up."

He jerks awake, and removes the pillow from his face, turning his half-closed eyes toward me.

"What is it?" He sits bolt upright as if something's wrong and then he sees his hand in mine and pulls it away. "Don't touch me."

"Julien!" I try to take it back, but he resists. "Why are you being like this?" I try to connect with him again, but for some reason, I can't. "Are you blocking me?"

He says nothing for a moment, just runs his hands through his hair, his eyes not meeting mine. Finally, he speaks, his voice low.

"You shouldn't touch me. You can't connect with me either."

"Why?" I try to take his hand once more but he turns away from me and stands up, trying to hide his morning erection by pulling his t-shirt over it.

"Just don't even try," he says, his voice harsh.

He leaves the living room and makes his way to the bathroom. I follow him, my gut in a knot. Has Soren compelled him to avoid touching me?

When Julien reaches the bathroom he starts to close the door. I stop him with my shoulder, sticking my foot inside. He glances down at my foot and then at me.

"Don't come in."

"Julien!" I'm angry now, and push against the door, trying to get inside. "We need to talk."

"I have to take a piss."

"So?" I say, pushing the door all the way open.

He lets me in finally and turns his back to me, standing at the toilet for several long minutes before I finally hear him urinating.

"What do you want?" he says, his voice a bit shaky.

I stand behind him while he pees, waiting for him to turn around. He finishes, then goes to the sink to wash up. I just watch him, wondering what I can say.

"Soren's compelled you to stay away from me and not let me connect with you."

He says nothing while he washes his hands and then throws water over his face. He dries off, glancing at himself in the mirror before moving his eyes to my reflection briefly.

"Did you hear me?" I say, my voice near breaking. "I said Soren's compelled you to stay away from me. Not let me touch you. For us not to connect."

"Are you going to class this morning?" he says, sidling past me to the closet, where he takes out a clean shirt and then to his suitcase for a clean pair of jeans.

"Julien!" I say and grab his arm.

He glances at my hand on his arm once more like it's some foreign thing he doesn't recognize. He turns away, pulling his arm from my hand.

"Don't," he says, his voice low. "You can't touch me."

"Why not?"

He shakes his head as if he doesn't know the answer. "You just can't."

"Julien, don't you realize that Soren's compelled you not to let us touch? It's just to punish us. To torture us."

He pulls his jeans on and zips up awkwardly, then pulls on his white shirt, saying nothing while he buttons it. Finally, he looks at me, his face hard, but he says nothing.

"Don't you *want* to touch me, to connect with me?" I say, stepping closer. "Don't you want to *kiss* me?"

He says nothing for a moment. Then he sighs, exhaling loudly.

"Of course."

"Then do it."

"I can't."

I grit my teeth. *That bastard...*

I step even closer and the closer I get, the more uncomfortable he appears, his face showing actual panic.

"*Please,*" he almost hisses.

"Kiss me," I say and take another step. Now he's pressed against the wall.

"Eve, don't do this. I can't kiss you."

"Why?"

"I just *can't!*" he says, chopping his hand down between us as if to demark where I may not pass.

"What will happen if you do?"

He slides away from me and I follow him to the kitchen where he starts filling the coffee maker with water. I come up behind him and slip my arms around his waist and he inhales, his breath sounding as if he's in pain. He pulls my arms away as if my touch burns him and steps away backwards. He holds his hands out, palms forward, like he's trying to ward me off.

"Eve, you can't touch me. I can't touch you."

"But you *want* to, right?"

He nods after a moment. "God, I *want* to, but I can't. You can't. I can't let you."

"Soren's done this."

It's like he doesn't hear me.

"Julien," I say and finally, he turns to me and looks in my eyes. "We can't touch, but we can watch. Each other."

Immediately, he knows what I mean. For the next fifteen minutes, we watch each other touch ourselves without touching the other.

It's not much, but it's better than nothing.

THE SCHOOL DAY passes quickly without incident and my shift at the Cove is busy. Before I know it, I've cleaned my twentieth table and it's almost ten. Julien shows up and is sitting at the bar, talking to the bartender while I finish up and sign out.

"How'd it go?" he asks as I get in the car. "Think you can manage two shifts a week? I was thinking we could stretch our stay here so you could at least finish one semester, get some credit. I don't want you working too hard so that it affects your grades."

I shake my head. "It was fine. Boss said if I work out OK, I could pick up a shift or two as a hostess. Get me out of bussing."

"Yeah, they like keeping the sweet young thangs for the front, attract the customers in." He glances at me, smiling.

I want to squeeze his arm but don't. "And the hot young studs behind the bar."

He laughs.

"Hardly young or hot. I mean, temperature-wise." He has that playful sparkle in his eye.

I'm glad the tension has been eased between us and he feels able to speak to me now that we had our little mutual-masturbation encounter. But he was right before when he said I could easily get caught up in the whole university junior world if I let myself. I've always told myself my lack of normal didn't matter. That I had a larger purpose in life – to protect our world against vampires. But in truth, in my secret heart of hearts, I really just wanted it all to go away, and for me to be ordinary. To have had my real family, friends and a boyfriend who loved me.

Julien knows how I feel. He understands how and why I'm so different. As much as I want to escape my previous life for normal, I know I can't ever do it, so being with him is a comfort.

I don't have to pretend with him. He knows me, inside and out.

"Eve, you have to understand that, every now and then I forget what you are," he says as we pull in the driveway at the cottage. We sit in the car for a moment. "I have to keep reminding myself that you're actually very strong. Competent. Dangerous." He turns to me, his expression serious. "I look at you and see this sweet young girl-woman who's seen way too much blood and violence, experienced way too much heartbreak. I want to protect you. I've got to remember that you're my partner so," he says and looks away. "That's my *mea culpa*. My confession." He holds his hands up. "You said I was over-protective? Guilty as charged. I have to back off a bit."

"Thanks," I say, warmth spreading through me at how honest he's being.

I SHOWER and dress as quickly as possible, but my hair is still damp despite the blow dryer. I put on this little black lace top, my jeans and heels. I put on some drop earrings and a bit more makeup than normal.

"How do I look?" I say as I turn in a circle in front of Julien. "Will I pass muster?"

He shakes his head as he looks me up and down. "You look," he says and hesitates. "Good enough to eat. I might just have to take a shotgun into the pub with me."

I laugh at that. "You look pretty nice yourself." He wears a black sweater and jeans, with a black belt and looks like he might have stepped out of GQ with those whiskers growing fashionably on his jaw and the dark hair. I allow myself to see him as a man. The other female students will swoon over him.

If they knew he was a self-described day-walking super-warrior-vampire-hunting vampire killer, I wonder how they'd feel.

That's someone only I could love.

JULIEN DRIVES to the fourth pub on the list after I finish getting ready and we enter and walk into the dimness of the bar. There's a small dance floor and a VJ had set up with a big screen playing music videos. Some students are dancing while others stand around in small groups. I stop beside Julien at the edge of the dance floor and watch, my heart beating faster than it usually did when I was in a fight. I think of how different this is from last night at Soren's. This is where I belong – feeling nervous and awkward at a college function, not an organized vampire and slave orgy.

I scan the floor looking for people I recognize, but don't see Nate – thankfully. I see Sarah Rhys and Brenda as well as several others at a table. Brenda waves at me and motions for me to come over. I nod and make my way through the dancers to their table, Julien behind me.

"Hi, Eve," Sarah says. "Glad to see you here."

I smile. "Thanks. I'm a bit nervous. I've never been to a pub crawl before." I turn to Julien. "This is Julien. Julien, this is Sarah and Brenda from my history class."

They turn to him and he smiles and bows mock-formally, that grin of his starting.

"Such beautiful ladies!" He bows to Sarah and then takes Brenda's hand and kisses her knuckles as if he's trying to see if she's an Adept. "How am I so lucky to be the only man here?"

Sarah smiles and I see Brenda's eyes widen. When Julien lets go of her hand, she looks down at the table for a moment. Julien pulls up a chair from another table and Brenda makes room for us. I sit down.

"I'll go get us a drink. What will you have?"

I make a face. "Just whatever you're having."

He leaves us.

"You've never been to a pub crawl?" Sarah says. "How come?"

I shake my head. "I was a bit of a nerd."

"*We* almost didn't come," she says.

"Why?" Then I cringe. "Oh, right. Your friend Christie's funeral was yesterday. I'm sorry."

Brenda looks quickly at Sarah. "Thanks. It's hard, but she'd want us to come. She helped organize tonight."

I'd completely forgotten why I came to Davis Cove, so wrapped up in the petty psychodrama of my so-called college social life.

"I read about it in the paper. She was your friend?"

Sarah nods. "My best friend."

"Do they know what happened?"

Brenda shrugs, glancing at Sarah. "Overdose, from what the coroner said. It was weird because she never took drugs. Someone maybe spiked her drink, but the coroner ruled it accidental."

I nod. Yes. It certainly was weird. But I know the real cause. She was an Adept and a Blood Slave.

They're silent for a few moments and then someone changes the subject, and talks about an upcoming football game against an old rival. Maybe I imagined the whole thing the other day when Brenda gasped when she touched me. Maybe she did get a static shock and I didn't notice it.

I start to relax once the focus is off me and on to other subjects.

It's then that Nate strolls up, looking very handsome as usual, in a dark blue shirt and jeans. He says hello to everyone and then turns to me, holding out his hand.

"Eve, would you like to dance?"

"Not really," I say, glancing at the dance floor where a few people are dancing.

"Come on. Don't be a buzz kill. Besides, I have something to tell you in private."

I frown and stand up, taking his hand, because, what am I going to do? Refuse? I'm sure it's a message from Soren.

"Sure."

He leads me to the middle of the dance floor and we wait for the next song. The music starts and it's a slow dance. *Crap.*

"I better not," I say stepping back from him. "Julien's a bit jealous."

I try to walk away, but he grabs my hand and pulls me against him. "You don't have a choice, Eve," he says and smiles. "Soren wanted me to tell you something and this is the best way to convey his message."

I give in, but I glance over at the bar, where Julien is chatting with the bartender, his back to me while the bartender pours our drinks. Probably talking bar stuff.

"You're on the wrong track if you keep investigating these murders," he says into my ear.

"What do you mean?" I put on a fake smile, not wanting Julien to get upset if he sees me.

"They're nothing. Just business. Not part of anything ominous."

"Like I believe that."

"Believe it. Soren doesn't want you to keep investigating them. You're raising all kinds of unnecessary questions. Back off or he says your little problem with Julien will continue. "

The song ends and I turn away without another word, going back to find that Sarah's table is joined by a tall dark-haired young man I hadn't seen at school before.

I take my chair and Sarah cranes her head to me. "Dylan, I want you to meet my new friend Eve. Eve, this is my big brother. He's only a year older than me, but he likes it when I call him that. He's back from Boston for the weekend. He's doing a degree in engineering at MIT. He's studying nanotechnology."

I smile at him. He looks a bit uncomfortable, but then smiles back at me. It looks anything but friendly.

"Nice to meet you," he says stiffly. I figure he doesn't like being introduced to all Sarah's little friends like he's some trophy on display. I wonder why he came if he's uncomfortable.

"I told you about Eve," Sarah says. "She's a classically trained pianist. Her father played violin for the Prague Symphony." She raises her eyebrows at that.

I feel my cheeks burn. Her father or mother must have spoken about me.

"Yeah, I was my father's performing monkey for a few years," I say, trying to downplay it. Then I feel bad, saying something mean about my father, considering. I just don't like the limelight.

"Our mother said you made the first cut at Julliard for the pre-college program. That's something you should be proud of," Dylan says.

I look at him more closely to see his expression. He's darkly attractive, with longish black hair and hazel eyes.

I shrug and turn away, hoping the conversation will shift away from me and my background. I don't like lying or telling too much of the truth and most of all, I don't want anyone to talk about the fact that I lost my parents.

Finally, Julien returns and sits beside me on the chair, which he's turned around. Then, out of the blue, Dylan offers me his hand when the music starts.

"Care to dance?"

I smile and glance at Julien, who raises his eyebrows. What is it with these people and hand-holding? I don't want to say no, so I breathe in deeply and take his hand but get nothing strange from him when I do. The song turns out to be another slow one and so once again, I've broken Julien's rule about touching strangers. He can't come and rescue me either. We can't touch.

"You're lucky to be able to play piano," Dylan says, his mouth next to my ear, one hand on my waist, the other holding my hand. "My mother tried to teach me, but it didn't stick. Didn't get the talent genes, I guess. Sarah did, but then she got sick."

"What's wrong with her?"

"Inherited neuromuscular disorder. Incurable. She'll likely be dead by the time she's thirty."

"I'm so sorry."

He shrugs. "I've known most of her life. It's hard to watch. She's still pretty good though."

He has the same accent as his parents and sister, called 'Scouse' to those who live in the region. When we lived in England, in Wales, I became familiar with the different accents.

An awkward silence passes.

He takes in a deep breath. "How come you didn't go to Julliard?"

"After my mother died, I focused more on science and never went to the audition."

He shakes his head and frowns. "That's sad," he says.

"I was in love with medicine, like my mom was," I say, remembering my foster parent's insistence that I go back to full academics in high school.

"That's too bad," he says, and his voice actually sounds sad. "The world has more than enough doctors but hardly enough really gifted musicians."

"So, you study nanotechnology?" I try to change the subject. "That's amazing."

He pulls back and checks me out. "You're interested in science?"

"I've loved science since I was a kid," I say. "I had a telescope back when we lived in Wales and I take pictures. I took one of Andromeda and a few nebulae that turned out well. Some time lapse video of the Milky Way rising."

"Really?"

"When we moved to Prague, I hated it because there was so much light pollution, I could hardly see anything."

"Wales, Prague. Sounds like an interesting life. How did you end up in Davis Cove, of all places?"

I hate to lie to him, especially since he and his sister are being so nice to me, but what else can I do?

I repeat the lie. "My dad stayed here as a kid and so I thought it would be a good place to come, get away from it all."

"It certainly is away from it all."

I look up at his face. He's smiling.

"Some weekend when I'm back, I'll bring my telescope and we can do some star gazing," he says, his voice light. "I have a great Takahashi and a pretty good camera for astrophotography. The Draconids are coming up next week – it's supposed to be a great show this year. A thousand meteors a second."

I smile. "I have a boyfriend."

"I have a girlfriend," he says and smiles. "Just being friendly."

I feel heat rise in my cheeks. "Sorry. I just didn't want..."

"No offense taken." We dance in silence for a few moments, and it's then I feel it – just a tiny sense that he's trying to get into my mind.

I immediately put up my mental blocks.

I don't know what to do. Do I act as if nothing happened? Do I confront him? I feel conflicted. I decide to pretend nothing happened.

Then I see Julien walking across the dance floor to us.

"I guess I overstayed my welcome," Dylan says, smiling. The song ends and now it's a fast one. Dylan bows to me and gestures to Julien. "She's all yours."

Julien tilts his head in acknowledgement. "She always was."

Dylan smiles and catches my eye before he leaves.

Julien and I dance, but we stay our proper distance away, and I try to tell him what Nate said.

"Nate told me that so long as you and I investigate these cases, our problem will remain."

"Fucking bastard," he says. "He knows we're here because of the murders."

Then I tell him about Dylan.

He frowns. "This is why you shouldn't be dancing, Eve. If he's an Adept working for Blackstone, they'll know I'm here."

"I thought you wanted to infiltrate them?"

"Yeah, but on my terms. Now, we'll have to see how they respond, if this Dylan guy is with them and if he knows who I am."

"How could I know? I'd written the Rhys family off because I never got anything from Sarah or her parents."

He shakes his head and inhales deeply.

"I guess we'll find out now."

Finally, we sit back down at the table.

"Eve," Sarah says to me. "Why don't you come by to my place some afternoon? We have a concert grand piano that my mother bought when she was in New York one year. I'd love to hear you play. I used to play before…"

I look at her and then to Dylan, who's smiling. His smile looks pleasant enough, but his eyes are hooded.

"You should come by," he says. "Supposedly, Glenn Gould played on it when he was still a student in Toronto."

"Glenn Gould?" I can't help but sound impressed. Gould is one of my favorite musicians. "I'll do that," I say, trying to find a reason to say no. I just will never go. I glance at Julien, who's frowning.

"Come by after school some day when you're not working." Sarah smiles so brightly. Perhaps she's unaware of her brother's gifts.

"I'll try."

We stay there for another half-hour and Julien and I listen to their talk about the community and then it's on to the next pub. I glance back to watch Dylan pushing his sister's wheelchair. Ahead of us, Nate and his friends leave the building, laughing amongst themselves, on their way to the next pub on the list. They all look so normal. But they're really just like me.

We're all performing, evaluating each other.

Once we're in the car, I turn to Julien.

"Let's go home," I say. "I've had enough."

"It's only 11:30."

"I'm tired and being around them is stressful."

He nods.

I slept poorly last night and we do have some work to do tomorrow. Our test results from the three deaths that drew our interest are due in and they'll determine just what our next steps will be. If they come back positive, with abnormal levels of oxytocin and dopamine, signs of being a blood slave, we'd start examining all their contacts to try to narrow down who our suspect – or suspects – are.

But I already think it's either Soren or one of his minions. Or Blackstone.

Why has Soren called us here if he knows we'll investigate these murders?

I stare out the window as we drive back to our cottage overlooking the ocean, wondering how Dylan Rhys fits into all this.

CHAPTER 18

D. H. Lawrence

ON SATURDAY, we have lunch and then Julien and I sit at the computer and read over the email Sheriff Conyers sent containing the results of the blood and tissue tests we'd asked for. Every one of our suspected cases reveals the telltale evidence of being a blood slave. There is enough other evidence to confirm that someone in Davis Cove is using Adepts as blood slaves. Of course, I think it's Soren.

"Soren said these murders were just housekeeping. My thought would be that he's weeding out the ones he thinks aren't loyal enough, or are tempted to join the Council."

Julien says nothing and I wonder if Soren's new compulsion overrides the last one. He totally ignores me.

"Did you hear me?" I say. "Soren said these murders are housekeeping."

He frowns at me. "Eve, I can't touch you. Stop."

Well, he's left them both in place. So I can't talk to him about Soren's guilt and I can't touch him.

He's trying to drive me crazy.

I think immediately about Dylan – he comes back each weekend. If he's an Adept working for Blackstone, he might be involved in some way. He wasn't at Soren's party but he was supposed to be in Cambridge at school on Thursday.

"Do you suppose Dylan's being prepared to be one of Soren's Adepts? Like I'm supposed to be? Or is he with Blackstone?"

Now, Julien looks up. "Soren's creating some kind of army of Adepts to take power once Blackstone strikes. Davis Cove may just be a retreat for him and his coven. A place to train Adepts while he waits for Blackstone to make their move. Or he located here because there's a Blackstone cell here and he wants to keep an eye on them. Dylan could be part of either."

So he can talk to me about Soren but not his guilt in the River Man case or this case. Did Soren or one of his servants kill them all? A sense of horror spreads through me at the thought Dylan is involved with either Blackstone or Soren. He's attractive, pleasant, and non-threatening – except for the last moment when we were dancing and I felt him reaching out to my mind.

Why hasn't he challenged me if he knows who and what I am? It doesn't make sense to me. This makes me think he's with Blackstone, which makes him even more dangerous.

"Julien," I say as we sit in silence, reading over the files. "All those first murders that were part of The River Man case – they were all like you, weren't they? Vampire warriors created by Blackstone? That's why they were beheaded. They were all vampires, not Adepts."

He glances up from his file, his brow furrowed. "Yes."

"Why didn't Michel and Ed tell me that right away?"

He says nothing for a long moment as if deciding whether to tell the truth.

"Blackstone's killing off members of my unit. I don't know why. If we can track down the killer, we may find out why but it has to be linked to Dominion."

Of course, I know it's Soren killing off members of his unit. Why? As a threat to Julien? Warning?

He comes over to me and sits beside me on the couch, careful to keep a distance between us. I cross my arms, trying to keep my hands away from him, because my first instinct is to reach out and touch him.

"Why did Soren stake you?"

"To get to Michel. To get him to comply."

"He never really meant to kill you."

"No, but he could have. He used me as his trump card if Michel didn't comply."

"Michel refused him?"

Julien nods. "Yes. Michel didn't want to cooperate with Soren. But then, he found you and was unable to keep you hidden…"

"So Soren found out about me and tried to push you and I together by making Michel stay with him in Pittsburgh."

"That was his plan from the start."

"That you and I would be lovers?"

"He'd use you to get to us both."

"So, he wanted me to be with both of you. He'd use you both to get to me and use me to get to both of you."

"That's about it."

"He's a bastard."

"The supreme manipulator," Julien says and shakes his head.

Now, I'm even more confused. I wish there was someone else to talk to about this. Someone who is compulsion free. Someone else like me.

JULIEN and I pore over the cases that we now know are the result of blood sharing and draw up a list of contacts each one had, to see if there were any people in common who might be linked to either Soren's coven or some Blackstone cell. With the help of Sheriff Conyers, we create a tree of contacts. Being a relatively small town, there are many shared connections between the four victims. All of them go to the local Catholic Church. They all went to the family medical clinic to visit their doctors at some point in the year or had one of the doctors attend to them. They all received mail, had the same telephone and internet service. As we build up our list, one thing kept cropping up.

The Rhys family.

"But none of them are vampires," Julien says as he looks at surveillance photos he's taken of them. "I don't understand. They're linked – tenuously – to every one of the dead, but then, so are a dozen other people on the list." He turns to face me and looks at me from under a furrowed brow. "Maybe you *should* go to the Rhys family for a visit after all."

I shrug and try to act as if it's just work, but I'm a little scared and curious. "Maybe I was mistaken about him trying to enter my mind."

"I doubt it. It wouldn't hurt for you to go there, check them out. You might turn up something."

"I'm surprised you'll let me go alone."

"I'll wait on the street somewhere close, just in case you run into any trouble. You can text me if you feel under threat since we can't connect."

Julien closes the file on the Rhys family, moving on to a fisherman named Colville Black who moved to town the previous year from Maine. He's single and lives alone. The story is he'd passed through once on a road trip and liked the town so much, he came back when he'd lost his job in a downturn – which, of course, sounded suspiciously like our cover story. He'll be first on the list for surveillance.

THE WEEKEND PASSES without incident and classes are pretty much ordinary all week. I work on Tuesday night, and again on Thursday night, but I have Friday night off because another busgirl wanted to switch shifts.

After history on Friday, Sarah calls me over in the hallway.

"Can you come over today, see our piano? We're ordering in Chinese and you're welcome to stay for supper. I'd love to hear you play."

I nod. "Sure, I haven't really played for several weeks and would love to."

"Why haven't you played?" Sarah asks, her eyebrows raised.

"Don't have a piano at the cottage."

"I'm sure my mom would be happy for you to come by any time and play." Sarah smiles brightly, her green eyes crinkling at the corner. She doesn't look at all like Dylan, but then again, the Rhys parents have very different coloring. I decide to investigate their family a bit more closely and will ask the Council for any records they might have in their files. If there are none, I'll ask them to use Homeland Security and CIA to create a file to see where they've lived and what they've done for the past couple of decades.

I call Julien at the end of the day and let him know I'll be going over to the Rhys house after school to play the piano and stay for supper. He'll find a safe place to park like we discussed. If I feel at all threatened, I'll text him and he'll come right away.

I'm certain I have nothing to fear from them.

Professor Rhys drives us to their house after loading Sarah's wheelchair in their van. The house is a large bungalow on the side of a hill overlooking the ocean. They have a huge bank of solar cells on the roof.

"You have solar power?"

Professor Rhys nods. "We're completely off the grid just in case it goes down." He pushes Sarah's wheelchair up the ramp to the front door. "That's Dylan's thing – solar power. Sarah needs a source of power 24/7 and if the grid went down for any length of time, she'd be in danger."

"He means I'd die," Sarah says. "Dylan insisted. He's afraid there might be another Carrington Event during solar maximum and the grid might fail so we installed the panels. Now we feed the grid, instead of taking from it."

"Carrington Event?"

"A huge solar storm that would disrupt power transmissions – maybe for months."

I make a face. "That's a scary thought. How likely is it?"

Professor Rhys laughs. "Not likely, but Dylan is all about preparation for the worst."

I frown. He is, is he? I wonder why... This just adds another tick mark beside the potential Blackstone cell member possibility.

The house has a beautiful view but the inside of the house is most interesting. Art covers every wall, modern art, posters from films and plays on Broadway, concerts at Carnegie Hall. This is the kind of house I would like to have lived in growing up. My foster parents are wonderful, but I didn't feel at home with them and all my memories of them were lost. This house is big, warm, full of art and culture. The Rhys parents are smart and seem kind.

"Here it is," Sarah says, wheeling into the conservatory. The piano stands in front of a wall-to-wall picture window overlooking the bay. Across from it is a huge bookcase with hundreds of books. A fireplace is off to the side and beside it two loveseats face each other.

Sarah's mother goes to the piano and stands beside it.

"Gould played it when he was a student in Toronto at the Royal Conservatory of Music," she says, touching it almost with affection. "We got it at auction in an estate sale."

There's nothing spectacular about the piano – an old Steinway grand. The only thing that makes it special is that Gould had played it when he was still unknown. It shows its age, but the mere fact Gould had played it makes my heart beat faster. I sit at the piano and run my fingers over the keys lightly, thinking of Gould himself touching them when he was even younger than me. Just to warm up, I play some scales and soon, I feel familiar enough with the instrument that I decide to play the Aria from the Goldberg Variations.

Sarah lets out an "ohhh" when she recognizes the piece and I smile to myself. Another Bach freak. I play it with a slower tempo, like Gould's final recording rather than faster, like his first.

"I can almost hear him humming," Sarah says as I play. I glance at her and see that Dylan has appeared and is standing behind her in the darkness of the doorway. I turn back to the keys, trying not to let Dylan's appearance throw me off. I stumble a bit but keep on going until I finish the Aria. Then, I move into the first variation and play it till the end.

"That's it for the Goldberg Variations," I say and shrug. "I didn't learn all of it."

"Play something else," Sarah says.

"What would you like to hear?"

"Play more Bach," Sarah says. "He's my favorite." She smiles so winningly, I can't resist.

I play Bach's Prelude in C Sharp Minor, a piece from *The Well Tempered Clavier*. It's one of my favorites. I like the darkness of the piece. It reminds me of Prague.

While I play, Dylan comes over and stands beside the piano, watching me. I try to block out thinking of him and what he might be, focusing instead on the music, on the feel of the keys, trying to get my touch right for Bach. When I finish, they all clap and I bow as a joke, and then start to leave the piano, but Sarah's mother stops me.

"Please," she says and holds out a hand. "Keep playing. It's so nice to hear someone with real talent and training. Most of my students are just putting in time."

I sit back down. "What would you like to hear?"

"Debussy," Dylan says.

I think for a moment and then start playing a piece from *Pour le Piano* – the Sarabande, which I like due to its chromatism. When I finish, Dylan leans against the piano.

"Did you know," he says, "that Debussy composed according to the golden ratio? You can find evidence of the Fibonacci Sequence in his compositions."

I frown, remembering something about that – Michel mentioned it as well.

"The Fibonacci Sequence is a mathematical progression of numbers," he adds, as if to explain.

"Yes, I know," I say, trying not to sound defensive. "It seems the opposite to my sense of Debussy, which is so much passion and beauty that it goes beyond math."

"Math is beautiful," Dylan says. "Numbers, patterns, built right into the universe."

I frown again. Sounds like what Michel said to me on the beach when he showed me the shell.

"That's Dylan," Mr. Rhys says, patting Dylan on the shoulder. "Always into the math of things. You play beautifully, Eve. Why aren't you studying music? You're in pre-med, from your records."

I shake my head. "I haven't taken lessons for years. My father was so involved in my training." I stop, suddenly overwhelmed by emotion. "I don't have the heart to study music any more since he was institutionalized."

"I'm sorry," Mrs. Rhys says. An awkward silence passes and Mr. Rhys clears his throat.

"I love science now," I say and force a smile, trying to counter the mood. "I'll probably do my MD and then a PhD." I stand and close the cover on the keyboard. I smile at them, feeling very much the center of attention, which I don't like.

"You won't play more?" Mrs. Rhys says, her head tilted to one side.

"I've played enough for now."

We go into the kitchen, and the parents start to remove containers of food from the oven where they are warming. Sarah leads me to a table in the great room.

"If you like marine biology, you should see my room later. I have a great collection of seashells."

"I'd like that," I say.

Once the food is on the table, we sit around it and after Mr. Rhys says grace, we eat, the talk about Dylan's classes, Sarah's project in our marine biology class, Thomas – the oldest brother – and his last year in Seminary, the upcoming drama production of the Chekov play, for which I will only be a lowly stage hand, and news of Davis Cove.

It feels so amazing to be here, sitting around a table with them, the fireplace flickering in the corner, Brahms playing on the sound system. A family – a *real* family. Mother, father, son, daughter, talking and laughing and sharing their lives. I sit and watch them and a feeling of such loss fills me, I bite my lip to keep tears from my eyes.

They seem so real, almost perfect – except that their daughter is a quadriplegic who will probably die before she reaches age thirty. I Googled her disorder – Kugelberg-Wellander Syndrome Type II-III variant. When I look at her, I can't help but feel my heart squeeze at the thought she'll endure a slow decline and then death. Dylan's an Adept who might be working for either Soren Lindgren's coven or Blackstone, out to destroy modern civilization and bring about Dominion.

They'll need that solar power if the grid does fail because of Blackstone. I wonder if Dylan knows something about that and this explains his insistence about the solar panels.

After dessert and coffee, Sarah asks me to come to her room. I follow her down the long hallway to her bedroom and am amazed. She has a hospital bed in the room with a bank of electronic machines like I expect would be in an ICU. But other than that, the room is beautiful, with art all over the walls depicting seashells, the sea, sailing ships, lighthouses, everything nautical.

"I'm sensing a theme," I say and smile. "I love the sea."

She nods. "The oceans are so amazing. If I'd been healthy, I'd have become a marine biologist," she says. "My mother and father took us to Florida when I was younger, before I was on a respirator, and I swam with the wild dolphins there. I'd want to study dolphin and whale communication or the deep ocean, down where it's dark and the creatures communicate with bioluminescence."

I sit on a chair in her room and look around. On the top of her dresser are huge conch shells and a tray of seashells of different colors. Starfish, corals – everywhere you look there's something from the oceans.

"Do you like my seashells?" she says and moves her head to the side. "I've gone a bit overboard, but Dylan collects them for me and brings me something new and different each week."

I walk around and touch them, picking up the conch and listening.

"They say you can hear the sea when you put these up to your ear," I say and hear a roaring sound when I hold the conch up to listen.

"That's a myth," Dylan says from the doorway, where he stands, leaning against the doorjamb, hands in his pockets. "It's just the result of ambient sound echoing inside the shell due to its structure."

I put the shell down carefully, my cheeks a bit hot. I feel like telling him I already knew that, but I shut up instead.

"Party-pooper," Sarah says. "It's much more fun to believe you're really hearing the ocean."

"The truth is always better than a myth," Dylan says and looks at me. "Isn't that right, Eve? What's the saying – *better a cruel truth than a comfortable delusion?*"

I freeze. He's quoting something back to me that I said to Michel… Was he able to read my mind from that brief moment when he tried to connect to me at the pub crawl?

"I guess some people need delusions," I say. "Gets them through the day."

"Not me," he says. "I prefer the cold, hard truth." He leaves the room.

"Don't mind Dylan," Sarah says quietly. "Sometimes, he's far too serious for his own good." She grins at me.

I follow her back to the conservatory and the piano that Gould once played. What a strange turn of events – here I am, in the house of a suspect, playing piano for him.

I don't feel like I'm in danger, so I don't text Julien. I'll tell him later.

I play the Bach Fugue in C sharp minor that accompanies the Prelude I played earlier. It's very slow and somber. I could play something lighter, but I love it so much, I have to play it while I'm able to do so on such a famous piano. Gould recorded the C sharp minor – he recorded the entire Well-Tempered Clavier. I think of him as I play – he was such a strange creature. Other-worldly with his Asperger's reclusiveness and social awkwardness. But such genius. I try to put as much into the piece as I can, as much precision as I can muster.

When I'm done, my audience is silent for a moment as if not yet ready to have it end. Finally, Mr. Rhys seems to come out of a trance.

"That was lovely, Eve. Please," he says and clears his throat. "Feel free to come over any time you feel like playing."

I stand and catch sight of Dylan standing off to the side, his long bangs hanging in his very hazel eyes.

What *is* he? Who is he with?

Julien picks me up and is impatient to hear how my evening with the mysterious Rhys family went. I give a very sketchy account, telling him about how normal they all seem, with the exception of Sarah's disease. How I didn't think any of them are involved in anything nefarious – except for Dylan. It's all the truth – but I'm lying by omission by not telling him my suspicions about Dylan and what he said to me, quoting me back.

"I don't think the family is involved in Blackstone or with Soren," I say. "But Dylan might be."

He nods in agreement. "I'll check him out but I'm liking Mr. Colville Black for this. While you were in class today, I did a bit more sleuthing. Seems he's been in a few locations where there've been other suspicious deaths. I'll be paying him a visit tomorrow to see what's up. We may have our case solved a lot sooner than I thought. Wonder if we could get a refund on the rent..."

I glance at him to see if he's serious, for I had my heart set on staying in Davis Cove for a semester.

"Just kidding," he says and laughs. "I'm not going to ambush him. We need to find his contacts, check them out. If there's a Blackstone cell here, that's the way to find them. Then, we have to find a way in."

After Julien goes to the Cove for his late bartending shift, I go out to the patio and sit in the darkness so I can watch the stars as they appear, one by one as darkness falls over the ocean.

I'm torn in a way I never thought was possible. Part of me hopes Dylan is just another Adept who's living here, and is completely unconnected to the murders. I really like Sarah and don't want her to lose her beloved older brother. Even as I think that, guilt fills me. I'm letting my personal feelings affect my work and that's dangerous. If Dylan is involved in these killings, either working for Soren or Blackstone, he's a threat.

I don't know what Julien has planned, but I can't imagine it involves letting whoever is guilty go free. Not for long, anyway.

My heart breaks for Sarah already.

CHAPTER 19

"*Sometimes the heart sees what is invisible to the eye."*

H. Jackson Brown, Jr.

THE NEXT DAY, on my way home from town where I've gone to pick up something for dinner, I catch sight of Dylan walking along the road towards his parent's house. He takes a shortcut through the park and I almost call out to him, but hold back when a group of men from town follow him inside the cover of trees.

I don't know them personally, but I remember them from the bar in the Cove Bistro one night when I was working. Some good old boys who work on the wharf on the fishing boats. Something about the way they follow him puts my nerves on edge, so I trail them, hiding behind trees so they won't know I'm there. They laugh amongst themselves and one of them pushes the larger guy forward as if egging him on. The guy calls out to Dylan.

"Hey, you – freak!"

Dylan seems to ignore them.

"I said, hey you freak!" the guy repeats. He runs up to Dylan and pushes him on the shoulder. My muscles all tense when I see the violence, my body ready by instinct, and I crouch, ready to run to him if he needs my help. I could beat all four of them in a pinch so long as they're not Adepts.

Dylan turns to face them, and then I see he had his earphones on. He speaks, but his voice is too low to hear. He waits as the others stand in a semi-circle in front of him.

"Oh, yeah? Do you think so? Who's gonna make us?" the big guy with a beard says, his voice mocking. He pushes Dylan on the shoulder again as if to pick a fight but Dylan turns and walks away. The guy grabs him, pulling him around by his jacket, throwing him to the ground. When he lunges at Dylan, I'm just about to step out in the open, ready to take them on. Then, Dylan sweeps his right arm in an arc. A shock wave emerges from his hand and the young men are thrown back several feet, falling to the ground. They lie silent and unmoving on the grass. I stay where I am, hidden behind a tree, my heart racing.

Dylan rises and brushes the dirt off his clothes, then he lays his hand on their necks for a brief moment, one after the other. He walks away, leaving them on the ground. When he's out of sight, they wake up, sitting up slowly, rubbing their heads.

"What the fuckin' hell?" the one who challenged Dylan says, rubbing his head. They all seem stunned, rising slowly, glancing around as if they're confused. "What the hell are we doing here?"

I slip away through the trees and walk home, my pulse racing, hands shaking. I'm determined to speak to Dylan about what happened the next time I see him.

He's no ordinary Adept. He's no vampire, either. I don't know what the hell he is, but whatever it is, he has powers I've never heard of.

JULIEN'S WORKING LATE at the Cove and I'm alone for supper. After I finish my meal, and put the rest away for Julien, I go down to the

beach and take a walk along the shore as the sun begins to set. When I round a bend in the beach, I come across Michel, sitting on the sand alone, his feet bare, his shoes on the beach a bit higher away from the surf.

I stop up sharply and gasp. He turns to me, and when I see his face, I can't help but feel my heart squeeze just a bit. His hair is a mess, blowing around in the wind, his skin so pale in the last rays of sunlight.

"Michel," I say when he turns back to the ocean. "What are you doing here?"

"I thought you might go for a walk. I was hoping to speak with you."

"I don't want to talk to you."

He exhales heavily and he rises, wiping sand off his jeans. He comes over to me and just stands there, looking down at me, his hands in the pockets of his jacket. He looks so sad. Almost fearful.

"I want to say how sorry I am for what happened at Soren's."

I say nothing, not wanting to admit anything to him.

"I know what Soren's done to Julien," he adds. "He'll try to torment you until you comply, Eve."

"What do you mean, comply?"

"Come with me. Be my Adept."

I turn away, my cheeks heating under his intense gaze. "You have a new Adept."

"She's not for me, Eve. She's Soren's. I don't want her."

"You sure looked like you did."

"I didn't. Not really. She was just to make you jealous."

"I'm not," I say, but of course, I'm lying. "I was just disgusted with Soren for what he did..."

He takes hold of my shoulders and turns me to face him. Then he cups my cheek with his hand, touching me to make me relax. When I do, he connects with me and I feel him enter my mind, the sensation so familiar I almost welcome it after this dry-spell with Julien.

"Eve," he says, his voice soft. "I *know*. I know how you feel without even having to touch you. Don't lie to me. Don't lie to yourself."

I stare into his eyes, which are so huge right now, his beautiful face filled with pain. I don't say anything to deny what he's said or to confirm it, for he's already read me. He knows how I felt, how I feel.

"I hate you both," I say, squeezing my nails into my palms to stop the tears, which threaten to well up in my eyes. Like Julien said so long ago, pain and anger are preferable.

"No," he says and shakes his head. "You don't. You love us both. You can't choose."

"I *did* choose."

He smiles softly. "In that moment, yes. But now?" He brushes hair from my cheek. "You'd go with me if I pressed a bit."

"You're wrong."

He shakes his head slowly. "No, you would go, but I won't ask. You'll go with me when the time comes. That's all that matters."

He bends down and kisses me, and despite everything, or because of it, my body is so ready, aching for his or Julien's touch. I can't help but respond to the feel of his arms around me, his body pressed against mine, his mouth on mine. I keep my eyes open while his eyes close as we kiss, so I can remember who he is.

He looks and feels and smells and tastes so much like Julien.

And he's right. The way I feel when he kisses and embraces me... Just like in the Abbey, I could so easily just go with him wherever he took me. I could fuck him right now in the sand with the fading rays of sun on us as it sets on the horizon.

He pulls away and presses his forehead against mine, his eyes closed.

"*My sweet girl*," he says, his voice filled with emotion. "*I will imagine you Venus tonight and pray, pray, pray to your star like a Heathen.*"

I recognize the quote. Keats – a letter to his Fanny Brawne written before he died. My throat chokes that he knows my deepest heart of hearts and can quote my favorite line from Keats's letter.

Then he turns away, goes to his shoes, and he walks down the beach, away from me.

Part of me wants to run to him, to go with him, but I can't.

I *can't*.

Julien would never stand it.

JULIEN ARRIVES home around eleven and when he comes to me where I'm sitting on the couch, he just looks at me, as if waiting.

"What?" I say, frowning at his dark expression.

"How did your evening go?" he says, his voice soft, his eyes hooded.

"Fine. I had supper and then went for a walk on the beach. I came back and have been reading. The meteor shower's later tonight. I'd like to watch."

He sighs and then he reaches into his jacket pocket and pulls out a small book. He looks at it, and then drops it on the couch beside me.

"I'm going out. I don't know when I'll be back."

Then he turns on his heel and leaves, the door slamming behind him.

I pick up the thin book. It's a hardcover volume of Keats' letters to Fanny Brawne, old, with a dark blue cover. I pull off the pale blue ribbon that has been hastily re-tied around it. Julien's opened it and has looked inside. I open it and see it was published in 1878. Inside is a letter from Michel.

Eve,

Forgive my visit earlier, and for my kiss, but I had to see you to apologize for what happened the other night. Know that I never wanted to be with Gabrielle, but I must comply with Soren. I realize it hurt you deeply. You must know that I would never hurt you intentionally.

Come to me when the time is right. I know from touching you that it's what you truly desire but you're afraid of hurting Julien.

I love you. Only you.

Michel

I go to the door and watch Julien as he gets into his car. I run to his door and put my hands on the handle, trying to open it. He starts to drive away and so I bang on the window. Finally, he stops and rolls the window down.

"What?"

"Don't be mad at me. I didn't ask him to come."

"You kissed him."

"He kissed *me*," I say, frustration filling me. "There's a difference. I refused him. I told him I chose you."

He shakes his head. "I can't even touch you to know if you're telling me the truth."

"I *am*," I say. "You'll have to trust me. He kissed me, Julien. I didn't kiss him."

"But you still want him."

"I chose *you*."

"I'm going to the bar for a drink. I don't know when I'll be back."

"Julien!" I say, but he drives off, leaving me standing in the darkness.

AROUND MIDNIGHT, I take a blanket and walk to the hill overlooking the beach and watch meteors fall. As they blaze across the sky, I feel incredibly lonely lying here by myself, thinking that by all rights, Julien should be here with me to watch the meteor shower. That thought just upsets me more and so I indulge in misery, wondering where Julien is and why he's forsaken me.

When a few drops of rain fall on my upturned face, sending a shiver through me from the chill, I think it's strange. Other than a few high clouds streaking the heavens, the sky's clear, the storm system having moved off into the distance over an hour earlier. The Draconids are unspectacular due to the moon, so when Julien drives up after two o'clock in the morning, I fold up my blanket and go inside to meet him.

"Eve!" he said when he sees me, pointing at my face. "What happened?"

I frown and go to a mirror in the entry to examine my reflection. Crimson dots cover my face and hands like so many drops of blood.

"It rained."

"That's not rain," he says. I lick a finger then wipe one of the dots off my cheek. It smears on my fingers and I hold it up closer.

"What the hell is it?" he says, alarm in his voice.

I shrug. "I have no idea. I was out watching the meteor shower. It rained but the sky was clear. The storms passed hours ago."

I go to the bathroom and wet a washcloth and wipe the red dots off my face and hands but there are stains in my hair as well. I get in the shower and stand in the hot spray. After I dry off, I put my pajamas on and go to the office, where Julien stands in front of one of the computer monitors, speaking on the secure phone.

"What was the extent?" he says, his voice hushed. "How far did it reach up the coast?"

I sit on a chair and listen as he speaks to Vasquez.

"OK," he says, running his hand through his hair. "I'll keep an eye out. Call if anything develops."

He hangs up and stands for a moment in silence, contemplating the screens in front of him. On them are maps of the world and of the United States. Sections have been marked off in red, covering the whole Eastern Seaboard of the US from the Carolinas to Maine and beyond into Canada.

"What's happening?"

He shrugs. "Some kind of strange weather phenomenon. It's probably algal spores."

"I've read about that before," I say. "There was a scare a few years back. People thought it was extraterrestrial."

"It's from algal blooms." He clicks on a link in the web browser. "Gets sucked up into the high atmosphere and then falls when the weather conditions are right. It's just weird. So far, the experts think it's from a massive red bloom due to warm waters off the coast. Don't eat oysters for a while, I guess."

We read reports from the CIA and Homeland security for a while, side by side at the two computer desks. Finally, I yawn and turn to him.

"How are you feeling?" I say, wanting so badly to touch him, for us to fuck. "Better?"

He doesn't say anything for a moment but then he shrugs.

"Nothing a little tequila won't fix."

"Are you coming to bed?"

He shakes his head.

"You go. I'm going to monitor things for a while."

"Julien!" I say. "Come to bed with me. Even if we can't touch, we can watch each other."

"Not tonight," he says without looking at me.

I want to argue but it's pointless. Instead, I exhale and go to bed, but I leave the door open. I can see him sitting at the desk alone, the light from the screen illuminating his face.

THE NEXT MORNING OVER COFFEE, we listen as the news channels report on the fall of red rain. At first, there are suggestions that the rain was part of the meteor shower, but that was just fanatics and conspiracy theorists talking.

Later in the day, scientists report that the substance was a lichen-forming alga belonging to the genus *Trentepholia*. The spores were likely picked up in a storm, mixed with the rain high in the atmosphere, and then dropped on the East coast of the US. The fact that it took place during the meteor shower was pure coincidence.

Since there is no cause for alarm, people go about their business, washing off the red drops from their cars, their houses and the streets and only the crackpots raise alarm, calling it the start of the end of the world. I think nothing more of it, except to bring in a sample to my marine biology class where other students and I examine the spores under a microscope. They look like red blood cells, except they have a nucleus and visible organelles.

Everyone's interested in the strange phenomenon for a few days, but by the end of the week, people's thoughts turn to a plane crash off the coast of France that killed over a hundred passengers and crew. Soon, the red rain is forgotten, my samples placed in a box and shoved to the back of a cabinet in the laboratory.

THAT WEEK, I pretty much carry on as a normal college student again. I try to forget what I saw that day in the park, but I ask Sarah about Dylan when I see her in class on Tuesday.

"How's Dylan?"

She follows me down the hall to our class.

"He didn't go to Cambridge. He's still in town."

"How come?" I say and frown.

"I don't know. After the red rain fell, he was strange, like it spooked him." She rolls her eyes. "I don't know what's up with him lately," she says. "He's been so mysterious."

I shake my head. "I never had a brother. You have two."

"I know – I'm so lucky." Sarah smiles.

THE INVESTIGATION into the identity of our killer continues, but at a slow pace. Julien orders a full background check on our mysterious Mr. Colville Black and it seems he's spent some time in prison and was hoping to start a new life in Davis Cove. He isn't an Adept or a member of Blackstone after all, for when Julien meets him at a service station by accident, he scopes the man out and there was nothing when he made sure to touch the man. Just an ex-con trying to start a new life somewhere where his ghosts couldn't follow him.

A dead end.

I find it really hard to go through the motions. All week, I drag myself from class to class, confused about Julien, who's remained aloof, not wanting to be with me, sleeping on the couch still. I'm uncertain about what to say to him about Dylan – if anything. I know I should tell him what I saw in the park, but something makes me hold my tongue. Part of it is that I don't want him to be jealous. I followed Dylan into the park. I've kept it from him for this long, and I know he'll be mad about that. Part of it is that it shows a lack of judgment on my part that I don't want to admit.

I *should* have reported everything to Julien immediately. I want to understand myself before I raise the alarm with Julien.

I start having lunch with Sarah and crew at school, and that's nice. I get no more strange looks from Brenda, so I finally let that rest – maybe I was just too paranoid to recognize ordinary behavior.

On Wednesday, Julien's home waiting for me after classes are over. I walk in and put my backpack down, removing my books so I can start homework. He's sitting at the island that separates the family room from the kitchen, several files opened in front of him, a glass of blood in his hand.

"Hey," he says, glancing up from his papers. "Come here, look at this."

I go to his side and look over his shoulder, careful to keep my distance. "What is it?"

"List of all patients at the hospital the night that Bobby Wilson died. That boy with terminal cancer in palliative care?"

I remember it from our first week. It's one of the cases that convinced us we had a vampire in town.

"Oh, yeah. I remember him. Parents left him alone that night for the first time and went home. When the nurses checked in the morning, he was dead."

Julien nods. "Guess who was in the hospital at the same time?"

I sit on the stool beside him. "I have no idea."

"Your little friend in the wheelchair. Sarah Rhys."

"What?" I reach for the file. In it is a sheet of paper with a list of names of all patients in the hospital on the night Bobby died. There it is, about six down from the top. Sarah Rhys.

I read the nursing report. Sarah and her family were new to Davis Cove at the time. She'd been sick with a respiratory infection and had been in the ICU. When the death happened, she was on a medical ward after improving. She was discharged a day after Bobby died.

"It's probably just a coincidence," I say. "She's not a vampire, Julien. She's on a respirator. She can't walk or even stand up."

"Yeah, but here's the thing. When our older woman died in palliative care at the nursing home? Guess who was staying there in a respite bed while her parents went to New York City for some family event? None other than little Sarah Rhys."

I grab the sheet of paper he holds up and read over the patient roster for the night the woman, Ginette Longman, died. Sure enough, there's Sarah's name. Nursing records indicate she'd been admitted on the Friday night into a respite bed so her parents could go to visit their older son at the seminary outside of New York City.

"Oh, my God," I say, shaking my head. "Once might be a coincidence, but twice? There's no *way* it's an accident. But how?" I say, frowning. "How could she move into someone else's room and share blood? She's a quadriplegic."

"Maybe she had help. You said her friend touched you and said she got a shock, right?" Julien says. "I wonder if there's some kind of new Adept. Maybe there are several here, and we're just looking for the wrong things."

Now is when I should have come clean about Dylan. I don't.

"Why would Sarah be blood sharing? She's not a vampire. It's not like she can be a hunter."

Julien says nothing, just continues to flip through his file. "What about the brother?"

"He isn't a vampire. His skin is normal tint. He can go out in the sun."

Julien shrugs. "Maybe they've found a way to make vampires look more flesh colored."

Now, I wonder if both he and Sarah aren't some new kind of Adept, as Julien suggested. One who can use telekinesis to move objects from a distance.

"I'll talk to Vasquez," Julien says. "I'll have to start getting all touchy-feely with folks. All we have is telepathy and good old-fashioned investigatory work to find whoever's doing this."

"What do we do about Sarah Rhys? She's become a friend," I say.

"Her brother as well." Julien eyes me.

An awkward silence passes between us. I press my fingernails into my palm, because I don't know what to say. "He has a girlfriend in Cambridge. I have you. Don't be jealous."

"I'm sorry," he says. "You have to realize this is driving me crazy. I can't touch you, I can't connect with you. Just knowing that Michel came to you, kissed you, is so hard."

"I miss you."

I sit quiet for a moment and let that set in. Finally, I leave the kitchen, and go to our room. After I shut the door, I stand at the window and stare out at the ocean. Night falls very fast and soon, the ocean is lit up by the full moon.

The door to our bedroom creaks open.

"I didn't mean to make you so upset," Julien says, as he stands behind me. "I've been so jealous of Michel."

I turn to him. "Just be with me tonight," I say, my voice breaking. "Don't make me sleep alone again."

"Oh *cheri*," he says and steps closer. "I've left you alone too much." This time, he reaches out and runs his hand down over my body, about a foot away, his hand moving to mime my curves, to cup a breast, and over my hip. "I want you so much."

"I want *you* so much," I say.

He shakes his head. "I've been a fool. I'm sorry," he says. "I should have been more attentive."

"Just lay with me," I manage, and go to the bed, starting to undress. He does as well and I lay on the bed and sigh as I watch him strip down naked, his skin glowing in the light from the moon.

CHAPTER 20

"$\mathcal{A}$ flower cannot blossom without sunshine and man cannot live without love."

Max Muller

SCHOOL GOES ON AS usual the rest of the week. I act as if there's nothing different. I sit with Sarah and have lunch with her and Brenda, but when she invites me over to play piano, I decline, saying I have a lot of work to do for a project. Meanwhile, Julien tries to track down any links between our other suspicious death and Sarah, but can't find one.

That Friday night, after my shift at the Cove, I'm home reading a book I've taken out from the library when Julien comes in after his shift. Outside, a fierce wind blows. When he walks through the side door, I gasp.

"What happened to your face?"

"What do you mean?" he says and reaches up to his cheek. It looks like he's cut himself for a streak of red mars his cheek.

He wipes the red from his cheek.

"It must be the algae again," he says. "It rained a bit when I was walking to my car. Strange weather we've been having."

It's been unusually stormy the past week, with heavy rains and winds from the East battering the coast. Still, I think it strange that algae would be so abundant at this time of year.

Because of the last red rain, we don't think much of it until Saturday morning when we sit at the island at breakfast and listen to the news reports on the television. A news reporter stationed in Boston says that this rain was the same as the last one so there was no cause of concern except for one thing – there are isolated reports of power outages in areas where the red rain fell.

While we're clearing up from breakfast, the satellite feed fails and the flat screen goes blank.

"That's strange," Julien says and goes to the office. He tries to switch on the computers, but then the power fails, the lights snapping off. I go to the phone but when I touch the receiver, it burns my hand – it's hot. I drop it and rub my palm. A tacky crumbly material sticks to my skin.

I smell smoke in the air, like burning plastic.

"What the hell?" Julien goes to the computer. The plastic casing starts to smoke, the plastic itself melting, deforming right before our eyes. All around the house, everything plastic starts to smoke and melt – even the couch cushions crumble to the touch.

"This," Julien says, glancing around, his hands up as if in surrender. "This is something different." He looks at me, his expression alarmed. "This is an attack. Everything plastic – it's degrading, falling apart, or burning up in some kind of chemical reaction."

Julien tries his cell phone but it won't even turn on. We go outside and run to the next house down the street. Sure enough, the Godwins report that everything plastic in their house is falling apart or burning up.

Julien and I do an inventory of everything in the house that's affected. So much has plastic in it – even our clothes start to disintegrate, and I search for pure cotton or wool fabric so that my own clothes don't burn me. Large appliances that aren't even turned on are made unusable due to the extensive use of plastic in the material used in manufacturing. The seal that keeps the fridge door airtight disintegrates. Inside the fridge, containers of food and milk rupture, leaving a hideous mess. I grab some glass serving dishes and try to salvage what I can, but a lot is just spoiled by the degrading plastic.

Everything that isn't made of natural fabrics or materials becomes unusable.

We sit in the room on wooden chairs, our couch a ruin due to the cushions, and try to think what else will be affected.

Julien runs out to his car, which because of its age, has less plastic in it. He's able to turn it on, but it won't run.

"The gasoline," he says, tapping the gauge. "They've attacked petrochemicals and everything made from them." He gets out of the car and sits on the ground, his arms resting on his knees. "It's actually brilliant," he says, looking up at me. "Our entire economy, our civilization, is premised on them." He looks frightened, his lips pressed thin. "This will destroy us. They're disabling us so we can't fight back. We can't even contact Vasquez," Julien says, his voice frustrated. "All the phones, the computers use plastics in the motherboards, in the components. It *has* to be linked to the red rain."

"Maybe someone has an old HAM radio?"

He nods.

I sit beside him and try to think through the implications. I think of Dylan and his plans for failure of the power grid. Did he know *this* was coming? Was he helping Blackstone or trying to stop them?

Then, my thoughts go to Sarah. There's no power, but she has the backup energy source – the solar panels. But then I feel as if I've been hit in the stomach. Her respirator has tubes made out of plastic. She has a tracheotomy and an indwelling catheter that feeds her. Who knows what else made of plastic – all of it keeping her alive.

"I have to go," I say and stand, my hands shaking. Julien follows me to the road.

"Where?"

"To Sarah's house," I say. "She's on a ventilator."

"Eve, maybe you shouldn't go…"

I ignore him, walking the few blocks along the road to check on her, running the last block as panic sets in. When I get to the house, I knock but there's no answer. I open the door and call out, but no one comes.

"Sarah?" I say and peek down the darkened hallway to her bedroom.

I go inside the room. Mr. Rhys sits on a chair in the corner of the bedroom, his eyes red-rimmed, his cheeks wet. He turns to me when I enter and I cover my mouth when I see Sarah on the floor, her skin dusky, her chest unmoving. She's dead, her red-gold hair spread out over the hardwood. Her wheelchair is on its side.

"There was nothing we could do," Mrs. Rhys says, holding up her hands, a brownish-yellow powder on her fingers. "The ventilator tubes all disintegrated. We couldn't even bag her manually. The unit was made of a plastic- rubber mix and dissolved in my hands."

Finally, I sit beside Sarah, and take her hand in mine. I stroke her skin and blink away tears.

"Dylan's here," Mr. Rhys says. "He didn't go back to Boston after the first red rain. He went looking for you."

ON THE ROAD HOME, he's there, walking towards me. Through my tears, he fades in and out of view like film stuttering in the broken Kinetoscope at the antique store in town. For a second, I think I'm imagining things, because I see wings spread out behind him. When I blink, they're gone. What is he? Is he a vampire who has ascended like Julien and Michel? Is he an Ancient?

My heart beats faster as he approaches. I don't know how to respond, and dig my nails into my palms.

"Dylan," I say, my voice breaking. "I'm so sorry…"

He seems so in control when he comes to me and stands there, waiting, but his eyes are very bloodshot, his lashes wet and clumped together.

"What's happening?" I say, my fists clenching.

"Something bad," he says, his voice sounding as if he's close to losing control. "I made sure we got solar panels, back-up generator, but they were useless to save her. . . "

My throat closes as I think about Sarah suffocating to death when the respirator stopped working, the respirator bag and tubes disintegrating so that her family couldn't even bag her and keep her alive manually. No matter what she was, death is still death.

"I knew it would be an attack on the power grid," he says, his voice breaking. "But I didn't expect *this*." He holds his hands up and I see the same stain on them that I saw on his mother's hands. He shakes his head. "I thought it would be a Carrington Event to coincide with solar maximum."

I stand in silence for a moment, trying to understand.

"Can... they," I start to say and stumble, wanting to ask '*can Blackstone do that?*' but I don't, not wanting to give too much away. "Can whoever did this create a Carrington Event? How could anyone *create* one? They'd have to be able to manipulate a star..."

He shakes his head and then covers his eyes with a hand, finally overcome. I stand and watch him, feeling helpless. After a moment, he seems to regain control, glancing away.

"I'm sorry," he says, after clearing his throat. "I just wanted to make sure you were OK. I have to go."

"Why did you want to check on me?"

"Because," he says, wiping his eyes. "You're my sister."

I'm stunned into silence. I watch him walk away for a moment then I snap out of it.

"Wait," I say and run to him, grabbing his arm. "What do you mean, I'm your sister?"

He nods and pulls me into an alley. "We have the same mother and were enhanced in the same batch. They took more eggs from her and implanted us in different women. They made a dozen of us but only we survived."

"What parents? Is Natalia our mother?"

He nods, but says nothing more.

"Tell me!"

He stops and seems to struggle with himself. "We're both enhanced Adepts. I've just," he says and shrugs. "Been turned. Transformed."

"You're a vampire? Your skin isn't pale."

"Vampires are pale because they have little circulation in the skin. Blackstone developed a genetic fix that makes the skin retain its peripheral circulation. You won't look pale either when you're turned as well."

"I don't *want* to become a vampire."

He shrugs. "To get your full powers, you must. It's your destiny."

I squeeze my hands into fists. "I don't believe in destiny. How can you? You're a scientist!"

"Science is just one way of knowing, Eve. There are others, like religion and faith. They're not empirical. They're spiritual. They can't be measured or quantified."

We stand there for a moment in silence. In my mind, I fight what he says.

"I saw you in the park with those men," I say. "You had some kind of power that threw them a dozen feet in the air."

He nods. "We're weapons, Eve. We're meant to fulfill the prophecy."

"Prophecy?"

"St. Therese of the Reeds."

It's then I remember reading my journal about the document Seth gave me.

"Now I have to go back to my parents," Dylan says. "But we'll talk again."

"What are you doing? Who are you with?" I say, not wanting to let him go.

"Blackstone," he says and shakes his head. "But you already suspected. No one knows about me, Eve. This must be just between us. *Please* don't let anyone know about me. Put up your blocks. Keep people out."

I let him go without another word, too stunned to say anything because I have a brother.

Problem is, he's also my enemy.

I WALK BACK to our house, my arms wrapped around myself against the cold wind.

"Sarah Rhys is dead," I say once I'm inside the door, barely able to hold back my tears.

"Oh, *God*," he says and shakes his head slowly, looking at me with alarm on his face, his eyes wide. "I'm so sorry about Sarah." He stands there, his hands in his pockets as if he's trying to keep them off me. "I know you were becoming close to her. I wish I could hold you." He runs his hands through his hair and stares at the ceiling. "This is it." He glances back at me. "This is what we feared and we're too late. I had no idea they were so close."

WE GO to the town square, joining the crowd that formed spontaneously, waiting to hear from someone in authority. The new mayor and the sheriff stand at the statue of a mariner in the center of the square and wait until the crowd hushes. There are almost a hundred people waiting, speaking with each other. We wear strange clothes – probably the only clothes that are natural fibers – cotton, linen, wool. There are no plastic rain slickers. There are no rubber boots – just various versions of leather shoes.

"If I can have your attention, please," the mayor says, speaking through an old megaphone with no power. "This is what we know, or the best we can piece together about what's happened. According to local scientists, this second fall of red rain appears to have been the catalyst for the destruction of anything made from plastics and petrochemicals where the rain fell, including gasoline, fuel oil, coal and all byproducts. You'll all be familiar with this as it's affected each one of us. We don't know how it was done and we haven't been able to get any updates from Washington since we have no power, and our communications technology either relies on electricity or has plastics in some part of it and is no longer functional."

A sense of unreality takes hold over me. We're completely cut off.

"We've sent out scouts to see how far it extends, but we haven't heard back yet from any of them. We have a HAM radio operator gathering information but he's using a very old HAM radio from the Pre-WWII era, and it's spotty. We know the red rain fell along the entire eastern Seaboard, up to one hundred miles into the continent so we have to assume it extends at least that far and that what happened here happened there as well. Jed Thompson took a horse and went south to see if power was on, but there wasn't."

He pauses for a moment, flipping through hand-written pages that flap in the wind. "We've taken a preliminary stock of food in stores in Davis Cove, but a lot of the perishable food that's been kept in freezers will start to degrade quickly if we don't get power back. A lot of food was lost due to being packaged in plastic containers. We're working on an inventory of food and medicines in grocery stores, restaurants and our stockpiles for emergencies, but a lot are either stored in or made with some form of fossil fuels."

He pauses for a moment and glances down at a sheet in his hand.

"We've had several deaths in our community due to this disaster and it's impossible to tell how many have died in the affected areas but we anticipate it's in the thousands, if not more. Cars and boats made with plastic parts have fallen apart. We assume some airplanes have as well. Possibly – probably in flight. Everyone we had who relied on respirators has died. That comes to twenty-three in total who died immediately in the entire county. Several people had heart attacks and died when we couldn't do anything to help them because there was either no electricity or the batteries used in technology – or the technology itself – failed. In total, the death toll is about fifty-seven but we expect more once the full count is in."

He pauses as if to gather his composure. People take that opportunity to speak to each other, a murmur running through the crowd.

"I've declared a state of emergency for Davis Cove. Until we have a better sense of the extent and whether we'll be getting any aid from outside the affected areas, community events and all school has been suspended. I'm asking all able-bodied adults aged twenty-one and over to volunteer to help with disaster assistance. If any of you have experience in emergency management or response, please indicate so when you sign up. We need folks who have experience planning for and responding to this kind of emergency. We're asking you to sign up for four-hour shifts." He put the paper down and stared out at the crowd.

"We'll pull through this if we cooperate. Until I indicate otherwise, a ten o'clock PM until six o'clock AM curfew is in place. That's all for now. Thank you and may God be with us in our time of need."

The crowd murmurs in response, and I see some of the Catholics making the sign of the cross. Of the hundred or so people gathered in the square, a good number form a line and start signing up for community service shifts.

Julien joins the line to sign up for us and I go home, deciding to spend my time trying to find candles and wood I can use in the fireplace to keep warm while Julien signs us up.

We spend the rest of the evening sorting through what had become junk and what survived the 'plague', as Julien calls it. I find some old beeswax candles in the bathroom cupboard that appear intact, and some safety matches that work. We'll have some light at night for a while if we conserve it. We have some flashlights but they've been made of plastic. Besides, the batteries look weird, because they had plastic wrappers. The batteries might still be useful, except everything that might have used them has plastic in them somewhere.

As far as food goes, our dry goods that aren't in plastic containers are fine. We have lots of oatmeal and pasta, tea and coffee, flour, sugar, cans of beans and soups. Boxes of crackers. Rice in plastic bags spilled out onto the cabinet shelves, but most of it is reclaimable. I store it in empty glass jars that the cottage owner had in a cupboard in the pantry. Our food might last a week, if we conserve. We still have running water, but I wonder how long it will last or how safe it is. I find an old tin kettle in the bottom of a cupboard and decided to make tea to keep us warm.

The fireplace isn't designed for cooking, but we'll make do. We also have a barbeque outside on the porch, but there's no natural gas or charcoal to use. Julien starts a fire in the fireplace, and soon, I have some beans and rice cooking in pots near the fire. I pour him some tea and we sit at the kitchen island and eat in silence.

"I hate this not knowing," Julien says finally. "I'm so used to instant communications with Vasquez. This is going to be a test of our adaptability."

∼

I SPEND most of the next day in bed and Julien lets me mourn Sarah without forcing me to do anything. Of course, he tries to comfort me with words, but I just want him to hold me.

A funeral is held on Tuesday for many of the victims who died in the initial hours of the plague. I see Dylan there and Sarah's parents. I go to them, giving him and them my sympathies.

"How are you, Eve?" Mrs. Rhys says, taking my hand in hers.

"I'm fine," I say, squeezing her hand. "How are you holding up?"

She smiles sadly. "We always knew she'd die early. She knew it as well. She viewed life as a journey with death at the end, but she wanted to live as long as possible. This was cruel, but it was fast. She passed out immediately from lack of oxygen and died within a few minutes."

I can't help but tear up again at the thought and she squeezes my hand again.

"Are you getting enough food and water?" she says and puts her arm around my shoulder.

I nod. "We have enough for now."

She drops my hand. "Come to our house and have something to eat. We have lots. I used to stock up at the warehouse store in Gloucester each week, just to keep Dylan happy. He was always going on about having six-months of food in case of a disaster so we're all set. I know he'd like if you came by." She squeezes my arm, and I think it's a sign she knows who and what I am.

"I'll drop by later," I say.

~

WHILE JULIEN GOES to do his first shift in the command center, I go to the Rhys house. When I arrive, Mr. Rhys is sitting in the semi-darkness of the conservatory, staring out the window.

"Oh, hello Eve," he says and stands. He's disheveled, his hair messy. "You'll excuse my messy clothes but we have no electricity for an iron. The solar panels use batteries with plastic in the casing. They're useless."

I shake my head. "Of course. You don't have to explain."

The Gould Steinway has music spread out on it – I imagine from Mrs. Rhys's lessons from the previous week. I doubt she'll be teaching anytime soon.

"Play for us," Mrs. Rhys says, urging me forward.

I shake my head. "I'm not really in the mood…"

"Please," she says. "We've been so sad. Something pretty would lift our spirits. Play some Bach. Sarah would have liked it."

I sit at the piano with reluctance and force myself, just to please them, for they've been so nice. I play scales for a moment to warm up. Then, I start to play the repertory I learned before my father went into an asylum, starting with a Bach prelude, but I'm just not in the mood and stop. I glance up and catch sight of Dylan standing in the doorway. I stop, turning to him.

"Don't stop because of me," he says and motions for me to continue. "Play something – play your most favorite piece."

I take in a deep breath and play the first few bars of the Chopin Nocturne. The memory fills me with a sweet melancholy that could easily change into grief. When I finish, I sit there in silence, emotions roiling inside of me. No one says a word.

"Come," Mrs. Rhys says and holds out her hand. "I have something for you."

I let her take my hand, feeling close to tears. She leads me down the hallway to Sarah's room. It's been cleaned up and all evidence of Sarah's death is gone. Mrs. Rhys goes to the desk on which is a tray of seashells.

"Here," she says. "She said you liked them. She'd want you to have them to remember her."

I hold the tray and examine the shells. Conch shells, mollusks, bivalves, starfish, sea stars, sand dollars. All these Dylan collected for her, the beloved brother.

"Dylan doesn't want these? He gave them to her."

Dylan stands in the doorway.

"Take them. It would make me happy for you to have them, of all people. And this," he says and goes to a drawer in the dresser and removes a small box. Inside is a leather bracelet made with cowrie shells. He fastens it around my wrist. "I gave it to her for her sixteenth birthday. It should go to you."

Mrs. Rhys retrieves a box from the closet and we start placing the shells inside. She shoves handful of tissues in with the shells so they don't move around.

"I have to go," I say, feeling close to tears.

Mrs. Rhys nods. Dylan doesn't argue or try to convince me to stay and I leave, my emotions almost overwhelming me.

PEOPLE MEET in the town hall during the day and at night by candlelight to exchange information and assist those who need it. People resort to using horses to travel and when plastic items are brought into the area of contamination, they disintegrate, so whatever it is that caused the destruction is still active.

It's so hard to be in the dark like we are – almost no communications with the world outside into the affected area except by messenger, but even then, Julien tells me that they are dropping packages with food and messages into the affected zone using air balloons. No planes fly over the affected zone. Barbed wire had been run along the perimeter, with warnings that no personnel are permitted to leave on pain of death. Reports came back to us that people have been shot trying to cross the perimeter.

We're totally cut off.

THAT SATURDAY AFTERNOON, about an hour before dusk, Julien and I go into town to collect our ration of food – a glass jar of peanut butter and a tin of canned tuna. Evidence of the red rain is still present in dots on the sidewalk and on the roofs of the buildings for the weather has been exceptionally dry and no rain to wash off the surfaces. A few abandoned cars line the street running through the center of town, their doors opened, trunks and hoods gaping like the mouths of dead fish. The seats have disintegrated, the material now like sludge that sticks to my fingers when I pick up a piece. Parts of the car have also disintegrated, so that the metal bits hang off or have fallen to the ground.

Off in the distance, the road leading to the highway is silent. Usually, the traffic's audible in town but it's quiet enough to hear a rusted street sign swing in the breeze. Now, cars sit abandoned on the road. I can just make out small figures walking along the highway. Others ride horses. All appear to be on a trek out of town.

Julien comes to my side as I shade my eyes and watch the exodus.

"Where are they going?"

"Who knows?" he says. "We're in quarantine. There's nowhere to go."

"What do *we* do?" I ask, meaning us as hunters. "Do we go back to Boston?"

"We'll stay in place for now until we get orders. We have to try to understand what their plan is."

"*Their* plan?"

He shrugs. "Whoever it was who did this. Right now, all I know is that it's Blackstone for sure." He shades his eyes and watches the exodus in the distance. "Whatever, we can't leave the affected zone. The National Guard is lined up to keep people from leaving so the contamination doesn't spread, but even so, the wind's spreading it day by day. People already left the affected zone and took the contamination with them. There are spots of growing infection around the world. We have to stay here, try to survive until they find a way to neutralize it."

The world changed the night the red rain fell but in my grief and shock from Sarah's death and revelations about Dylan, it's unreal. Seeing people walking west finally makes it real for me. I turn to him, examining his face, which seems even more somber than usual.

"How do we survive?"

He shrugs. "We're fine for now. We'll be hungry, but we'll probably survive if we can maintain law and order. I've got a shift for the next four hours."

He turns to me and reaches for me but then stops. "Sooner or later, Blackstone will make a move." He shakes his head. "After that, all bets are off. Vampires will no longer feel they have to remain in the shadows."

Then, Julien smiles, a rare event during the last few days. "Maybe you could cook us up some beans and biscuits, like an old camp cook on a cattle drive."

I nod but don't smile back, not in the mood for any form of levity. I watch him walk towards the center of town for his shift. Alone now, I cross the street, walking down the center of the deserted road to the pier. The world is falling apart around me. Blackstone has succeeded in bringing down modern technology as Julien said they would. Now, we wait for the vampires to make their appearance. So far, nothing has changed and I wonder what Blackstone has planned.

Things are manageable right now in Davis Cove, although we'll run out of food soon and who knows what else – medicines, treatments. So much of our world is based on petrochemicals.

I'm afraid. Michel said I was key to preventing Dominion, that once the end started, I'd realize that I had made a mistake and would go to him. I'm afraid that Michel was right and I was wrong not to go with him back at the Abbey. If I had, would we have prevented this? I can't believe that could be possible... How could my going with Michel have changed things so much that Blackstone didn't release the plague?

Still, doubt nags me. I'm sick to think that my selfish desire for

Julien and happiness has led to this. That Sarah and so many others have died because I was afraid of going with Michel – afraid of what I'd be expected to do when I was with him.

Part of me wishes I could go back to that day at the Abbey and go with Michel instead, just to see if this would still have happened.

As I walk along to the pier, lost in thought, I look up to see Michel walking toward me. I stop in my tracks at the railing overlooking the water. I didn't call him so why is he here? Did he read my mind and know I was feeling regret and fear?

This is the moment – the one I didn't believe would really happen.

CHAPTER 21

"*A* kiss makes the heart young again and wipes away the years."

Rupert Brooke

WE STOP on the pier and stand side by side, looking out over the ocean as the sun starts to set.

"I didn't call you," I say. Beside me, he's silent. I expect him to be all I-told-you-so, but he seems just as upset as I do.

"Did you really need to call me?"

Finally, he exhales and turns to me, leaning on the railing. He tilts his head to one side in that characteristic de Cernay way, his skin so pale, his blue eyes intense. His expression isn't judging. It's sad.

"You saw all this?" I say, anger in my voice. "Why couldn't you have told me?"

"I saw this happen as one of many scenarios," he says. "This was the most likely, but depending on what everyone did and chose, it could have been slightly different. I knew we would meet and talk. And that you would come back to me. I already told you that if I told you exactly what I saw, you'd die. I can't have that."

"I haven't said I would come with you."

"You will," he says and reaches out, touching my cheek. "It's the only way to stop it from getting even worse."

I shake my head and pull away from his touch.

"I only have your word on that."

"Isn't this enough to convince you?" he says and points to the town and then to the dock. Down below us, the dilapidated remains of several boats and yachts float and bob on the water. Everything with any plastic component either melted or disintegrated, leaving non-plastic parts to either sink or float depending on their material. A brownish sludge coats the surface of the water.

"All this tells me is that Blackstone was successful in attacking technology. I have no way of knowing if my being with you is key to stopping them from taking more power. All that prophecy stuff is just too hard for me to accept."

"You think I made it up so I could have you as my own? I could have forced you long ago if I wanted that. Like Julien did."

"He didn't force me."

"He took you. Didn't listen to you. Pushed you because your mind and body are torn."

"I wanted him, Michel," I say and finally look at him straight in the eye. "You've lied to me so much since I met you, either directly or by omission that I don't know what to believe any more."

"Come with me and learn for yourself if you don't trust me. You can leave at any time."

I shake my head.

"Why would my being with you have prevented this?"

He just shakes his head. "I don't know exactly how, but it did. Now, that's not possible. The genie's out of the bottle. We have to try to put it back in before the whole world falls."

"And my being with you does that how?"

"I said I don't know the details, just the cause and effect."

"How can I just leave Julien?"

"He'll understand."

"You think he'll just let me go to be with you as your little pet?"

"He will. All you have to do is tell him you're going with me."

I frown and turn away.

"You couldn't be more wrong. Julien's extremely jealous of you. He found your book and note before I did. It upset him so much, he's not even sleeping with me."

Michel says nothing. I imagine what Julien would say to me if I was to tell him I was going to be with Michel. I can't imagine he'd be as accepting as Michel seems to think. "If I was to go to you, it would break his heart. He loves me."

"He does love you and he will accept it. He'll think it's for the best," Michel says, his voice soft. "He may even suggest it."

"How can you know that?"

"He's been compelled."

"What?" I turn to him. "Soren compelled him to like the idea of me being with you?"

"Yes," Michel says, glancing away. He looks back at me, his face guarded. "Soren doesn't want his heart to break. If you were to tell him and he wasn't compelled to accept it, he'd give up. Soren wants him in fighting mode. He has work to do. Besides, we need him to help in the end. When it comes to destroying Soren."

"No," I say, fisting my hands, digging my nails into my palms. "I won't come to you, no matter what."

"If you don't, Julien will grow more and more distant, and finally, he'll tell you that you must come to me. He'll get angry with you. He'll kick you out, eventually. Then, he won't speak to you again unless you come to me. Soren wants Julien at his side. The other night at the party, he compelled Julien to accept you being with me."

I frown as I try to process this.

"Soren wants the three of us together as his servants," Michel says. "If Julien is too jealous, it will impede his performance. Soren plans on performing miracles to convince people he's a god. We'll help him at first, or appear to," Michel says, but then he takes my shoulder in his hand and leans closer, his lips beside my ear as if he's afraid Soren will hear us. "And then, when he's secure in our obedience, when he thinks he's ready to take power, we'll strike. We'll kill him and all the Ancients. Then we'll finally be free of them all. This is what my group in the Council has been planning for years, Eve. This is endgame. I tried to keep you out of it, to find another way, but I failed."

I stand in silence for a moment and consider. "Why do you need me as your pet?"

"He wants us to be his servants and if we don't comply, he'll kill us all. He needs your compliance, but because you can't be compelled, you must be controlled through other means. Love is the perfect lure."

I just look at him. "Has this all been a charade? Do you even love me? Or have you also been compelled?"

"Of course I love you," he says and closes his eyes, leaning in to me, his forehead against mine. "More than anything. How can you even ask that?"

"Maybe you're playing me so you can have your own endgame. Maybe Soren's compelled you to tell me all this."

"No," he says, his face so serious. "He can't compel me. Not anymore."

"What do you mean?"

"When I ascended, I became uncompellable."

"Why didn't Julien?"

"What Blackstone did to him prevented it. They needed vampires who could be compelled. When he ascended, he was still susceptible."

"So Soren wants me as your Adept so you can control me. So you can make me do his bidding when he needs me for his rise to power."

"Exactly. He fears you, and needs to be reassured that you're under my control. When he is, he'll let down his guard and then we strike."

"Why does he fear me?"

"Because he knows you can either make him a god or destroy him."

"Why does he think that?"

"It was prophesized."

I sigh, shaking my head at the nonsense these religious people believe. Dylan included.

"And Julien? How does he fit in?"

Michel sighs. "Soren gave you to him, hooked him in, and now will deploy him like a weapon. Julien will be the most powerful warlord a god could want. He'll be obedient because he thinks he'll be protecting you, even as you and I are lovers again."

"I *love* him," I say and turn to Michel, tears in my eyes.

"I know," Michel says, and wipes my cheek.

"I *want* him."

"Not now, Eve. One day if we succeed, you may have him again. But not now."

He takes me in his arms, wrapping them around my body, his face buried in my neck and I let him hold me, needing some contact because of all the fear and stress and loneliness I've felt since the red rain fell.

Finally, I pull away and he lets me go.

"I have to think about this."

He nods. "Don't take too long. Once vampires feel secure that humans are helpless, they'll come out from hiding. You'll have to fight to stay alive every day, Eve. People in town will start to die. Then, the enslavement will start. This is a test-run of their weapon to see how it goes and how people respond so they can adjust their strategy."

His words fill me with dread.

"Tell me how we're going to kill him or else I won't believe you. This could all be a way to reel me in, to make me obey so Soren can become this god you speak of."

"I can't tell you. Soren could find out."

"I'll block him."

"You can't be compelled, Eve. None of this would have happened if you could because I would have wiped your memory and sent you back to oblivion. But you can be tortured. He'd torture his way into your mind if he had to. This way, you don't know any details."

"I have to go," I say and walk backwards away from him, my arms around myself. "I can't go with you if you can't at least tell me what we're planning to do."

"Don't do this Eve. This is your fate. Come to me before nightfall," he says, his voice soft. "You won't be safe after that."

I WALK BACK to the cottage and sit in the dimness with my weapons by my side, facing the door so I can watch in case some vampire has compelled the owner to let them in. I figure I have a fighting chance so long as I see them first.

Is Michel right? Will vampires now start to claim Dominion now that Blackstone has struck?

JULIEN ARRIVES home from his shift at the community center sometime later. He takes off his jacket and comes into the room. It's dark out and I can see just a bit of light in his eyes as he stands by the fire and looks around the room for me. I'm sitting in a chair in the darkened corner, my stake and gun beside me.

"Eve," he says, and comes towards me. "What are you doing?"

"Michel says that vampires will start claiming Dominion now that Blackstone has struck. He says we're not safe at night any longer."

He sighs heavily and stands in front of me.

"He's right. It's still early, but there's enough chaos despite our efforts that some may be willing to risk it."

"He also says I should come and be with him now."

He says nothing for a moment, but then he glances away, his gaze moving to the picture window looking out over the ocean as if he's fighting with himself.

"You should. Now's the time. I should go south to Boston. That's where I should be."

My heart squeezes to hear him give in so easily. "You think I should go and be with Michel?"

He nods, but doesn't look at me. "Looks like it. It's the only way to stop Dominion. It's the price we'll have to pay to preserve humanity. I'll have to set up surveillance on known Blackstone cells in Boston."

"You won't be upset if I go to Michel? Become his pet?"

"It's for the best. You have to go. You'll be safe with him. We'll be together again one day."

He looks back at me and in the low light from the fire, I can see tears in his eyes, as if his words and his emotions are at odds. Without thinking, I go to him and he's still unable to embrace me. He tries to pry my arms away, grimacing as if touching me hurts.

"Don't touch me," he says, his voice rough.

"Why? What will happen if we touch?"

I persist, pushing him, and finally, he practically throws me down onto the couch, which is covered in wool blankets, and looms over me, his hands beside my body, not touching me.

"I'll have to kill you, Eve!" he says, his eyes wet. "Don't touch me!"

Then he rises and cradles his head as if he's in pain.

"Just go!" he says, pointing to the door. "Go to Michel. Do it now. I have to get ready to go south."

I struggle to get up from the couch and wipe my eyes. "I won't go. I'm coming with you."

"You *can't* Eve," he says, his voice breaking. "You *must* stay here."

"You'll have to make me."

He stands there in silence, struggling, his breathing hard. Finally, he goes to the bedroom, hauling out a large black duffle bag from a closet, which he starts packing with what little remains of his clothes – all those that have no synthetic fibers. He pushes past me and goes to the kitchen for some food and then to the closet for his coat. After he packs up his weapons, he turns to me.

"There's a horse and cart at the stables I can use. I'm going south."

I grab my coat and a few things, the Keats book, my shells, some food, and a worn wool blanket.

"I'm coming with you."

"It's not safe for you to stay with me," he says as he goes out to the yard. "You should go to Michel."

"I'm staying with you."

He shrugs. "If you can keep up."

I follow him down the road to a farm on the outskirts of town, struggling with my heavy backpack, my weapons in a case over my shoulder. He practically ignores me.

When we arrive at the farm, I stand in the driveway and he goes to the barn. In a few moments, he brings out a horse and cart. He throws his things in the back of the cart and takes a seat on the bench, the reins in his hand.

"I suppose you've driven one of these before," I say as I throw my backpack and weapons bag in the cart beside his duffel bag.

He shrugs. "Not for most of a century, but I know my way around a horse and cart."

I climb up beside him but he doesn't even look at me.

"I'll drop you off at Soren's place."

"No, Julien!" I say. "This is my choice and I choose to stay with you!"

He says nothing, and gives the reins a shake. The cart jerks forward and I hold on to the side rail.

We ride along the darkened streets in silence, the clip clop of the horse's hooves the only sound. I stare at the trees that border the road, whose branches sway and move in the wind. A storm is brewing. I wonder if what Michel said was true – that soon, vampires would start asserting themselves. It doesn't matter. I can beat them, if I'm prepared.

"How long will it take to get to Boston?"

"Depends on how rough going the road is. I expect there'll be quite a lot of abandoned cars on the roads. It's about thirty miles to Boston.

"Shouldn't we wait until daylight?"

"I have to get there as soon as possible."

"Why?"

"Work. Gotta provide security for Soren's estate and work on our battle plan."

I just stare at him. Where did my Julien go? It's like he's another person entirely.

Soren...

He has all of us exactly where he wants us. He has Michel at his side, he has Julien preparing to defend him against Blackstone. Blackstone succeeded in starting a technological apocalypse.

I doubt it's possible to hate Soren even more than I do now.

WE MAKE slow progress for the first hour due to the abandoned cars that block the main roads, their owners abandoning them, car doors open, hoods up. Soon, the cars thin as we reached the more rural areas along the coast with less development, but that's also a problem. The older dirt roads are clear, but they've been worn down over the years so that there are deep ruts where wheels have carved through the soft earth. A storm hits while we're on back roads, and I pull a blanket over my head to keep from being soaked by the rain. Julien doesn't seem to notice.

Then, an unanticipated problem -- the ground softens under the heavy rain and quickly turns to mud. Despite the blanket, I'm completely soaked, the blanket around my shoulders offering little cover.

Soon, the cart founders, its wheels stuck. I hold a lantern up that uses cooking oil as fuel while Julien takes the horse by its reins and tries to maneuver the cart out of the rut.

Other than the occasional boom of thunder in the distance, there's no sound except the rain on the leaves and in the puddles surrounding me. Then, the wind picks up and the flame falters. I shelter it, hoping to protect the flame but the wind blows it out, casting us into darkness.

"Quick," Julien calls out. "There are more matches in my bag on the seat."

I run to the wagon and find a package of safety matches, light one and rekindle the flame. Its light casts long shadows amidst the trees. I see movement at the edge of the road ahead, a dark shape moving across the path but there's nothing more.

"I saw something in the shadows."

He glances at me but shakes his head. "Nothing we can do but stay alert. If anything stops us, for any reason, keep your wits about you."

Finally, Julien's able to get the wheel out of the rut and we drive on, the lantern casting a feeble light ahead. As we make our way into the deepest part of the forest along the coast, I worry about the movement I saw earlier. Behind the cart is nothing but darkness, the light from the lantern quickly dissolving into black as we pass. I catch brief glimpses of trees and brush as we drive on when lightning flashes, but as we enter the center of the forest, the trees thicken and soon the rain falls in torrents, obscuring my vision even further.

We drive on like this for an hour, and fatigue grips me, but the wagon banging over the ruts on the road keeps me awake. A crack of thunder overhead shocks me into alertness, adrenaline coursing through me.

Then, Julien pulls up the reins, the wagon almost slamming to a halt. Ahead on the road lies a fallen tree bough, its thick branch making passage impossible. The wind is strong but I immediately feel unease at the thought that someone or something has done this deliberately to stop us.

Julien whispers. "Watch the back."

He takes the lantern and inspects the fallen tree. I join him, my nerves tingling

"Look," he says, pointing to the tree. "Lighting strike."

I examine the fallen bough. Sure enough, there by the side of the road is the tree trunk. It's blackened where lightning struck, cracking the tree in half, one half remaining and the other falling to block the path. The wood's still smoking where the lightning hit, so it must have been recent.

Julien drags the branch out of the way and I begin to feel a bit safer. The sun won't rise for a long time. Then, I see something out of the corner of my eye - something at the back of the cart.

I wave to Julien to draw his attention and he immediately stops dragging the fallen tree and holds a finger to his lips. He grabs his dagger from the ground and motions to me to go on one side of the cart, while he goes to the other. We circle it and end up at the rear of the wagon.

Julien shakes his head and then I see movement at the front of the wagon -- just a flick of ghostly white in the darkness. I hear the clink of metal on metal.

We run to the front, Julien's gun at the ready, but there's nothing to see.

"Get in," he says to me, his voice filled with fear. I do without question. The only thing I can look to for comfort is Julien's crossbow, armed with silver-tipped arrows. Then, when Julien tries to urge the horse forward, it refuses, stamping its feet and snorting as if frightened.

"What is it?" he says, pulling the reins again and again. "Something's spooked him."

I glance at the trees as the shadows shift, and what looks like men in long cloaks come into view.

"Julien!" I point to the trees lining the road where several men approach, and from the color of their faces, I know they're vampires.

I drop into fight mode and Julien is right there with me and together we leave the cart. I grab my weapons and we're on top of the three vampires before they can respond, easily taking them out. I take on one of the three, my weapons at the ready, and stake him because he's like a statue. He falls to the ground, lifeless and I then take my metal sword and hack his head off, thankful that we were trained to do so without thought at the abbey, even though it was just on straw-filled dummies.

Julien is fighting both the other two vampires and takes them down with a couple of quick moves and beheads them as well. I look to the three bodies – the first time Julien and I have fought together and the first time I've actually killed a vampire.

I'm barely out of breath because they were helpless against us and I realize the importance of Adepts with fight skills.

"You did great," he says and there's pleasure in his eyes. He reaches out to wipe off some blood from my face but then stops, remembering.

"This is what I was meant to do, Julien. Not be some pet of Michel's."

"You really do have to go to him, Eve. You'll be safe."

I shake my head. "I'm not going. I belong with you."

He sighs heavily and starts to go back to the cart. I follow him, but before he gets there, a flash of light strikes so blinding, a boom so loud, that I'm thrown backwards, my senses leave me.

What feels like an eternity passes before my vision clears of bright sparks and stars, the brightness fading slowly, but my hearing is still dulled. *Flash bangs*. Hands drag me from out of some inferno, someone carries me and I grasp instinctively to hold on.

Before my eyesight returns, I can barely make out the face of my – savior? Or captor? I don't know. All I see are blue eyes and a pale face, still out of focus, framed by dark hair. Behind them a pair of dark wings outspread. Is it Julien?

Blackness surrounds us for a brief moment and I feel the whoosh of air on my cheeks, and then those eyes recede into the distance, up into the sky, into the stars above.

Finally, consciousness leaves me completely.

CHAPTER 22

"The one thing we can never get enough of is love. And the one thing we can never give enough of is love."

Henry Miller

I REGAIN CONSCIOUSNESS, my vision coming slowly into focus. When I can finally see clearly, I'm inside a covered wagon, the cart banging against the ruts in the road. Michel sits on the bench beside a man with grey hair. Now and then, I hear a hint of conversation from Michel and the other man, but I can't make out what they're saying for the sounds are muffled.

I feel a bit dizzy and so I reach out and touch the side of the cart beside me to try and steady myself. Then I remember the attack and sit up, my heart racing. I glance around to see where Julien is, but he isn't in the back of the cart. When I sit up fully, an intense pain strikes my temple and I gasp and grab my head, lying back down once more.

Michel turns and sees me. He speaks to his companion and then comes to me, crawling over the bench, sitting beside me where I'm lying.

"Let me see," he says, leaning over me. He tilts my face so that I look in his eyes and I see only tenderness in them. He runs his fingers over my temple, and soon the pain disappears and a sense of calm descends over me.

"Try and rest. You've had a shock."

"Where's Julien? What happened?" I try to sit up again but he presses me back, his hand firm on my shoulder.

"He's fine. Just rest."

"Where is he?"

He keeps his hand on my shoulder, holding me down. "He's in another cart. You needn't worry about him. Just sleep now."

Whether it's due to shock from the explosion or him manipulating me, I don't know but soon, I can't keep my eyes open.

WHEN I WAKE, Michel's carrying me through an alley into an old building in Boston. It's day, but when I catch sight of the sky, it's grey and cloudy. Even so, the light bothers my eyes and I shade them. He carries me up some stairs to the third-floor offices. The grey-haired man from the cart opens the door for Michel and he carries me inside.

"We're here," Michel says as he lowers me onto the small couch in Ed's old office.

I sit up and glance around.

"Why are we here?"

"This is one of the only building on the waterfront that still has working fireplaces. We have no other way to heat buildings that relied on electricity for heat."

Michel brings me a blanket from a chest against the wall. "I have a house in the north where we'll live until Soren calls us to be with him. I have some business to attend to before we can go there." He hands me the old wool blanket, which has faded from use to a soft blue. "Use this to keep warm. These old buildings don't have much insulation so it'll be cold until we can get some kind of heating system set up and running."

The grey-haired man comes over and stands in front of me. Michel gestures to him. "This is Ethan. He's a police officer who's joined our cause."

I guess that Ethan is in his fifties, for his eyes crinkle at the corners when he smiles.

"Hello, young miss," he says. "Pleased to see you're better. We had a bit of a scare there for a while with your head injury but Michel was able to fix you."

I frown at Michel. "Where's Julien?"

"He's at his residence."

"I didn't consent to come with you so this is abduction."

"Eve," Michel says, exasperation in his voice. "Why must you always resist me? Resist reality?" He sits beside me on the couch and takes my hand. "You know this was inevitable. Best you just come with me now, rather than later when it might be too late."

"It's already too late," I say. I try to pull my hand out of his, but he's too strong.

"I thought you understood," he says. "Now is the time to obey, Eve. Now is your last chance."

I don't want to be petulant, but it scares me, this future with Michel.

"I'm afraid."

"I know," he says and leans down, his forehead against mine. "You should be, but I'll do everything in my power to protect you. Right now, everyone is fighting just to stay alive. Speaking of which," he says and stands. "You must be hungry. I'll get you some tea."

He goes to the fireplace, which has a small fire going and pours some hot water out of a tin kettle into a cup. "Milk, one sugar?" he says.

I nod.

"Would you like a sandwich?"

I shake my head. "My stomach's a bit off. Just the tea will do for now."

He comes back and stands in front of me once more. "I have some work to do, but please, if you do get hungry, let me know and I'll get something for you."

"Michel, you can't just abduct me and force me to comply."

"I don't want to force you to do anything," he says and sits beside me again. He leans closer and cups my cheek with his hand, stroking my skin with his thumb. "I want you to freely join me. Haven't I told you that a dozen times?"

I glance away, not yet ready to do this.

He goes to a table on which are files and papers. "I don't have much that would interest you," he says as he flips through materials. Finally, he pulls out a newspaper.

"Here's *The New York Times* if you feel like reading."

I take the paper and glance at the headlines as I sip my tea. Football stories and scores along with a political scandal dominate the front page.

"From before or after?"

"Just before production stopped."

Then, it strikes me just how much things have changed if all I have to say is 'before or after' and he knows exactly what I mean. Before the red rain.

Before the start of the end of the world.

AFTER I READ the paper from cover to cover, I eat a cheese sandwich. Then, I close my eyes for a while as sleep sets in. In the background is the conversation between the two men, their voices rising and falling, lulling me to sleep.

MICHEL FINISHES up his work a few hours later. He lets me walk out of the building to the cart. He sits beside me, his arm over the back of the bench while Ethan drives. I watch Michel for a while.

"You knew, didn't you?" I say. He turns to me and he knows exactly what I mean. He looks devastated. "You should have been more convincing if you actually saw all this."

"I tried, but you were too in love with Julien and too afraid of yourself to listen."

"What's happening?"

"War, Eve, between two groups of fanatics who want to bring about an apocalypse. They don't care who they hurt or how many die because to them, humans are nothing more than food and toys. Both sides are ruthless and so must we be."

We drive southeast, through the old industrial part of the city center.

"Look at it," Ethan says, shaking his head, pointing to the devastation. "This whole area was revitalized but now it's a wasteland. Shame that people take their anger out on their own city."

I have many memories of big cities. The dividing line in my life is my mother's death and then the bombing. Everything that happened in between is a fantasy world and I have a hard time believing actually ever happened. The city we drive through is like a huge crumbling garbage heap. There are few people out, only several men pushing carts filled with scraps of wood.

"What are they doing?" I ask, pointing to one.

"Collecting wooden furniture, building materials, they're ripping up hardwood floors in old warehouses for firewood," Michel says. "Without gas, without heating oil, the people are freezing, living in the dark."

"Why are we here?"

"It's where Soren will try to take power."

We pass warehouses and docks, and streets littered with abandoned cars that have been junked, seemingly out of anger and frustration, the windows smashed in, the tires slashed, rude symbols or slogans spray-painted on the hoods. The same is true of the storefronts and office buildings, which have been similarly attacked. Huge plate-glass windows hang in broken shards, the streets and sidewalks littered with fallen glass. Stores have been looted, and as I catch sight inside the deserted buildings, I see row upon row of empty shelves.

We drive to Michel's mansion in the center of a thick grove of trees, which stands atop the crest of a hill. There's barbed wire on top of the high stone fence circling the property. We drive past an open metal gate to the house and the cart stops by a huge entrance with heavy wood doors. Michel helps me out of the old cart and takes my hand, leading me up the stairs and inside. The entry is enormous, with marble floors and columns. A staircase winds to a second floor and to the left and right are large reception rooms filled with ornate and antique furniture.

"I haven't seen anything like this since I was a child in Prague."

"You've been here before, but you don't remember."

He leads me up the stairs to the top floor to a bedroom and I think, I can't just do this. I can't just go from Julien to Michel.

"Stop," I say. "Don't do this. Not yet."

"If not now, when?"

I shake my head and pull my hand away. He lets me. We stand facing each other.

"What do you want from me?"

"I've already told you. I need you to play the part of my blood slave, my pet, so that Soren is assured you're under my control and will obey."

"Will you at least tell me the truth when we're alone?"

"I'll tell you as much as I safely can. You'll have to trust me."

I sigh. Back to the old 'just trust me' demand.

"I'll give you some time," he says, "but it's the one thing we don't have."

He closes the door, leaving me alone in the huge room. I sit in silence for a long time, trying to gain control over my emotions.

Finally, I wander around and touch the wood and velvet drapes, the silk coverlet, the tassels on the throw pillows. The furnishings are very luxurious.

I go to the washroom and pour water from a pitcher into a basin. I splash water over my face, examining my reflection in the mirror. Too much has happened in too short a time.

I don't know what I feel any more.

I go to the huge bed and crawl under the coverlet, pulling it over my head to block out the light. Soon, I'll need to feed. I don't know how Michel will handle that, but I have an idea.

CHAPTER 23

Khalil Gibran

I wake later after the sun has set and the room is in darkness except for the fire flickering in the hearth.

Michel sits by me on the bed.

I sit up and rub my eyes.

"Dinner will be ready in an hour." He raises my hand to his lips and kisses my palm. "We'll talk about the way things have to be between us to convince Soren that I truly control you."

WHEN MICHEL RETURNS some time later, I've fallen asleep and he wakes me when he sits on the bed. I sit up, and rub my eyes.

He moves to kiss me and I push against his chest. "You just expect me to be your lover again?"

"What do you think?" he says, frowning.

I swallow. "I can't just do this right now, Michel. It's too soon."

He sighs, frowning. "Do you mean tonight or this week?"

"I don't know."

He looks away and I can tell he's fighting with himself. Finally, he turns to me, his blue eyes huge.

"I'll give you a few days. That's all I can spare, Eve. With each day, the plague spreads and we get closer to Dominion. Soren gains more power on his own, without your help."

He stands and turns away, but I stop him. "Before you go, can we talk about a few things?"

He turns back, sitting on the bed beside me.

I clear my throat. "I can't do *this*," I say. "Servitude."

"I understand," he says softly. "But you must understand that Soren needs to truly believe you're my pet."

"I don't want to be your pet. I don't want anything to do with it."

He moves closer and runs his finger over my bottom lip.

"Can you trust me enough to stay, for the time being?" I look in his eyes and he's so determined.

I nod. "I'll stay and I'll think about it. But only because of what's happened. I need some time."

"Fine. I'll give you a few days. But only a few, Eve."

He stands once more and turns, leaving me alone on the bed.

A FEW DAYS pass and he leaves me completely alone as if punishing me for delaying. Servants come in to bring me vials of his blood, food and pour a bath for me when I need it, carting in pitchers and buckets of hot water.

I go over things in my mind, wondering if I can do this. Part of me says to just give in and agree to be his pet, but part of me resists. I gaze out the window at the city and there are fires burning because there's no way to put them out. Water stopped working a while ago, and without a pump and well, there's no fire service. When a fire starts, it burns until it's completely razed to the ground.

The servant brings me the hand-printed news that's limited to a single sheet and every morning I read it with my morning coffee and toast. People are dying of diseases that once were treated with our medicines, but they've run low and plants that once made them no longer operate. If we can't find a way to stop the plague, it will circle the globe and civilization will crumble completely.

ON THE THIRD NIGHT, I sit at the piano and play my repertory, but it offers little comfort. Finally, Michel comes to me while I sit at the piano staring out the window at the dark city that used to sparkle like glittering diamonds. He sits beside me at the piano and leans close to me.

"Eve, I need you to agree. You need to practice being my pet so we can perform for Soren when he calls. Perform for the others who'll be watching us."

"I know," I say, my throat closing. "I just hate it – having to do it."

"I understand."

We sit there for a few moments.

"Play something for me first," I say, feeling melancholic for the time when we were happy. I read about it. I felt his memories of it, but I have no real memory of it.

"What would you like me to play?"

"Chopin."

I move over on the bench and let him sit in proper position. He hesitates, his hands resting on the keys.

"Nocturne No. 11 in G," he says and starts to play. It's a sad piece that makes my throat choke. He would play such a piece, as if to drive home how serious everything is. When it's done, I sigh.

"Play something happier," I say.

"I shouldn't be playing," he says. "You should play."

"I *love* to hear you play. It's a side of you that made me love you in the first place."

He relents and plays another Chopin piece. "Tristesse," he says. "Etude in E Major."

It's less somber, but still very emotional, the movement starting off slow and dreamy, but it builds to a crescendo and it's just as intense as the other piece he played. And I think that *this* is Michel – these pieces he chose to learn to play. Despite his attempt to be controlled and calm, inside there's this fury and passion.

When he's done, he turns to me, leaning against me, his arm pressed against mine as if he craves just being able to touch me. He reaches out to touch my face with the backs of his fingers. "I love you. I need you to help me fight Soren. My only desire is to stop him and to save you, Eve. Nothing else."

I take in a deep breath, and while his words make sense some-where in my brain, I fight it out of fear.

"Just obey me without hesitation. Do as I command. When we're around other vampires, and especially with Soren, obey me. Show deference. This is the only way he'll trust you. Once he trusts that you're all in, we strike."

"You've seen it?"

"I've seen it. We don't have the luxury of time," he says and strokes my hair.

"Okay," I say. "I agree." I smile, but it falters. "What happens first? Will we be lovers again?"

"Yes, Eve," he says, and strokes my cheek. "The first thing I'll do is kiss you." He strokes my cheek with the backs of his fingers, looking at my mouth. "Stop trying to control everything. Stop trying to *know* everything. Let this happen. But, if it makes you feel better, we'll have supper. Go for a walk. Share a bath later. You'll need to feed and we'll go to bed."

"It's so hard," I say, my throat tight. "To trust someone enough to obey."

"I know. You have every right not to trust anyone, especially me," he says and pauses. "Perhaps I should say, trust me to move as slowly as I can, given the circumstances we're in."

I nod, and take in a deep breath. He turns back and brushes hair off from my cheek, his eyes searching my face. He cups my cheek and leans in, his lips brushing my other cheek softly before bending down to kiss my neck where he bit me, his tongue wet against my skin and it sends a shock of desire through me that surprises me.

He moves back to my face, his lips poised just over my mouth. Then he kisses me, his mouth soft on mine, his lips together. A tender kiss that surprises me, for I expected him to overwhelm me. Instead, it's such a sweet, sweet kiss that goes on for a long moment. He pulls away and just smiles at me, his gaze moving over my face, his hands stroking my hair.

"You're mine. Together, we'll kill him."

CHAPTER 24

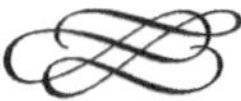

"The way to love anything is to realize that it may be lost."

Gilbert. K. Chesterton

"Now, you must be starving," he says and takes my hand. "From this moment forward, you have to obey me without question. You need practice in obedience."

"I do need practice," I say sarcastically.

"Our meal is ready. Please put on one of the dresses in the armoire. I think I want you in the white dress with nothing on underneath. Then, once you're dressed, we'll eat."

He pulls me over to the huge antique armoire, and opens it. Inside, it's lined with cedar and on a rack hang a dozen dresses – gowns of different colors and fabrics, all of them looking like they're out of couture shops in New York.

He takes out a white gown and holds it up to me. It's a diaphanous shift with thin straps and is made of a material that feels like the finest silk.

"Here," he says and takes it off the hanger, returning the empty hanger to the rack and closing the armoire. "Dress while I watch."

He pulls up an ornate chair and sits, his hands on the armrests, his legs wide, his head to the side. I stand in front of him and hesitate. He watches me expectantly.

"Don't be shy, Eve. I've seen you naked before. Every inch of you."

I shrug one shoulder. Of course he has. But still… Things are different now.

"Eve, there's nothing you can't try, nothing you can't feel with me. No reason to be embarrassed. Please, change into the gown."

I hang the dress over the foot of the bed and undress while he watches, acutely aware of his eyes on me. I remove my sweater and jeans, and then my bra and panties, folding each item and placing them on the chest at the base of the bed. I quickly pull the white dress over my head, and while I have the dress just around my neck, I catch sight of him and his eyes are fixed on my nakedness, his nostrils flaring, lips parted.

It arouses me – that look of complete possession.

I slip the gown down over my body and adjust it. My nipples are hard from the chill in the air and clearly visible through the thin fabric as must be my pubic hair.

"Is this appropriate for dinner?"

"Don't question my choices, Eve. If I picked it, you can trust that it's entirely appropriate."

"You're enjoying this whole control thing, aren't you?" I say.

"Believe me, I'd much prefer that you and I were living as a couple somewhere on the coast of Wales rather than this, but we have to play this game to convince Soren and every other vampire in his coven that you're truly my pet. When you're a pet, you're expected not to speak until I ask you a question. If I want to know what you think about something, I'll ask. For the first while, until you're used to it, when you answer a question or if you need to ask me something, start with *Please, my Lord,* or *Please, Sire.* Do you understand?"

I nod.

"Say it out loud, Eve, so I know you understand."

"Yes," I say and force out the words. "*My Lord.*"

"You don't mean it," he says and his voice is quiet, "but you have to convince everyone else."

"I've never been a good actor," I say. "I'll try."

"There is no try."

I smile sadly, remembering an entry in my journal describing him talking so long ago about me being his Adept. I had no idea this was what he meant.

He takes my hand and leads me out of the bedroom.

"What about my feet?' I say and look around.

"I want you barefoot, and please, remember the rules."

"Oh, I'm sorry," I say. "*My Lord.*"

"I know it will grate on you, but when this is all done, you'll be free to be your own person again. Free of all of us, if you want." He pulls me into an ornate dining room lit by dozens of candles. A long dark wood table that could seat thirty people has a place setting for Michel at the end and one for me at his side. Michel pulls out my chair and seats me while the servant lays a napkin on my lap. Michel takes a seat and removes his own napkin and I hope my table manners are up to his standards as a member of the former Occitan nobility.

"I'm not sure if I know the right fork to use," I say and smile, checking out the array of cutlery. Michel leans over and places his finger over my lips.

"Eve, remember – speak only when I ask you to or when you have a question."

I grimace. "Sorry," I say when he removes his finger, flustered at breaking the rules again so soon. "*My Lord,*" I add quickly, but then my back stiffens just a bit. He doesn't want me to just speak when I feel like it. A flush spreads over my cheeks from anger. But then I remember how Luke's blood slave behaved and I understand this is part of teaching me what's expected of me when we're on stage in front of Soren.

"Can I call you something other than '*My Lord*'? What about *Sir*?"

He shakes his head. "You called Julien 'Sir' and I don't want you thinking of him unnecessarily. Always *My Lord* in public."

I sigh. I don't know what feels the most natural. "*My Lord*, then."

"If you misbehave in public, I'll have to punish you. "

He raises his eyebrows at that.

"My Lord, if I may ask," I say, after taking a sip of wine. "What would you do, exactly, to punish me? Do you have a dungeon somewhere in the depths of this house? Will you go all medieval on me if I disobey you?"

"I *am* medieval, Eve. I was born in 1194. I grew to be a man in that time. I try to keep up with modern trends, but unlike Julien, my psyche is medieval. You have to understand that. And no," he says. "I don't have a dungeon in the basement. If you disobey, you'll get a good spanking, usually with my own hand."

"You wouldn't actually spank me in public?"

"I'd have to threaten to," he says.

The servant comes over to our table and holds a tray of food out for Michel to inspect.

Michel examines the dish – some kind of roast meat. He nods and motions to me. The servant holds the tray out and I shake my head and turn back to Michel expectantly.

"Eve, you must eat," Michel says. "The roast venison is excellent."

"I'm a vegetarian."

He frowns and waits.

"My Lord," I say and exhale.

"Eve, there will be little protein for you, given the food shortages. I doubt tofu is in big supply in the stores and the cheese will run out very soon because of supply chain failures. You must eat the food we can get and not be so picky. When did you become a vegetarian and why?"

I sigh. "I don't remember," I say. I give in and take a slice of the roast. It looks good and smells good. Then I shake my head. "My Lord," I say, exasperated.

He grins while he inspects a tray of vegetables and roasted potatoes. "Be thankful you don't have to call me *My Lord Bishop* or *Your Excellency.*" Then he glances at me, his blue eyes wicked.

"Don't make me call you *Your Holiness,*" I say and laugh, remembering that Soren wants him as his Pope. Then I cover my mouth. "*My Lord,*" I add quickly.

He's smiling as he helps himself to some food. When the servant leaves, Michel takes my hand and bows his head. He makes the sign of the cross and says grace, something I remember from my own days when I still believed in the God of the Catholic Church.

Father of us all,
This meal is a sign of Your love for us:
Bless us and bless our food,
And help us to give your glory each day.
Through Jesus our Lord.
Amen

He makes the sign of the cross once more but he can't expect me to profess a faith I don't possess.

"You see, Eve," he says and lets go of my hand. "We are all obedient to someone. Even a former Viscount, Bishop for a Week and eight-hundred-year old vampire."

I smile and then we eat. I haven't eaten with him very often – never in such a formal way and despite everything we've been through, I barely know him.

I didn't realize how hungry I am and eat with relish, having eaten mostly peanut butter, beans and rice since the red rain fell. Roast venison and root vegetables from the garden are so much better.

I don't say anything while we eat, nor does he. I wait to see what he wants. Finally, he turns to me, chewing thoughtfully, his brow creased.

"So, Eve," he says. "Tell me how you're feeling."

I put my knife and fork down and pick up my glass of wine.

"My Lord, I was just wondering, are you expecting me to be your servant as well as your pet?"

He adjusts his position and considers what I've asked. "Do you mean, will I expect you to wait on me? Pour my wine, wash my hair, dress me?"

I nod. "I wondered…"

He raises his eyebrows.

"Oh, sorry. *My Lord*…" I say, emphasizing the title. I heave a sigh. This is harder than I imagined.

"Only if we're in public, or if someone is with us. Then, I expect you to attend to my needs, whatever they are."

I nod and smile. "Very good, my Lord. Just so I know. Tell me, do all vampires like this kind of thing? This whole human pet game?"

"We live for it," he says and pours me more wine. He returns to his food and I watch him eat for a moment. He looks so at home in this sumptuous setting, dressed in a white shirt open at the collar and black tunic like he wore at Soren's party. I could see him with lace at his cuffs and neck. Against his pale skin and dark hair, lace would be very attractive.

"Why did you want to be a priest? You're so handsome. I can't imagine the girls of Carcassonne were happy to see you take up the cross."

He glances at me and picks up his glass of wine, but says nothing. Finally, he puts his glass down and waits, staring straight ahead.

I inhale sharply when I realize I haven't used the proper form of address.

"*Crap,*" I say. "I'm sorry, my *LORD.*" Exasperation fills me. "Can't I just say it once and have that count for the entire meal?"

He turns a jaundiced eye towards me. "That's not how it works, Eve. Each time you address me, you must use the appropriate title. It shows respect. Deference. It reinforces our power difference. That's the whole point of this. Soren expects you to be my pet and blood slave. You must always show deference to me and every other vampire."

"It's just that I don't know if I can remember to use the proper title all the time," I say. "*My Lord.*"

"It would be easier if you start out with *My Lord* rather than using it at the end of a sentence. For example, you might say, '*My Lord, I was wondering if you're planning to fuck me senseless tonight?'* That way, you won't forget to use the title. Concentrate…" He smiles wickedly at me, his eyes hooded. I can't help but smile back, heat rising in my cheeks, the thought of him fucking me senseless tonight sending a stab of desire through my body, making my breath hitch.

I take a big sip of wine.

"My Lord, after you've said something like that, how can you expect me to concentrate? But I'll try."

"As to what I said about fucking you senseless tonight," he adds, "you can expect it every night at least once. And every morning at least once. You don't have to wonder or ask. Expect it."

"You're enjoying this," I say, frowning.

"Eve," he says and reaches out to me, taking my hand. He kisses my knuckles. "I love you. I would love to do anything with you. Even the smallest thing. Never forget that."

My body can't help but respond to what he's said and for a moment, I'm a bit flustered.

"Now, I feel like a walk around the grounds for some air." He motions to a servant standing at the side of the room. "Bring Miss Hayden's white sweater and her sandals from her room." The servant immediately bows and leaves us.

Michel takes my arm in his and leads me out of the dining room and into the main foyer, which is grand, the centerpiece a huge chandelier lighting the area that has been fitted with real candles.

The servant returns and Michel helps me slip on my sweater and sandals. I feel a bit exposed with this thin shift that's so transparent, but the servants are very good at not looking at my body. I expect Michel's given them orders. This must be the way things were run back when he was a human. His father *was* a Viscount.

"Soon, we must be more careful," Michel says as we leave the house and start walking around the grounds. There are lanterns on the path spaced out every twenty feet or so, but still, it's dark. "The vampires will start coming out at night. I'm safe, my grounds are likely safe, at least for a while. They know who and what I am, but at some point, Blackstone may consider attacking me because I'm with Soren."

"Are you?" I say. "My Lord? Are you really with him? I thought you were just there to watch and wait for the right time to destroy him."

"I have to appear to be with him, just as you have to appear to be completely under my control. He must believe we are both his creatures. The average Blackstone operative must think I *am* with Soren. Only our own people who have infiltrated Blackstone know what my plans are so I can defend myself. Once human authorities recognize the threat Soren poses, they'll come after me as well. I hope we can deal with Soren before it comes to that."

"What's the plan?" I wait, but then remember. "My Lord, forgive me."

He says nothing, just keeps his hand clasped over mine, which is resting on his forearm as we walk.

"You have to give up your need to know. *I* know. That has to be enough for you. You must stop asking and just let things happen. Take your cues from me. Let me lead. All you need to do is obey. I'll take care of everything else. Trust me, Eve."

I say nothing for a moment. "My Lord," I say finally. "Trust is the hardest thing for me."

"I know. You have no reason to trust me, considering. All I can do is ask that for once, you do. Wholly and completely."

I look at him as we walk – at his pale skin, his dark hair that hangs below his collar, a bit wild. His blue eyes, so intelligent and determined. I *want* to trust. I'm craving it. I want to feel completely relaxed for once in my life. Not on guard.

I just don't know if that will ever be possible.

CHAPTER 25

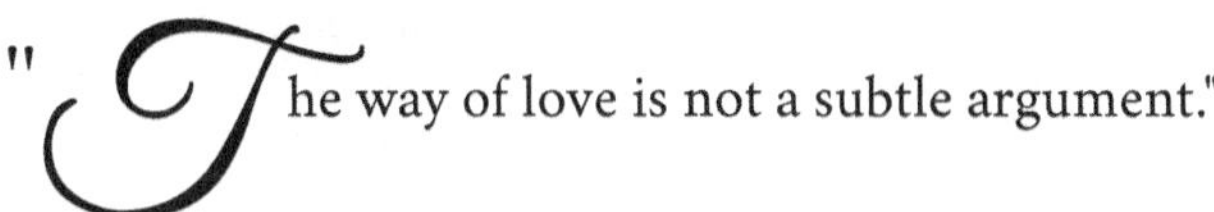

"The way of love is not a subtle argument."

Rumi

WE ARRIVE BACK at the front entrance and enter the building through open double doors. He stops and drops my hand, speaking with a servant for a moment. Then he comes back to me and takes my hand, leading me into another room where sits a huge grand piano.

"Play for me, Eve."

I take my seat on the bench. Michel sits beside me and leans against me, his arm touching mine. He smiles, and it's so soft and affectionate, it makes my throat a bit choky. At times, he seems so formal and commanding, and at others he seems so open and tender.

"My Lord, what would you like me to play?"

He sorts through sheet music on the stand and selects one.

"Chopin, the Ballade of course."

I play the piece as best I can, and when I finish, he leans closer to me, pressing against my arm and shoulder when he does. He turns slightly and nestles his face in the crook of my neck, inhaling to smell my perfume.

"I think that's enough piano for now," he whispers, his mouth at my ear, his hair tickling my cheek. "Your scent intoxicates me." He pulls back, looking in my eyes and I can see his desire on his face, in his half-lidded eyes, his parted lips. He's breathing a bit faster now.

"Here," he says and pulls me deeper into the bedroom, leading me to the bed so that I sit on the edge. He reaches for the box and opens it to reveal a thin black velvet choker with a small black and white cameo pendant. "This is a gift for you – the symbol of my family. You have to wear it all the time."

I take it from him and examine it. The cameo is beautiful, made from what looks like onyx, and in the shape of a white *fleur-de-lis* against a black background. It's about the size of a nickel and delicate. He fastens it behind my neck and positions it so that the cameo falls just at the base of my throat.

"Beautiful."

He takes my hand and leads me to the antique bureau with a large mirror and stands me in front of it so I can see what it looks like on me. I stand there with the cameo choker around my neck and examine my reflection. He pulls my hair away from my face, holding it up in a loose ponytail so that long tendrils fall around the nape of my neck. He bends down and places his mouth over his bite mark possessively.

"You are so *lovely*," he says and pushes me back, lying on top of me. "You are truly all mine. Keats never had Fanny the way he wanted, Eve, but I have you. I've always thought how tragic was his love story with Fanny. He so capable of loving her entirely and completely and unable to have her that way. I've wanted you so long and now you are mine."

"My Lord," I say, enjoying his weight on top of me. "We've only known each other for four months. You haven't waited long at all."

"I feel like I've known you for eight hundred years."

I frown. "What do you mean?"

"I was there when you were conceived, Eve," Michel says and

strokes my cheek. "I saw your mother's ultrasound at eighteen weeks when we discovered your siblings had all died in utero. I was there when you were born, waiting outside the delivery room. I saw your first recital. I saw your last recital before your mother died."

He kisses me and I respond despite my confusion.

"You were there when I was conceived?"

"Soren's scientists used your mother's egg and father's sperm. They infused the fertilized egg with selected DNA that had been manipulated to include some from an Ancient, and some from another human."

"What other human?" I say, a sense of dread filling me.

"You have some of your mother in you – what we needed. Your fight skills, your telepathy. You have some Ancient DNA that gives you the ability to act as a conduit between vampires and Ancients."

"Which Ancient?" I say, alarm filling me. "Not Soren..."

"Yes," Michel says. "You are his creature."

I can't even think at this point. Soren is *not* my father. I have some of his DNA – that's all.

"Who else? What other human?"

Michel doesn't say anything for a while. Finally, he takes a lock of my hair between his fingers and holds it up to his nose. "Danielle."

Danielle? "But," I say and can't speak for a moment, confused. "She *died*... You killed her!"

"We dug up her bones and used her DNA. There are techniques, Eve, that never existed until now to extract DNA from hip bones. There was enough to use to make you look like her. Your hair. Your eyes. Your build. The shape of your nose. Your chin. Your long neck. But your dimples, they're your mother's. Your freckles? They're from your father."

My eyes widen.

"But why?"

"Soren promised me that if I was at his side, he'd make you for me. You see, he played us both. Promising us both a copy of you in return for our obedience and compliance with his plan. Then, your siblings died in utero and there was only one of you. He thought that was even better – to have us both enslaved to him, fighting over you."

I'm unable to speak or even think, while he kisses my neck. I try to understand – I'm *not* Danielle. I look like her, but I'm my mother's daughter. I'm my father's daughter. I have her dimples. I have his freckles.

Michel calms me and I don't cry although tears threaten at the corners of my eyes.

"Soren created me for you?"

"His scientists created three of you, one for me and one for Julien and one spare. You were the only one to survive."

"Why are you telling me this now? You should have told me before!"

"Would it have made a difference? Would you have felt differently?"

I don't know if I would. All I know is that my hatred for Soren is growing so great, I feel as if I might explode. Michel kisses my neck and releases more endorphins to calm me and my body relaxes but my mind won't shut down.

"So you and Julien were waiting for me to grow up to see which one I'd choose?"

"No," Michel says. "I lost you on purpose so neither of us would have you. So Soren wouldn't use you. Then, you had to get those files from the university. I had no idea where you were or that you'd try. I had no idea that Julien gave that manuscript to your mother. I did everything I could to stop this from happening. Fate had other plans for us, Eve."

I let the knowledge wash over me. No wonder he and Julien are unwilling to give me up. They both wanted Danielle when they were human. Now, here I am, looking so much like her, even with some of her DNA in me. Soren is *such* a bastard to manipulate them through me...

I close my eyes and try to shut my brain off. When Michel feels me give in, he starts kissing me again. I try to not think for the thoughts are still too confusing and upsetting.

I shut it off. I'm so confused, and Michel is so insistent, kissing me, his hand stroking down my body. When he opens himself to me so that I feel his love, his desire, I give in.

This is what I wrote about in my journal – how I wanted him. Our connection makes it all the more intense as I feel what he feels, and it's like fulfillment to him.

I'm what he's waited for since he saw me in the Linguistics Building – that day which feels as if it never happened and even before that, when Soren first proposed the deal that would have Michel and Julien as his servants.

Once he's secure that I can obey him fully and without question, we'll kill Soren.

CHAPTER 26

"True strength lies in submission which permits one to dedicate his life, through devotion, to something beyond himself."

Henry Miller

He kisses me one last time before he blows out the candle.

"Good night, Eve," he says, his face nestled in the crook of my neck.

"Good night, Michel."

I feel his smile against my neck. I'm going to call him Michel when we're in private. I don't want to forget that I'm not a pet every hour of the day.

I'm me.

We're Lord and servant because we have a mission. I turn over and face him and he adjusts his head on the pillow. Despite the darkness, I can see his face with my hunter vision and because of the moonlight flooding in from the window.

"When we kill Soren," I say and tuck his hair behind his ear, "Will we go back to being an ordinary couple?"

"Whatever you wish, Eve."

"Have you seen it?" I ask. "Us being normal?"

He clucks his tongue. "You don't believe I can see the future."

I say nothing for a moment. I *don't* believe it. But still…

"In your," I say and hesitate. "Visions, or whatever they are, are we together after we kill Soren?"

"Yes. After a fashion. Not like this in every possible future." He smiles softly. "It's enough that you're alive and that I'm with you."

I just look at his face, at his eyes – those thick black lashes that belong on a woman, not a man. That square jaw that's all man.

"What about Julien?"

"What about him?" Michel says, his words clipped.

"You know what I mean. You said he was expecting to have me. It explains a lot."

"Forget about that. I don't want to talk about Julien, Eve. I just want to be with you. And right now, I want to sleep," he says and closes his eyes.

He doesn't want a future with Julien in it, at least, not one with Julien trying to get me back. I can't help but wonder how Julien is and I feel traitorous. How can I think of Julien when I'm here with Michel and am so happy? I feel so possessed. So wanted. So desired.

I sigh and turn over so that my back's toward Michel and close my eyes, trying to shut my mind off. Michel squeezes me, his naked skin against me. He must do something to me for I finally relax and stop thinking, just listen instead to the sound of his breathing.

WHEN I WAKE, I catch a glimpse of Michel through the open door to the bathroom. He's dressed in his robe while servants pour buckets of hot water into the tub. I sit up and keep the blankets around me, watching as Michel pours some bath salts into the water. He turns back to the room and sees me sitting on the bed.

Before he can come to get me, another servant enters the room and goes to his side. They speak briefly and then Michel shakes his head as if upset. He speaks to the other servants and then comes into the bedroom.

"Eve," he says. "I'm called out to see Soren. I have to go right away, but you go ahead and have a bath, then eat your breakfast. Wear something from the clothes I've provided for you. I've picked them out myself. I'll see what he wants and then be back."

"Yes, my Lord," I say because one of the servants is in the room, stoking the fire, and I don't want to show disrespect.

"Good," he says and reaches out to stroke my cheek. "Thank you for understanding," he says quietly, his voice almost a whisper.

I have a nice long soak in the tub and then dress in one of the dresses in the armoire. They're all formal and more fitting to a night out than a day spent at home. I pick the most casual dress, a long black silk dress with a very low décolletage, a square neckline and fitted bodice. I feel like a lady from some medieval court and smile to myself, wondering if Michel will just take it off once he gets back. I probably should have stayed in my robe and nightgown.

I eat my breakfast of poached eggs, orange juice and coffee and wonder what Soren's up to, calling Michel away so early in the morning. It can't be good. I wonder what new form of torture he'll inflict on us all. I wonder what Julien is doing and if he's unconcerned about my being with Michel. I kick myself mentally for even thinking of Julien when I've been with Michel.

I will *not* become Marguerite.

It's while Michel's away that I start to explore the mansion a bit, checking out the library where I find thousands of volumes, old and new. Then I find a dark wood-paneled room that seems like an office and go inside. In the corner is a huge wooden cabinet and I open it, curious to see what's inside.

Bingo...

Boxes from my apartment – my own things, *and* my mother's files. Immediately, I know the one document I want to read more than any other – that report prepared by the Council on the prophecy Dylan mentioned. St. Therese of the Reeds.

I start to sort through the files, sitting on the floor by the closet. I find the file after about ten minutes of flipping through the file box contents. Inside is a typewritten report titled *"Revelation of St. Therese of the Reeds"* – *Analysis and Conjecture.* Included is a photocopy of the original document written in the Third Century in some language I can't read, and a typewritten translation.

I lean against the closet and start to read:

THIS BEING *the revelation of The LORD God, as shown to His humble servant Therese of Aquitaine, by an angel of The LORD to whom God sent, bringing the prophecy and news to all who have ears to hear. Blessed are those who read the words of this prophecy, and blessed are those who hear it and take heed what is written in it. Let it be known that the time will come when the children of God shall weep and moan, for an ancient evil will rise. Only the Sword of Megiddo shall free those who suffer slavery to the Fallen Ones who pollute the earth with their pestilence.*

I, Therese, your sister and daughter and companion in the suffering and kingdom and patient endurance that are ours in Jesus, was among the people of Persia, where I sat by a river along the Euphrates, in the place that Adam and Eve once lived, called Paradise, or Eden, and I heard behind me a loud voice like a horn, which said: "Write what you see and send it to the seven churches: to Ephesus, Smyrna, Pergamum, Thyatira, Sardis, Philadelphia and Laodicea."

I turned to see the voice that was speaking to me. And when I turned I saw a being with wings of grey dressed in a uniform with leather breastplate and helmet, a huge sword in its hand. Behold, an angel of The LORD, an Archangel, come to bring news of the end of days. His skin and hair was as white as snow, and his eyes were like blazing fire. His face was like the sun shining in all its brilliance.

I fell to my knees before him, my eyes burning from the brightness of his countenance. When he touched me, I saw a vision of the future and fear was in my heart for a rain of blood fell from a cloudless sky and all was cold and dark. One would come, the Angel told me, who would take over the holy Church, and fight those who would enslave the Children of God across the world. He would wield one weapon that could save those who faced the blood tribulation – a double–edged sword of dark and light, but the one who wields the sword must be pure of heart for the blade is a harsh mistress and he who wields her should regret the day they raised it not in service of The LORD.

"Woe is to him who wields this weapon who is not pure in the ways of The LORD for it shall destroy them," the Angel of The LORD said unto me. "Write what you have seen, and what will come to be. Let those who have ears to hear and eyes to see take heed, and find the one who wields this weapon that The LORD has provided to fight this pestilence. Follow him and heed his word for it is he whom The LORD GOD sent to save the world from perdition.

JUST A LOT of mumbo jumbo from a young woman visiting Persia, probably suffering from some kind of tropical disease and having visions. But something nags at me. A rain of blood? That sounds too much like the red rain for my comfort. All would be dark and cold? Sounds like what's happening in the areas hit by the red rain. A being with grey wings and white hair and skin? With eyes that burn like fire... It sounds too much like Soren – or at least another vampire – for it to be a coincidence.

Was it Soren? Did he plant this prophecy so long ago as a way of manipulating us? Or, like Michel, did he see the future and was trying to use it to his advantage? I just don't know what to believe but whatever the truth, I suspect that it's part of some grand plot of his to take power.

I put away the boxes but keep the file from Seth and a few of my mother's on angels and go back to the bedroom. I sit on the bed and open a document and search for what angels are supposed to look like, and the descriptions come back very similar to what St. Therese described – huge wings, white skin and hair, red eyes, blinding brilliance, booming voice. Not that I believe in angels, but perhaps all accounts of angelic beings really are just accounts of Ancients trying to appear to be angels as a way of manipulating poor religiously-susceptible mortals.

Then I read the report prepared by some nameless researcher for the Council. It reads like a serious paper with footnotes and annotations, referring to other authors and to literature on angels, on ancient prophecies, to swords of power in myth, on the Plains of Megiddo where the battle of Armageddon is supposed to take place – somewhere in Palestine. It says that the battle will be fought by two opposing forces – those mortals who want to rid the world of vampires and the vampires who seek their Dominion over mortals. The Ancients will jockey for power over what remains.

The Sword of Megiddo itself is seen as either real or symbolic. If real, it is judged to be the sword that the Archangel Michael used to defeat Lucifer in the original battle before the creation of humans. It is not known where this sword might be located but there is a section on speculation as to its location in Palestine, perhaps in Jerusalem itself, buried somewhere in the ruins of King Solomon's Temple. There's a section that speculates about the role of the Knights Templar in protecting that sword and keeping it safe for the future. That they carried the secret of its location away from Palestine when they were disbanded in the 13th Century and that it is now hidden somewhere in Scotland.

Other speculation is that the Sword of Megiddo is metaphorical and refers to people or a person instead of an actual sword. This line of thought has the weapon being a powerful warrior who will fight against the Fallen, against the Ancients, and will destroy their leader and them. I think of Julien, an ascended vampire, former knight, manipulated by Blackstone to be a day walker. I think of Soren, who was so prominent in the peace negotiations in Palestine, with his militia and soldier of fortune business and his goal of becoming the God of War reborn.

It's as I'm reading the final page that Michel returns and finds me absorbed in the document.

"What have you got there?" he says as he enters the bedroom and sees me reclining on the bed with papers spread around me. He comes to the side of the bed and touches my cheek when I sit up and face him. "That's quite interesting reading," he says. "And was never meant for your eyes."

"Seth gave it to me – one of the techies at the SCU."

"I know who Seth is."

I hold up the photocopy of the scrolls written by Therese. "Do you believe this?"

"It's hard to know what to believe with these apocryphal gospels." He scans the Council report. "I remember reading this when it was first sent out to Council members. There are some pretty shocking parallels in it. The rain of blood seems to refer to the red rainfall we had. The description of the archangel sounds a lot like an Ancient."

"I've only ever seen Soren, my Lord. Do they all look like him, with white hair and skin?"

He nods. "They're northern because the Nephilim were up north looking for new peoples to conquer and those were the only group to survive the flood in the Middle East."

I sigh, not knowing what to believe. "Speaking of the devil, what did Soren want?"

Michel pushes the papers away and sits on the bed beside me. He takes my hand and waits.

"I'm sorry," I say and roll my eyes. "*My Lord.*"

"He wants us to go to his estate and live there. Today. He's having a grand party tonight and wants you to be with me."

"Why do we have to live there, my Lord? Will Julien be there tonight as well?"

"Of course he will," Michel says, exasperation in his tone. "How better to torture Julien and me than to have you there with both of us in attendance? As to us living there, he wants you and I and Julien to be with him all the time, the way it was back when we were first under his servitude."

Apprehension fills me. Michel must sense it for he releases something in my brain and I relax, leaning against him, my head resting on his shoulder.

"Now," he says and runs his finger over the tops of my breasts. "Put those documents aside. No more snooping and no more reading things you don't have to know. The servants are fixing me that bath I missed and I want you to do all the work, washing every single inch of me."

I look up in his eyes and see that lopsided grin and smile back.

Once the servants finish filling the bath, I wait for Michel to give me my orders. He stands beside the tub and feels the water. Finally, he turns to me.

"You should be naked when you do this, Eve. I don't want that gown to get wet."

"My Lord, that sounds like an excuse to get me naked," I say and can't help but smile, so I turn away to try to hide it.

I hear him cluck in mock disapproval and smile more widely, angry at myself for enjoying this as much as I am but I said all in.

I expect that's what this means.

CHAPTER 27

Elizabeth Barrett Browning

WE ARRIVE at Soren's mansion in time for the evening meal after a day spent either in bed or walking the grounds. I'm nervous as we enter a huge mansion in Cambridge that looks to be right out of *Pride and Prejudice*. Michel does everything he can to relax me. I remember reading about that night in Franklin Park when I first was in the presence of other vampires and how Michel calmed me. He's doing that now and I'm thankful, for otherwise my heart would be pounding, my instinct just to run. That or run to Soren and kill him with my bare hands. I must be on my best behavior, but not too good. Soren won't believe it. He has to see Michel discipline me.

Thankfully, Michel's left it up to me to decide what it will be.

I don't want to please Soren too much through my misbehavior. At the same time, if I'm too well-behaved, he might feel it's just an act. He wants to know whether Michel will do what it takes to ensure my compliance.

I can't be compelled. I *can* be controlled – at least, that's the purpose of this whole blood-slave-pet thing. To control me so I'll be the good little Adept when Soren needs me.

A host of servants greet us. Some take our trunks out of the cart, while others take our coats. I walk beside Michel but a pace behind him. Michel's instructed me to keep my eyes averted unless he speaks directly to me, addressing me by name. I'm not to let my eyes wander around the room. No matter what I hear, I'm to sit at Michel's side like a good pet and keep my eyes down, waiting for his questions or orders.

We enter a large salon and Soren is seated at a table playing backgammon with Julien. When I see Julien, my heart does a little flip flop and I hate Soren more than anything. He's truly a bastard and despite what Michel's done to calm me, my heart rate increases. Michel can sense my emotions and turns to me briefly, squeezing my hand as if for courage. He releases a little something in my brain to ease my anxiety and I walk behind him, keeping my eyes on his back, slightly lowered so that I don't meet anyone's eyes.

I can't see Soren like this, but I can hear him.

"Ahh, here's the *lovely* couple," he says, his voice ebullient. "All flush with hormones from their day of fucking."

So much for Michel's efforts. When I hear that, and the tone to his voice – mocking and ridiculing, and knowing that it was meant to injure Julien – I have to clench my fists, digging my nails into my palms to block the feelings of hatred that fill me.

"Come, child, and let me look at you. What did Michel dress you in tonight?"

I stand still, frowning. Am I supposed to go to him? I wait for Michel to command me.

"Go, Eve."

I glance up at him and he nods, his face calm, but his lips are pressed tight.

I walk to where Soren stands by the backgammon table, trying not to look at him or Julien directly, but I can see them in the periphery of my vision. Soren's dressed like some eighteenth-century Lord in a navy morning suit with lace at the collar. Julien is wearing a dark grey suit with a white shirt open at the collar. I feel his eyes on me, and it takes every ounce of strength I have not to look at him to see how he's taking it. I hope Soren has compelled him to not feel jealous, but I suspect it's precisely Julien's jealousy that Soren is trying to elicit with this charade. I clench my fists, anger boiling inside of me.

"I love your gown. What color is that Michel? Violet? It brings out the flecks in her eyes, I'll bet. May I?"

Soren takes my chin in his hand and lifts my head so that I look at his face. I try to avoid his eyes, but he moves his head around until I can't avoid meeting his gaze.

"There, let me look at your eyes, Eve. Yes. They're *just* like hers, aren't they Michel? Julien, wouldn't you agree? Just like lovely Danielle."

Soren's smirking. Neither Julien nor Michel says a word. Soren takes my hands and turns my palms over, inspecting the damage I've done to them with my fingernails.

"Tsk tsk, Eve. So *angry*. So much passion! No wonder Michel would move heaven and earth to keep you to himself. Or should I say bomb his own entourage? Leaving poor Julien to imagine you dead. He grieved, Eve. Did you know that he wept like a baby when he saw what he thought was your dead body? Can you imagine his broken heart? No you can't, can you? Here," he says and takes my face in his hand. "Let me show you."

I pull away. "Stop," I say and turn my face away. I can't imagine it. I don't want to see it.

"I don't think so, Eve. You *should* see it. Quite the heart, our Julien has, despite the bravado and denial."

He takes my face in his hands and I can't resist him. I see Julien through Soren's eyes.

After the phone call, they rush to the site of the bombing only to find that Michel is gone, as is Vasily. The coroner is there inspecting the dead, and there's a body on the ground by Michel's limousine, a sheet over top.

Julien leaves Soren's car at a run and asks the police officer on scene where I am.

The cop asks who he is and Julien says he's my boyfriend. The cop makes a face and points to the body.

Julien stumbles to what he thinks is my body and kneels beside it, bending over it, one hand resting on the body while the other covers his eyes. His shoulders are shaking. Soren can't believe it himself and comes over, lifting the sheet from the body to check. The face and torso are burned horribly, as is a lot of the hair, but it's fair like mine and about the right length. The woman is about my height. It looks like it could be me. Then Julien reaches to the corpse and fingers a golden crucifix on a chain around its neck.

Julien finally covers his face with both hands and bends down close to the body, and I can hear him sobbing. He's actually sobbing. Soren rests his hand on Julien's shoulder for comfort, and Julien turns to him, leaning against Soren's leg like a child might a parent. Soren calms Julien with a touch and he soon stops weeping, his face wet, his eyes closed. Soren bends down to pull Julien up, one hand beneath his arm but Julien resists, turning back.

"I want it!" he says, and reaches down to take the crucifix from around the dead woman's neck. Soren lets him, watching while Julien gingerly removes it and slips it around his own neck. Then, Soren helps Julien up and he's like a zombie, almost dragged to Soren's vehicle.

The vision stops and I can't help but respond to the emotions I see. Tears fill my eyes that Julien would cry. It's so unlike what I expected of him.

"He gave you back to Michel when Michel returned from Pittsburgh despite his fears that Michel would get you killed," Soren says. "Can you *imagine* how he felt once he thought you were truly dead? He thought he'd been right to fear that fate, blaming himself for your death. Then – a miracle and he finds you alive! You go back with him, stay with him and become his proper lover, only to go back with Michel? What a little siren you are. Neither brother can resist you."

I bite my cheek until I taste blood to stop my tears. I won't give him the pleasure of my response. Soren says nothing for a moment, watching me.

"So much self-control, Eve. You surprise me." Then he turns to

Michel. "Please, come and join us by the fire, Michel. Take a seat. Drinks are served."

Michel comes up behind me and places a hand on the small of my back, whisking me to a chair by the fire. He sits and then points to the chair beside him. I imagine that's where I'll be seated. I sit and he lays a hand on my shoulder, stroking my hair like I'm the household golden retriever.

I can't believe I'm here, doing this, with my mother's killer sitting across from me, smirking. All I want to do is lunge at him and slit his throat but I know that would do nothing. I don't know how to kill him. I don't even know what he is. All I know is that Soren is my mother's true killer. I no longer blame Michel for her death. I know he was horrified at what he'd done, just as he was with Danielle. It was Soren who was truly responsible and it is Soren who will pay.

I have to keep calm and bide my time until we have the opportunity and the way to do it.

"So, Eve," Soren says, unable to leave me alone, trying to get some kind of response from me. "Are you enjoying your liaison with Michel? I think so, based on what I can glean from your memories of earlier when he was fucking you from behind in the bathroom against the vanity. You looking at him in the mirror while he did, thinking about another time and another vanity. That time with Julien. You love them both, don't you – the beautiful identical twin brothers. Fucking them both... I *love* it! I love you with them. Shameless little thing you've become under Michel's and Julien's tutelage. So glad I pushed the three of you together."

"So am I," I say. It slips out. He's just being such a bastard, gloating, and I can't hold back despite knowing this is exactly what he wants.

"Ah, there's that saucy mouth I enjoy so much," Soren says and grins. "I don't know where you got it from – certainly not Natalia or Danielle. Was Sean like that, Michel? I don't think so. Her father was quite the stuffy fellow if I recall correctly, all focused on turning her into a little Mozart. Too bad your mother fucked things up, isn't it Eve? You might have had an entirely different life if she'd only cooperated with me."

"She was a hero and you're a bastard!" I say, my voice breaking.

"Now, Eve, we've already had this conversation. Bastard is not a term that applies to gods."

"You're no god."

"How would you know? You don't even believe in one!" Soren says, laughing.

"Certainly not one like you."

Soren smiles, but his eyes betray him. He's not pleased at *what* I've said, just that I've disobeyed.

"Michel, you really *must* do something to shut your little minx up. Teach her to show proper respect."

"Eve," Michel says, his voice stern. "Apologize to Soren."

I say nothing, fuming, my breath fast.

"Eve," Michel says, his voice commanding. "Apologize."

I turn to Michel. "I'm sorry I disobeyed your rules, my Lord," I say, trying to wheedle out of apologizing directly to Soren. I bow my head, but he stops me. He tilts my head up and looks in my eyes.

"A proper apology to our host, Eve. *Now.*" He turns me around so that I'm facing Soren, and for a moment, I feel Michel's pleasure that I've resisted apologizing and now that I'm allowing him to discipline me. It's necessary. Soren must believe the charade.

I avert my eyes and mumble an apology. "Please accept my humble apology, my Lord Soren, for showing disrespect towards you."

"Apology accepted, although I doubt it's truly humble, but it's good enough. Now, let's go to the dining room. I believe our meal is ready."

Just then, Gabrielle joins us from another room. She's dressed in a black velvet gown with a very plunging neckline that displays her sumptuous bosom so well. She walks to Julien and threads her arm through his. They walk behind Soren into the dining room. Michel places his hand on my waist as if to steady me, for I feel slightly faint when I see Julien so calm with Marguerite as if they've been together forever. She's talking to him and leaning in more closely, touching him possessively. Has Soren compelled Julien to be happy being with her?

Soren turns around when he reaches the door to the dining room and smiles back at us, wagging his eyebrows.

"As you can see, Eve, you don't have to worry about dear Julien's broken heart. I've given him a toy to play with. Rather pretty pair they make, don't you think? Just like old times…"

Michel squeezes me, as if to keep me from responding. Soren waits for us.

"You know, Julien was a bit more fond of my Marguerite than Michel ever was. Almost *liked* her. I think he enjoyed her saucy mouth and I know he enjoyed fucking her. He even protested when Michel decided to kill her. Michel hated her with a passion. Hated that he loved fucking her. Hated being debauched by an eighteen-year old girl. I chose her wisely when I turned her. I hate being bored with a female. Only one with fire can keep my interest."

"Why did you leave her, then?" I say, unable to shut up. "You left her to her own devices and she turned Michel and Julien against their will."

Michel squeezes me again. "Eve, use the proper form of address."

"My *Lord*, " I add, my tone still impertinent. "Please forgive my lapse."

Soren grins. "Don't be too good, Eve. Michel's probably dying to spank you. Make sure you at least do something to merit it." He walks into the dining room and a huge table that is fit for fifty diners. We're clustered at one end of the table. He waits for us.

"Don't blame her for turning them. She needed someone to make her look respectable. Remember the age, Eve, when you judge her. Back then women weren't allowed to be on their own without male protection. As for me, I had to get some distance from her. Saucy becomes downright annoying after a while. Besides, Julien didn't want to die. He *wanted* immortality."

I watch Julien with Gabrielle and he seems happy and attentive to her, pulling out her chair, sitting close to her, leaning in to speak into her ear.

"I know you've compelled him to be happy with her, my *LORD*, " I say. "If you're trying to make me jealous, it won't work."

Soren shrugs. "You are jealous. I need him happy."

Soren sits at the head of the table, a servant pulling out his chair. Michel seats me and then sits down beside me.

We're served a delicious meal and I wonder how many people are going hungry given what's happening in the world around us. There are roast meats and vegetables, potatoes, sauces, breads, and fruit. A feast. There's wine. Servants hover around us, and as we're being served, a string quartet of musicians enter the dining room and start to play something light, Baroque. Geminiani. *Concerto Grosso*. I recognize it because my father played in a string quartet for a while.

It feels like we've been transported to the eighteenth century, with the music and décor and candles. I realize that these vampires are used to living without technology. They know how to survive. This is likely why Blackstone decided to attack modern technology. Technology and science give us humans an edge. Without our machines and energy and electronics, we're as helpless as children compared to them with their powers, speed and strength, and knowledge gleaned from hundreds if not thousands of years of existence.

Michel would know how to survive without technology as would Julien.

It's then that I wonder if Michel and Julien truly *want* to stop Dominion. Julien said he didn't want Dominion because he didn't want humans to be cattle. He likes being a vampire, but also likes humans to exist as we are. For humans to choose vampires as lovers. Michel said he hated the idea of Dominion – he hated vampires and being one.

But here they are, both of them enjoying themselves in this setting. I wonder if, when it comes to it, whether either of them will stop it. Or will they just let it happen and see what the fallout brings?

Michel can't be compelled. From what I've read of him in my journal and from what I've felt from him due to our shared connection, he hates being a vampire. He wants vampires and Ancients dead. He wants to die himself, hoping that his efforts to stop Dominion will win him back his immortal soul.

Soren sits there and watches Michel and Julien, drinking his wine and smiling to himself as if he's a puppet master and we're all his puppets. I sit beside Michel and watch Soren covertly, my hatred boiling over despite everything Michel has done to calm me.

Finally, Soren turns to me and I avert my eyes.

"Eve," he says. "How are you doing? Is the food to your taste? I see you've given up your silly vegetarianism."

"My Lord," I say and keep my eyes averted. "I don't remember being a vegetarian so it doesn't bother me to eat meat."

"Good. When I and the Twelve share your blood and you ours, we'll be counting on you. We need you nice and healthy, full-blooded."

I freeze at that. I know he plans on using me as his 'medium' – I'll share his blood and that of his group of Ancients, and through me, they'll be able to connect to each other the way they once did – or so Michel told me.

At that moment, I realize that I've never seen Soren drink blood. Of course, I've seen Julien and Michel drink blood, but I've never seen Soren. Michel and Julien both have crystal goblets filled with it, and are drinking it to augment their meal of food. Soren has none. He's drinking wine only.

Is he even an Ancient? Is he even a vampire at all? He suggested he's more than what we think he is...

I sit and think of this while Soren chats with Michel about the Council. I listen with half an ear, the other half of my mind wondering what he is. Julien and Gabrielle are leaning in close together, laughing over something private. When I see him with her, I feel a twinge of regret, remembering our time together and how happy I was. How much I enjoyed being with him.

"Michel, have you filled Eve in on what I'm planning?"

Michel takes his napkin and wipes his mouth.

"I've given her a minimal briefing on it. Nothing specific."

"She knows my plans to claim Dominion once we've taken care of Blackstone."

"Yes, in very general terms."

"What do you think, Eve?"

I say nothing. I can't lie. I just can't. I try to hide behind Michel's body, my eyes not meeting Soren's.

"Come on, now. Tell me the truth. What do you think?"

I struggle not to reply in a snarky or impertinent tone but I can't hold back.

"If you think I'll help you, you're crazy."

"Eve!" Michel says, taking my chin in his hand, staring in my eyes. "Remember your manners."

I feel tears bite at the corners of my eyes and press my nails into my palms, to get control.

"I'm sorry, my Lord, but I don't approve of Dominion. I can't willingly support you."

Soren rises from his chair and comes over to where I sit. I cower a bit as he stands over me. He's so tall and has such a strong build. He's a bit terrifying with his white skin and hair, his eyes so clear blue they look transparent.

"I don't expect your willing support. I expect your support only through coercion. I'm not an idiot. But I will get it. I have the perfect tool to gain your compliance. I have the twins."

He tilts my head up and even though I try to avoid his eyes, I can't. I put up my blocks, squeezing my nails into my palms to ensure he can't read me.

"When I get my blood into you, when you have the blood of the twelve in you, you won't be able to block me, Eve. Shall I give you a demonstration?"

I try to pull away. I don't want to have his blood in me.

"Please don't," I say and shrink away.

"Oh, I think so. Here," he says and runs a nail over his wrist, drawing a thin line of blood. "It doesn't take much, my blood is so powerful." He forces his wrist to my mouth and I can't help but take some of his blood onto my lips and tongue. Before I know it, I'm under some kind of drug-like spell, my body numb, my senses focused in on his wrist and the blood that drips from his wound.

"Yes, that's it, Eve. Drink a bit more."

Then he lifts me up and I'm helpless to resist because of his blood, and he pulls down the shoulder to my dress and bites me. His mouth is cold on my skin, the pain of his teeth sharp. He feeds only for a brief moment and then lets me drop back to my seat. I see into his mind when he steps away, see myself momentarily from his point of view, how my head leans against Michel's shoulder, how Michel tries to hold me up, his brow creased with concern, his lips pressed thin.

It's so good, isn't it? Soren says to me in my mind.

"Michel, feed on her just a bit. Then feed her your blood as well."

Michel complies, biting me over his mark, taking only a mouthful of my blood. He presses his own wrist to my mouth after he's made a wound there and I swallow, unable to resist.

The three of us are connected. Soren takes us back, far back in time to when he sent Marguerite on her quest to find and turn the de Cernay twins.

He's away in Germany and can't be with her, and so he sends her to find them and turn them for him. He plans to start a coven in France and Carcassonne is his desired location. He needs servants who know the area and can get a safe home for him and his entourage.

He'd do it himself, but he finds that using a woman to enslave men is one of the easiest and most fool-proof approaches to gaining their compliance. Men are such slaves to their cocks and hearts. He thought women were slaves to the heart, but men are even more so. They're such weaklings when it comes to cunts and their attractions.

Marguerite was one of his favorite mortals, and when he turned her, she became his primary lover. He'd grown quite fond of her because she couldn't be compelled. He had to spar with her mentally, use pain and threats, use coercion and promises, use pleasure and love, to control her and even then, he failed more often that not. It was that which made him love her —he realizes that when he sees me with Michel and Julien.

They can't help but fall in love with me because they have to treat me like a person – one who looks almost identical to their first love, Danielle .

When he comes back to Carcassonne to find her and see the results of her seduction, he learns she was burned at the stake by the very brothers he hoped to have as his servants.

He is livid when he realizes that the young whelp of a priest and his warrior-brother had the audacity to kill Marguerite. Burn her at the stake like a common witch? She was a princess from the Norse family – the daughter of kings!

He wanted the brothers enslaved, but he wanted her to be their constant source of torture. He misjudged her ability to keep them both under her spell.

He failed. He finds the charred remnants of her bones and takes them with him, keeping them safe in a golden casket until one day in the future when they will once again be of use to him – when she will once again return to him and be his plaything and servant. Until then, he plans on torturing the brothers as often as possible as just retribution for their crime.

He lets Michel and I separate from his mind so that I'm back in the room with Michel at my side and Julien watching me from across the table, concern in his blue eyes. Michel and Julien will play a role in the future he has planned, only because he's become fond of Michel. A priest who has fallen – Soren can't resist him. Michel still believes, even after everything. He still longs for a place in the Church. Soren's promised him one, as his own High Priest. As his Pope. Michel couldn't be one among humans because of his vampirism, but now, in his ascended state, he is no longer in danger from mere mortals. Only Soren can destroy him.

Together, the three of them will rule the new Church. The Twelve will rule the world. I'll make that possible.

I'll comply, Soren thinks, because when it comes time, Soren will kill them both if I don't. He's counting on my love for them both to make me help him gain power.

He knows that I want to kill him. He knows that Michel has promised to help me. It doesn't matter what the two of us plan. In the end, he knows I *will* submit. That whatever little plan we have to use against him, I won't let him kill Michel.

He's counting on it.

CHAPTER 28

"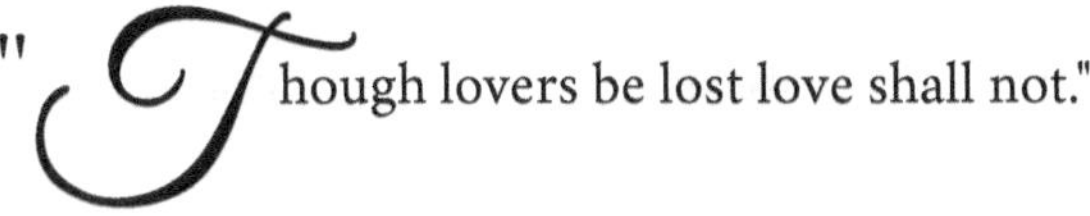hough lovers be lost love shall not."

Dylan Thomas

SOREN SAYS nothing for a few moments as Michel and I recover from sharing Soren's and each other's blood. We're speechless, for the experience is far too intimate. I feel as if I've had sex with them both, without the pleasure, for it puts me right into their point of view, into their bodies and them into mine. Now I know why drinking a human's blood is so sexual to vampires.

Once we recover enough to speak, the five of us leave the dining room and sit by the fireplace, the three men talking about the Council and its plans.

While I listen, Michel rubs my shoulder, then strokes my neck affectionately. I think of being in Soren's mind. He didn't hide his thoughts from us. Soren *knows* Michel and I are planning to destroy him, but he doesn't care. He knows we must try. He also believes that ultimately, he'll use me to keep Michel from doing it himself and he'll use Michel or Julien – or both – to keep me from doing it.

He figures the bond we three share will be all he needs to keep himself safe, no matter what scheme we cook up.

Our task will be to find a way to kill him where he can't use us against each other.

As I sit at Michel's side, I dig my fingernails into my palms and it's then I know Soren is no Ancient. He *is* a fallen angel just as Terri suspected – or at least, he sees himself that way. He took physical form and was made a vampire in a moment of weakness with a female vampire he knew.

He doesn't care. He loves being a vampire, loves the connection to mortals he feels by having a body and requiring our blood to keep alive. He thinks it's the final joke against a god who cast him out of heaven. The greatest joke of all – he, an angel, forced to worship humans by a god who loved us more than the perfect creatures he created first, now drinks the blood of those very mortals who replaced him in God's heart.

His own brand of heavenly-father vengeance.

Now, with me under his control, he thinks he can create a new pantheon of gods from other fallen angel/vampires and reign over us all.

Finally, with Soren no longer apparently interested in harassing me, we leave, each couple going to our own rooms on the second floor. Michel closes the door behind me and turns the lock. I stand in the semi-darkness by the fireplace and wait for him. It's late, but I wait to see if he has something else planned for us. I don't need to feed now – not after drinking both his and Soren's blood. The way I feel from Soren's blood alone is like ten times the effect of Michel or Julien's.

Michel comes right to me and embraces me, kissing me, his passion overwhelming me and I can't help but respond. But just when I think he's going to push me down onto the floor and ravish me, he stops and presses his forehead against mine.

"Now do you believe?"

I pull back and look in his eyes. "Believe what?"

"That angels are real. That there is a God."

I say nothing. Soren identifies himself as a fallen angel. One of the two hundred around the world who took physical form as shape shifters after a battle with heaven.

"I thought the fallen angels were cast into the pit. That's what the Bible says..."

"It was a figurative pit, Eve. Being separated from each other and from God, cast onto the mortal plane was hell for them. They've been seeking some kind of heaven to replace it ever since."

"I take it 'The Twelve' are all vampires, like Soren?"

"Yes. It's the key to their creating a new heaven, using the Church to give them access to worshippers, and you to channel that worship so they can take power. They can do small things individually – shape shift, heal wounds, manipulate matter on a small scale, but nothing big that would impress a humanity inured to special effects, nuclear bombs and trips to the moon. They need to do something impressive to really show their powers and gain believers but they need to be connected to really mass their individual power together into one force."

"And that's my role? Collect that power through sharing their blood?"

He nods. "Soren is planning his own version of Ascension, using the Twelve and you. Do it in front of a mass of worshippers, use the sharing of blood to pool their powers. Impress the worshippers. Do that over and over until he has the whole flock believing he's a god. That they're all gods. A new pantheon, like the Roman gods before Christianity."

"They're not gods. They just have a way to manipulate matter."

"What *is* a god if not precisely that?"

I say nothing for a moment, trying to process this. Michel brushes the hair from my cheek, tucking it behind my ear.

"How do we stop him?"

Michel tilts his head. "I can't tell you."

"I just go into this blind?"

"Yes. Your ignorance of the plan is key."

"You said that to me before. I ended up brain damaged, living in Ipswich."

"This time, there's no alternative. We *have* to do this. Blackstone has struck." He sighs. "If humans can't find a way to stop the plague, the whole of civilization will fall and vampires will claim Dominion. Soren wants to strike Blackstone and the Council members who support it first. We have a way to kill them all or gain their compliance. Then, Soren will start locally, displaying feats of power to collect followers. Once he has power over Blackstone and the Church, he'll be in a position to claim Ascendance for himself and The Twelve. That's all I can tell you."

"We'll stop him before that happens."

"That's my plan. And that's all I'll tell you. Now," he says and bends down to kiss my neck. "You did very well tonight. You were obedient enough at times and resistant enough at times to convince Soren you were really willing to be my pet. He's counting on it."

I nod and play with a button on his shirt while he strokes my hair. I wait for him to do whatever he will do. He tilts my head up and looks in my eyes.

"I want you. *Now*."

The abrupt turn in his demeanor, the sound of urgency in his voice makes me almost shudder with desire.

"I can't believe I'm doing this," I say, guilt and a touch of sadness suddenly welling up in me. I bite my lip for emotion is rising in me, bringing tears to my eyes.

He stops what he's doing. "Shh," he whispers in my ear. "Eve, you *love* me. You *want* me. That's the only thing that's kept me going despite everything that's happened. Don't feel guilt for your love and desire. It's good," he says and kisses me softly. "It's pure."

Then he kisses me and he must do something to calm my emotions, because I feel acceptance, the guilt and sadness dissipating.

He opens himself to me and I feel a rush of warmth from him.

He loves me...

CHAPTER 29

" _L_ ove is a springtime plant that perfumes everything with its hope, even the ruins to which it clings."

Gustave Flaubert

THE NEXT DAY, Michel, Soren and Julien are out on some business, leaving me alone. After I dress for the day in one of Michel's gowns, I play my entire repertory, and then read for a while. Finally, I wander around the mansion, bored out of my mind. A guard stands at the window, watching the grounds and the road outside the mansion. There are other homes just as rich along the streets bordering Soren's, with the same tall stone walls with barbed wire. I stand behind the guard and examine the yard, noticing several guards patrolling the perimeter of the grounds. A horse and cart pull up and waits at the gate. A guard goes to speak with the driver and then passes the cart on.

It drives up and stops in front of the rear service door and a couple of men in uniforms emerge with large tool boxes in hand. One of them wearing a cap and sunglasses sees me, then pulls his equipment into the hallway outside the library.

"Eve, come with me." When I stay where I am, he grabs my arm. "I need to speak to you."

I frown. When I look up, he removes his sunglasses.

It's Dylan.

"Come to the back door."

He lets go of my arm. I follow him to the rear entry, knowing I probably shouldn't leave but I do anyway. One of the guards pulls a crossbow and points it at him and Dylan immediately holds his hands up, and he uses that strange power I saw him use once before to send the weapon flying, the guard falling to the floor in a heap. Dylan goes to the man and touches his neck like he did to the men in the park. Then he turns to me and pulls me out the rear door and into the cart, pushing me down, covering me with a tarp while another man drives the cart away. I glance out the back of the cart and see a number of Soren's guards running after us, but they're too slow and we're outside the gates and driving down the road before they can respond.

Dylan turns my face to his. "Eve, just keep quiet and do what I say."

I nod and lay on the hard floor of the cart as it jostles over the road, wondering who the heck Dylan is working with.

WE DRIVE for some time along the coast road, past an old cemetery and stop at a small park by the sea. Outside, it's very warm for this time of year. Dylan ushers me out of the cart. He points to a small seating area along a sidewalk looking out over the water. I walk over to the bench and glance around. A few meters away stands a woman with her back to me. When she turns, I don't recognize her. She smiles at me and walks over to where I stand.

"Eve," she says. "It's been so long. I know you don't recognize me. I'm Terri Starr. I worked with you at the SCU before the accident."

I look closely in her eyes, but I don't remember her. She has large brown eyes, wide cheeks, and short steel-grey haircut in a masculine style.

She embraces me, and it feels so strange to be hugging her – a complete stranger.

"I'm sorry, Eve, but all this cloak and dagger stuff is necessary."

I nod and follow her and Dylan down a path to a small cottage on the beach and enter the whitewashed house that feels like it belongs in California instead of Boston. Inside the home, we sit at a small wooden table on a quiet patio.

Terri and I sit in silence and watch as Dylan prepares tea. Sunlight shines on his skin, the paleness contrasting with his dark hair. He bends over the small jade-green teapot and swirls the hot water inside. He stirs the tea and then looks up at us, smiling.

"May I offer you some tea?"

Terri nods and I do the same. I see a very sharp sword in a scabbard on his hip. A Samurai sword.

Dylan pours the amber liquid into our cups, and then sits back on his seat. We sip at the fragrant jasmine liquid and the scent calms me.

"I wanted to see you, to talk to you about what's happening," he says.

"I thought you were working for Blackstone."

"I am, but on behalf of the Council. We know you're with Soren and Michel. He's busy preparing for conquest. We have a plan to stop him."

"Michel has a plan as well," I say. "But I don't know the details."

"Michel can't be trusted any longer," Dylan says. "We have to move on our own."

"You don't think Michel will follow through on his plan? I thought it was the *Council's* plan."

"He can't be trusted. We're moving forward. We need you. We think Michel is now truly siding with Soren. That he's seen Soren and the Twelve as the lesser of two evils."

In all honesty, I don't know what to believe any more. I can't imagine that Michel sees Soren's rule as the better choice. He *hates* Soren.

A breeze blows through the courtyard making a wind chime sound. My anxiety dissipates as I listen to its soft melody. I close my eyes and try to imagine what life would be like with Soren as a god ruling over us. Probably not much better than if vampires ruled us in Dominion.

We sit for a few moments and I sip at the last of my tea and feel a heavy weight of sadness descend on me. Dylan reaches out and squeezes my arm, but I pull my arm away, not wanting anyone to take away my feelings, however bad they might be.

"Now, we have to talk about the plan."

"What plan?"

"The plan to kill Soren."

"If you tell me the plan, Soren will find out. Michel will find out. He's making me share his blood with his group of would-be gods."

"We have a way to stop them from reading you, Eve," Dylan says. "Even when you share blood with them, you'll be a blank to them. You'll forget it until the right time. Then, when you hear a code word, it will come back to you. You'll know what to do."

"I can't be compelled."

"This doesn't involve compulsion."

He turns and smells the breeze. I look out at the courtyard and smell it too – the salty scent of the sea. Finally, I turn back to Dylan.

"So, tell me about this plan."

He tilts his head. "I already did."

"What do you mean? You were going to tell me the plan."

"I did."

"No you didn't!"

Dylan smiles at me. "I told you everything. Then, I made you forget. Now, you'll only remember when you hear the right phrase."

"I can't be compelled!" I say, frowning.

"You can't, but your memories can be ..." he says and frowns. "Short-circuited. Michel tried something similar but he had to destroy the neurons involved in your memories. We're only temporarily rerouting them until you hear the right combination of words. Infiltrating Blackstone has given us access to the latest in neuro-biotechnology."

"So you're not going to tell me your plans for me..."

"I did Eve. You agreed to them." He shakes his head sadly. "It's to protect you and the plan. You must understand. As soon as you leave this place, you won't remember we even talked about a plan. You'll think we just talked about our families. Our losses."

I sigh. "I hate this."

"Don't hate, Eve. This is what you've wanted to do. Michel won't do what's necessary, because he loves you too much, but we will and you will."

"How do you know he won't?"

"We can't take the risk he won't."

"What happens when we stop Soren? Will the Council be able to stop Dominion?"

"We don't know, but with Soren and the Twelve neutralized, we have only Blackstone to fight. Soren and the others want power. They're going to use you to take it. We have to prevent that. Some of us have to sacrifice. You're willing to sacrifice to stop it, just as our mother was."

I sit and look at my hands. "I agreed to help?"

"Yes. You'll remember at the right moment. Now, it's time for you to go back to your little heaven."

Dylan takes my hand and the three of us return to the cart. Terri embraces me and I take one more look at her.

"I know you don't remember me," she says. "One day, maybe we'll work together again."

I sigh and Dylan helps me inside the cart, covering me up again. We drive off and I watch Terri recede into the distance.

The driver takes me back to the mansion and drops me off at the front gate, driving off when guards run out to meet me. Michel emerges from the door and comes to me and grabs my arm, clearly angry. He turns to the guard.

"You should have called me the moment anyone approached the building. I told you, the moment someone approached her."

"We did. They said barely anything and then were gone."

Michel pulls me into the mansion. "Do I have to put a leash on you?"

I shake my head as he pulls me up the stairs to our second floor rooms.

"I was taken."

"My guards say you went willingly."

"Yes," I say. "I went with my brother. I have a brother, Michel."

"I know who Dylan is."

I frown. "How do you know?"

Michel shakes his head. He pushes me onto the bed.

"He was worried about me," I say. "He convinced Terri to take me away so he could make sure I was all right."

"Eve, you can't just go without my leave. Not even with Dylan. How do I know he hasn't been compromised?"

"He's with the *Council*, Michel."

He looks in my face, in my eyes. "Don't lie to me, Eve. Please."

"I'm *not*."

He sits beside me on the bed, turning my face to him. "Look in my eyes."

I do. We sit in silence and he grips my hand tightly. I can tell he's upset.

He just sits there and watches me. Then, I hear him exhale heavily.

"I was so *afraid*..." He leans forward and pulls me close and kisses me, his kiss almost desperate. The pressure of his lips on mine, the softness of them, his tongue wet against mine as it pushes between my lips and into my mouth finally overwrites the sadness I feel from seeing Dylan.

"You're alive," he says, stroking my hair. "I thought whoever took you would kill you. Eve, you just can't ever leave this place without my permission. Why *did* you?"

"I don't know," I reply. "It was Dylan. He's my brother."

He kisses me again, running his hands over my body.

"I'm so glad you're safe."

"He wanted to see me. We met and talked about our families. That's all."

The door opens and Soren strides into the room, his face dark, his brow creased. I'm still in Michel's embrace and we're kissing, but we stop when Soren comes to the bedside.

"What the fuck happened? I get this panicked call from one of my guards that Eve was abducted?"

"She's fine. She was with Dylan," Michel says, brushing hair from my cheek. "He wanted to see her."

"He should have contacted me. He can't just come and take her."

"Would you have let her go with him?"

"Of course not. Michel, you must ensure she obeys the rules. We could lose her in the blink of an eye."

"You think I don't know that?" Michel replies, his voice tight.

"They took her without any difficulty."

"She's not used to having her movements controlled. Yet."

"I'm very angry, Eve," Soren says and rubs his forehead. "Michel was very scared. Look at him, see the fear in his eyes. He was afraid he'd never see you again. You should be whipped."

"She made a mistake," Michel says, looking in my eyes. I nod.

"I'll whip her if you don't."

Michel turns to Soren. "She made a mistake. I *will* punish her, but I want her in a good frame of mind for later."

"Yes, of course, by all means, punish her later," Soren says and laughs. He sighs and shakes his head. "Eve, you really deserve a good spanking right now. Consider yourself lucky."

"Thank you, my Lord," Michel says to Soren, his voice properly subservient. He pulls me into his arms, his face pressed into my neck, his mouth covering his bite mark.

Soren chuckles softly. "Enjoy."

LATER THAT NIGHT, I attend a meeting of 'The Twelve' to discuss the plans to reveal Soren's powers to the congregation in Boston. It's part of his plan to gain followers and amass power. I was supposed to attend with Michel, but he and Soren are in a meeting and have been delayed. Vasquez picks me up instead in his cart. We drive through the deserted streets of Boston. People stay in off the streets for there is a heavy police presence on horseback to enforce order.

"What's going to happen? Why am I attending?"

Vasquez leans closer to me. "You must join with the Twelve today. Try out those skills of yours we value so highly."

"I drink their blood and they drink mine?"

"Precisely. We need a test run of your abilities. We don't want any snags when we do this publicly."

I stare out the window at the scenery and then my stomach is all butterflies as we approach the Cathedral of the Holy Cross. It's a beautiful old cathedral, and I'm nervous, wondering what it will be like to drink the blood of twelve fallen angel-Ancient-vampires and share their consciousness. If what I felt with Soren is any indication, it will be intense.

I *don't* want to do this, but I know I must.

Before Michel left for his meeting, we shared blood, because he wants to be able to access my mind at all times, to make sure I'm all right. He then calmed my nerves, assuring me that this dry run would be important. Soren has to believe I'll do it – that I'll help him get power. Otherwise, he'll kill me and create someone else, but he wants to seize the day now that Blackstone has struck.

I want to kill him. Nothing more. But I'll cooperate because I trust Michel. Despite the fact he hasn't told me everything from the start, I know now that it was to protect me. He wants to stop Soren as much as I do. He's wanted this since Soren killed Danielle so long ago.

Vasquez and I arrive and enter the cathedral through the side entrance and go immediately into the nave where the Twelve and their entourages have already gathered.

They turn expectantly when Vasquez and I arrive.

"My Lords, please excuse our delay," Vasquez says, all obeisant to them. "But Lord Soren has been detained due to some urgent business and will be another fifteen minutes or so. Please, partake of refreshments, if you need any. We will get underway soon."

Vasquez leads me to a seat next to a large throne on a dais at the front of the boardroom. There's a chair on either side of the throne, where I expect Michel and Julien will sit as Soren's two lieutenants. My own seat is a stool to the right of Michel. Vasquez sits on Michel's chair and glances around the room.

I'm dressed in something a bit more conservative than the usual revealing gown Michel prefers, but still, I look like I'm attending a medieval ball rather than a secret meeting in a cathedral in the center of Boston. Michel directed that my hair should be styled in an up-do. I sit quietly and wait, my stomach in knots as I survey the Twelve, as Soren refers to them. They're his equals, vampires, Fallen Angels all of them. Why they would choose this existence I don't understand except, as Soren said, to get revenge on the god who punished them because of their refusal to worship mortals.

Now, they feed off us like cattle and want our subordination as their worshippers.

I don't know what Michel's planning but I hope it works. I can't stand the thought that these monsters will be our gods. No wonder the Romans thought the gods were devious and under them, life was precarious. They are monsters with more power than morals.

Finally, the doors open and a balding priest in vestments rushes in and goes right to Vasquez. He bends down and whispers in his ear and Vasquez nods. The priest leaves, closing the doors behind him.

Vasquez stands and addresses the Twelve.

"There's been a delay. Our Lord Soren and his entourage were attacked on their way here. Lord Soren is unharmed, of course, but Michel has been injured in an attack with Molotov Cocktail bombs infused with liquid silver. I'm told his injuries are not serious. They will arrive momentarily."

A murmur rises from the Twelve and their advisors as everyone discusses this development. My heart races when I think of Michel being injured in the attack. It must have been Blackstone.

Vasquez leans over to me and takes my hand. "Don't worry, Eve. Michel's wounds were minor."

Finally, a few moments later, the double doors open once more to admit Julien and Michel, their wings extended fully. Michel limps over to the dais at the front of the room, Julien holding him by the arm. His clothes are burned, the skin on one cheek scorched and he has a large wound on his calf. I stand and concern flows through me. He sits beside me on the chair and immediately, I bend down and pull the ripped fabric away from his calf.

"It's nothing, Eve," he says, waving me off. "A piece of glass cut me and some liquid silver burned me. I'll heal."

"It must hurt."

I ignore him and go to the anteroom where there's a small kitchenette and search through the cupboards to find a basin and a roll of paper towels. I fill the basin with warm water and take them to the room, kneeling down at Michel's feet.

"Let me wash your skin."

"It's really not necessary," he says, but I insist. I remove his shoe and sock, then daub the wound that runs from his mid-calf to his ankle with a moistened paper towel to wash off the remnants of silver nitrate from burned skin. Michel grimaces and inhales sharply from the pain. As I kneel administering to Michel's wound, his foot in my hand as I clean the damaged skin, I feel the eyes of the Twelve on me. I can almost feel their thoughts from here, despite not having drunk their blood. Michel looks down at me indulgently.

Then the doors open again and Soren enters. I know because someone announces him and when I crane my head around, I see all the Twelve stand and bow low to him.

"Stand and bow, Eve," Michel commands. I do, standing in front of Michel's chair on the dais, and feel his hand on my shoulder for support as he stands behind me. Soren strides in, nodding his head to everyone he passes and then he steps up onto the dais and stands in front of his throne. His wings are fully extended as well and he looks formidable, dressed in something vaguely resembling military fatigues, as if he's always prepared for war.

"Please be seated," he says after folding his wings and seating himself, his arms outstretched on the armrests of his ornate wooden throne. The Twelve and their advisors follow his lead. I return to my ministrations to Michel's wounds, which are already healing before my eyes.

Finally, Soren turns to Michel and me.

"How fitting that Eve is kneeling at your feet like a good slave, Michel. I know it pleases my brethren to see her so subservient to you. I can feel their pleasure from where I sit for they can feel your love, Eve. They long to feel such love from their own mortals. Once we join through blood, it will be even more amazing to share your emotions for him. Speaking of which, Eve, I'm impatient. Let's get this started."

I put my paper towel away and sit on my stool, smoothing my skirts.

Soren motions to one of his servants at the side of the room, who brings a tray with a large glass goblet in the center and what looks like a very sharp knife. I imagine they'll bleed me and each other and then we'll all drink from the goblet. My hands are shaking as I wait.

"You first," Soren says and extends his hand. I take it and stand in front of him. He takes the knife and holds my wrist over the goblet. Then he runs the knife's edge over my skin, beside the scars from my own self-inflicted wounds. The image of them side by side makes me feel so small and helpless. Here I am, some instrument of power by these fallen angels, a girl who hurt herself to deal with her pain.

I grit my teeth as the blade slices through my skin and my blood drips into the goblet. He lets it drip for quite a while – not quite a pint of blood, but close. Then he runs his fingers over the wound and it closes up so that there's only a thin pink seam where the cut once was. He follows with his own blood and then goes from one of the Twelve to the next until the goblet is quite full. Finally, he takes some of Michel and Julien's blood.

"This will unite us as we once were united," he says, and then drinks from the goblet before passing it to the others. "As we drink, let us rejoice that we are once again as we were before we were cast out, condemned to this plane of existence."

After Michel and Julien, I'm last to drink and there's only a mouthful left. I swallow it down and when I do, the effect is immediate. I feel as if I've been hit by a truck of emotion, my body almost slammed with the minds of thirteen fallen angels, and I'm nearly struck unconscious from the intensity of their emotions as they connect once again after thousands of years alone. I feel little else but their euphoria, their ecstasy, and my knees give out. Michel grabs me and holds me in his arms. I have no idea what's going on in the room around us, for my hearing is dulled, the sounds drowned out by the minds meeting in what feels like my own skull.

This seems to go on and on forever, and there are no words to describe how I feel and what I experience. Finally, it's too much and darkness closes in.

CHAPTER 30

"A man that studieth revenge keeps his own wounds green."

Francis Bacon

I WAKE up long after the meeting with Soren and the Twelve when Michel sits on the bed beside me.

"Eve," he says, a hand shaking my shoulder.

"What?" I sit up and rub my eyes. "Is something wrong?"

"Soren wants us back tonight for a special mass."

"Mass?" I say, frowning. I look him over. He's wearing vestments and a clerical collar, a large wooden cross on a thin leather strap around his neck. "Don't tell me you're going to say Mass?"

"He wants me to. I'm the only priest—"

"Former priest."

"Eve, once God has you, He has you forever."

"How can you do this?" I say, anger filling me. "Pretending to be his priest. Or, do you really want this? Do you really want to be his High Priest? Head his bastardized church?"

He sits in silence for a moment and I can see I've upset him. He takes his hand away from my cheek, where he's been stroking my skin with his thumb.

Finally, he exhales and leans in closer to me, pressing his forehead against mine. It makes my heart soften.

"Please just *trust* me," he whispers.

"I'm sorry," I say. "You have to understand…"

"I do. Now please, try to follow the rules from now on. I don't want to have to remind you in public. Not tonight."

"Yes, my Lord," I say, nodding. He kisses me and it's such a tender kiss, so gentle that it makes my throat constrict. He's afraid for me.

"Why are you afraid?" I say.

He shakes his head and just kisses me again, this time more intense, as if he's trying to make me forget his fear and my own. A thrill of desire goes through me when he joins with me, and I want him right now, but we have to go.

"Just knowing you want me is enough for now," he says. "Later tonight, when we come back."

I smile and tuck his hair behind his ear but I know he's afraid there won't be a later tonight and I wonder if this isn't something dangerous – what we'll be doing at the cathedral.

"Wear the long black dress in the armoire and put your hair up."

I nod and get up from the bed, dressing quickly.

He stands watching me, and I don't feel lust from him. I only feel fear.

When I'm finished, I go to the bathroom and wash my face. He stands in the doorway, leaning against the doorjamb, his brow furrowed.

"No makeup," he says.

"Why?" I say and look at his reflection in the mirror. "My Lord?"

"Just don't."

I shrug. I look much younger without makeup but he must want that. I brush my hair and twist it up, securing it with a few clips. I turn to him and hold my arms out at my sides.

"Well, here I am, for what it's worth."

"You're priceless, Eve."

I smile. "You're exaggerating."

"No, I'm not." He comes to me and puts one arm around my waist, pulling me against him, and gently he pulls a few tendrils of my hair out of my makeshift bun. "You look ... angelic. The way they're supposed to be."

"Obviously, I'm no angel."

"You are. Now, let's go. Just follow my lead. Remember to keep your eyes down."

"What are you planning?"

He places his finger over my lips. "Shh," he says. "Just obey tonight."

I nod. "Yes, my Lord."

WE DRIVE to the cathedral in the old vehicle rigged up with a hydrogen cell battery. It's a rough ride through a dark city, only a few lights in a few locations where once there were thousands of offices lit all night. We arrive at the Holy Cross Cathedral and once more I'm struck by a deep sadness, remembering the last time I was here, for Mass the Sunday before my mother died. I stop at the door at the side entrance reserved for clergy.

"Don't be afraid," Michel says and squeezes my hand. "Tonight's just a dry run. There will be only a small congregation to see how things will go. Just do as you're told and we'll be finished soon and will go back home. Soren's not planning anything big for a while."

"You were nervous earlier, my Lord," I say. "I could feel it."

"There is always danger, Eve. I'm always concerned for your safety, given who and what you are. We'll be fine."

He pulls me inside and we go to a small office, where we sit for a moment. Finally Soren enters and strides over to us. He's dressed in something military, an old Roman uniform with blood-red leather breastplate and split leather skirt, greaves and has a Roman crested helmet under his arm.

"Well, here they are, my lovely couple. Priest and Priestess looking all holy and ready for Mass."

I want to shout at him that I'm not his priestess, but Michel squeezes my hand and I avert my eyes.

"Soren," Michel says. "I imagine we will proceed as we discussed."

"Yes." Soren turns to me and takes my chin in his hand so that I have to look in his eyes. "Tonight, Eve, we'll test-drive your channeling powers. I have a congregation filled with believers. I want to perform a little miracle so they can be given proof of my godly powers. After we share blood, the Twelve and I will join our powers and let's just say, a few sparks will fly. My followers need to see me smiting evildoers. This country seems to love seeing them suffer. I'll give them some and you'll help channel their adoration and faith, giving me even more power."

I nod and say nothing, a bit scared now at this ability I have.

"Good. Let's get this show on the road."

He puts on his helmet and Michel and I follow him out of the small office and through a narrow hallway to the side entrance to the altar where the Twelve are already assembled, standing with their wings unfurled. Soren unfurls his own as does Michel and I see Julien standing beside the altar, waiting, looking like a Roman warrior wearing a uniform similar to Soren.

Soren takes his place on a throne behind the altar, with Michel to his right and Julien to his left. I stand between Soren and Michel. Michel takes my hand and leads me to the altar where a crystal goblet sits on a gilded cloth. He takes a sharp knife and cuts my wrist, letting blood drip into it as we did yesterday. Then, Michel takes the vessel and goes to each of the Twelve in turn and repeats this until the goblet is once again filled. We repeat the process. I drink last from the goblet and an overwhelming sense of emotion fills me as I connect with all thirteen.

I barely hear what Michel says as he speaks to the congregation, some words of Latin mixed in with English, something about the blood of the sacrifice uniting all the angels of the Lord but I'm too overcome with the Twelve and Soren to really make much of it. I stand staring out at the congregation and I can feel their awe when they regard Soren and the Twelve with their wings outstretched. In that moment, I understand how awe-inspiring the sight must be to a group of humans in fear from the calamity around them, the red rain, the destruction of technology, and now, the apparent return to earth of angels.

Then I see what Soren is planning – he's amassing the power of his flock's worship, joining it with the powers of the Twelve, and will create a miracle in front of his follower's eyes. There are several hundred in the nave. I can almost feel each and every one of their emotions, their fear and worship entering me, making my heart pound. I glance to my left and right and Soren and the Twelve have their eyes closed as they feel the congregation's worship fill them, making them stronger.

The side door opens and soldiers dressed in uniform with weapons enter, and following them are a dozen men dressed in prison orange. They're shackled together in chains and shamble inside the nave, their faces dark. They stop in front of the altar and wait, glancing around nervously.

"My children," Soren says, his voice booming as if coming from a loudspeaker. "Before you, see twelve sinners. They're all killers and rapists and child molesters. They have forsaken the commandments for their own pleasure and gain. They deserve holy fire, and that they shall receive."

Then Soren raises his arms, his hands inches apart, and I see something bright between his palms. It's a small spark of light, tiny, perhaps as big as a grain of sand. But soon, it grows larger, now the size of a marble, spinning on its axis, burning bright as an acetylene torch. He spreads his legs as if the spark of energy weighs a great deal, his face a grimace, the muscles of his bare arms flexing with strain.

The spark grows even larger, perhaps the size of a baseball, the light from it so bright I have to squint. I step back, alarmed, but I can't tear my eyes away, and neither can the congregation. They gasp in shock as the spark is now the size of a basketball. The ball of lightning-like energy hums and buzzes, the scent of ozone filling the room.

What is it?

I have no idea what's happening, only that it's like a small nuclear reaction is taking place between Soren's outstretched palms, the white fire-like plasma forming strange shapes as it grows and morphs.

Soren speaks, his voice booming through the nave.

"And the fourth angel poured out his vial upon the sun; and power was given unto him to scorch men with fire. And men were scorched with great heat."

Then he throws the spark, which is now the size of a beach ball, forward and it stops in mid air above the shackled prisoners and then explodes, showering down onto those below, incinerating them in front of us. They writhe and scream, flames burning them almost instantly into charred statues, the scent of roasted human flesh making my stomach turn.

People scream and run, but the doors are closed and they can't leave. I want to cut the connection I have with Soren and the Twelve and between all of us and the congregation, but I can't and now Soren raises his hands and everyone stops, turning to watch him. He's shining like the fire he cast into the congregation, so bright my eyes hurt.

"I am your God," he says, his voice so loud it sounds as if it's coming from everywhere at the same time. "I am the God of War reborn and you will bow down and worship me or die."

He glares down at the remaining congregants, who crouch or stand in mute horror. Finally, they start to bow, falling to their knees, their hands on the floor in front of their faces the way Muslims bow down in prayer.

He rises up over the altar, levitating, as if his power is growing even stronger as the awe of the congregation increases and I'm as helpless as a baby to stop what's happening.

It's too much and I fall to my knees, unable to hold myself up any longer.

~

MICHEL COMES up behind me and puts his hands under my arms, lifting me up so that I stand in front of him. "It's okay, Eve," he whispers in my ear. "Not much longer now."

Then, when everyone is on their knees before us, their heads bowed, Soren descends and his feet touch down to the marble floor. He clenches and unclenches his hands as the glow of light dims and then he turns to the exit. Michel holds me up as we follow him back to the side room. Following behind us, the Twelve. Julien takes up the rear.

"Well, that was fun!" Soren says, rubbing his hands together as if he's just performed some kind of parlor trick instead of controlling some force of nature and killing a dozen people in front of us. "Tell me that wasn't fun, Eve! We smote some bad guys, regaled the congregation with some shock and awe. I think it was a resounding success. Imagine the talk around town tomorrow! I can just see the headlines – *'Mars, the Roman god reborn, reveals power, smites evildoers!'*"

I ignore Soren, unable to speak. Michel seats me on a chair against the wall and kneels down before me, holding my hand in his, brushing hair from my face.

"You did really well, Eve," he says, his voice soft.

I stare at him, still reeling from joining once more with the Twelve and Soren, channeling the congregation's awe and worship. I feel as if I've been infused with electricity but at the same time, I might collapse if expected to stand on my own.

"Just imagine what we'll do in Vatican City once I take that as my residence," Soren says, a gloating expression on his face as he paces the room. "Thousands of worshippers all in one place, watching feats of wonder. We're a great team. Word of this will spread fast, people will return to the churches when they start to really believe that the old gods have returned. I may have to heal a few cripples, make the blind see. Bring the dead back to life. That sort of thing."

Julien stands off to the side of the room and watches Michel with me. Our eyes meet and I can tell he's concerned about me and doesn't like what he's seen. I wonder when either he or Michel will tell me of the plan to stop Soren – if there even is a plan.

"Tomorrow, we'll deal with Blackstone," Soren adds. "I intend to get the formula for the plague so our own scientists can control it. I don't like that Blackstone can start or stop it at will and I have no say in how it's deployed. I've asked the Chairman to add my item on the agenda at their weekly board meeting – it's a ruse of course. I just want them all in one place. Make sure you're in top form," he says to me and wags his eyebrows. "They have to know we mean business. I intend to give a small demonstration, but I'm sure by tomorrow night, they'll have heard about my miracle and powers. I doubt I'll have to do too much convincing."

"As you wish," Michel says quietly. "My Lord," he adds. Even Michel must be submissive to him.

"Good," Soren says, smiling. "Julien, make sure you put extra security in place for when we go. I don't want some crackpot soldier trying to screw things up."

Julien bows to Soren.

"Well," Soren says to one of the Twelve, the rest of whom are standing or sitting in the room, watching him. "I'm starving. I think I'd like a bit of redhead today. Who do we have on tap?"

They leave the room, filing out in Soren's wake, leaving Michel, Julien and I behind.

"Let's get you home," Michel says, helping me up. We pass Julien on the way out. He nods to me, his expression dark.

"Soon, Eve," Julien says to me. "Soon."

I look back at him as we leave the room and make our way to the exit and out to the vehicle. What does he mean, soon?

Soon this charade will be over and Soren will be dead?

Soon, he and I will be back together?

As Michel and I drive back to Soren's mansion, I wonder what the board meeting will be like.

CHAPTER 31

" 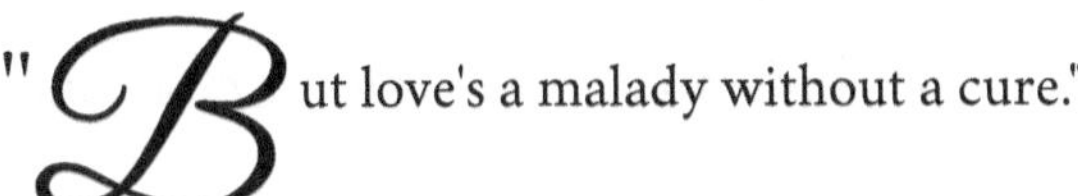 ut love's a malady without a cure."

John Dryden

THAT NIGHT, Michel assists me into our bedroom and helps me undress, but I'm absolutely so exhausted, nothing happens between us. Instead, Michel lies beside me, his arms around me while I fall asleep. I'm so tired I can't even say goodnight.

I sleep without waking for nearly twelve hours. In the morning, Michel's away on business so I eat alone at the table by the window in Michel's bedroom, looking out over the city while I drink my coffee. Michel finally returns in the late afternoon, but he's busy with meetings, and I barely see him. He slips into the room where I'm curled up on the settee with a soft blanket, dozing. I hear him close the door. He comes to my side and bends down to kiss me, tilting my head up with his finger under my chin.

"How are you?" he says, his expression concerned. "I'm sorry to put you through more, but it's important that Blackstone sees you're with

Soren and the Twelve. They need a demonstration of your powers. It will make them realize he means business."

"Blackstone's board of directors will agree to meet with him?"

"The Board already agreed because their spies were in the congregation yesterday. I imagine Soren's little show of fiery power was convincing enough that his request to attend was granted."

LATER THAT NIGHT, the vampires and Ancients on Blackstone's board sit in the boardroom of one of Blackstone's office buildings surrounded by images of the military corporation's many training facilities around the world. They're convening in a special session to meet with Soren and the Twelve. While we all wait for Soren to appear, I sit with Michel and Julien in one corner. I overhear them discuss the plague, which is spreading every day, bringing more and more of the world to its knees.

Then the side door opens and in walks my brother, dressed in some kind of black uniform with Kevlar armor.

I frown, shocked to see Dylan here. He comes behind me but Julien stops him, one hand on his chest.

"Hey," Dylan says, holding up his hands as if in surrender. "I just want to say hello to my sister."

Finally, Julien nods. Dylan leans down to whisper in my ear.

"Hello, lovely sister."

"Hello," I say back, but a sense of tension grips my body. Michel leans over to me, a look of concern on his face.

"What did he say?"

"Just hello, lovely sister."

Michel turns to Dylan, who leans against the wall behind the chairman.

For some reason, I reach to my throat where I feel the crucifix Michel gave me dangling beneath my leather collar, and take it in my fingers. It has a sharp pointed end, and without thinking, I press the point into my palm, hard, harder, until I feel a sharp pain and I know

I've punctured my skin. I look at my palm where the point is piercing me, and blood wells up as I continue to press down hard.

While I sit and jam the point into my skin, I try to listen to the other board members talking to each other. Dylan is standing, watching me when a scene fills my vision from the other day when I met with Terri and Dylan.

❧

We're sitting in the courtyard in the shade of a tree. Despite it being October, it feels like summer and the fragrance of the sea fills my nose. Dylan turns to me. "Eve, give me your crucifix."

I remove the crucifix from around my neck and hand it to him. He examines it and then removes a tiny vial from his pocket. Inside the vial I see what looks like a fine black powder. Dylan removes the lid and then dips the tip of the crucifix into the powder. After he seals the vial, he examines the cross.

"Amazing what nanotechnology can do." Dylan turns to me, meeting my eyes. His face is deadly serious. "This is a substance that will enter the bloodstream and replicate, building tiny copies of itself using atoms in your blood. It contains a targeted killer molecule that will seek out specific sequences of DNA in any vampire that it infects. If it locates specific sequences, and only those sequences, it destroys the vampire at the cellular level, taking over the nuclear DNA first, using it to rupture the cell wall. Tissues dissolve. The vampire disintegrates, converted to mostly plasma and protein. Anyone with that very specific sequence of DNA in their cells will be killed."

"You're going to use this against Soren?"

He nods. "And the Twelve."

"They're infected when they drink my blood."

"Yes, but even more than that. Anyone who's been turned by Soren, and anyone who's been his blood slave or shared his blood, no matter where they are, will be destroyed."

"They don't have to be directly infected?"

"No. We use quantum entanglement to create instantaneous identical state in anyone with that sequence of DNA. It doesn't matter where they are.

They could be on the other side of the universe and will still be affected, still die."

"What about me? I've shared blood with Soren twice. I'm Michel's blood slave and he and Julien were turned by Marguerite who..."

"We've tried to alter the molecule so that Michel and Julien will both be protected. We're using the same technology Soren is planning to use to kill off his enemies. We've tried to find specific sequences in Michel and Julien's DNA that will slow the effect, give their bodies time to heal, but we can't be sure if it will work for you because you don't self-heal. If Michel or Julien survive, they may be able to save you with their blood, but they'll have to drain your blood from your body entirely, and then feed you theirs so that their blood can heal you."

"But won't that..."

He inhales. "Make you a vampire?" He nods.

"I don't want to be a vampire," I say, horror filling me. "Dylan, please – don't let them turn me. If it comes to that, let me die. Promise me!"

He shakes his head. "It's not all bad, Eve. You can drink donated blood. You don't have to kill. It would be great to have you on our side as a vampire."

"I thought you wanted to eradicate vampirism like our mother did."

He turns away and exhales slowly. "I used to but how does that poem go? 'For life's a shabby subterfuge and death is deep and dark and huge,'" he says.

"Who wrote that?"

"Updike. He was right, Eve. I'd do almost anything to bring Sarah back. I don't want to lose you, too. Don't give up the chance at immortality."

I turn away. "I'll only agree to do this if you promise to stop Julien if he tries to make me a vampire. I know Michel won't turn me because he doesn't want to be a vampire either, but Julien," I say and sigh. "He will try to turn me."

"I'll do what I can," Dylan says. "I promise to try."

"Do or do not," I say. "There is no try."

He frowns. "Yoda?"

When I nod, he smiles.

"I will do everything I can to stop him. I promise."

Then, I think of something. "Soren self-heals. Why won't he be able to just heal himself of the damage the molecule does to him?"

"Too fast for even an Ancient to fight off."

"He's not an Ancient, Dylan. He's something different. He claims to be a fallen angel."

"He's an Ancient, Eve. Actually, more powerful than an Ancient because he killed his own father, who was a Nephilim, and he drank the waters of life, activating his angelic inheritance. But he's not a fallen angel. That's just a story he tells to make people fear him."

"Michel and Julien also drank it."

"And I did as well. This substance – it's what the Church was prepared to kill for, what Crusades were launched over. The Holy Grail for vampires that would allow them to day-walk and become more powerful than any other being in existence. The substance was protected by the Cathars for centuries. After the Cathars were murdered in the Crusade, it was protected by the Knights Templar and after them, by various other groups. You'll take it as well and then, we'll have a chance at preventing Dominion. You and I together were meant to do this. It was prophesized."

"What do you mean?"

"St. Therese. The Sword of Megiddo. The prophecy spoke of a double-edged sword. That's us, Eve. You and me. We can make them powerful. Or we can kill them. If we're used by someone with a corrupt heart, we will destroy them. That's what the prophecy was all about. Soren's trying to use us both. We'll destroy him."

I sit in silence for a moment, thinking about 'The Pure' mentioned in the literature in Julien's emails I read back so long ago.

"Soren isn't just an Ancient." I have a bad feeling about that. "I've been in his mind. I think you're wrong."

"Eve," he says. "Don't believe everything he tells you or even everything you think you've discovered when you've connected to him. He's the most powerful Ancient ever. He can block you or make you see and feel what he wants. He just can't compel you."

I look out at the courtyard, wishing I was still just a college Junior studying biology and the college archivist refused my request for my mother's files.

"When you hear me say, 'Hello, lovely sister', take the cross and puncture your skin with the point. A very thin coating of this nanotechnology will adhere to the cross. It will only dissolve in blood, so no matter what you do, shower, swim, as long as the cross doesn't touch blood, the material will stay on the tip. There are millions of molecules on the tip. It will take only a few moments for the molecules to start replicating, and within several heartbeats, the agent will have spread through your body. It won't harm you until Soren drinks your blood. It has to affect the progenitor first. When you share blood with Soren, the Twelve and everyone else he's sired or shared his blood with will be affected and once it goes through them, every vampire they've made and every blood slave will be instantaneously infected. It should take about five minutes for each one to die. Thousands will die immediately. It will be a massive strike against the Twelve and Soren."

I put the cross back around my neck and take in a big breath.

"I'll do it."

THIS MEMORY TAKES ONLY the briefest of seconds because I relive it in that strange time shift I experience when fighting.

So this is it. I've probably just signed my own death warrant. But I've just done what I've wanted to do since I learned that Soren killed my mother – or as I found out, that he compelled Michel and forced him to kill her. For a moment, elation fills me and I feel heat rise in my cheeks at the thought Soren will soon be dead, destroyed, a mass of denatured protein and plasma.

Then sadness fills me. It means I'll likely die. It could mean Michel and Julien die as well. It will certainly mean that every single vampire and blood slave that Soren and his Twelve created will die.

There's no going back now. Soon, my blood will be infected. I'll be teeming with nanovirus and they'll infect Soren when he drinks my blood in order to demonstrate to the board that he's more powerful than ever.

Finally, Soren enters the boardroom. We all stand while he enters and then take our places at the large table while the servants bring out a large crystal goblet like the one we used yesterday during the ceremony at the cathedral.

I sit behind Michel and behind us both stands Julien, who is acting as Michel and Soren's bodyguard for the night. There is no head of the table, but Soren sits in front of the huge floor to ceiling window with Michel at his side, just a bit behind him. His and Michel's wings are fully unfurled – emblems of their status as the most powerful beings in the room.

The Blackstone board members are seated to Soren's left and right at a round table. Each Board member is protected by a bodyguard. They all wear the Blackstone logo – a blazing white sun surrounded by a black circle.

The Chairman of the Blackstone Board is a portly man in his fifties named Sir Peter Gregoryk, from Indianapolis. He stands at his place and reads off the items to be approved, his Eastern European accent thick. I wonder what Soren is planning to do to convince the board of his new powers. Julien stands behind Michel, and I can almost feel the tension in his body at a distance.

The Chairman reads over the first item – a request from the coven leader from the south of Boston, for rights to annex the neighboring coastal areas where there's still seafood to be had. The food will go towards keeping the mortals fed, and that's a priority in these days of shortage. The assembled vampires agree to his request without discussion. He moves to the next item – something about using Blackstone's banks to safeguard vampire wealth during the plague years, and that passes without any debate as well.

I can tell Soren is barely able to wait any longer. He taps his fingers on the table as if impatient for the lower orders of business to be completed. Before the Chairman gets to the next item, Soren stands at his chair, his hands resting on the tabletop.

"I've had enough of this pissant stuff. Let's move on to my item, shall we?"

The vampires and Ancients on the board almost shrink back, turning to the Chairman to watch his response.

The Chairman, flustered by the out-of-order demand, purses his lips for a moment and turns to his fellow vampires, looking for their counsel.

"My Lord Soren, my apologies, but this is highly irregular," he says. "Usually, the board must vote on whether to amend the order of items, and only then can you speak to it."

Soren raises a hand as if deferring to the Chairman, but the side door opens and in walk the Twelve, their wings unfurled in a massive show of power. While they enter and take their places behind Soren, Julien slips behind one of the board members, looking as if he's going to the table where the tea and coffee are located.

"As you all know," Soren says, his voice firm and strong. "Vampires are hard bastards to kill. No wound can kill a vampire with the exception of wood to the heart and only after we've been staked can our limbs be severed. Until now, the only way to really destroy a vampire permanently was to first stake them, then behead them and burn their bodies, then pulverize them to dust." Soren glances around at the other vampires, who sit tense, some leaning forward, some cringing away, looks of surprise or horror on their faces.

"Now, that's changed. The Council's genetic research is very useful," Soren says. "Tonight, if you don't cooperate, I'm going to demonstrate just how useful. What I show you against one, I could use against each of you. I have a drug that will infect any vampire I choose, which will destroy them at the cellular level. The vampire will disintegrate, becoming nothing more than bodily fluids. I control this power and now demand your total compliance. I want the formula for the plague within the hour or you and all your covens will die."

I frown – this is exactly the technology Dylan and the Council are using tonight against Soren...

One of the Blackstone vampires motions to Soren.

"Get my science advisor, James," he says. "He's in the anteroom, waiting."

Julien goes to the door and calls his name. Michel leans back to me.

"That's Professor Miles Fourney, from New York. Head of research for Blackstone."

Soon, a young man in a rumpled suit with dark horn rimmed glasses enters. He looks confused. He goes to Fourney's side.

"James," Fourney says. "We have a bit of a *problem...*"

"Yes," James says, glancing around at the vampires in the room.

"Soren claims he has a drug that can make a vampire, well, dissolve. He says he'll use it unless he gets the formula for the inhibitor tonight."

"Jesus *Christ*," James says, whispering as if we won't hear him. "That wasn't our plan. We were supposed to let it run its course. What the hell is going on?"

"Change your plans, James," Soren says.

James looks up at Soren and adjusts his tie nervously. "I have to hear from the head of Blackstone first, " James says. "He's the one who funded development. I take my orders from him."

"James," Soren says. "I know you're trying to be a good employee. Let me repeat what I told Dr. Fourney. If I don't get the formula for the inhibitor in one hour, Dr. Fourney and everyone in this room will die and every vampire you've turned and every blood slave you have will die as well. Do you understand?"

"I don't believe you," James says, shaking his head. "With all due respect, no one has that kind of power."

Soren smiles. "Do you really require a demonstration?" He looks around the room. "I believe Colonel Drake from Blackstone's board of directors is connected by blood to his aide." He turns to Drake, who's frowning. "Open the door so we can speak to his aide from the other room, but don't let him in."

Julien does that, going to the door to the boardroom.

"Colonel Drake?" comes the voice of a young male. "Are you in need of assistance?"

Drake turns to Dr. Fourney. "For God's sake, tell your man to give him the fucking inhibitor!"

"I'm not releasing the formula until I hear from General Blackstone himself," comes James's reply.

"Release it!" Dr. Fourney says, but James shakes his head.

Soren nods and Julien goes to Colonel Drake, who's trying to get up but Julien's too fast and is at Drake's side before Drake is even able to leave his chair. Julien easily scrapes a blade down his cheek so that a line of crimson drips off his jaw. Drake whimpers, breathing fast.

"How are you Cooper?" Drake gasps, craning his head to the door.

"I'm fine," comes his voice.

"I didn't think they could affect us all," James says, his voice dismissive. "How could that be? If it's a virus delivery system, it would have to infect us all and there'd have to be some kind of contact first, either physical or aerosol. If it's a toxin, we still have to be exposed. It would have to be aerated, the particles small enough to enter the bloodstream through the lungs or skin."

Fourney looks relieved at that, his eyes closing.

"Don't relax too fast, Dr. Fourney." Soren smiles, and his expression sends a chill down my spine. "Think spooky action at a distance," he says. "Quantum entanglement. What happens to you happens instantaneously to everyone you've turned or made into a blood slave."

Fourney frowns, a look of panic back on his face. "You mean…"

"Yes," Soren says. "A change of state in the sire causes a similar state change in every other vampire or blood slave who has that same sequence of genes."

Fourney closes his eyes.

"How are you, Cooper?" Drake says once more.

We hear a cough from the other room. Then, Colonel Drake starts to cough as well.

There's a silence in the room. I can't believe that James is still considering, his brow furrowed, as if he still doesn't believe this.

"James," Fourney says, his voice desperate. "As your sire, I order you to release the formula. *Now!*"

"I can't," James says. "I'm sorry. I just don't accept that research on quantum entanglement is that far advanced." He glances around the room at the others. "I've worked for Blackstone for a dozen years and we haven't even gone beyond some experimental entanglement of photons in two different labs in the same building. Certainly not entire molecules or sequences of DNA across the globe." He shakes his head. "They're lying."

"I'm not willing to take that risk!" Dr. Fourney says.

"I'm sorry, Dr. Fourney," James says, "but as your science advisor, I have to tell you it's just not possible."

"Listen to me," Fourney says, his voice breaking. "Give Lord Soren the fucking research *now!*"

Then, Colonel Drake starts to disintegrate before our eyes. First his eyes tear and the tears are stained pink. Then, a crimson fluid starts to ooze from his ears and nose. He coughs, and gags, then a pink frothy foam bubbles out of his mouth. Julien grimaces and turns to the room. He runs a finger over his throat to indicate the man is dying. He steps forward. "Turn over the formula or suffer the same fate."

"All *right,*" a reluctant James says. "I'll have to go to my offices and get the research, collect the files for you but you have to know everything was on computer. All I have are the basic research papers and workbooks. You'll have to rebuild the molecule from those."

"What's stopping you?" Soren says, smiling, his expression feral. He motions to one of his guards. "Go with James. Make sure he doesn't try to get away. Now, for our next demonstration, how about showing you what our dear Adept Eve can do," Soren says, rubbing his hands together. "She's a very special Adept, which all of you have no doubt heard about. Natalia's daughter. She has the ability to channel the emotions of followers, transferring that power to me and members of the Twelve. Eve," he says and waves me over to his side. "Come and let me show my new board members what we can do together."

I glance at Michel, who motions to Soren. I catch Dylan's eye and he nods almost imperceptibly. I go to Soren's side, offering him the wrist of my unwounded hand. He takes a sharp knife from Julien and cuts my wrist as before, dribbling it into the empty goblet on the table. Then, he hands the knife to Michel and motions for him to add his blood to the mix. Julien follows Michel, mixing his blood with that of Soren and the Twelve. They then share the blood and finally, Soren takes his share and passes the remaining mouthful to Michel, Julien and then to me.

I look at the goblet and I know this is it. If I drink it, I'll unite all of us and soon, the dying will start.

I glance at Dylan and he nods, a slight smile on his face.

I drink it down.

Then, I'm assaulted by the emotions of the Twelve who shared the blood. They're gloating, having enjoyed the sight of Colonel Drake dying. I survey the board members, who look on in awe of Soren and the Twelve standing behind them. I'm almost overwhelmed with emotions but I manage to steal a glance at Soren and he has his head down, his hands resting on the table. Then, he raises his hands and stares at them as if he's trying to create that spark again, but nothing happens.

"Something's wrong," he says and tries to hold his arms out in front of him, but his hands shake. "What's happening?"

Behind us, several of the Twelve start to frown. One stumbles and has to lean against the wall while one and then others fall to their knees as if they don't have the strength to stand up under their own power.

Beside me, Michel puts his elbows on the table and holds his head. I can hear his breathing, which is fast and hard. Julien leans against the wall, dropping his sword to the floor where it clatters against the hardwood. His hands are spread on the wall at his side as if to support his weight and stop from sliding down.

Soren finally turns to me. Now, he joins minds directly with mine and he's searching my memories. He finds the one of me meeting with Dylan and sees him dipping the crucifix into the black powder. Then Soren manages to grab my hand and turns my palm up only to find the small puncture wound, the blood having already clotted and dried.

"You fucking *bitch*..." he says, and tries to reach for me, but I pull away and he seems suddenly helpless to do anything but stare at me, his face contorting in anger. He turns to Dylan. "You're too late," Soren says, his voice weakening, growing barely above a whisper. "The new world has already come, no matter what you do to delay me."

His strength is slowly being sapped, but unlike Colonel Drake, he isn't dissolving. He doesn't cough, his skin is intact, and he's still whole as are the Twelve. He does slump back in his chair, barely able to keep his chin off his chest as if all his energy is being drained. Soon, he can't even keep his eyes open.

Michel and Julien are still all right, but then I feel something on my cheeks. Pink-tinged tears. Something is warm on my upper lip and when I reach up, I find that my nose is bleeding.

Michel turns to me and then leans over, wiping my lip.

"No, Eve, *no*..." he whispers. "Not this way." He takes my hand, pulling me into the chair with him. "I didn't see *this*..."

Dylan comes over to us as I start to cough.

"Drain her blood," Dylan says, his voice filled with urgency. "The infection's slower in her because she has more of your DNA than Soren's and you're healing fast. I don't know why Soren and the Twelve aren't disintegrating, but you'll have to act fast. Slit her carotid. Cut her femoral and jugular. Drain out all her blood and feed her yours just before her heart stops completely. Both of you feed her your blood. Your blood will heal any damage that the infection has caused. She'll die with your blood in her, and she'll be a vampire, but she'll survive. Your blood should now be immune to the infection."

"Dylan, you *promised*," I manage to whisper as Michel searches my face.

"Sorry, sister," Dylan says. "Some promises were meant to be broken."

"Eve, what should I do?" Michel whispers to me.

"Don't turn me," I say, shaking my head.

"I can't live without you," he whispers. Then, Julien drags himself over and when Michel hesitates, Julien reaches out to touch me, hesitantly, and then I remember Soren's compulsion. The battle Soren's waging with the infection must have weakened the compulsion so that Julien can touch me again. He grabs me and pulls me out of Michel's arms.

"Don't make me a vampire!" I say. "I don't want it!"

"Too fucking bad," Julien says. "You're not dying today. I won't let you. Michel, you better help me or I'll kill you."

Julien sweeps his arm over the tabletop, sending cups and papers flying and lays me on it. Then he takes his dagger and slits my throat and wrists, the pain overwhelming me. Next he hikes up my skirt, cutting the femoral artery on both legs so that my blood spurts out of me with every heartbeat. I feel the effects immediately, almost fainting from loss of blood, and he holds his hand against my chest to feel my heart.

He slits his own wrist and when my vision starts to fade, he presses his wrist against my open lips. Michel looms over me, as he too cuts his wrist and they take turns feeding me their blood. I feel the blood drip into my mouth and the last coherent thought I have is that I have to spit it out. I can't become a vampire. Before I can, darkness closes in.

CHAPTER 32

*E*ach moment of a happy lover's hour is worth an age of a dull and common life."

Aphra Behn

I WAKE up in Soren's home in Boston. It's day, and the light streaming in from the huge windows assaults my eyes. Julien's on the bed beside me, and he pulls the drape on the canopy so that there's more shade.

"The light won't hurt you. The windows are all UV screened, but it may bother your eyes for a while until you feed."

It's then I remember what happened last night in the boardroom. I'm transitioning and have to decide whether to feed or die.

"Where's Michel?"

I try to sit up but my head pounds when I move. He appears in my field of vision from the other side of the bed.

"I'm here, Eve. Just lie down and try to relax."

"You promised me," I say, anger filling me. "You said you wouldn't turn me."

Julien shakes his head but says nothing for a moment as if he's overcome with emotion. Michel takes my hand but I push his away.

"And you – you of all people. You told me you didn't want to be a vampire. That when you destroyed Soren, you'd gladly die yourself."

"Soren isn't dead, Eve. He's merely in stasis, his body in a continual battle with the infection, trying to stop it and it's taking all his energy. As a fallen angel, he's able to fight it off, but not completely. We've got him and the Twelve in tanks at the SCU. Nothing happened to all those vampires that they turned, although every blood slave they created died. Like you, they weren't able to self-heal the way vampires can. Blackstone still has their agenda. We have to recreate the plague nanotech virus so we can find a way to stop it or slow it, but the plague is spreading, and we have no easy way to get to everyone quickly with this technology. Destroying them will take a long time."

"I won't drink any blood."

"We won't let you die, Eve," Julien says, his voice emotional. "We'll *make* you drink."

"Eve, don't ask for the impossible," Michel says. "I can't bear," he says and looks at Julien, shaking his head. "Neither of us can bear to let you die."

I turn my face away from him and close my eyes. Something's building in me and I know what it is – it's bloodlust and it's completely different from anything I felt when I was just a blood slave, but I remember the feeling for I felt it when I was in both Michel's and Julien's minds.

Before, I felt sick when I went too long without vampire blood. Now, I feel a craving that is beyond anything I felt when human.

"I hate you both for this."

"Don't hate us for loving you too much," Julien says.

"If you truly loved me, you would have let me die!" I cover my face and finally, tears fill my eyes.

"That's not human love. That kind of love is only for the saints, Eve. Neither of us are saints," Michel says and I can hear a touch of humor in his voice, as if he's indulging me. I open my eyes and he's gazing at me, his head tilted to one side.

"You're both bastards."

"Oh, that we are," Julien says, and he's smiling now, despite his eyes being wet. "You need to drink some blood. I have some here," he says and holds up a bottle. "No humans were killed in its production. All volunteer fans of us fanged types. Drink some and you'll feel much better."

I push his hand and the bottle of blood away. I look between them, sitting on either side of me, Michel with his longer dark hair falling in his blue eyes, Julien with his shorter hair and several-days worth of stubble on his jaw, that telltale scar on his cheek. They're both so beautiful and so different. I realize I love them both and despite everything, I want them both.

But I don't want *this*.

"Where's my brother? He's not innocent in all this either."

I watch as Michel waves to someone and the door opens. Michel and Julien rise from the bed and Dylan strides over and stands at the bedside.

"Eve," he says, smiling. "How are you?"

"You promised me that you wouldn't let Julien turn me."

He shakes his head. "Do you really think I could let you die? I already lost one sister to this war."

"I barely even *know* you."

"Don't you want to?" he says, exasperation in his voice. "If you drink some blood, we'll have time to get to know each other. Eve, we're *family*," he says and sits on the bed beside me. "*Real* family. I love my parents but they were always my *foster* parents and they let me know who my real family was. I grew up wanting to meet you. I knew that one day, fate would bring us together and it has. Don't leave me, just when I've found you. Besides, we still have work to do."

"Fate," I say, tears in my eyes as I think of him as a small child hoping to meet me one day, knowing that his real mother and father couldn't raise him to protect his role in some predetermined destiny foretold by prophecy.

I struggle to sit up and he helps me, fluffing up the pillows behind me. I examine his face and he does look like me in a way, even though his hair is dark for he has hazel eyes. He smiles at me and he even has dimples. Our mother's dimples.

He takes my hand and squeezes it and I can see into his mind. He saw me at the same recital where Michel met me in London. He felt so excited to finally see me in real life and after the concert, he and the Rhys family came backstage to meet me. I don't remember the meeting because I met so many people that night, but he remembered it.

'*Sister,*' he thought to himself. '*One who will live,*' for he knew even then that Sarah would die before she reached age thirty.

I look over at the fireplace and see Julien leaning on it, his head in his hand, staring out the window. Across from him, Michel stands, looking out at the cityscape.

How can I fight the three of them, all of them wanting me in their own way?

"Give me the bottle."

I hear a muffled sound from Michel and he turns his back to me, covering his eyes. Julien turns toward me and watches as Dylan takes the bottle and pulls out the cork stopper. He hands it to me, exhaling loudly.

"Thank you."

I drink.

CHAPTER 33

" *To* witness two lovers is a spectacle for the gods."

Goethe

DYLAN TAKES me to the SCU stasis tanks once before we return to Davis Cove. He shows me where they keep Soren and the Twelve so that I know he's really imprisoned and is unable to hurt me.

The chamber where all the Council prisoners are kept is deep beneath the ground beside the SCU's main offices near the waterfront in Boston. The entire block is one big cement warehouse that used to house vampires found guilty of crimes under the Treaty. All of the tanks failed after the second fall of red rain, the plague eating away all the plastic in the tanks so that the vampires emerged, recovering once the gel leaked out of their bodies. It was impossible for the few techs and guards who monitored the warehouse to fight them and all two hundred of them escaped. Just one more threat for the Council to manage.

Now, the only residents of the huge chamber are Soren and the Twelve, kept in cement tanks filled with tank gel. They use all their reserves of energy and all their powers just to keep the infection from my blood at bay. There's nothing left over to actually animate so they're as good as in stasis. Now, the aqueous silver gel infuses their system, and they are effectively in a kind of purgatory. They are probably conscious only of the battle they are waging to keep the infection from taking over completely and killing them.

The Council's only hope is that the infection and the stasis gel will keep them in suspended animation until Council scientists can find a way to destroy them completely.

We walk down the narrow paths between rows and rows of crumbled stasis tanks, the cavernous underground facility like a huge parking lot, dimly lit using lanterns fueled with animal fat that has been processed into oil. Here and there are old computer monitoring stations, with blank screens, and melted casings. There's no energy to run them. The Council is working on setting up solar power systems, but as with everything in this new world, it's slow going.

"Here they are," the guard says and leads us to a special room set off from the others. The tanks in which Soren and the Twelve rest are different from the normal stasis tanks. They're made of cement and look like crypts with glass covers. Soren floats naked in the tank, his pale skin almost glowing, his white hair floating like weeds in water. He's really quite terrifying even in suspended animation, with his perfect musculature and height. His eyes are sewn shut.

"Why are his eyes sutured?"

"He kept opening them. They figure it's an involuntary motion, but it was bothering the guards to have his eyes open. They felt like he was watching them."

I walk down the row of tanks that hold the Twelve and they are similarly entombed in the stasis gel, floating like they're sleeping. Angels, fallen to earth – whatever that means. I still don't buy the Biblical explanation. To me, there's a scientific answer to this.

Council scientists haven't found a way to kill Soren and the others yet and with the plague ravaging the civilized world, it's extremely difficult to work around its effects. So much of our modern technology relies on plastics and fossil fuels. Scientists are busy finding workarounds, but it's very slow and tedious. Everything is a huge effort.

Council scientists didn't believe Soren and the Twelve were fallen angels and what they designed to work on Ancients was not powerful enough to destroy them. Dylan is determined to keep trying and so am I. I'm going to start back at Boston U in January and I'll keep working part-time at the SCU to help on cases. Only a few stalwart professors continue to hold classes – primarily those that will help develop new technology to replace the old, which relied on fossil fuels. While Dylan works with scientists at MIT to perfect the technology used to infect Soren and the Twelve, I'll work with Council scientists trying to find a way to cure vampires of our need for blood. If we can understand it fully, we may be able to do it. What makes us immortal is also an important area of research that will benefit not just existing vampires, but all of humanity.

That's for the future. I'm just not ready to return to real life yet.

We leave the SCU and take a horse and cart along the back roads to Davis Cove. The Council is working on getting an old steam locomotive up and running so there's some kind of transportation along the old Amtrak line that threads its way along the eastern seaboard, but it's not ready yet.

I stay with Dylan at a different cottage in Davis Cove – one that is better designed and fixed up after the ravages of the plague. We're close to the Rhys family and far from Boston where Michel and Julien are. Under his tutelage, I drink blood and learn to deal with the cravings, determining how long I can go without feeling out of control and how much I need to keep cravings at bay.

Nothing diminishes the craving, except blood.

I drink from the glass bottle filled with blood, and feel immediate pleasure and then relief but soon, all too soon, the craving returns and builds over the course of a day or so. By the end of twenty-four hours,

I'm almost beside myself with bloodlust and even the older woman with shabby stockings and floppy grey hair who comes to clean the house looks appealing.

Dylan sees me staring at her one morning as we're reading the latest edition of the Davis Cove Register, printed using some old hand-powered printing press. We've had our breakfast and are sitting in the warmth of the kitchen with the morning sun streaming in through UV shaded glass.

I'm trying to push my boundaries to see when I lose control and I can't help but notice her bending over a pail as she mops the entry floor. I can smell her blood from where I sit and it smells so much better than the blood in the bottle. It smells warm. I can hear her heartbeat and it's so inviting. I want to bite her flesh and my teeth elongate the way they do when I drink from the bottle.

I have yet to actually bite a human and drink their blood. Dylan promised to let me decide when I was ready for such an event. There are still volunteers who want to be bitten and there will be several willing, when I'm psychologically ready.

"Don't wait too long," Dylan advises. "You need the human connection of a blood feed to keep your humanity from fading."

I feel ready now but the cleaning lady is not a volunteer. Dylan must see my face change into hunter mode and he takes my hand and shakes his head. He pulls me out of the kitchen, and I keep my face hidden so she doesn't see me and freak out. We go into the bedroom and he hands me a bottle and I drink it down in nearly one pull I'm so in need.

"You really must feed on a human," he says to me, watching me as I finish the blood, sucking down every last drop. "Don't be so stubborn."

I wave him away. "I will, I will."

"When? If I wasn't here, I suspect you'd have had her already and who knows if you'd be able to stop?"

"Okay," I say, annoyed that he's right. "Soon."

There's just a part of me that wants to postpone that first real feed as long as I can. It seems too intimate to do with a complete stranger. Even I know how sexual it will become and that scares me. There have only been two men I've ever really been sexual with – that I've really wanted.

Michel and Julien.

I haven't seen either of them for two weeks. I've spent this time trying to figure out what I'm going to do about them.

I love them both. They love me, each in their own particular way. How can I choose between them? How can I be with one and not with the other? Whose heart do I break besides my own by choosing one over the other?

I lay on my bed and Dylan leaves me alone, closing the door behind him. He knows that after a feed, I must try to deal with the arousal in some way and so he gives me time and space.

With the blood flowing through my system, I'm so aroused and I can't help but think of both Michel and Julien. Where are they even now?

Is Michel sitting at the piano in his cottage in Ipswich with a glass of blood, playing his sad Chopin piece, wondering how I am? Is Julien staring out the window of his warehouse in Boston, thinking of our time in Davis Cove, wishing he were here with me?

As I fight my desire, I write a separate note to each of them with my decision. I'll send them in the post tomorrow. There's a new pony express to take written messages between cities along the coast. Now, everything old is new again. I grew up in an age of iPhones and wireless internet and instantaneous communication. Now, we use HAM radios from the pre-WWI era, and pony express. We haven't even got the telegraph system up and running yet. All the wiring used plastics.

My decision isn't the kind I want sent over the radio.

A FEW DAYS LATER, I'm alone in Davis Cove, walking the beach. It's a cold evening and I'm dressed in a thick wool sweater and old leather boots, a woolen scarf around my neck against the cold wind that blows in off the ocean. Dylan's going to try to find the formula for Blackstone's day-walking drug because I don't want to drink the waters of life – not yet. I will take Blackstone's drug so I won't be trapped inside during the day, but it may be a while. Things are so disrupted because of the plague.

Dylan's gone to stay in Boston for the next week, staying at his apartment so he can attend a few lectures at MIT where some stalwart professors have decided to keep the institution running despite the lack of power. He leaves me alone with a phalanx of guards to watch over me and an icebox filled with bottles of blood, one for each of the five days he'll be away.

I walk along the shore, aware of the two guards trailing behind a hundred yards away. Ahead, I see a figure walking towards me. The moon is out and shines on the sea foam, making it glow. As he nears, I see him more clearly and once he's close enough, I see his smile. Such a brilliant smile.

He says nothing, just comes to me, wrapping his arms around me, kissing me deeply, squeezing me so tightly I think I'll break, except I'm a vampire now and bloody hard to kill.

"Julien," I say when he pulls away. "I'm so glad you decided to come."

"How could I ever deny you anything?"

He kisses me again, and when we connect, I feel his need and it ignites my own.

"I want you right now," he whispers in my ear, pulling me against his body. "Right here on the sand. Tell your guards to fuck off."

"I'm not getting sand in my," I say and laugh. "My… *you know*…"

He grins at me. "Your *you know*?" he says and laughs with me. "*Eve*…" He nuzzles my neck, his mouth against my ear. "It's your *pussy*," he whispers. "And I missed your sweet little pussy so much, you just *can't* imagine."

"Just my… *pussy*?" I say, smiling back, still awkward with that word.

"You *and* your pussy. It's a package deal," he says and wags his eyebrows.

I take his hand and pull him back towards the cottage.

"I want you in a warm bath with me and then in my bed. And later, in front of the fire, and then maybe on the couch."

"Gotta love a new vampire," he says and shakes his head. "Insatiable, are you? It must have been difficult stuck here with only your brother as company."

"It's been wonderful in one way, but hell in another."

We walk back to the cottage, hand in hand, and he tells me about the goings-on at the SCU where he's working, trying to get it set up again and working despite the lack of power and technology, but his voice is a bit shaky and I know it's lust. When we arrive, the guards return to their positions around the property and Julien and I go inside. There's a palpable sexual tension between us as both of us know what's going to happen.

I go to the bathroom and pour one more bucket of hot water from the fireplace into the bath, pouring in some of the sandalwood bath salts. Julien comes into the bathroom and I turn to face him. He stands a foot away from me and looks me over from head to toe.

"I was afraid I'd never be with you again," he says. "I was afraid I'd never be released from the compulsion. I was afraid you'd choose Michel. Or neither of us."

"I considered throwing you both over for celibacy, but that's just not in the cards."

He smiles and runs his fingers over my cheek and then down over the curves of my breasts, touching the crucifix Michel gave me.

"That thing safe?"

I bend my head and look at it, touching it with a finger. "Yes, Dylan assures me it's no threat to us. If there's any residue left, we're immune."

Soon we're in each other's arms and I feel drunk on lust as we kiss.

"Oh, God, I want you so much," he says.

"I want you so much," I whisper, almost choking with desire.

We feel so much bliss, I don't know how we can bear it.

But we do.

THE REST of the week passes this way, with Julien and I spending our time back together in bed or on the floor in front of the fire, or against the wall in the shower. At night we walk the beach when the weather permits and sleep during the day. Finally, it's Friday and Julien must leave. He rises early, after we've only been asleep for a few hours.

"Why so early?" I say, as I watch him dress.

"I have a meeting with Terri tonight and I want to make it there with some time to go over a few things with security at the residence."

I watch him from the bed, the sheets around me against the chill in the room. A vampire's body isn't as warm as a human's but we still can feel cold and heat. I still prefer warmth to chill.

Julien comes over and bends down to kiss me one last time before leaving.

"Next Friday?" he says, his voice light, but there's a note of regret in it that he has to wait so long before we're together again.

"Next Friday night, same time. Meet me on the beach if the weather's good."

He sits beside me and leans in to kiss me again.

"Back in October after you left me to go to Michel," he says. "I thought we'd never be together again. The only thing that kept me going was Soren's compulsion."

"I know," I say. "I felt so bad, but I also felt responsible. I thought it was my fault that Blackstone released the plague. I didn't leave because I wanted to. I love you, Julien."

"I love you."

He kisses me once more and then leaves me. I hear the door close and the lock click behind him and I lay back, listening as he walks to wherever his ride is waiting.

DYLAN'S back that night from Cambridge. He brings with him a crate filled with bottles of blood from the local volunteer group packed in chipped ice. We sit by the fire and talk in quiet voices about the classes he attended and how people are trying to keep society together, keeping a skeleton crew of faculty working, and a roster of classes going, working day and night to find work-arounds for technology that failed due to using plastics. We spend the weekend talking about our families, our pasts, and telling each other stories about our parents and growing up.

I ask him about the deaths Julien and I investigated. The woman in the nursing home, the boy with cancer, and the man whose wife took her life – Dylan gave them all painless deaths at their requests. The young female adepts were Soren's work, as I suspected. He was weeding out Adepts who were loyal to him and those who chose the Council.

Finally, Sunday morning comes and it's time for Dylan to go back to Boston.

We hug, and for the first time, I feel like I truly have a brother. He feels real to me now.

"So, I won't be back on Friday, I guess."

"You have Amy," I say. "She must be getting fed up with you doing 'sister duty'."

He smiles. "No," he says. "She understands. Her parents are in Boston so she stays there on weekends and hangs out with the girls."

"Are you going to turn her?"

"That's up to her."

"How come she gets a choice and I didn't?"

He shrugs. "She may not either." He smiles and picks up his duffel bag and goes to the door. "If you need anything, use the HAM radio in town to send me a message. I'll come right away, but you can always ask mom or dad to help. They're up to speed."

I nod and wave to him as he goes out to his car. I close the door and turn back to the empty cottage.

I SLEEP ALONE ALL DAY, and it's cold outside so I get the fireplace stoked when I get up, eating a light breakfast when I should be eating supper but until I get the day-walking drug, my days and nights will be mixed up again like they were when I first met Michel.

I soak in the tub because it's really chilly in this cottage. I know I'll have to move to a winterized house soon, but I can't leave the coast right now. I *need* to be here. I need to adjust to life as a vampire. I have to feel more certain of my choice before I move back to Boston and start life over as a vampire hunter for the new Council.

Once the sun sets, I get dressed in something warm and wrap a scarf around my neck. Then I get my ancient binoculars and a blanket and climb down the hill to a spot on the beach that's sheltered from the wind. It's a brilliantly clear night with no moon this early so I can watch the Taurid meteor shower with no worries of clouds or the moon affecting the show.

It's when I'm standing on the blanket, spying the Orion Nebula – a tiny smear of white in the belt of Orion – that Michel shows up, walking towards me from around a huge dune, stepping over a spit of sand that stretches out into the surf. He smiles when he sees me, his hands stuffed in his pockets, his hair ruffled by the breeze off the surf.

My heart does a little flip-flop because he's so beautiful.

He doesn't say anything when he gets to me, just takes the binoculars out of my hands and wraps one arm around my waist, pulling me against him. He kisses me, the fingers of one hand tangling in my hair. Our kiss goes on and on, and when we connect, I feel his emotions and he's so happy to see me, so relieved that I gave them my ultimatum and demanded that they either share me or give me up completely because I couldn't choose.

He *thought* I'd choose Julien.

He hoped I'd choose him, but he knew from our connection that I was also just as in love with Julien as I am with him and couldn't pick one.

My heart would break if I had to have one without the other. It was an impossible choice. This was the only way – one at a time, separate from each other. I won't become Marguerite and make them watch each other with me. I'm not that cruel.

"Eve, I don't want to watch the meteor shower right now."

I pull away and try to slip out of his arms.

"Michel, I just got everything set up…"

"It lasts all night and I need you, Eve. *Now*," he says, his voice husky. "I can't wait."

"You waited three weeks," I say and laugh. "I just got things ready for us. I have a thermos of tea, even some cookies for you to eat."

He makes that sound in the back of his throat and smiles, his smile lopsided. "I want to eat *you*," he says.

I turn back to the sky, smiling to myself.

"Shh" I say and pull away completely. "You're distracting me."

I turn my binoculars towards another star and think of Betelgeuse – a red supergiant, which makes me think of Julien and his story of the two stars colliding, setting off a supernova. I push Julien from my mind. It's not fair of me to think of him when Michel's just arrived

"Such a saucy mouth," Michel says. I smile to myself and finally give up when he steps closer from behind me and wraps his arms around my waist, resting his chin on my shoulder, his face beside mine. "Have I told you I love your saucy mouth? I want your saucy mouth on me." He moves my hair out of the way, but when his lips press against my skin, I remember Julien fed there the other night and he feels my memory. He pulls away and moves to the other side, kissing me where Julien hasn't fed.

Part of me feels incredibly bad that I'm making them do this – share me. I feel rather like a selfish little girl wanting a pony *and* a new bicycle for my birthday, but it was either this or neither of them.

I could never choose.

Julien is so open now, so willing to just love me, and he lets me know it without reservation. I read over my journal and see how frustrated I was with his demands that I just have sex with him, back when we were living together in the warehouse. He said he couldn't give me what I wanted, what I thought I needed, but he was wrong. Now, he wants to give me exactly what I need. I fell in love with him despite his seeming inability to love me. There is a sweetness to Julien that makes my heart glad to be with him.

I know he loves me with a wild abandon.

But Michel? I fell in love with him at first sight, with his unruly black hair below his collar, his blue eyes and thick lashes. He gives me something that Julien can never give me. His calm strength, his quiet passion, his desire to protect makes me weak. When we're together, I feel completely possessed and safe for once in my life.

I laid out my offer in my letters to them and let them decide if they could do it. If they could learn to share, one week on, one week off with time for me to be all alone on the weekend if I chose. So this was them deciding that they could try.

I wasn't sure if Michel would show up tonight. I was sure he'd feel slighted that I spent time with Julien first. I sent Michel a message through the HAM radio operator to explain.

I flipped a coin. Julien won.

As I watch a falling star streak across the sky, Michel's busy with his hand up my sweater, and I think he's not hurting too much right now. I close my eyes and finally give in trying to watch the meteor shower. When he feels my resistance wane, he grabs my hand, pulling me away from the beach.

"*Now*, Eve," he says, urgency and a little bit of amusement in his voice. I let him pull me along the shore and up the hill to my cottage, enjoying his urgent need, smiling as he takes my keys and opens the door, picking me up and carrying me over his shoulder like some caveman. I squeal and pound his back lightly with my fists but I'm laughing because he seems so much better than I expected and it makes me happy. He closes the door and turns the lock, then carries me still giggling to the bedroom. He throws me down on the bed, undressing me with an urgency that ignites my desire.

"I see you still want to control everything," I start to say, but he shakes his head.

"Quiet," he says and silences me with his mouth. He kisses me forcefully, his hands reaching up under my sweater to cup my breasts. "You talk far too much." He kisses me once more, slowly, deeply.

"Michel, we have to talk about--."

"Shh," he says and places his fingers over my lips, stopping me from speaking. "No talking. Not now." He takes off his sweater.

"There's more time than you can imagine for talk. I want you right now."

"I want *you* right now," I say and grin.

He makes that throat sound again and shakes his head. "Oh, those dimples," he says. "They're my undoing."

"I like the thought of undoing you, Michel," I say, closing my eyes as he slowly and very deliberately kisses my cheeks, one after the other, his tongue touching my skin. "I like the thought of doing you and undoing you and then doing you again."

He stops his motions and for a moment, I wonder if he isn't angry at me because I'm refusing to be quiet, but he just lies there, his face in my neck, his mouth open, tongue pressed on my skin. He wraps his arms around me, sliding them under me and pulling me against his body so tightly. He does nothing but hold me, his face in the crook of my neck, one hand in my hair.

"Michel," I say, trying to connect with him, but he's blank. I try to pull away. "What is it?"

He shakes his head and kisses me, but when he finally opens himself to me again, I sense his relief, his lingering fear just now dissipating that I'd leave him because he killed my mother. I feel his horror when he thought that I'd die in the boardroom from the poison he had no idea Dylan and I were going to use against Soren and the Twelve. I feel his dread that we'd never be together again because I'd choose Julien. All the fears finally evaporate and he's momentarily overcome.

He pulls away finally, breaking our kiss, which has become more about love than lust, and presses his forehead against mine.

"I thought you were going to die in front of me." He looks in my eyes and I see that his are wet. "Eve, I couldn't bear to lose you."

"Oh, *Michel*," I say and cup his face, tuck his hair behind his ear, my own eyes tearing up from seeing his.

"I love you," he says, and runs his fingers over my cheek. "When you learned about my role in your mother's death, I thought I'd lost you forever."

""You could never lose me. I *love* you, Michel," I say, my throat choking with emotion. "I have since that day in my flat when you stood at my piano and said music was your passion. That it made existence bearable. I even wrote that down as the last line in my entry that day. I wrote, '*I think I'm in love with him and I've only just met him*'. Nothing has changed that. If anything, I love you even more."

His gaze moves over my face as if he can't believe what I'm saying. Then he closes his eyes and leans in, kissing me so tenderly that I feel as if my heart might explode. Soon, the love turns back to lust and I can't wait any longer. The bliss is almost too much.

Almost.

∼

END OF BOOK THREE

Mr. Big Shot: Book 1

Mr. Big Love: Book 2

Mr. Big Daddy: Book 3

Mr. Big Deal: Book 4

THE MCINTYRE BROTHERS SERIES

Tempt Me: Book 1

Tease Me: Book 2

Tame Me: Book 3

Military Romance / Romantic Suspense

THE BAD BOY SERIES

Bad Boy Saint: Book 1

Bad Boy Sinner: Book 2

Bad Boy Soldier: Book 3

Bad Boy Savior: Book 4

THE BOYFRIEND SERIES

Boy Toy: Book 1

Man Bun: Book 2

STANDALONE BOOKS:

Matched

If You Fall

ABOUT THE AUTHOR

S. E. Lund lives on the side of a mountain in the shadow of an active volcano with her family of humans and pets. Besides writing paranormal romance, urban fantasy and contemporary romance, she dreams of living in a warm climate where snow is just a word in a dictionary.

If you would like updates on new releases and sales, special promotions and other news, sign up for S. E. Lund's newsletter. She hates spam and so will never share your email with anyone!

https://www.subscribepage.com/x8t1t7

www.selund.net
selund2012@gmail.com